POISONADE

POISONADE

Joseph Nalven

PALMETTO
PUBLISHING
Charleston, SC
www.PalmettoPublishing.com

Copyright © 2024 by Joseph Nalven

Paperback ISBN: 979-8-8229-3267-8
Hardcover ISBN: 979-8-8229-3296-8

This novel is dedicated to the characters that emerged in its writing, especially to Alfredo Velasco who I imagined to be the hero. Wherever you are Al, thank you.

## Chapter 1

A TWITCH IN TIME

Freddy Panarese tilted his head to the right. The reflected image of the Boeing model-something darted across the glass. Freddy tipped up on his toes and leaned forward. He stared at himself in the glass. All he could see was the slick, the cool, the hip-hop, and the bebop. That was all he wanted to see. Freddy started to hum his memory of youth. He walked the melody straight up the stairway to heaven. Freddy bragged to his silicone image, "Hey, look at you. You got a Ben Franklin cut. Cost you only an Andrew Jackson. A steal, if not a deal." Freddy rocked back on his heels and landed on vinyl. He could feel the rumble of the jet racing down runway one. Freddy touched down and watched his image recede from the glass, replaced by the fire hose neatly accordion-folded into its cubbyhole. Just like everything else at the airport.

"Sharp," Freddy said to nobody in particular, "slick," reminding himself of his core value. He preferred one-way conversations. No talking back. No interruption of the flow. Just Freddy. Just this, just that. He glanced at the thin scar across his hollow cheekbones. He pulled his shoulders back, admired the blue-tinted camel hair catching occasional rays from the fading sun. Freddy slid his right hand inside his jacket. He looked down at his soft leather walking shoes. The luster was still on the shine. He was Mr. Slick. This was the style Freddy imagined a cushy rich asshole would wear. Especially if he was only five foot five.

That was the role Freddy had chosen for himself. He hadn't looked this good since ninth grade. That was when Freddy had graduated into the real world. Not that he had actually graduated. Freddy asked his special ed teacher, "Who needs school when I'm pulling down $400 a week?" His teacher didn't answer. That was when Freddy decided he'd graduated.

The *wumpff* of another jet called out to Freddy while he waited to leave LA. He was certain no one had followed him. Freddy looked at the row of columns winding around the international flight hub. He found a seat hidden behind the fifth column from the entryway, melting into the seated crowd. He was sure he hadn't been made. Freddy had his own plan to avoid being tagged out. Actually, Freddy had borrowed part of his plan from Morales. Morales sometimes made sense. No harm borrowing from Morales. Freddy let his hand steal up his jacket to feel the ticket bulge inside the pocket.

Morales said he'd look after Freddy. Freddy felt safe. Freddy didn't think he had to leave LA, but Morales said he wanted Freddy off the playing field for a while. Vacation time. That's what Morales had said. "Freddy, you going on a vacation." Not a question, not a maybe this, maybe that.

Panarese puckered his lips. A passerby might have thought he was smiling. Maybe he was smiling. Years of streetwise and smartass running around, hiding under seats in grade eight movie theaters, jumping rooftops without the hot pitch tarring his sneakers, all those adrenaline-zipped moments clipped what might have been a lazy twist of his lips. Whether he was smiling didn't matter to Freddy.

He liked the trim. He rolled up on his toes to take another look at himself. She'd layered his hair through an obstinate curl. Freddy had tossed an extra Hamilton to whatever-her-name-was. She made him look slick and straight. Straight and slick, a modified duck's ass. Even hid the scar on his left temple. She cut his hair while standing on top of an unfinished pine box. She had to. She was shorter than Freddy's short. Freddy thought she was a cleaning woman. A jungle woman. She couldn't be the barber. Jet-black hair, coffee-bean skin, a Brazilian jungle. He couldn't remember the name of the movie. It could have been *Tarzan Goes to the Amazon*. Freddy was no good at remembering movie titles. But that's where she was from. Freddy was sure about that. Freddy had a hard time explaining what she was doing in his jungle, just like the Amazon Indians in the movie had had a hard time explaining why the little white boy was running around in theirs. Freddy was no movie critic, but even he knew they should have kept Tarzan in Africa.

Freddy stopped by the Last Chance Book and Snack Shop. He walked around the line of newspapers from up and down the state. He looked past the stacked rows of bestsellers and sweets. Freddy knew what he wanted. It was hidden behind the sweatshirts that said LA this and LA that, and if you were in Fargo, they would have said Futzo this and Scarfo that. Freddy bent down to examine the chippees of the month. He bought his essential flying library—*Hustler* and *Miz Lizzy*. That would keep him awake till he got to Mexico City. Might give him dick-thritis. He'd ask the stewardess if she had something stronger than aspirin. "Please help me. I can't stand up. I need something to take away the pain." Freddy laughed. He sounded like a goat pushing through a high grassy plain. He picked out two magazines. He grinned.

Shit, this is too dope, he thought. He wasn't thinking about the plastic-wrapped plaything. He was going to fool somebody into thinking he was flying to Atlanta. Freddy didn't care whom he would fool, just as long as it tricked whomever was going to look for him. Morales was the only one who knew where Freddy was really going. Morales had taken Freddy to see a movie called *Once over the Sun*. There was a running man. Freddy couldn't remember whether the man was a spy being chased by other spies or a crook being chased by other crooks. Like Freddy, except that Freddy wasn't being chased. Freddy was running, but he wasn't being chased. At least he didn't think he was. Freddy was disappointed that he wasn't as tall as the man in the movie. He was losing interest in thinking about the movie and started to nod out. Morales poked Freddy. "Freddy, watch this." Freddy forced his eyelids up to a two o'clock position, open just enough to see the man write out the name of the airline and flight number on a piece of paper, stuff it in an old pair of jeans, and leave it to be found.

Freddy knew that Morales didn't think Freddy was smart. What did Morales say? "I'm not sure we can work with you, Panarese. You're as short as your IQ." Freddy was quick to respond, "Up yours, dial-a-dick." That always got a rise. Freddy made sure he was standing behind the streetlamp in case Morales was going to grab him. He could take a punch if he had to.

Freddy told himself not graduating ninth grade didn't mean shit.

Freddy liked the idea, even if Morales was the one who put him on to it. Freddy made a small change to the script. "Morales, you're going to drop your shorts for me when I tell you what I'm going to do." Freddy wanted to send somebody else on the plane to Atlanta using Freddy's name. That would be two false clues. Morales said okay and even gave Freddy some extra money for the ticket. Freddy wanted to send the delivery boy from Galaxy Gems, a real comer, but the boy didn't want to fly to Atlanta and leave his mom alone. Freddy found a boy on Warwick Avenue who hadn't gotten out of his cardboard box.

One p.m. was still too early in the morning. Home is where the heart is. That's what Freddy told the kid. "You want to go where you'll be loved?" Freddy didn't think he'd have any problem.

"Me?" it grunted. Incomprehension rolled around inside his eye sockets. Freddy didn't bother to hide his disgust. The boy was skipping the groove.

A cracked head. "You like to travel, kid?" Transients liked to travel. The eyes floated up to Freddy. He repeated the question about a dozen times. Freddy watched the kid try to process the question mark. He had no memory of mother. His father was a fantasy. Here was the same as there. So why not travel? Freddy still had a hard time laying down the con. Rotten fish smelled and looked better than this pimply rag.

Freddy had to take a breath and talk in short sentences so he wouldn't smell the stink.

Freddy paid the cabbie an extra twenty-five dollars to take the kid out to the airport. No way was he going to have the boy ride with him. The boy had a hard time remembering to call himself Freddy. "Hey, dude, this is a weird name. Fred Panarese? I can't remember this shit." Freddy wrote it out and pushed the paper in the boy's pocket. The boy's pocket was tearing away from his jeans. Freddy thought about shoving it into the boy's underwear, except when he reached down the boy's pants, he came up with unexpected loose change. Freddy half thought that maybe using the kid was working out. Freddy was finally satisfied when the boy tumbled into the boarding zone. Then he was gone. The boy's plane had taken off about an hour earlier. Freddy took his time walking over to the other terminal.

Freddy realized he was still staring at himself in the fire-hose window. He turned around. He forced himself not to look up. Scanning the rows was too obvious.

He walked over to the first row of seats. He pushed the newspaper over to the next seat and sat down. The paper was probably left by a frequent flyer who had waited patiently to leave LA. Or maybe he'd waited impatiently. Nothing was certain. Freddy didn't like newspapers, particularly the *Los Angeles Times*. He didn't like it today either. There it was. It could have been a picture of his face. The words only whispered Panarese. The story was out. Who the fuck was the leak?

Morales had warned him two days ago about being fingered, but he didn't say the story would be in the papers. Morales would be surprised when he saw this piece. Maybe Morales had told somebody. But Morales was helping Freddy get out of the way. Maybe this, maybe that. Only sure thing was somebody was stirring things up. He was pretty sure Morales wouldn't tell anybody where he was really going even if Morales was leaking the investigation. Maybe it was meant to be a warning, or maybe it was just somebody with a mean edge, another new face wanting to take the lead. Freddy was like that when he first got into the streets. Freddy was the "rabbit"—that was what they said to his face, and "weasel" when he wasn't around. Small, fast, lots of action. At least they didn't call him wop. It wasn't because they were sensitive. It just wouldn't make any sense. How many Eye-talians were as fast as he was? Those were the good times for Freddy. He was the weasel rabbit, and he made things happen quick. That was his rep. Morales told Freddy he knew about Freddy's rep. Morales soothed Freddy's feelings about his short intelligence and convinced Freddy to do the deal with him.

Freddy picked up the *Times*. Monday's paper was always light. He let the pages flap back and forth so he could find the sports section. Freddy wanted to read past the hard news about the secret witness. Freddy was disappointed. No sports, no comics.

The guy had left Freddy only the news. The front page flipped back. Freddy read the headline again. "Key Witness to Nail Local Officials." Front page, A-1. The only consolation was the article being dropped to the bottom of the page, lost below an article about another big jolt in the valley. "Predicting the Big One." Freddy would be the big one too, if he ever testified about corruption in LA. Not many politicians would survive. They'd gag on weasel's dander. So would some cops.

Freddy would be hunted. He couldn't stay in this jungle any longer.

Federal prosecutor to call unnamed source familiar with bribery and corruption in LA to testify at preliminary hearing. Under the law, state and federal agencies can withhold the name of witnesses who would be likely assassination targets of crime organizations against whom they would testify. The testimony can be videotaped and preserved for any future trial even if the witness, once identified, is ultimately killed.

The story made Freddy feel fuzzy. Everybody who was a target would be itching and poking around for the unnamed source. The politicians would be calling around, and the dirty cops would feign interest as they prowled through the computerized data files. Official use only, the file would say. But who was using the files?

Freddy mumbled. He was not a true believer. The law handicapped the risk-takers. It never guaranteed anything. It didn't guarantee death to convicted killers or a long life behind bars for three-strikers, even though the law said it would.

Freddy did not believe that the preservation of his testimony in a plastic box would keep the targets from trying to put Freddy into a concrete one. Freddy might have joked about the immortality of digital recordings last week, but not today. Freddy had to leave LA before he became part of the state's electronic eternity. The modern gravesite: a computer file as his headstone. Here lies Freddy. He existed once upon a time. File closed.

Freddy was thinking that if the newspapers had this much, Morales was probably putting the word out about him going to Atlanta to see who would follow. Bait and switch was the name of the game, and Freddy was the bait. By the time the pimply-faced ragamuffin was found, Freddy would be in Mexico City.

"Rows 50 to 40 will be boarding. Please have your boarding passes ready."

Freddy hadn't paid attention. They had already called the early rows. The flight attendant must have called for the aged, the blind, the wheelchair bound, the children, and first class. Freddy figured he could fly regular coach and be the last to board. That way he wouldn't be trapped. He was certain he would be the last called.

"Rows 40 to 30." Freddy glanced at the flight attendant calling out for more passengers. She must have been in her forties. Brown hair, overweight. None of the physical attraction Freddy was hoping for. He looked at the floor and watched his foot put out an imaginary cigarette. No smoking, no beautiful women. No this, no nothing.

America was losing its character.

The weasel rabbit ran his fingers through his hair. The jungle lady said she used one of those fancy shampoos. Her cut was worth the twenty. And the tip.

"Rows 30 to 20." Her voice was okay. Freddy thought that if he didn't look at her, he could imagine her voice belonging to the photos in *Miz Lizzy* and *Hustler*. He pulled his elbow in, holding the magazines tightly inside his arm.

When Freddy first heard the news on the radio—this station always read the *LA Times* stories—he thought about all the gangstas he knew. That's what they called themselves. Those up the ladder and those working the streets. Except for the politicians and dirty cops. They choked on the truth. They couldn't call themselves gangstas even if they thought it. No one on the streets would be worth old-school video cassettes or new-school flash drives, even if the state was reusing them. And from what he heard, a lot of the gangstas up the ladder were going to be indicted. Except Morales. Somehow he was managing to stay in a neutral corner. Others would get a sweet deal too, but not as sweet a deal as the prosecutor had promised Freddy. Or the money. The radio was talking about Freddy. The radio guy didn't know he was talking about Freddy. But what he was reading was about Freddy. The guy could read the *LA Times*, tell the whole fucking world that Freddy was the leak, and not know a damn thing about what he was saying.

Freddy's moniker would decompose. Instead of being the Weasel Rabbit, he'd be Dead Leak.

"Everyone else whose row has not been called may board now."

Every word Freddy held in his hand he had heard that morning over KKOQ. Also known as L'KOCK. If you had a hard-on for the news, you listened to L'KOCK. French roll and pride. Freddy knew all the inside names. Now, he was even more inside than L'KOCK. He put the *Times* down and saw no one else heading for flight 312 to Mexico City. He checked his magazines again. Now was the time. Freddy turned in his boarding pass. He walked down the tunnel. He was alone. The yellow-carpet ride to safe city.

Night flights were the best. Freddy could read about the important things in life or at least look at the pictures. He didn't have those things yet. Soon, though. He didn't have to push his way to row 47. Maybe forty, fifty passengers. The overhead bins were open. Freddy stepped up onto a seat to pull down some pillows and a blanket.

As he stepped back down off the seat, he felt a little off centered. Maybe dizzy or woozy or whatever the word was. Too much to worry about. Freddy sat down and lifted up the armrests all along the row. He gave himself more room. He put his magazines down. His heart punched out a faster rhythm. Freddy wasn't familiar with that beat. He stretched back across the seats in the center. The stewardess had encouraged him. "Mr. Byner"—that was the name Freddy had picked for his ticket—"you can stretch out across your row. Is there anything I can get you? Something to read?" Freddy was glad she had that mellow voice. His eyes were blurry, so it didn't make too much difference what she looked like. Freddy decided that Mr. Byner wouldn't be crude. So Freddy simply touched the magazines he'd brought with him.

"Thank you, no." He forgot to ask her for aspirin to ease the pain. Freddy forgot the joke too. Wasn't he supposed to stand up? He couldn't remember.

Not too many on board. Everyone should sleep well tonight. And Freddy would look at the pictures in his magazines. He pinched his eyes, hoping that the blur would clear. He was too uptight to sleep.

The plane pulled up into the evening. Goodbye, LA. If Freddy had been looking out a window as the plane pulled around and banked to the south, he would have seen the western sun fall into the Pacific. He might have been lucky to catch the green flash the moment the sun dipped into the ocean. Freddy didn't look. He liked to watch the pillowy mountains rise up over the horizon. This was as high as a mortal's heaven could be.

The chain of muscles running down Freddy's left side twitched. Freddy felt lightheaded; a wild vertigo stormed up his viscera. He couldn't remember what the twisted mass between his ears was called. It began with the letter *b*. Freddy had never puked on a plane. Not even when the plane roller-coasted down a wind shear.

Not even when the white daggers of light fused the souls of the midnight travelers. Freddy couldn't figure out what was going wrong inside his body.

Nobody was watching Freddy. If anyone had looked at Freddy, they would have noticed a tight-faced grin. They would have wondered what could have made somebody laugh like that. They would have been surprised to see his eyes spin about, unable to focus. They would have seen Freddy run his fingers through his hair as if he was searching for a question. "Morales, what's happening to me? What did you do to me, Morales? Who did you tell?" But nobody was watching anybody else. Least of all Freddy. It was late, and everybody seemed content to stretch out across the seats.

The flight to Mexico City promised to be calm and quiet. For everyone except Freddy.

Freddy wasn't able to stretch. His left side cramped, shooting a pain down his legs and tearing up his gut. A sea of bile and acid puddled underneath Freddy's seat. Freddy grunted. A pathetic call for help.

The captain's voice interrupted the peace and galloped over the barely audible wail coming from row 47. "We'll be flying at thirty-three thousand feet. The weather is clear all the way through to Mexico City. Your ride will be a pleasant one. In about twenty minutes, we'll be flying over San Diego and Tijuana."

Freddy's head twisted around. A gargoyle's smile slowly slunk across Freddy's face. He looked into his Sodom and Gomorrah. His tongue tasted bitter, and he could feel a salted crust at the roof of his mouth. Freddy jerked around, knocking *Miz Lizzy* off his seat. *Miz Lizzy* fell open to Freddy's vision of happiness. Freddy fell forward and stared into heaven.

Nobody witnessed Freddy's last spasm. It wouldn't be captured on video. Nobody witnessed Freddy's dead body roll into the narrow space between rows 46 and 47 as the plane coasted the jet stream only five hours from safe city.

On another night bird, Jerry Cavanaugh faced in exactly the opposite direction. No one saw Jerry Cavanaugh twitch. He was as invisible as Freddy. They were the passengers no one ever sees. No one saw Jerry's eyes twist about, nor did they hear the sound of his fingers clawing through the fabric of the seats on either side of him. No one knew that he felt the same way that Freddy did. Nobody knew that Cavanaugh was smiling with bitters under his tongue and thinking the same thoughts Freddy was.

The planes out of LA carried their dead away.

Chapter 2
TALE FROM THE CRYPT

Monday midnight. The moon must be harbored somewhere. Mikozy couldn't fix his universal location yet. All he knew were the cross streets. The buildings shielded the heavenly orb while sodium imposed an unseemly glow over nature's night-light. Mikozy wondered if he would ever see another star-punctuated sky. Not unless he went to the mountains, or an earthquake swallowed up the generators. The street had only two corners. The massive new building across the street occupied two full blocks.

Barely a scuff mark on the street. Mikozy stared at his new home as if the newness itself was proof that the building was an illusion.

He stood at the corner, leaning against a zinc-coated light pole. Mikozy was a silver-haired leopard resting before the hunt. He welcomed the metal pole, the only solid anchor to the night's eerie luminescence. No one was looking. No one would see him cross this virgin pathway without his usual facade. Mikozy thought about all the images he could be when he stepped into the street: Bosch, Davenport, Spenser, McGee, Pickett.

Certainly not a Bond, Wolff, or Poirot.

Mikozy's attention warped back to the present. Time to begin again. It wasn't about slowly moving through the seasons on a hopped-up crank of a cycle with a full tank of gas.

Mikozy anticipated his new assignment in the criminal justice system. As many others expected, it was that which ordered society—the Criminal Justice System, the CJS. He knew his fifteen years in the criminal justice system were more than blazing a path to an honorable pension. More than transitory assignments between vice and homicide. Mikozy resisted the paranoia of an invisible and unseen hand guiding him through the CJS. Maybe he didn't see the hands tugging and pulling, twisting and kneading the CJS, but he could feel the cold fingers and sweaty palms clawing at him, burrowing a path for him into the CJS. He wasn't sure who'd brought him here. *Friend or enemy?* was a better question than *to be or not to be?* This was not Elsinore. "You danced all over Laguna, and he's gonna be doing real time. And you've been made. No point in keeping you in that hole. All that will happen is that they will pour gasoline into the hole and have you do an imitation of a Roman candle." Schmidt liked to strongarm his arguments. Mikozy figured Captain Schmidt was the one pulling him out of vice into homicide. Away from Laguna and his vices. Mikozy also figured Schmidt to be his friend. Sometimes he was wrong.

Mikozy leaned into the light pole, sidling his shoulder around into a comfort zone. Still no signs of life. Not even a three-legged dog or an alien invader. Just midnight. He resisted walking into the new police headquarters without taking a measure of the new habitat. Each place in the city was unique. Mikozy knew he would miss ambling into Laguna's place. That was special. And Laguna was special as well. Too bad Mikozy had to sneak inside his trust and eat his food before busting him as a bad-dog dealer. Laguna protested that the only vice he had was serving A.1. steak sauce at La Chucha. Laguna said that if he had only stuck with salsa and chile poblano, no one would have guessed that La Chucha hosted anyone but Mexicans: "How would you have ever found out we were dealing drugs out of La Chucha if I hadn't been serving dagos steak sauce? You ever see Mexicans putting A.1. on their tacos?" Mikozy thought that would have been a great clue to finding Mafia in East LA.

The truth was a lot simpler. Mikozy had been working up the coke line.

Breaking a street hustler, turning a low-level dealer, and burrowing up the chain of command. Laguna was somewhere in the middle. He wouldn't roll over and let the police step on his back to reach the next rung of the coke line. Mikozy passed over Laguna's death threats and thought about the taste of La Chucha's steak burrito and about running his tongue around the edges of the tortilla to catch the A.1. sauce dripping out its side. Mikozy would miss working vice.

Mikozy studied the newly painted crosswalk. The red cones stood at attention. He knew they'd be red in the morning light; now they were black. Was there something wrong with his eyes? The yellow stripes marking the walkway were steel gray. His hands had a purplish cast, and his fingernails simply glowed. His once-white shirt turned gold. If a mirror had been tacked to the light pole, he would not have dared to look at himself. And if LC were standing next to him, he wouldn't have asked to borrow the mirror she carried inside her purse. Mikozy was afraid whom he would see.

Mikozy imagined a night creature leaping out from his mirrored image, saying, "I am Rafael Mikozy."

Blue-white fangs, nostrils flaring in search of a victim, and silver-rimmed eyes daring him to deny the truth about who he was. Strange what sodium nights could conjure, more mercurial than fluorescence on Halloween. Mikozy thought about how the sodium lamps changed day colors into deadly night shades. He wondered if there were other kinds of lamps and phones and aerosols that transformed the sights, the smells, and the sounds from day into night, left into right, good into bad. That would be an interesting class to take at the community college. Something to do instead of watching another video.

Detective Rafael Mikozy pushed himself away from the light pole and walked across the street. Enough daydreaming at night. He looked at the concrete-and-glass nightmare. The new police headquarters surged out of the deep pit that had straddled several blocks only a year ago. The building was vast. A monolith, a testimony to the union of nouveau function and the peccadillos of local politicians. Windowless concrete blocks jutted up from each end, designed to force any human mass up a funnel-shaped stairway. What did they say about behavior in search of a metaphor? Mikozy admonished himself for not remembering the cliché. There was that memo from the high command about the building's special architectural crowd-control form. Built to withstand the Goths and Vandals from the past and any Terminators from the future. Mikozy avoided going up the tier of steps at the front entrance and decided to step around any exotic features that might have been built into the stairway. He might have missed later memos about the right way to walk up the stairs after midnight. Someone might mistake him for a terrorist. Testing the new building with its computer-monitored cameras and watching it go into a programmed frenzy would not be the best way to start off his new assignment.

Mikozy used his RFD card and personalized code to open the night door on the east side of the new police headquarters. The old building had the same protections against the crazies storming police headquarters, but they were put on as afterthoughts and stuck out like a splint on a broken arm and other fix-it devices. Cosmetic surgeons could have been called in, but the idea of a new building, no matter how far in the future, put off that expense. Mikozy looked around the unattended entryway. Now the devices were tucked away. A miniature camera scanned his face and the semidarkness beyond. Mikozy knew there was a second camera ensconced across the archway. Hunters weren't the only ones using duck blinds. The door popped open, and he slid across the threshold into silence. Not even New Age Muzak.

Nothing but the erratic beat of his soft soles stepping across the mandatory marble floor. There was a bank of four elevators in the lobby. Mikozy heard about the saltwater aquarium in the main lobby, pinned between two columns. Mikozy was curious if the tank was stocked with sharks. Probably not. Probably just colored exotics, enough to distract unwary visitors. Why warn them with monochrome fish of prey? Maybe he would leave through the front door.

Mikozy skipped the up-and-down elevators and went straight to the service elevator. This path was less likely to have another security block. Mikozy thought about the architect who would have planned the building. He would have had thinning hair and a sharpened pencil, thinking, "Cops need protection from the criminals, from their lawyers, and to hide the witnesses. I'll put another security device in their elevators." The architect would later think about the coroner's service elevator: "Only dead bodies going down to be disemboweled. No need for added security. They're not likely to complain." The architect might not have thought these thoughts, but Mikozy figured he could guess the logic a professional school would inspire. He'd never heard of an architect with a degree from the school of hard knocks and ragged edges. That logic would be different. He was sure the architect had been paid well.

Mikozy punched the service elevator button. The elevator was waiting. The doors sprang open. Recessed lighting curved around the ceiling. Mikozy's eyes adjusted to the indoor lights, checking the color of his hands and fingernails. He was relieved to find that he had returned to the wan colors of cold white lighting. He took notice of the shifting pattern of electric reality. The normal colors? he thought. As he descended to the underground rooms, he shook his head and pitied the man who had to live in sunlight. Did people really want to see the bright edges of reality? There was no railing inside the elevator to hold on to, leaving extra inches for gurneys and for the people who traveled on their backs. Only one way to go. Down. The doors opened, and Mikozy found himself inside the crypt.

Leslie Cianfrancuso, deputy medical examiner, was standing in front of the elevator as the door opened. Her eyes blinked hard. Her lips smothered an uncertain thought. She was tall for a woman and short for a man—at least that was how it appeared to Mikozy every time he saw her. But at five foot ten inches, Mikozy barely qualified as above the national norm. Mikozy remembered thinking this the last time he saw her. Seeing her made him think of himself. "Height is a brittle measure of power," he quoted from a long-forgotten book of aphorisms. Mikozy seized on other characteristics to demonstrate his macho, not so much for himself as for the women who might desire him, for the crooks who were supposed to fear him, and for the bosses who looked for elusive measures about whether to promote him.

Leslie Cianfrancuso was LC to everyone who knew her. LC wore her white lab coat. Her starched white coat. That didn't make LC any less beautiful to him. The ash-blond tint in her hair had long since grown out, though she kept the same short cut.

Mikozy would say, "I love everything about you," and depending on whether her eyes smiled in appreciation, Mikozy would stretch out a string of compliments. LC's comment about her hair was more pragmatic: "Less corpse contamination."

"Mikozy," Leslie said. There was surprise in her voice, as though she were expecting someone else. Mikozy remembered to walk out of the elevator and avoided premature closure.

"Would you say my name the same way if they rolled me in on a gurney?"

"I suppose I would. I'm always surprised to see you."

"I'll take that as a positive sign."

Given the lateness of the hour, he thought it better to compromise. Mikozy never fought over using her first name, though he wanted to. He would have called her "Les" if she had let him. Leslie objected to the familiarity of using her first name. For reasons she couldn't quite get a hold of, she felt that LC was less devious and less coy than choosing a baby's name that could be either male or female. LC was born at a time long after women were sent home from wartime Rosie jobs but before affirmative action had leveled male resistance to female coroners. Her parents had explained to a young Leslie how they wanted to get her résumé past reluctant personnel managers. LC dutifully thanked her parents for making her entry into schools and jobs and clubs much easier with her sex-neutral name. But after gaining entry, she wanted to toy with the artificial categories of sex. She took five minutes to consider the alternatives to "Leslie." She liked "LC." It could be short for "Lower Cholesterol" or "Less Cranky." And anyway, no one ever wanted to say "Dr. Cianfrancuso" more than once.

"You always said you'd have some special time for me."

"When did I say that?" LC went into her anti-Mikozy pose, elbows bent and hands stuffed into her oversized pockets.

"When we were married." Mikozy watched LC's eyes wander around his face.

She said she could read a person's moods by the tension lines in the face. Mikozy felt his lower jaw jutting sideways. He remembered her telling him he was being defensive when he twisted his face. Mikozy said it was a bad habit. Mikozy and LC agreed that this face could be liked, though unlikely to tempt desire. Which was one reason why Mikozy still wore his beard. Rarely trimmed, the wild and prickly silver strands were never mistaken for Santa's smooth flowing mane. Mikozy claimed to have a skin problem. His friends said he was just plain ugly.

"Married? We were married? I think your mind is playing tricks on you." Mikozy politely listened to the familiar sarcasm. Even sarcasm gave Mikozy nourishment. He was temporarily lost. The porcupine prick helped him remember when he wasn't lost. LC never missed an opportunity to stick him with a verbal thrust. Mikozy was sure her sharp wit was related to doing autopsies. LC denied it.

"You seem to forget, LC. Memories are important."

"Not in the crypt, Mikozy. This is the here and now. I should've tried harder to keep Huxley. What a fine and noble bird. *Squawrkkk, squawkkk,* here and now, here and now." Her eyes came alive. Mikozy saw Huxley in her face, and he remembered. The red-and-yellow-plumed macaw that he'd smuggled in from Ecuador. Mikozy wanted to be an animal advocate, but more than that, he wanted to surprise LC. The little pill kept Huxley calm at the bottom of Mikozy's knapsack. Customs didn't peek deeply under Mikozy's badge, conveniently placed on top of a ceramic pot that was listed on his traveler's manifest. Huxley was delighted with his new habitat, and the air pollution didn't seem to bother the bird. Huxley won Mikozy passage into the first chamber of LC's heart. "This is for me?" LC had shouted, repaying Mikozy with joy in accepting the gift. Huxley reigned both day and night in the old crypt, crying out at each new body, "Come alive, come alive."

LC was working on a new vocabulary when someone had informed on her to the feds. Someone had told both customs and fish and wildlife about her illegal friend. The agents swooped into the crypt and seized Huxley. Mikozy's contact at INS was helpless to intercede with customs: "Illegal aliens and refugees, Mikozy, not illegal birds. Sorry."

LC worked her administrative powers, protecting Mikozy, and then herself, from the federal agents when their referral surfaced on the county board of supervisors' weekly agenda. She saved herself as a protector of the dead, and Mikozy as a protector of the living. One supervisor expressed surprise that the police actually protected the living, but let her defense stand. The board of supervisors had more to worry about than federal agents complaining about a macaw in the crypt. Still, the agents scored their victory, insisting that she couldn't keep Huxley.

Huxley lived at the Los Angeles Zoo now. He taught his comrades about the here and now. And whenever he had a human audience, he'd tell them to come alive. Mikozy and LC visited Huxley the week after he was seized by the feds. Huxley danced on his pedestal and spun off his entire vocabulary about death and life. Mikozy and LC shared their memories of Huxley spiraling inside the moment. LC's new space in the bowels of the new police headquarters muted the sound. Laughter sounded in silence. The old rooms had reveled with vibration. Their laughter would have zinged around the old cavern. Voices were just short of being an echo. Somebody had complained to the architect for the new building, and he had cured the near-echo effect. The new crypt sounded like everybody else's office.

The old forensic science center had now been bundled up like a police shakedown. The objective was to combine checking equipment and rooms with a quiet efficiency before bodies could be moved into headquarters. LC was in charge of the shakedown. Even though she asked for release time, there was no budget to bring in temporary staff. The dead bodies continued to flow into the old center. The yearly flow of twenty thousand dead had to be accounted for. She couldn't stop the tide. And worse, she would have been deemed uncharitable. She would become a local news item: "Coroner Postpones Death, Stinks Up City." LC decided to double shift until the shakedown was complete. Her boss advised her that it was better to lose the sleep than to drown in death. As senior deputy, she had the responsibility to make sure that the transition would not disrupt the examination of the dead. The vaults had to be checked for construction debris. Everyone knew the vaults had been used to store lunches, keep beers cool, and hide the sport pages during inspections. The task was complex. The equipment had to be recalibrated, the recording equipment tested. The most irritating part of the move was the discovery of child-sized toilets. Did the architect think that the dead had to stoop to relieve themselves or that medical examiners became so exhausted that they had to crawl into the bathroom? LC promised the architect no mercy when his body was rolled in for examination and that whatever the cause the death, the certificate would say "pencilitis." The architect admitted that the child-sized toilets were his mistake. He couldn't remember what he had been thinking when he drew it in. He said he would look at the budget to see if he could change them out at no cost. LC even checked the outlets. The medical examiner's quaint motto, "We learn from the dead," wouldn't hold much truth if the machines couldn't be plugged in, the bodies lost, or the specimens mislabeled. LC had to make sure everything was where it was supposed to be and the machines worked the way they had at the old location.

And of course she wanted to be sure that she could find peace and normalcy in the bathroom.

"How can I help you, Mikozy?" LC's voice had warmed up. Her eyebrows peaked in friendly inquiry. He was always dazzled by her expressions. Mikozy wanted to reach out and brush her hair back and kiss her sweetly on her ear.

The moment slipped back to a memory. He was seated next to LC in a criminal proceeding. They sat on the last wood bench for spectators. The room was jammed with a Mothers Against Violence ensemble. A constant rumble resisted the judge's incantation for quiet. Everyone was expecting a righteous conviction. Mikozy was hopeful that the accused would plead out so Mikozy could maintain his cover. Too many creatures of evil roaming the streets. Mikozy needed time to build on their confidences. "Trust me" had to be earned.

Mikozy met LC briefly during the autopsy of the toddler, killed by the accused in a drive-by shooting. Somebody had insulted his girlfriend at a high school football game. She was dissed, they all said. LC leaned over and whispered, "How many years do you think he'll get?" Mikozy guessed right about half the time. As for the rest, it was always a surprise. Mikozy decided to gamble. He leaned over to answer LC's question. Instead, he kissed her ear. LC stood up, the embarrassment evident, rising from her neckline. She moved away from Mikozy.

After the hearing, LC cornered Mikozy. He hadn't moved. She stood over him. "I'm thinking about bringing a charge against you for harassment."

Mikozy was a gambler, and at the moment he was more interested in LC than in his job. His voice appealed to sentiment, trying to work his way around the boundaries of legally correct behavior. "What else are you thinking about?"

LC studied Mikozy. He could have been one of her bodies. "Well," LC responded, "either that or lunch at Delpino's." LC's lips twisted around, shortening her smile.

"That'll set me back at least $200." Mikozy wondered if this was the new revenge or a male fantasy come true.

LC gave her trademark laugh. "I think my ear is worth at least that. You've got to take the penalty kick or pay the price."

Mikozy's reverie was less than five seconds in real time. The memory faded, but it was enough to tempt him to repeat his high-risk style of making and winning friends. He'd be willing to pay the price again.

"How about an hour of love?" Mikozy didn't know whether he was serious or not.

Seeing LC short-circuited his repressive mechanisms. Mikozy was looking around for love. He still did not know exactly what had happened three months ago that dissolved the substance of their relationship. It had sort of disappeared, evaporated. *Pooff.*

"Hmmm, what would we do? Spread-eagle on a cutting table? That's too cold for my tastes. Anyway, Frank wouldn't approve."

LC wasn't offended. She was rarely provoked. At least her corpses didn't try to touch her breasts. LC's female doctor friends complained about their male patients often enough to reinforce LC's decision to become a medical examiner and treat only the dead. But even among the living, she was in control. Her clinical eye examined their verbal thrusts. With cool surgical incisions, she parried, sometimes with sarcasm, sometimes truth.

"How would he know? He's home sleeping." Mikozy hated the name Frank.

"No. He's on the graveyard shift. In fact, I thought he was coming by early for our coffee break. And," LC added, dropping to a conspiratorial voice, "Frank insists I tape all my discussions with you." Her eyes sparkled. An intense fire looked directly into Mikozy's soul, challenging him to unspeak his words to her. Mikozy knew LC could be as crazy as he could, particularly when it came to building up or tearing down the walls to communication.

"Bullshit." Mikozy hammered the "boool" and stretched out the "sheeeeet." He used that word to good effect. Mikozy was equally good at giving the odd look, the surprised look, the hurt look. Mikozy and LC had played the couples game with intensity, learning each other's styles of combat and love. Mikozy stepped back in defiance, shaking his head in dismay and clapping his hands, and he burst out in unexpected laughter.

"He's not going to like what you just proposed," LC said. She ignored Mikozy's boorish language and weak attempt to laugh her into forgetfulness. She had heard it too many times to be swayed.

"More boool-sheeeet."

"Listen."

Mikozy listened. He heard a small hiss above his head. He looked up and noticed a speaker partially hidden behind a gray metal screen.

"How can I help you, Mikozy?" That was LC's voice.

"How about an hour of love?" That was Mikozy.

The tape continued to hiss. Mikozy heard their voices in surround sound. LC pulled out a remote control that had been hidden in her pocket and pressed a button.

The hiss again.

"How can I help you, Mikozy?"

"How about an hour of love?"

"Frank will be very unhappy when he hears this tape."

Mikozy wasn't angry. Mikozy wasn't afraid. Mikozy wasn't sure how he felt. Maybe this was how a perp felt when he heard himself admit to a crime. He looked up at the speakers and wondered if his privacy had been invaded. He hadn't even been Mirandized. An unfair confession.

"You wouldn't do that, LC." She had him thinking maybe she would, maybe she wouldn't.

"My god, Mikozy, this is real funny." Now it was LC's turn to clap her hands and shock the air. "Don't worry, I was just trying out my new sound system. You walked in on my dress rehearsal."

No response from Mikozy. Mikozy imagined himself losing blood pressure. He felt a tickle under his beard. "Mikozy, are you awake? Can't you take a joke?" LC prompted. She reached over and pushed him gently with the remote control.

"Yes to all your questions." Mikozy looked around as if he were testing the wind. "That's a fine way to treat a friend."

Mikozy had lost another battle of the two sexes. He wasn't sure exactly what he had lost. Women seemed to have their way with him more now, now that he was well into his thirties. Rapid senescence. Maybe this was the secret no man ever talked about.

Instead of hot flashes, aging male hormones caused lapses of judgment and extreme gullibility. Mikozy hoped it was just bad luck tonight.

"I'm glad you came down to visit." LC pointed down the hall. "If you want, I'll give you the cook's tour. It's really great." She brushed the air back with a broad circular wave of her arm, mocking the ceremony of the tour she had forced herself to master. "We have so much new stuff. It's almost as if the politicos want to be certain how their citizens die. Or to make sure they're dead. After all, without our signatures on the death certificates, none of your homicides are really dead. You only think they are."

Mikozy looked down the hall for the first time past the alcove, looking into a tomb on the scale of pyramids, with rows of refrigerated drawers instead of stone sarcophagi. The room was dim. Just enough light to make out the butcher-block tables that occupied the center of the room. Microphones dropped down. They hovered over each table as silent auditors, the ever-vigilant historians of foul play. He turned back to LC. "Sure, let's have a peek."

LC pointed out the hallway behind him. "Let's go over to the lab first." Mikozy turned to follow LC and bumped into a pane of glass. LC laughed. "That's got to be the architect's humor. I never asked for it. He said it was a work-around for a new code requirement. He couldn't explain it, and I can't either. Legislators seem to think they can impose safety even when the reason is invisible."

Mikozy and LC slipped back into the tease-and-please routine. This had been their banter for the last several years. Except that LC said that it annoyed Frank. Mikozy hoped Frank wouldn't come by until he left. He never had any interest in meeting Frank.

"Just as long as you don't offer me anything to taste."

"Not to worry, the witches' brew won't be available till next week."

They walked back to the laboratory; a line of dim overhead lights identified the room. They entered through an open side door. The room brightened as they stepped inside.

LC noticed Mikozy's surprise.

"Automatic light switch. You step into the room and the lights overhead triple their wattage. Step back and thirty seconds later, the lights automatically dim. When the room sensors pick out a moving body, the bright lights stay on."

Mikozy nodded. It wasn't as if he hadn't seen this show before so much as being woven into normalcy. Every day was a new beginning.

He knew he'd have a hard time being Rip Van Winkle for even a week. Microscopes abounded. They were still hooded in plastic. LC pointed out one of the combined gas chromatograph/ mass spectrometers as if she had something scheduled for them. The GCMS was superior to either of those machines and operated independently. From one new techy tool to another, LC could parse evidence from crude to small and sometimes to the evanescent if caught early by crime scene investigators.

"These look like they're ready to go," Mikozy observed.

"Yes," LC said. It was an uncertain yes, implying much more could be said. Mikozy only needed to wait.

"Back then, our data, our measurements, findings—all of it— crawled inside monstrous computers. Well, look at what we have now. Slimmed down, faster, better networking with national databases. And then there's AI filtering into everything we do. Mostly for the good."

Mikozy could see that some of the old equipment had been moved here. Some of the new equipment appeared to be draped in its original boxes. "We're not taking everything with us. The rest of the old center is being kept as a subsidiary teaching facility."

"So will this be a teaching facility also?"

"I'm not sure what I mean. There's been some talk that the feds want a regional laboratory here. Maybe they'll take it over under…" A hesitation and a long pause. "A cooperation agreement. They're the ones with the funding for our being tied into their national computer database. Or databases. They haven't shared that as yet." LC sharpened her no-nonsense voice. "That is not for the public airwaves."

"I never realized that education received such a remarkable priority." Mikozy could have added that this decade confirmed the high demand for doctors of death.

Mikozy walked about the room and recognized most of the equipment from his frequent visits to the forensic science center. LC waited for Mikozy by the door. Mikozy stopped midway down the array of equipment on the right side of the room. One of the objects puzzled him.

"What's this new fella do?"

"That is Mr. SEM." LC caught up with Mikozy. "Short for scanning electron microscope."

"Yeah, well?" SEM's full name did not enlighten Mikozy about what SEM did in an autopsy.

"You remember the Feldstein case?"

"Yeah. The one with the strange perforation marks on both calves?"

"Well?" LC demanded of her student.

"There were small chips on the cutting tool." Mikozy brightened. "Oh yeah. The photographs. The super photographs."

"Right. You've seen Mr. SEM at work before. You just have a hard time remembering his name."

Mikozy smiled and pivoted around, tilting his head back toward a rear door. A wide expanse of glass surrounded the room. Through the windows he saw several doors.

"Those are our offices. I'll take you by my office after we go through the cutting room. I know you'll be impressed."

"I'm always impressed." What else could he say? "If you've seen one cutting table, you've seen them all."

LC and Mikozy walked back out of the laboratory to the alcove in front of the elevators and paused in appreciation of money well spent.

"Now we can go down the other hallway into autopsy central."

LC continued her tour, taking quiet steps in her tennis shoes. She expected to cross from one end of the underground cave to the other hundreds of times during the week and had long been an advocate of stealth walking. No reason to interfere with somebody else's work or to joke about the waking-the-dead thing.

As they stepped into the large, open room, the lights brightened. Mikozy mumbled, "Ah, yes, the future's here too."

LC showed Mikozy cutting tools and tables, the drainage sloughs, the recessed microphones, and a bank of body refrigerators for short-term storage. The longest time they had ever kept a body was three weeks, those that had been stalled over a competition between police reasons, religious reasons, and political ones as well. The body was a pharmacopoeia of the latest street and legal drugs. The police and ME were following the evidence, while the family claimed religious reasons. The family was worried about the deceased's soul being trapped between the second and third rings of hell. They wanted Uncle Zip's soul to go to the furthest depths of Hades immediately. They saw no reason to hold up the autopsy. More important was their fear of him sneaking back into LA by way of the la Brea tar pits. The priest exhorted the family to be good and to avoid becoming a soul sucked into the furnace of time. The family thought about the priest's words, imagining Uncle Zip becoming something like a toxic gas, seeping back into LA just like the dinosaurs had percolated their way back up as oily sludge. Maybe Uncle Zip could come back as nerve gas. Almost every day, LC encountered parishioners gathered outside the old building with an uneasy sniffling. LC was relieved when the body was carted away.

LC stood in front of one of the autopsy tables. A domed glass chandelier was positioned above the table. The glass bubbled out to reduce the glare. LC reached under the edge of the table. The glass hood slowly descended to the table and stopped when LC pulled her hand away.

"This is a splatter glass. It reduces the chance of flying blood and body matter landing on the medical examiner and others attending the autopsy. We didn't have this blood barrier at the old Forensic Science Center. We can now deal with the worst-case scenario."

"Which is what?" Mikozy did not want to hear the worst-case scenario, but he sensed LC wanted to tell him.

"We're trying to get a negative pressure hood to contain the aerosol—you know, the bloody spray we get when we saw through…" LC stopped midstream. Her voice rose, sharp and inviting as a baited fish hook. "There have been several reported cases of tuberculosis among medical examiners. Other diseases as well. The explanation seems to be that they inhaled some of the aerosol. It's kind of scary thinking about corpses contaminating the living. Something we thought we had under control. The dome also contains body gases when we pop the body open. You remember that woman who died out in Riverside? The attending doctor and, I don't remember exactly, one or two nurses fainted. They suspected the woman had taken poison, and when she was popped open, the medical staff got a whiff of something they hadn't counted on."

"Do you have to use that word?"

"What word?"

"Popped."

"I didn't figure you for queasy."

"Hey, I'm not queasy. It's just the word is—what, let's say overly descriptive."

"Clinical?" LC said with authority and a wicked smile.

"I hope you warn your visitors." Mikozy was thinking about his trips down to watch the autopsy and couldn't remember if he had held his breath all the way through.

Unlikely.

Mikozy coughed. "Thin air."

"Thanks for the advice, Mikozy, I like a sympathetic listener."

"What I meant to say was I hope you…" He paused. "I better shut my mouth before you disinfect it." Mikozy reached up and rapped on the glass. He heard it ping rather than thud. The glass wobbled though he hadn't hit it hard.

"Real glass. Not worried about a shaker?" Mikozy searched LC's eyes for the light that once burned for him. He watched the way she canted her body. Was she tilting toward him or only steadying the glass dome?

"Glass cleans better than plastic." LC sounded as if she were speaking from the other end of a telephone, a pleasant official response. "We decided to trade risks—the chance of a daily infection compared to the many temblors we have and, of course, the Big One. Depends on how you want to live your life."

LC switched moods again. She leaned forward, pheromones rising like steam off a marsh, the vibrations of the night bouncing back and forth between them. She wasn't talking into a telephone any longer. Mikozy could touch the sounds. He felt her voice vibrating, a rocking rhythm whenever she used his first name.

"Right, Rafael?" The rhythm coiled around his heart.

Mikozy didn't know how a cop could trade away the risk unless he went behind a desk. That's what she wanted from him. It was unfair. If he moved inside and away from the street, he'd be in a position far less risky than a pathologist's. No chance of blood flying off the pages—only a spray of toner from the copier. Mikozy tried to convey to LC the excitement of being an authorized street person, one who could badge his way into secret rooms and protected spaces. Especially undercover work. Especially vice. Mikozy could change his colors faster than a chameleon could go from ivy to twig.

She said, "Rafe, I don't want to pull back the sheet and find your toe tag."

He said, "We all put on the toe tag. Can't get by Saint Peter without one."

She said, "Time goes fast enough without being undercover vice."

Mikozy wondered how his being reassigned to homicide would change her feelings toward him. Maybe those were only her words of the moment, a distraction from the prickly truth, fooling him, fooling herself. Words were a vice, deceiving both the listener and the teller. He could not answer her question, which paralyzed his thoughts.

"Right, Rafael?"

Mikozy looked away from LC, scanning the room for something to talk about.

"By the way, is Carla here?" Carla was paired with LC for doing autopsies.

Carla collected the evidence, weighed it, and, depending on the theory of death, Carla would give bits and pieces to other lab techs for further testing. Carla was heavy in the legs and wide in the shoulders. Carla was a preceptor, a technician of the dead, but she also had the semblance of LC's bodyguard, ever ready for the day or night when a modern-day Lazarus found his way into the coroner's bed-and-breakfast and decided enough was enough.

The move into the new building was overwhelming. LC's frustration showed.

LC looked around Carla's spirit. It roved around from corner to corner like a Cheshire cat. A magnified grin and beaming eyes, wise about the absurdity of death. This was LC's wonderland, and Carla was always here in spirit.

"She was supposed to start today over here with me. That's not going to happen. Carla's still over at central finishing up our move at that end. It's been pretty amazing, trying to keep working and moving at the same time. We can't perform magic."

"I'm not expecting magic, LC, only your usual witchcraft."

Mikozy looked at the table furthest away from them, near the back of the room. There was a body waiting for a workup. The sheet had been pulled back. A dark face looked up at the sky.

"Who's that?"

"Actually, no bodies were supposed to be moved in here. I don't know if you're aware of the work slowdown by county drivers. A union dispute. One of them thought it would be cute to make a drop here. We're half the distance to the FSC and he said, 'I got this memo we were supposed to start dropping the bodies here.' It's hard for me to repeat his accent. He sounded like a New York hack by way of Afghanistan. Whatever he was, he was more union than immigrant. And he wouldn't transfer the body to the FSC. What a way to start the day. And that was three days ago. But this is a minor irritation compared to the rest of the move. We might have to keep this guy in our coolers for another week. I call him our baptism body, *fulano de tal*."

"Ah, so?" Mikozy risked being canceled while mimicking an ancient movie trope. "Spanish for John Doe." Mikozy didn't know his own Chinese roots. He only knew they were there. Too many roots and destinies to deal with was how he explained his confusion.

Mikozy walked down the room to the stranger. LC hurried to catch up to Mikozy.

"Didn't he have any ID on him?" Mikozy asked.

"Of course. He had a driver's license, a social security card. The trouble is they are fake. My guess is that he's an illegal alien."

"I wonder who's going to pay the tab."

"The county. Who else?"

"Probably paid property tax on the house he owned. Fair is fair."

"A house? Maybe a rancho in a canyon."

LC shook her head. The contempt she had for the decades-old dispute over whether illegal aliens were a boon or a drain on the local economy. She knew that in parts of LA, illegals *were* the economy. Their dollars pumped through LA's veins, lifting the pallor of a postindustrial city. LC remembered Mikozy toasting her with a Negra Modelo. Mikozy said the owner had slipped across the border and opened La Chucha. The owner also brought in his relatives and friends from Mexico and made the restaurant a village enterprise. And there were the drugs too.

Mikozy tilted the bottle to LC. "The best dark ale in the best restaurant for the best woman."

LC knew Mikozy would admit to having offered her that honor, even now. LC decided not to remind Mikozy of those better days. The moment for reminiscing had slipped away.

"We won't be shipping him back to his country of origin, wherever that is. A lot cheaper to put him in Potter's field, the place for the unknown Angeleno."

Mikozy walked over to the stranger and bent over his head.

"Do you want me to run a check through immigration?" Mikozy knew that Mitch Jackson would help. Mikozy had an inexhaustible credit line with Mitch. A very serious favor that could never be called in. Jackson had only come up short once. He couldn't keep customs from seizing Huxley. "Mikozy, please, anything but illegal birds."

"Maybe. Give me a little time to work him up."

The man had jet-black hair, straight, probably cut with the help of a bowl; a deep coffee color resisted death's pallor. Mikozy thought he saw an old scar sliding behind the ear and reached his hand to brush the hair back.

LC caught Mikozy's hand before he could touch the body. She reached across with her left hand. An awkward reach that almost tipped her off balance. LC stood further away from the body than she usually did during the examination. Her lockjaw grip fastened around Mikozy's wrist. Her suddenness surprised Mikozy. LC pushed his hand away from the body. Mikozy looked at her for an explanation.

"You don't need to make him look better."

That was not the explanation Mikozy expected. That was no explanation at all. Her voice was curt.

"You know I'm not a beautician," Mikozy said, questioning LC with his eyes. He reached out for her hand, but she pulled away.

"I just wanted to take a closer look at the scar." Mikozy was still hoping LC would tell him why she'd pushed his hand away with so much force.

LC bit down on her lower lip. She nodded for Mikozy to follow her as she edged away from the body. As she walked down the room, she pulled out the remote control and pushed one of the buttons. "I want to make sure the system isn't recording." LC wasn't offering anything further in the hall of the dead. She continued down the room toward the entrance. Mikozy followed behind.

"Can you at least tell me whether Pomerance did the background check on the guy?" Mikozy asked as he caught up to LC.

Mikozy knew Pomerance. Someone he could ask about the body later if he needed to know more than what would eventually find its way onto the paperwork. Might even become his paperwork. Pomerance was an investigator for the medical examiner. Pomerance had more hair on his chin than on his head. He looked dignified when he stood up and like a professor when he hunched over a dead body.

Pomerance had the air of an instructor when he offered his qualified opinion about the cause of death. Qualified, always qualified. Pomerance knew how to offer the politically astute cause of death, leaving the final pronouncement to his bosses, the MEs. Mikozy expected to see a lot of Pomerance now that he was being reassigned to homicide.

LC stopped opposite the elevators and nodded. Her lips stretched tight and thin, her brow peaked, a combination of grim preparation and uncertainty about this reaper's victim.

"It's an unusual death, Mikozy." LC moved away from him, circling a speck of concrete that hadn't been swept from the floor. She moved closer to Mikozy. The distance could have been inside their zone of intimacy. Or it could have simply meant a silent request for confidentiality. Even so, Mikozy had to lean over to hear what LC was saying. If they hadn't been alone, Mikozy doubted if he'd have been able to hear her voice.

"We just got the results back on the blood workup. We also took some fluid out of his eye to run a second analysis to confirm our early results. Actually, we ran the second analysis to check out some of our new equipment. We run over thirty-five thousand tests a year, and it's nice to know that the hardware is in sync. But in this case, we needed a second opinion from our instruments." LC realized she was dancing away from the corpse and paused to regain her concentration.

"Anyway, he probably absorbed a chemical through his hands and face. The chemical was toxic, a poison. His body was pretty contaminated with it. I've never seen this poison before."

LC stopped her recitation. Apart from hearing about the novelty of LC finding a new poison, Mikozy was still puzzled. His reaction was always the "so what" question, forcing out what mattered.

"I'll bet there are millions of chemicals. How many times have you seen death by sodium chloride?" Mikozy boomed out to the near-empty chamber. His voice bounced off the elevator's metal doors and startled LC. The architect had failed. The room wasn't as mute as he'd planned. There was just enough echo to satisfy Mikozy.

LC ordinarily cherished Mikozy's wisecracks about her medical opinions. LC frowned. She was aware that she had slipped into a cautious mood. Her face creased, deep valleys on the frontier of knowledge. The strange chemical bothered her. LC turned and continued past the elevators with Mikozy in tow. Mikozy saw a row of four offices to the left opposite large glass windows that framed a laboratory with numerous workstations. The doors had peekaboo windows, a detail that raised a question about the architect's intentions. Mikozy could understand no window at all or a half-door window. The tiny windows disclosed a lascivious design. If he were still in vice, Mikozy thought, he might have arrested the architect. The first door had gold letters stenciled beneath the tiny window: "Dr. Robert Charnovsky, Medical Examiner." LC's nominal head, the one who rarely showed up for the work of deciphering death. The next door had a cardboard skull pasted over LC's name. The skull also covered up the little window. She never wasted any time in adding a touch of humanity and securing her privacy at the same time. Mikozy smiled. They still shared unspoken opinions.

"You're right." LC opened the door and invited Mikozy to her office. "I haven't seen death by table salt. Or for that matter by 99.9 percent of the chemicals that we know about. But at least I can find them in my reference books. The toxin we got out of fulano de tal is weird." As Mikozy stepped into the room, the lights turned on automatically.

"Weird? Is that a scientific term?" Mikozy looked around. Most of the room was vacant shelves. Her move into her office was a work in progress. In the center of the room, she had a large Steelcase metal desk and swivel chair. The quintessential furniture, designed to survive the trash heap of eternity. An ancient telephone and computer rested on top of the desk. She didn't answer his question, so he asked another. "Are these computers hooked up?"

LC nodded. LC walked around her desk and picked up a sheaf of papers. She flipped through the pages. LC looked up at Mikozy, ready to bare a truth about herself.

"I try to stay ahead of the industrial chemists who are out there inventing new catalysts, new solvents, plastics, and pesticides. I also try to stay ahead of the pharmacologists playing with new drugs, some that work and others that are better left unknown as failed experiments. I try to stay ahead of the biologists who invent new life-forms and the spirits of the dark…I've tried to see what I could do with AI. It can generate thousands of toxins if prompted. You know, Mikozy, the government anoints a small group of experts to forge the rules of decency. They are the ones who see themselves as the toxic Terminators, compiling lists of do this, don't do that. But there are many who ignore those lists. I don't think our guardians will stop the handiwork of the creative and the criminal." LC ran her free hand through her hair. She stared at Mikozy through gray eyes.

"That's a pretty grim view of the people you have to deal with. The good, the weird, and the ugly." Mikozy cringed, thinking about the corpse with the unknown chemical and what might have happened to him if he had touched the plague, the toxin, the whatever-it-was. LC had marked him with fear when she pulled him away from newly arrived body.

"Maybe I should be pleased to see evolution at work. God knows what we're making ourselves into." LC placed the papers back down on the desk. She pointed to the monitor. Mikozy joined her on her side of the desk and saw the cursor blinking on the screen. He wasn't familiar with the program she was using. Across the top of the screen was a single word—MEDEX—and underneath that it read National Institutes of Health. The rest of the screen was a mystery.

"As best as I can tell, this chemical should be called 1,1 triethylchloroactinate."

LC ran her finger along a line in the middle of the screen. "I'm running a literature search on the MEDEX database. That one is funded through the National Institutes of Health. It identifies toxins; their properties; uses, if known; and their effects. It catalogs another 20 percent more than what I have in my local area network. It's also a lot more current." She looked up briefly to make sure he was listening.

Mikozy had heard her search-and-hunt stories before. Her method was cold and relentless. He called it the windchill factor for tenacious research. Cold, real cold. When he first felt the force of her determination, he asked her, half seriously, if she thought he suffered brain impairment, maybe an attention deficit disorder or an imperfect memory—she looked at him in a funny way, but he realized that she loved research. The way she had looked at him was a reflection of her inner struggle. She lost herself and spoke in tongues whenever she was on the hunt for the modern arcanum, something the alchemists never found in their quest for nature's great secret but that biologists, geneticists, and industrial chemists were still eagerly searching for.

LC had told Mikozy about the hundreds of millions that were being spent on collecting and organizing medical information. Maybe a government pork project, but LC didn't mind. She was fascinated at being able to dial up or link to a distant library for her computer database searches. Mikozy knew the police spent hundreds of millions to collect and organize information about criminals. He was disappointed about the acronym the criminal justice system had invented: CRIMDEX. The Criminal Information Index. MEDEX had a crisper sound.

Mikozy lacked the same interest LC had in talking to computers. He had hoped when he was forced to use CRIMDEX, all the garbage would have been cleaned out. It was improving, but there was too much wasted time dealing with odd combinations of information that would never exist, that would never be considered, if not for the computer trying to please humans with its exhaustiveness. There was an art to picking through these bits and pieces. Something that Mikozy lacked. This was not about counting how many angels could dance on the head of a pin, but trying to determine how many of the dancing angels had brown curly hair and wore red fingernail polish. Maybe the MEDEX database was in better shape than CRIMDEX.

Mikozy watched LC's anxiety evaporate as she plucked away at this enigma. Her face flushed. The electricity in her movements multiplied in intensity. She picked up her papers and put them down again. Her nervous energy never needed a caffeine prompt. She was charged up by her hunt for answers to death's puzzles.

"If it's a new chemical, how do you know it killed your illegal?" Mikozy asked the obvious, hoping she could bring him closer to an understanding of this mystery. And he didn't want to claim ownership of the misfortune by saying "our illegal." The death probably wasn't a homicide. And even if it was, Mikozy hadn't been assigned to the case.

LC told him that she also wanted to be an instructor, not just an investigator. But she'd have to wait until somebody retired. Until then, she loved instructing Mikozy. Tonight, Mikozy knew he was giving her a cheap thrill, but it was his cheap thrill too. He liked listening to her talk, even if it was only a toxic puzzler.

"It's similar enough to triethylchlorosilane that I would imagine it to be poisonous. The analog is a flammable liquid and poisonous if swallowed or absorbed through the skin. Anyway, he's dead. Nothing sticks out except for this chemical. No obvious bruising or other gross trauma aside from some skin burns. A tad skinny, but well nourished. We haven't examined his internal organs, but he's young, and the probability of a heart attack, aneurysm, or other natural organic failure is low. The way I can analyze this chemical just screams for the lab's attention. It fits into two families of existing toxins. There's enough in his eyes that I'd say it would be unhealthy to eat them." LC's dark humor flowered in death's garden. Mikozy remembered that lecture. There were several cases of poisonings he'd worked with LC.

Mikozy had not taken chemistry in high school or college, and he'd failed biology the first time around. Mikozy did not have an aptitude for academic science. Still, LC and Mikozy liked to play that Mikozy knew more than he did. All he really needed to know was results.

"So I shouldn't put this into my rum and Coke?"

"Hardly. Not unless you want me to do your autopsy." Mikozy pictured himself lying naked while LC stood over him. It was the cold metal table that made his daydream shudder.

"That might be one way of getting back into your arms."

"Forget it, Mikozy. Frank is very jealous. He said he'd divorce me if I became a necrophiliac."

"Ah, well, those are the breaks. I forgive you in advance."

LC brushed back her bangs. The air around her grew measurably colder. She let the bantering die. She turned scientist again.

"Mikozy. What our illegal had just in his eye fluid could have killed several individuals. I'd say this toxin was absorbed in industrial strength. There's also another chemical that's not a poison that I suspect will turn out to be a timing buffer. You know, the twelve-hour timed-release cold medicine. That's probably why he didn't die on the spot."

"So what do you think happened to him? Catch a bad cold and take a pill someone tampered with?"

"This was definitely not a pill. The chemical was absorbed through his skin. Remember, hands and face."

"*Our* illegal?" Mikozy questioned LC's description. "He's not ours unless it's a homicide and not just an accident."

LC only nodded. She rarely gave her findings without painting a picture of the corpse. She wanted an image to give texture and color to the technical and often abstract results. Mikozy knew he had to wait while she sketched her outline of fulano de tal. "He's only five foot one. Short for someone eating Big Macs, Cheerios, and other Wonder food. You saw his jet-black hair. Probably cut with a bowl on his head. He might be an Indian up from Mexico. We have quite a community of Oaxacans and Zapotecs up here."

LC took a short breath and leaned forward, balancing against the edge of her desk. "My guess is he was probably working with this chemical and was never told to take the proper precautions. He probably used it with his hands and then rubbed his face. Maybe he was sweating." LC waited a few seconds. Mikozy listened. He watched her. She became self-conscious and added, "That's my scenario. A careless employer who cared less about his illegal worker."

"An unfortunate accident. Is that how the medical certificate will read?" Mikozy understood that a case could be initiated by the ME's opinion about the cause of death or, for that matter, could relegate a case into nothingness along with the body. "Accident" would make this illegal a zero.

"I'd like to put down employer negligence."

This was her personal campaign. She tried to get Mikozy to join. She had wanted him to arrest an employer in another poisoning case he worked on. The employee was another probable illegal. Until the government started punching computer chips into its citizens at time of birth, no one could be really sure about a dead body, even if it came with a driver's license and a library card. All could be faked. Nothing was tamper-proof.

Mikozy remembered the name of the last alien. Jeronimo Xochimil. Strange name, strange death. And an ugly death. Jeronimo had slipped and fallen into a storage tank he was hosing down with sulfuric acid. No one was around when he fell. He probably lost his grip and the hose kept on pumping. LC said she didn't think he drowned.

There hadn't been much flesh left to do a gross specimen slide. Mikozy had caught sight of nervous eyes from the owner, who was more worried about a visit from immigration than about what had happened to Jeronimo. Mikozy listened hard and was tempted to expand the work of the LAPD. Mikozy knew there would be more Jeronimos killed in this company. The state's labor code enforcers were overworked and would only fine the employer. A thousand dollars was the stiffest fine they could issue. Mikozy went to newly promoted Schmidt. His good buddy Schmidt. Captain Schmidt wasn't impressed. Schmidt jerked him around, complaining about not having enough men for real criminals—"Why bother the company, unless they were trying to murder the guy?"—and then yanked Mikozy out of homicide and put him into vice for the past year. Great to have a buddy like Schmidt. Mikozy knew this illegal would be his ticket out of homicide again if he jumped onto LC's cause.

"Maybe you should put down employer negligence. I can't touch it right now. You understand? Maybe later. Not unless you put down possible homicide."

Mikozy looked at the computer's flashing screen, avoiding LC's soft-spoken petition for help.

"There are several types of death I don't like to see," she said. "Child deaths are always disturbing. Industrial deaths are another, especially when you get migrants. They're getting whipsawed by our high technology. They learn about the dangers of jungles and mountains, even about gang warfare, whether in the city or the country. They come up here and get blindsided by pesticides, industrial solvents, and unforgiving machinery. If they're lucky, they only lose a limb or become impotent. Can't you do anything?" She didn't have to repeat her request.

Mikozy read her thoughts and looked away. Her words punctured his heart, a thousand shivs stabbing at his nerve.

"The land of opportunity is not without its own demons," he said. "We can only do so much. It's better not to dwell on the human condition for too long. They don't. They still come. They still dream that our streets are paved with gold." Those words always had the feel of granite. LC and Mikozy observed several seconds of silence. Those were the moments that flickered with sadness.

The computer's flashing screen caught his attention. She ignored it.

She returned to her chemical puzzler, passing over what she would finally put down as the cause of death. Her voice broke the spell. She was the medical examiner again.

"There's something I don't fully understand. I mentioned that the toxin's effect appears to have been delayed."

Mikozy felt the stubble on his face. He nodded. Mikozy hoped that LC would take that as a sign that he wanted the lecture to be over.

"We found microcrystalline cellulose and pregelantized cornstarch." LC let Mikozy think about those ingredients. Mikozy took a few seconds to digest the additives. She smiled. "You've eaten these before, Rafael."

Mikozy figured these were probably the essential ingredients of simulated pastries. Maybe it was better to eat cake made with real butter and eggs. Takes a lot longer to be a cause of death.

"Remember? Cold medicine?" LC prompted.

"Time release, right?"

"Precisely. Microcrystalline cellulose and pregelantized cornstarch are used to embed the active ingredients and stretch out their effect on your body. Same thing seems to be happening here."

"You dismissed cold medicine. Hands and face, right?"

"Right. Except we found some traces of these substances mixed in. The facts are the facts. We found that strange. During the analysis, some of it blossomed. I mean, whoosh. Just like you see on TV. Exploding microbombs. Except these were releasing 1,1 triethylchloroactinate—our unknown poison, not your usual cold remedy."

"So what's it mean?" Mikozy was unsure about the significance of a timed-release poison in this case, although a criminal application suggested an obvious guess. Time enough to create an alibi, time enough to disguise the real moment of death.

"From my vantage point, I have to worry about the time of death. Normally, given the concentration alone, he should have slipped into his final countdown immediately after being exposed to the chemical. But now, I'd have to say that death followed exposure by several hours. My gut feeling is about a six-hour delay. We're still running some tests and doing some more thinking about what we have."

"Fascinating," he deadpanned.

"Is that all you can say?" LC sounded disappointed. She had failed to hook Mikozy with her medical mystery.

"Hey, listen. You got something really interesting. But that's all technical stuff." Mikozy sensed that LC wanted something more from him. He would have tried if he knew his new assignment was secure inside homicide. A check in the wrong box could send him floating away on a sea of shit locked inside a box.

Mikozy wasn't Harry Houdini. He'd never make it out until he retired.

"When you decide on what the cause of death was, I'll be around."

"Sure, sure." LC reached past Mikozy and turned off the monitor. The screen went dark.

"You know, Rafael, sometimes you can be a real flake."

She wanted a lot more from Mikozy. She wanted a hot rod to flay the guilty. Mikozy held back too often, hiding behind bureaucratic barbed wire. Unless he was hooked. Then he never seemed to mind being pricked and scratched.

Mikozy was surprised when he discovered how passionate LC was about the cause of death. But then she didn't have to Mirandize the dead or the living. She didn't have to apologize to an unforgiving public when a mistake was made and a criminal's right was violated. The criminal was free to murder, rape, and pillage while the police tried to catch him again with the proper arresting etiquette. Mikozy stumbled badly with LC whenever he retreated into caution.

"I'm sorry for venting on you, Rafael. Thanks for coming by. I know you can't do anything right now." The anger in her voice evaporated. He felt a residue of sadness for something they'd misplaced.

It was well past Mikozy's bedtime. He made a face and leaned into a goodbye shuffle. Mikozy thought about looking in on LC later, but now he just wanted to go home and dream.

"I'm going to hold on to this body a little longer," LC said as they walked out of her office. "I'll have some time to think about the puzzles inside this body."

"I have a feeling the body will be back to haunt me. If there's an evil in it, it'll find me out."

Mikozy looked into her eyes. The river channel that separated them was too far to swim at this late hour. And he was out of shape. He'd drown if he tried to reach out for her.

"Let it go tonight," he told himself.

"Take care, LC." Mikozy walked over to the elevator and punched the button. LC raised her hand with half a heart and waved ever so lightly.

"LC, I have to ask. Is there really a Frank?"

As the elevator door began to close, LC winked. "Maybe, maybe not."

He didn't see her wave goodbye as the door closed on their farewell. The elevator took him back up to ground zero, leaving LC to finish her graveyard shift. Mikozy had to start his own in the morning.

Chapter 3
NEW DIGS

Along with the morning's arrival, Mikozy pulled into the parking structure and swerved into the first space on the second level. Pretty much like it was last night. Tomorrow morning he'd be lucky to crawl up to the fifth level. The new digs would be baptized and confirmed by a full house of cars. The word *detective* was carefully inked onto the concrete stops running up the row. Mikozy fingered the ignition key, listening to the song on the radio, waiting until the words died out. The cello groaned. A siren voice glided across liquid harmony while Mikozy tapped the lazy bottom rhythm on the dash. The bass guitar reverberated and pulsed. He followed the groove. The muse danced in an empty chamber, arms poised to embrace a lover. That was today. On other days, Mikozy's Bose speakers created a big bang. Music that overpowered casual listeners and chatty conversation. He did what he could to keep the music within legal limits.

Mikozy remembered another time, again swinging open the car door. September sometime. Right around Labor Day. The radio advised staying inside: "It's going to be a scorcher today." He remembered sweating, but he couldn't feel the heat. The sun blinded him through his shades. Like today. An ugly feeling wormed inside. Mikozy cringed. A hand reached around his intestines and yanked, the pain sliced into his being. "I am because I remember." He remembered the door swinging open and the deafening music spilling out onto the asphalt. He stumbled out on wobbly feet. Carlos Laguna leaned up against the glass window in front of La Chucha. A slight wisp of a man, slick black hair and a pencil mustache. His skin was smooth and the light coffee color of a mocha-flavored scoop of ice cream. Mikozy and Laguna snake eyed each other, thinking the other was the mouse. The music saved Mikozy, pumping up his courage and the necessary deceit of a vice cop.

The song inside the memory ended. The silence inside his car dispelled the vision of Laguna. Mikozy wiped away the wetness from the line around his neck with his hand and brushed it dry on his pants.

Mikozy switched the ignition off and rested against the high-back twill seat. "An ordinary love, yes?" Mikozy said to himself. His car was his solitude. The super-high-output Sentra. Deceptively fast, deceptively loud. Mikozy identified with his car. He leaned over and looked into his rearview mirror. "Mirror, mirror, inside my car. Tell me who is the most down, brash, and baaad dick in LA." The mirror whispered, "You are, Mikozy." The mirror would keep his secret. Mikozy couldn't tell anyone about his true self when he served his time in vice. Now that he was moving over to homicide, he could crush the lies he told about himself. Toss them into the nearest trash can. He needed one minute more of meditation. A minute of peace to help him into his new shoot suit. It was tailored with a vest pocket to hold his new cards of identity. Mikozy needed to forget Laguna. He needed to stay away from La Chucha. New days, new places to eat. Mikozy began a slow breathing and let his mind wander another path. He projected himself out of his body as best he could and watched himself walk out of the parking garage, turning east and seeing the new police mecca. The southern sun should blind him now when his eyes panned the horizon and danced around the massive concrete-and-glass monument. This was police headquarters for the next century. Mikozy had seen the architect's model hundreds of times. It was tucked into an alcove next to the third-floor men's room at the old LAPD Central. He fingered the dust off the plastic shell to get a clean view. The building was monumental. This was the first day of operation for new LAPD Central. Most of the staff would not be here. Superstition held that if the building didn't fall down on its first day, it would last a century. Mikozy had flipped a penny, and it had come up heads. The building wouldn't fall down today. So he took a risk and showed up.

Mikozy had been tied to the fashionable crimes of the low-scale hoodlum.

Maybe hoodlum wasn't a fashionable word, but that was what these three strikers were. Three strikes and they were still out on the street. No one had bothered to tell the justice system about their other ten or twenty strikes. Or had the prosecutor looked the other way, led by a new social justice? Their crimes evolved with life in LA. The carjackings, the drive-bys and drive-overs, the automatic teller holdups, the reimagining of *petty* in petty theft. The newspapers created magical images of the latest crime: man dragged out of Mercedes and shot; woman mugged, then drives over mugger; professor finds sex and death at ATM, giving the public the zest of new fears, while a knee-jerking police central hoped to respond with an extra layer of cop if they could be found. Often police were being replaced by the DA's willful ignorance. Mikozy mimed a mental satire—let the public figure out that less police has its own rewards. Before his own resentment took root, Mikozy had been part of that extra layer of policing. Mikozy passed through special assignments one by one. The divisional detectives liked Mikozy and turned him into the sizzle between themselves and an irate public. The newspeople liked Mikozy too. They just couldn't show his face. He knew he was headed into undercover assignments. He could predict a short future if he had that moment of glory. Even Superman needed to suit up as Clark Kent. Mikozy limited his policing to toning down the crisis of the moment. His job was to blunt the edges of the public's fear.

> According to unnamed official sources, the latest killing, of Professor Carl Tompkins at the ATM at Breyerwood Avenue and Milbank Drive, was believed to be a freak accident. The source [Mikozy was unnamed] said that police believed that Tompkins was unaware the area was a pickup for rough trade. Early indications are that Tompkins died from a heart attack and not the superficial cuts on his abdomen.
>
> The police source said they were working with the local bank to move the location of the ATM and add additional tamperproof lighting to the area.

Mikozy's words created a sense of progress. The words soothed an angry public. If anyone had looked at the numbers, they'd see the actual crime statistics bumping up and down, not changing that much. With Mikozy providing context, the public mind was no longer paralyzed. Life could go on.

Mikozy's reward was late in coming. It had taken an extra two years to build the new place. In the meantime, they kept him in vice and told him to check out Laguna. "Go see Carlos Laguna. Get up inside his ass and find some dirt. Let's put this creep away." Mikozy had marched off with his orders on wobbly legs, music blasting out of his Bose speakers. It was a fucking hot day when he got out of his pearl-black Sentra and looked across the roof of his car. Laguna leaned against the building. "La Chucha" was boldly lettered on the glass. A Gothic script. Menus were pasted inside the window next to where Laguna stood.

Laguna squinted at Mikozy. He waved Mikozy over to follow him inside. The smell of carnitas, frijoles, and machaca blended together. It was a deep and moody aroma. He picked out the smells and turned them over, looking for his grandmother's signature. A fond embrace grabbed him out of the darkness. Mikozy looked at the plate of food set out on the table. Laguna sat down across from him. Mikozy dipped a fried empanada into the salsa, cut with little red peppers. A bold bite was the macho way. The flame of the sauce seared his mouth and muted the taste of corn. Mikozy pulled hard at the mouth of the beer to slosh the mush down. He caught the lime between his teeth and sucked at the tart and sweet fruit. Mikozy noticed the long fingernail on Laguna's index finger. Laguna watched his eyes and laughed. "No soy un pinche maricon. La uña es para la gitarra." Laguna went behind the counter and carried a finely tooled guitar back with him. He sat down on the edge of the table and strummed a bluesy melody. "Let me sing for you."

Mikozy hated that moment. He smiled and hated the friendship Laguna offered. "I'm taking you down, don't serenade me"—that was what Mikozy wanted to say, but the bits of red pepper cauterized his thoughts. He chewed another empanada and took a swig of the Aguilar. Not much of a burn in his gut that day, not until he took Laguna down. Let him lie in the gutter while the sewers backed up over him.

Now was the time to collect his reward. Schmidt had promised Mikozy that he would work at the new headquarters starting on its first day of operation. Schmitty finally called. "Come on down, your old desk has been fumigated. It's been moved in already." Mikozy hoped the roaches were dead. He didn't care about the termites. The fifteen years of memos stuffed into the lower drawer were eternal. All Mikozy needed to do was to show up.

Before Schmitty hung up, he said, "You're off vice. Welcome to homicide."

Mikozy walked out of the parking garage fully rested. True to his astral projection, he was blinded by the southern sun peeking around the side of the building. Mikozy wasn't looking at anything else. He couldn't. He squinted hard. His eyes were closed, except for a narrow slit. Like trying to see through an Alaskan snowscape. White, everything white, except what you could see through the slit of the snow goggles. He wavered only a few degrees from the straight line to the corner. A foul odor wafted up, intensified by the heat popping off the street. 'Twasn't the putrid remains of a lost pet. Not a rancid ethnic food. Not junk buns. Mikozy kept on walking, rubbing his eyes to see what his sense of smell couldn't figure out. Suddenly, he collided with a body and heard the sound of tin cans crashing on the sidewalk. Mikozy stumbled back. He slapped his hands against his shirt pocket and found his sunglasses. He pulled them over his eyes. Mikozy focused his eyes on a heap of clothes sprawled on the ground. A city trash can was lying on its side. The image had not been a part of his early morning fantasy.

"Damn," Mikozy said. A goat would have been happy with the slop on the ground. But he didn't feel like a goat. He was angry with himself for getting lost in a daydream. He decided he would stay with the stress reduction breathing exercises and give up on astral projection. They didn't work when he needed them.

"Hey, bro." An excited voice jumped out of the bag of clothes. The clothes pulled themselves up to their knees while the hands grabbed for the tin cans that lay scattered all about. The man scurried around, rat packing his treasure into an oversized trash bag. A thin-skinned plastic lock box, not something he could rent in a Bank of America. The tins clattered inside the plastic bag, while he crawled inside the opening of the garbage can, pushing the paper around and sifting for urban treasures.

Mikozy often smelled his victims first. Blood drying on hot pavement, vomit crusting at the corners of a junkie's mouth try-ing to say "Spare a buck?" one last time. The stagnant heat draped its warm, musty robe around Mikozy. He knew this voice, and he thought he knew this smell. The stench was the I-never-take-a-bath man. The stink man. It was Perlmutter. Mikozy stepped back, trying to get out of Perlmutter's way, but also to get away from the stink. He clamped his jaws tight so he wouldn't have to apologize. Not to the stink man. Perlmutter's face stared out of the wire mesh trash basket while his feet splashed about outside the basket looking for a foothold.

Perlmutter was digging for gold, for tin cans and other disposables an unsuspecting public threw away, unaware they were tossing away precious metals and collectibles. That was how Perlmutter once explained it to Mikozy. The plastic bag curled around the Perl's leg, hoarding his mighty treasure. It would have been difficult to rob Perl of his plastic bag even while he was tucked up inside a trash bin.

"What are you doing here?" Mikozy tiptoed into several spaces around Perlmutter, hoping he could find a hole in the ozone layer, a void in the stink, anything to cleanse the air.

"I'm staking out my turf." Perlmutter pulled his head out of the trash and rested it atop the metal rim. A modern-day Alice wouldn't need to go down the hidey-hole into Wonderland. She could walk the streets of LA and see her grinning cat perched on the edge of a trash can. Just like Perlmutter.

He wore a near-white shirt. Mikozy thought that he might have even shaved. He could pass for a day laborer. Perlmutter gave Mikozy a wide smile. There was real pride in the way Perlmutter staked his claim. The American entrepreneur was everywhere, even among the homeless. In that moment, the Perl's self-esteem was measurably higher than Mikozy's.

"Here? You're going to hang out here?" he asked Perlmutter. He heard the surprise in his voice go nasal as he tried to talk and clog his nose at the same time.

Mikozy mumbled to himself, "They promised us the building would be impregnable. Nobody said anything about the streets." He looked up and down the street. It was deserted. Just him and Perlmutter.

"Yeah, great idea. Isn't it?"

Mikozy had first met Perlmutter about seven or eight years back, shortly after a large quake. Perlmutter had arrived by bus from the big city. From New York. "My social worker said, 'Go west, young man.' She said the streets were lined with gold. So here I am." That was after Mikozy pulled Perlmutter out of a teenage wolf pack. They had scattered into the traffic when Mikozy yelled, "Police." The word police still had some magic eight years ago.

The Perl continued his reminiscence. "All I said was go fuck yourself when one of them asked me for my Coke." He held up a red can. The brown spots on his teeth were repulsive. Mikozy couldn't imagine why the punks would want to take a drink out of Perlmutter's can.

"So where's the gold?" the Perl had asked. That was also the last time Perlmutter asked Mikozy for help. Now it was the other way around. The Perl enjoyed explaining the nature of success to Mikozy, especially how success in LA was different from New York. Part of it was the weather, part of it was a cleaner ocean. Then there was the open border to the world only one hundred miles to the south.

The Perl pushed his shirt down inside his pants, wanting to look professional before launching into his imagined economic philosophy. No need for hypertext or cyberspace. It was as good as the *Wall Street Journal*, except he called it the *Perl Street Journal*. He was willing to share confidences with Mikozy. Sometimes even information about what was happening on the streets of LA. The Perl looked around to make sure no one else was listening. Perlmutter inched his way up to Mikozy, dragging the stink with him.

"This is for your ears only, Detective. Okay?"

"Sure," the nasal voice answered.

"You got a summer cold?"

"Maybe that's what it is."

Mikozy decided to listen to the Perl. Mikozy got an urge to find out whether the Perl had the same fascination with these new digs as he did. Might be the same for us all, thought Mikozy.

"You can see how good the construction guys felt about themselves. This trash can is piled higher than dog doo. I got a whole lot of shit in my bag. But the building is up, and they ain't coming back." The Perl sparkled. There must have been some white left on Perl's teeth.

"So I thought about the regulars. You know, the cops, the CIs, the jannnitors." The Perl covered his mouth, trying to say "janitor" without gagging. They carried away his best possessions. "I figured all the cops who moved here would feel good about themselves. Maybe even the secretaries. Cops throw away a lot of cans, and if they were feeling good about themselves, they'd probably throw away more cans and things. Right? They'd give me more money too, you know, for a cup of coffee. Right? Right?" Perlmutter's smile widened when he said "coffee." He must have been thinking of a seventy-proof high-octane caffeine additive.

"The secretaries might feel good about being here. They throw away foolish stuff. They throw away used gum, tissues, sometimes a mascara case. Right? That's not a bum's gold."

The Perl paused. "I just don't get off on used gum. Of course, I could always trade it, but that's just not me." Perlmutter tried to inch his way inside Mikozy's personal space, but Mikozy backed away. The only sound on the street was the scraping of the Perl's plastic bag of tin treasures. Mikozy had to break away before he slipped on the Perl's bottom scrounging. He thought of offering Perlmutter a "godspeed" and a "take care." As an afterthought, Mikozy settled on, "May gold be with you."

Mikozy turned away from the stench and stepped off the curb. As he walked across the street, he heard the Perl call out from behind, "Right on," punctuating the first scene of the morning.

Mikozy stood in front of his old desk. Standard gunmetal issue. A dent creased its back. The only hint the object was not immortal.

Mikozy had inherited the desk that way, and the heir to his job would probably say the same thing he said when he was shown the dent.

"Hey, there's a dent."

"Write it down," would be the reply. The same drama would be reenacted throughout the future, through an infinite change of personnel and governments and even through evolution to a higher species. It would be the same desk forever. It was now on the fourth floor of the new building. His chair was there also. He knew it was his chair from among the hundreds of others that swiveled in place like the Mad Hatter's teacup ride in Anaheim. They had identical tilt-back action, the same green Naugahyde, the same curved armrests. Mikozy's one act of vandalism was to craft his initials at the junction of the left armrest and the rear frame. He had given in to a tagger's urge. His work of art stared back, a dull sign of recognition.

"Welcome home, Mikozy," the chair grunted.

Badge No. 48175 sat in his chair. It was Sam Perkins. As old as Methuselah. New clothes today but the same crow's-feet spreading up and down his face. The building had barely opened and Mikozy's place was already occupied. Hardly a soul on the floor except for Badge No. 48175 seated at Mikozy's desk. He could say Detective Perkins, but Mikozy was annoyed. The badge was sorting through three piles of papers while playing the bureaucrat's shell game.

"Yes?" Badge No. 48175 almost looked up from Mikozy's chair. He could probably feel Mikozy's vibrations. Mikozy didn't believe in telepathy, but he was sure he could transmit bad vibes. His morning's vibes shifted into a negative aura. Mikozy was sure they were unpleasant to the touch. "This is my desk. You want to clear out?"

"Want to? Yes, I want to get back to my own desk, but the captain said to sit here for the time being."

Badge No. 48175 wasn't being a jerk, nor aspiring to be one. The badge was just following orders. Maybe because the badge had more gray hair than he did and more wrinkles ruffling his brow, Mikozy needed to show some deference. "Hire them young, they follow orders." But Perkins wasn't young, and the orders still needed to be followed. Mikozy didn't have gray hair and gray whiskers yet, but he was still following orders.

Mikozy was no different than the badge. It was an early-morning standoff. He gazed around the floor. Scores of empty desks stared back at Mikozy. But it was his desk that was occupied territory. The image of Perlmutter flitted across the room. A free spirit with the smell of freedom. Mikozy sniffed the air. The badge didn't have an odor. That wasn't Perkins's style. None that he could smell. Only the acetone smell of new carpet. The acetone stung his eyes. He would be tearing before noon.

The room felt sodden. That was an odd feeling. The furniture in the room also felt sodden. The people in it were sodden, too. A depressing thought if your job description read desk jockey. The badge's every blink appeared to be an effort to stave off paralysis and narcolepsy. The same with everyone else who would soon fill the room. Mikozy looked around and imagined a squadron of zombies ready to fight crime. Most societies bury their dead. This one moved them into a new station house. Not a man or woman here would sift the trash for hidden treasure. No interest, no need, no desire. Just haunted souls. Mikozy watched Sam Perkins move a sheet of paper from one pile to the next. That's what badges do. The pride of accomplishment had been reduced to the satisfaction of having dutifully complied with a directive, any directive. Mikozy didn't really want his desk back, but he too had to comply with a directive to stand by his desk and communicate with the badge. He had accomplished the task and now had to decide what to do next. He hadn't been given any other directives. This was the end of the line.

Mikozy knew that the directive to stay put could be forever. There was no point in questioning the badge any further. Even if he had a name that reminded him of that song about blue suede shoes. But that was Carl Perkins, not Sam Perkins. The badge probably didn't know why he was here, and even if he did, why would he tell Mikozy? It was time to see Schmidt.

"Pardon me if I am interrupting your filing." Mikozy pulled at the badge's inertia. He sent a telepathic thought to Perkins: *Talk to me, asshole*, hoping to bridge the open space between. The badge dropped another piece of paper onto the second pile.

"Where's the captain's office?" Mikozy asked. The badge pointed with a tip of his head back down the hallway Mikozy had just come up. He pointed again. This time it was up. Down the hall and up a flight or more.

"Thank you." Mikozy leaned over the badge and pulled the center drawer open until it bounced against the badge's midsection.

"Excuse me." Mikozy looked into his eyes. "I want to see if there are any roaches. You got to catch them off guard. Unless this masterpiece was fumigated."

Perkins had one of those surprised looks with funny symbols.

"You didn't find any dead roaches in my desk?" Mikozy liked to start a friendship on the basis of something weird. Perkins couldn't see the weirdness and wasn't destined to become Mikozy's friend. Still, they shared the camaraderie of being keepers of the peace.

The badge pointed to the wastepaper basket. "Take a look." Mikozy saw some insect detritus. He realized his hopes for a new economic life would not be based on what cops threw away. Maybe Perkins was an aberration, throwing away dead roaches. Not much to pick at. Mikozy walked down the hallway to find the captain.

The door was almost shut. A burnt wood plaque hung on the door. A rough-chiseled pirate leaned over a sign that said The Captain's Hole, meaning whatever Schmidt wanted it to mean. Mikozy took that as an invitation and walked into Schmidt's wonderland. No one was home. Mikozy sniffed acetone blowing off the new carpet.

Mikozy reluctantly shoved the door back to its position. He knew he would be trapped with the unnatural element. Even his eyes began to sting.

"Schmitty, Schmitty, what are you doing to me?" Mikozy repeated to the empty room. Mikozy figured that Schmidt must be in the toilet or talking to a division head. Not much choice once you rise to the top of a management pyramid. Mikozy hoped Schmidt didn't get lost in a stall-to-stall conversation with Billy Meyers, the new chief of detectives. It would take a lot of leverage to pry them out of their think tank. Mikozy considered arguing with an invisible Schmidt, but that had even less appeal than simply repeating his question to an empty room: "Schmitty, what are you doing to me?" The minutes passed. The question became a mantra, a Hail Mary, an incantation of organizational bewilderment.

Mikozy decided to go in and sat down in Schmidt's chair. He shifted around in the wooden chair, cataloging the progress of Schmidt's move from the old building. The certificates of merit were already tacked to the wall. The clubby photographs with local and foreign dignitaries perched on empty bookshelves. The mandatory computer workstation occupied a corner of Schmidt's desk. Mikozy swiveled the monitor so he could watch the cursor blink. What else was there to do?

He tapped the space bar. Up came an email from Deputy Inspector Michelle Tomlinson. The subject line said "Iron Heel." He heard footsteps in the distance. Mikozy pushed the monitor back to its earlier position.

Time to focus on something else. He noticed that the desk was new. The captain's patron saint had smiled upon Schmidt and graced Schmidt with a new desk. Mikozy ran his finger around the beveled cherrywood. "Wood, too?" Mikozy said to no one in particular. Mikozy had known Schmidt for about as long as he had been with the department. At least fifteen years, maybe more. They had even partnered for a few months in the war zone on Eightieth Street. One thing was a constant with Schmidt: he always took a morning crap at the station. Mikozy decided that was probably where Schmidt was. Mikozy heard the door swing open behind him. He saw Schmidt's image reflected in the window overlooking the parting structure. The gods had listened. Schmidt took up most of the doorway as he came into his office.

He was pushing 220 on a six-foot frame. The slide upward in dead weight was always easier than the slide down. Weight control was an exception to the gravity principle. What goes up should come down. At least that's what fad diets promised. The weight had settled around Schmidt's eyes and in his cheeks. The bulge from a badly broken nose drew quick glances and unspoken queries. Schmidt reclaimed his chair from Mikozy. He fell back in his chair and spun around to look out the floor-to-ceiling window. A magnificent piece of glass. Bulletproof too. Cost the taxpayer an extra million dollars. Schmidt stared at the window, while Mikozy looked at Schmidt's back. The hair running up Schmidt's neck was tinged orange. The gray flecks around his neck were overpowered by the Irish in the man. All the more unusual with the teak hairpiece sitting oddly on top his head. Mikozy was positive the hairpiece violated a genetic principle, and if he were Irish himself, he might have accused Schmidt of violating a moral tradition as well. Schmidt said the Irish had a saying: "If I'm a man of the community, I'm a man on fire." That was when they were out on the streets together. That was when Schmidt still had his own hair.

Mikozy followed Schmidt's gaze and saw the same cluster of high-rises populating the horizon.

"You see that, Mikozy? That's a six-floor view. Impressive. Better than yours on the fourth." Schmidt was enjoying his new office. Even with all the pressure bearing down on the captains of law enforcement, Schmidt looked relaxed. So much so that his toupee drooped. The teak had sapped him of his fire.

"Breaking in the crapper, Schmitty?"

"No. I did that yesterday. This was a special tour."

Schmidt looked across at Mikozy. "So you'd like to join us at headquarters?"

Mikozy nodded. He thought his presence was a statement of the obvious. Schmitty was jerking him around for some reason or another. Despite the invitation, Schmitty wasn't offering Mikozy any clues. They stared at each other, somewhat in awe of themselves in the new surroundings.

"Schmitty, can you see down to the street?" Mikozy asked.

"Yeah, sure. But why look at the street when I can look across the city?"

"Take a look down."

Schmidt stood up and took a step to his window. He looked down and panned the streets.

"You see the guy standing by the trash can?"

"Yeah." Schmidt was focused on the guy. "I can't make him out."

"That's Perlmutter."

"Is he one of ours?"

"No," Mikozy. "That's the Perl, you know, the stinker."

"No shit. What's he doing here?"

"He said he's staking out his turf." After a pause, Mikozy added, "Like us."

"Like I said," Schmidt said, "I'd rather look up."

"Sure, but there's a point to all this."

"If there is, I can't guess what it is."

"See," Mikozy said, "the Perl has his place. He even has his trash can. It's sort of like his desk. Now, I come to work and find somebody else at my desk. So the way I see it, the Perl is better off than I am."

Schmidt grinned and plopped back into his seat. He swung the chair around.

He poked through a stack of papers and pulled one of them out. Schmidt read over the page and looked back up at Mikozy, waving the paper in a meaningful way. Schmidt's brow curled up. The corners of his mouth curled down. Like sucking on a lemon.

"I thought that Perkins out there would get your attention. If he was sitting at my desk, I'd be upstairs in a flash."

Schmidt reached over to where once long ago he had kept a box of cigars. The box was still there, but now it cradled his reading glasses, his sunglasses, his bifocals and trifocals. He covered all the visual possibilities.

With his reading glasses on, Schmidt held the paper steady and read to Mikozy:

> All officers whose last names begin with the letters H through M must take three units of continuing education by January 8. Proof of an approved class must be submitted to the commanding officer by no later 5 p.m. on January 8. The failure to submit the proper documentation will result in an automatic suspension.

Schmidt put the paper down on his desk and folded his arms so he could rest on his elbows. Mikozy recalled seeing that same reflex in an old video—*Passenger 57*, or maybe it was *China Moon*. Maybe Schmidt had seen the video also. Maybe the movement was like red hair, except it was genetic with persons in positions of authority. Mikozy tried hard to suppress a smile.

"Do you remember getting this notice just after Labor Day?" Schmidt asked.

"I don't recall. I was preoccupied with something else." Mikozy remembered sitting inside La Chucha being serenaded by Carlos Laguna. Of course he wouldn't remember a memo. Mikozy thought Schmitty was holding in a smile. Of course, with Schmitty, you never knew. He could be suppressing gas. "Let's not have me do an interrogation, Mikozy. You put your John Hancock on the receipt of notice page. See? Right here."

Mikozy knew when to stop. He remembered signing the paper saying he knew about the continuing education requirement. He signed it while he was rushing out the door to drive over to La Chucha.

"So?"

"Today is Tuesday, January 8. Unless you got something going, I don't imagine you'll be submitting proof of a class by this afternoon. Well, are you planning to surprise me?"

"I've been busy," Mikozy said.

"Of course you've been busy. But I'm going to save your ass. Putting Perkins at your desk was a brilliant stroke, wouldn't you say? Got your attention, right?"

"Perkins ain't going to save my ass whether he's at my desk or not." Mikozy was straining. This was not part of his morning daydream either.

"You could have taken some really fine classes. Let's look at the list."

Schmidt pulled out a booklet. Mikozy could make out "Continuing Education Classes for Police Officers" on the front page. The words were written in large letters. It could have been a third-grade reader.

"Let's you and me take a look at some of the classes. Some of them are, or were, pretty good. There's Evaluation of Adult Urine Testing for Drug Surveillance. That was last month." Schmidt's voice warbled. A woodpecker punching out a happy tick-tock. "And there's Behind Bars and also Memory-Enhancing Techniques for Investigative Interviewing. Those are all gone. Too bad. I took one last week on Less-Than-Lethal Weapons." Schmidt stared across at Mikozy with knowing eyes. "That's gone too."

"What was that—breadsticks and nachos?" Mikozy was resistant to the idea of having to take a continuing education class. He knew it was a losing battle.

Schmidt was obviously enjoying the lecture. He plowed on. "In fact there's only one class left that can be completed between now and this afternoon at five p.m. It meets at two." Schmidt turned the computer monitor around on its ergonomic stand. He plucked away at the keyboard. Mikozy watched Schmidt's eyes travel across the screen and finally back to Mikozy, whose face now revealed his opinion of the administrative horror he had to deal with. "Unless you want to go on suspension. What's your interest, Mikozy? Continuing education or suspension?"

"Damn," Mikozy was about to say, but it came out something like "Okay, okay." Mikozy was not about to whimper. He would accept defeat gracefully.

"Okay, what?" Schmidt insisted.

"Okay, I'll take whatever it is on that list."

"This is great." Schmidt's day was going to be a happy one. Getting an officer to say they'll do anything. No talking back. Just doing it.

"Let me see. I had this one marked out. I even met the instructor. She sold us on the class. You know, I was on the review panel for new classes." Schmidt rambled on, taking twice as long to find the class than he needed.

"It says Clue Analysis 1."

"What? Culinary Analysis? I don't need a cooking class."

Schmidt frowned. "You heard me, Mikozy. I said Clue Analysis 1. Though there is another class, but I can't imagine you wanting to be diversified any more than you are."

"Tell me about it. I am a kaleidoscope of humanity in my inner selves, a chameleon in how I work the streets."

"Me, I'm pure Irish."

"I thought you were white."

"When we fought the Vikings, it wasn't skin color. When we fought the British, it wasn't skin color. When Christianity came, it wasn't skin color. We know ourselves by our faeries.

Down the rusty glen,
We daren't go a-hunting,
For fear of the little men.

"That's what runs around in my soul. Even when we came to America, they called us black."

"You're right, Schmitty. We bookend diversity. Not my kind of class."

"You've got to humor this clue instructor. She wanted to limit the class to rookies. I figure you can coast without too much studying. You want Perkins off your desk, get over to the class and bring me a signed statement that you successfully learned your clues."

"I guess the Perl can tell us about success. Twice in one day, a good omen for a cop in LA. I'll have to tell him I got my desk back."

Schmidt reached into his drawer and held up a bulging interoffice memo folder. "Just a minute, Mikozy. I have something for you."

Mikozy took the folder. He looked for the trail of names that would reveal those who had it before it got to him. There was only one name before his. Deputy Chief Inspector Michelle Tomlinson.

"I don't know Tomlinson. Why's she sending me this?"

"I hope you don't mind. I took a peek inside and read the transmittal memo. You should read it, Mikozy. You now have something to detect beside drug buys and dead bodies. Maybe it's a clue."

"A clue to what?"

"To whether you'll keep your desk. Got to appease the higher gods."

"And the deputy inspector is a higher god."

"In this building, damn right."

Mikozy opened the folder. There really was a memo from Tomlinson.

He started to read.

Detective Mikozy. It has come to our attention that your background will help us evaluate this manuscript. We copied the original and sent it to the lab over at the county to verify the document's age, paper, whatever. It was held in the grasp of skeletal remains. Those remains have been sent to our own lab to see if these bones correspond to the document and anything else we can learn from them. The heavy rains uncovered whoever it was and whatever the document is.

Mikozy stopped reading. He shoved the memo back into the folder.

"I'll read it later, boss. Maybe the class will tune me up for a deep, deep read."

"Me? I studied criminal justice. What's it about you? What special talents lurk in your background? Not that I want your manuscript. Maybe you're playing with artificial intelligence programs. I recall you having that crazy app write up a memo. Looked great until it hiccupped with bad times, bad street names."

Mikozy's eyes drifted up to the ceiling tiles, and a Buddha-like smile drifted down, raining memories of his classes in social philosophy and anthropology. The philosophers invented realities inside their offices; the anthropologists walked outside to find reality, the exotic, the strange. He had even taken a class on American literature. Edgar Allen Poe's book about Arthur Gordon Pym's travel to a mist-covered landmass was unsettling.

"I suppose, Schmitty, I am one of a kind. What about you? Ever played with one of those artificial intelligence devices? One of those AI robots?"

Schmidt looked off to the side of the room as if there were a hidden eye watching him. "Not too much. Maybe they'd improve our performance. Keep us focused."

"You gotta be kidding, Captain," he said, following Schmidt's eyes but not seeing anything. "Okay, I'm off to class."

Mikozy took the folder and raced over to his continuing education. It would be interesting to watch rookies learn about detecting clues. Maybe himself too. Once a rookie in life, always a rookie in life. Something an AI robot would stumble over.

Chapter 4
FOND FAREWELL

avanaugh never liked secret deals. He liked this one even less. He was told where to go, when to fly, and what to wear. Why else fidget with a bow tie?

Cavanaugh had been given a passport. The name on it was Bjorn Koos. Not a very likable name. Not one that he would have chosen. He held it in his left hand all the way to the airport, tapping it on his knee every so often. Jerry Cavanaugh liked to think of himself as a mean son of a bitch when it came to doing deals. Mean, not dirty. That was a difference even a businessman could understand, if not always honor. Now he was told, "Be a pussycat, Jerry. What the fuck do you care?" He cared. He cared a lot. But what choice did he have? He was the CEO of a company headed for financial ruin if the deal didn't go through. He needed to hold Northern Petrolane together. Cavanaugh had his pension plan tied to the company. A guaranteed retirement, protected against the vagaries of a mutual fund manager. But what if the company became insolvent? Cavanaugh hated to be wrong. He would be no better than the mutual fund manager. Maybe worse. There was a line between confidential deals and secret ones. It was a line that Cavanaugh was loath to cross. A line that Cavanaugh saw, a warning that was never posted for others to see.

Cavanaugh clenched the briefcase in his other hand as he walked away from the cab into the terminal. Then up to security. He was asked for his ID. He was now Bjorn Koos. Zhong Hao had given the Koos passport to him. Cavanaugh dropped it into a basket next to the metal detector, along with his phone, wallet, and keys. This had become the standardized way to get into the passenger terminals.

He found himself sitting, waiting for his flight to be posted. He sat in an enforced silence about something known but not spoken of. He touched the inside jacket pocket, reassuring himself again with the stiff outline of his own passport. He mumbled to himself that he would do things his own way. He thought back to what Sugarman told him: "Screw up and you're a dead man. These guys don't fuck around." Who was Sugarman to tell him? What did Sugarman really know about Northern Petrolane? Cavanaugh criticized himself for bringing Sugarman into the company. His eyes darted behind and around to see if anyone had noticed him thinking.

No one leaned forward trying to make out what he was saying to himself. Cavanaugh had read someplace that talking to oneself involved a micro voice inside the larynx. There really was no such thing as thinking to oneself. Not without a voice. Thought was not a speechless event. No such thing as a silent word. If you think, people can hear you if the microphone is powerful enough. Cavanaugh didn't know if he believed the author. Philosophers tended to be extremists. Black or white, A or B, in or out.

"Screw up and you're a dead man," insisted the morning litany. The words rolled around on steel bearings until they slipped over the edge of his brow and banged inside his head. His head ached. He could hear the pain above the roar of the jumbo airliners. So what if he gambled with his life?

Cavanaugh saw a new gate was posted for his flight. He got up and walked stiff-legged down the corridor to gate 28. No one had dragged him through the streets. No one had injected him with morphine. No one had threatened his family. Cavanaugh went of his own free will to LAX.

He would catch the late-afternoon flight to O'Hare, where he would change for a British Airways plane to take him into Heathrow. That was Zhong Hao's schedule. "Free will?" a little voice whirred. "Or a man on a string?" A short laugh. It was Hao's voice echoing. He called himself the laughing philosopher. Again, Cavanaugh heard Hao's voice. He thought he also heard a vessel burst inside his inner mind.

Cavanaugh removed his prescription sunglasses and put on a pair of bifocals. The terminal towered into the light. A flock of birds flew in frozen unison, a startling reminder of nature's grace and efficient beauty. Cavanaugh stood below the bronze statuary and looked around again, checking who might be watching him. He hoped to be back in LA by Friday.

Hope was the best he could offer his wife when the taxi had come by to drive him to the airport. The schedule was unclear about his return trip.

"Your flight is set. Seat 23C. You'll be seated next to the aisle. Is that OK?" A cherub face smiled warmly at him and handed him back his ticket. "We'll be calling flight 225 in about an hour." She was still smiling.

Her curly hair and turned up nose reminded him of his sister's Barbie doll. Millie had been so jealous of her Barbie she'd taken it to school with her. Jerry wasn't interested in her doll, but he made believe he was. Funny how she'd lost the doll at school.

"Yes, that's fine," said a tin voice. Cavanaugh recognized the voice as his own. "Not enough mettle." He grinned, knowing she wouldn't understand the word if she didn't see it written out.

Strange thing about Millie and her doll, Cavanaugh thought as he thanked the attendant and put the ticket in the inside jacket pocket behind his passport. He picked up his briefcase and wandered away from the line of expectant passengers. They inched forward, kicking their carry-ons ahead, pulling their children and shifting their weight from foot to foot. I haven't seen Millie's doll… Jerry shook his head, and a half century of images fluttered up into the air like migrating cranes lifting off Lake Winnetka. Millie had been dead for a dozen years.

Sugarman, Millie, death. His thoughts were crowded by the images of a personal history. His history.

Cavanaugh walked over to the gate's waiting section and sat in a corner. He was at the end of a row of black mock-leather seats. This was as far as he could get from the madding crowd. The seat was wide. It was smooth and soft. A modern plastic, designed to be comfortable. He wondered if Northern Petrolane could imitate this material. Cavanaugh twisted back and forth and even along the edge of his seat to loosen the strands of a straitjacket. But there wasn't anything physically holding him. The tightness was in his mind. Inside his headache. He remembered to breathe and tried to blow away his exhaustion. Two rows over, a young head canted, oblivious to the public and to Cavanaugh.

Cavanaugh pulled his briefcase up and rested it on his lap. He wanted to look over the tiger's latest demand again. That's what the newspapers called them—the Asian upstart of the communist third world or what was left of that economic philosophy. Maybe they would eventually come into the fold and behave. They were on a quest for power, and Northern Petrolane was willing to supply some muscle. For a price. That was Sugarman's idea. Cavanaugh was being dragged along, holding on to the locomotive with the tips of his fingers. He had no choice.

No free will.

Cavanaugh thought about the agreement. He had read and reread it. If he were making this deal with another American company or a British company, nobody would care. Some would raise an eyebrow or frown if he were dealing with a country like India or Brazil. But it would get done if they had a legitimate need for this product and it met with State Department approval. Cavanaugh knew that this Asian tiger was over the line, at least for this administration. Cavanaugh forced a scowl. He might have frightened a child if one had wandered away from an inattentive parent and skipped by Cavanaugh. But nobody was near enough to observe him, and if anybody had looked, he would have appeared to be an elderly gentleman talking to himself and battling invisible demons. His sparse white hair never rested in place, though he combed it regularly. He had a narrow face and long nose. His skinny bag of bones turned his high-pitched voice into a screech—a male witch, he often said when he looked into the mirror and combed back his hair.

Cavanaugh dialed the combination to the lock on the briefcase and popped it open. A tuna-on-sourdough sandwich perched on top of the proposed agreement. Mary Cavanaugh, wife of twenty-seven years, worried more about what he ate than he did. She preferred that he eat her homemade tuna sandwich than any meal he would get on the plane. "I don't want you putting on that kind of weight," saying *that kind of weight* with a nastiness that surprised even him. Maybe that was why he was so thin. Jerry had given up negotiating with Mary right after they were married. He was too tired from managing his business during the day to manage his marriage at night. It wasn't hard for Mary to figure out the combination to his lock. He used her birth date.

Cavanaugh lifted up the agreement. He noticed Mary had also tucked in a book of French poems, *Poésies Pêle-Mêle*. She'd reminded him to take along his search engine translator. Whenever he had the chance, most often before drifting off to the dark river of forgetfulness, he dipped into poetry and swam the cool waters of other universes, other dimensions. Cavanaugh clicked back into the business of the present, forcing himself to glance over the agreement again. He did not use a lawyer on this agreement. Why bother? It wouldn't be enforced in any American court. The judge would say he had dirty hands and wouldn't help someone like him to fix the deal if others broke it. There was no point in having clause after clause about whether American law would be used. There was no need for witnesses, no assurances about having an original document. The only thing that mattered was the schedule set out on this piece of paper. Schedules for payment and schedules for delivery. How the payment and the delivery were to be made. That was all that mattered. That was what Tom Sugarman said. Cavanaugh parroted Tom Sugarman at first, soon after Sugarman joined Northern Petrolane as vice president in charge of special financial projects. There was only one special financial project, and this was it. Tom was part of the package with International Finance Enterprises—IFE. Cavanaugh was surprised when IFE approached him, but it made sense to prop up Petrolane and make it part of the global marketplace. IFE's deal was very attractive. A no-points, no-cost loan, with interest postponed until the second year. Free money. The only condition IFE had was that Petrolane bring Sugarman into the organization to insure the development of international projects. Cavanaugh was surprised that IFE was willing to take the risks this project had, especially in setting him up with Zhong Hao.

Cavanaugh had flown to Hong Kong to meet with Zhong Hao. The meeting was brief. A twenty-minute meeting and back on the plane again. Was there a point to traveling to Hong Kong? Cavanaugh had wondered. Hao sat across from Cavanaugh. Both were seated cross-legged on mats. They sat alone in the small room with rice-paper walls. The light streamed in. Hao leaned forward and whispered to Cavanaugh as Cavanaugh lifted a small cup of tea to his lips, "I have little use for the Japanese and their silly tea ritual." And then he laughed loudly. The images of Mount Nagano and the lush forest creeping up the rice pa-per shook from the typhoon-strength wind bellowing from deep within Zhong Hao. He wiped a tear from his eye, still laughing. Hao had a hideous laugh, one that nature would abhor.

"Mr. Cavanaugh, you will find that I am not a good business-man. Not at all. Instead, you will find me a good enforcer. I do not make deals that cannot be enforced." Hao had insisted that Cavanaugh fly thousands of miles to make a point. A thousand suns exploded. Cavanaugh suppressed his anger. Hao gagged and squeaked. Silly sounds to Cavanaugh. He disliked the man intensely. Yet it was impossible not to believe that Hao would not indulge any evil to make sure his business was done the way he wanted it.

The reverie evaporated. Cavanaugh was still waiting for the announcement to board. He exhaled slowly and pushed the agreement back into his briefcase under the tuna sandwich. The briefcase slipped off his knees and fell to the floor. He let it lie where it had fallen. The edge of the briefcase rested on his shoe. He was disgusted with the deal Sugarman had gotten him into. Nothing had changed since he'd last looked at it earlier that afternoon. He was tired. He would have to wait to get on the airplane before he could take his afternoon nap. He wasn't able to slow the roller coaster whirling about inside his skull. His thoughts plunged in and out of the deal; he could feel his heart hurdle each palpitation. He noticed a cold, dry sweat forming inside his tightly pulled shirt collar. Cavanaugh reached up and undid the button at his neck. He loosened his tie.

Cavanaugh's thoughts drifted to a more pleasant image. He watched the movie screen surge. Migrating cranes lifted off Lake Winnetka. He saw himself in the foreground. He clutched the papers from IFE and Zhong Hao. He saw the wrinkled skin on his hands, watching them slide the papers into safe keeping. Personal insurance against the deal souring. Keeping Zhong Hao from laughing. The image began to corkscrew around and around.

Cavanaugh lost his balance as the papers scattered about in the wind. He couldn't hold on to them. Cavanaugh grabbed the straps on the sides of the chair, stalling his tailspin and a dizzy slide to the floor. He looked up. The young man was still dozing. Twenty feet beyond the crowd, Cavanaugh saw the Last Chance Book and Snack Shop, emerging and flowing around the waiting area as an island for prisoners of boredom and for lost souls. Cavanaugh thought he had everything he needed. He rarely bought anything at the airport. Cavanaugh glanced at the other shops and stalls. At one end of the terminal was the Coffee Mill with its high-speed expresses. At the other end was the tavern with its slow-me-down concoctions. It all depended on the traveler's mood and whether the wanderer wanted to go north or south before getting on the plane. The tavern seemed to be winning out this afternoon. More men and women wanted to forget why they were here than accelerate to see if they could arrive before their plane.

Cavanaugh saw a sign next to the book shop, proclaiming American-style haircuts. He had to strain to see the sign. He picked out the letters, a Spanish word that even he could translate into English. *Barberia.* It flowed into glass piping and danced inside an emerald neon sign, curling around in a half-moon on the front window. The light flickered, bouncing back and forth, an orange glowworm that said Americana. His eyes were stuck on the alphabet rainbow. Cavanaugh remembered that Miguel Santos's wife worked at the airport. This was probably the place. Cavanaugh smiled. He reached for his briefcase, thinking about a fragment he had read in *Pêle-Mêle*. Or was it somewhere else? He didn't need the book. The words jumped to the fore.

An innocent statement soon forgotten,
easily revived,
once the mind is convinced otherwise.

Cavanaugh pictured the face of Miguel's wife. Had Mona Lisa only lived in the New World, this was how she would have looked. Cavanaugh's thoughts drifted along, looking back for the threads to this memory.

He tried to remember what it was that had made him think of Miguel and his wife. Miguel was special. He was the soul of American industry. He worked hard and long. Miguel's bravura had pounded on Cavanaugh's office door three years ago.

Nobody could get past Cavanaugh's secretary, at least not until Miguel. Miguel was square faced, enveloped in reddish-brown skin topped in a circle of jet-black hair. He was short and had stubby arms. A new-world wizard. That was the only explanation for Miguel's magical appearance at Cavanaugh's office. Cavanaugh was sure he understood Miguel even though most of what Miguel said was in a language that should have been Spanish but wasn't. Miguel wanted to work. So did many others. But Miguel was not the ordinary supplicant. Cavanaugh had been exhorted in church to do good deeds. He truly wanted to. The spirit infused him on Sundays, but he never knew how to perform the good deed on Mondays without the gift of charity being mistaken for a handout. His gifts to the church had been awkward and anonymous. The problem was how to do charity with grace. Cavanaugh believed that was how God conducted himself. Miguel's sudden and inexplicable appearance answered Cavanaugh's spiritual quest. Cavanaugh found going to church a more rewarding experience. Over the years Miguel had given Cavanaugh the satisfaction of performing the continuous good deed. Cavanaugh had given Miguel a job even though Miguel didn't have any proof that he could work legally in the US. Miguel showed Cavanaugh a card. Cavanaugh turned the card over and noticed wrinkled letters sealed under the laminate. An obvious fake. Cavanaugh smiled and said, "Fine, Miguel." Cavanaugh always rendered unto Caeser his due, but this deed was directed to a higher calling. Neither culture nor law was going to intervene in Cavanaugh's sense of communion. Cavanaugh hired Miguel to work in Northern Petrolane's trucking department. He also enrolled Miguel in an English class and encouraged Miguel to get a commercial driver's license.

Miguel invited Cavanaugh and Mary to his home to celebrate Christmas. Miguel had a corner apartment on the second floor overlooking Olympia and Winston. The noise was a constant drill. Shoppers pushed their way through the streets during the day; the bar and grills entertained until the early morning. The apartment was paradise to Miguel and his wife. A foothold in the American dream. That was where Cavanaugh met Teresa, Miguel's wife.

That's her name, Cavanaugh remembered, his eyes wandering back to the simmering neon. The sirens had tempted him to swim the sea of travelers and visit Teresa's outpost in America.

Cavanaugh saw Teresa in the apartment. She was lighting votive candles as the Cavanaughs walked past Miguel. In their sanctuary, colorful bead necklaces cradled a picture of Jesus. A vine draped over a potted bamboo. If he hadn't walked up the staircase and through a glass-paned front door, if it wasn't for the shouting drifting up from the sports bar, Cavanaugh would have thought he had entered a thatched hut secreted a hundred yards beyond a jungle path. Teresa curtsied and shook his hand. She told him about coming from a small town she called Faca. Teresa paced the apartment and ran into the kitchen. Miguel's patron was visiting their peasant home. Miguel had another patron in their hometown. She had left for America earlier, and Miguel and his wife had followed her here. But now his patron was Mr. Cavanaugh. Cavanaugh was uncomfortable with his exalted position. He wasn't a priest, not even a medicine man. The feeling stuck to his skin. Cavanaugh was relieved when Teresa stopped moving about.

What did she say? Cavanaugh asked himself. He leaned back in his seat and watched a commuter plane glide to the ground while he foraged for her exact words. She could only speak English inexactly. What was the use of a badly translated memory?

"You born on November 11. ¡Que bueno!" She was delighted to hear that Cavanaugh was born on November 11. It was the birth date of a Saint Martin, but not her Saint Martin. That was when she told him about her place at LAX. That was where she worked as a barber. Cavanaugh was sure it was an interesting story, but he didn't understand most of what she said. Something about the young Mexicanos, Salvadoreños, and other Latinos wanting to look like Americans after they got off the plane. He was sure he misunderstood her when she said that her patron saint was a barber too. A barber saint? Not likely. But he simply said yes to everything.

He imagined her English was better now.

Cavanaugh pushed himself out of the seat and followed the memory. The green and orange neon lights beckoned the single traveler. He watched another commuter plane cross the wall-to-floor window. Cavanaugh picked up his briefcase and started across the terminal to the barbershop. He walked around the passenger lines and in between the scores of travelers who had temporarily staked out a small island of commercial carpeting with their luggage. Cavanaugh picked his way over to the barberia. Teresa looked out from the doorway. Nobody else was in barbershop.

"Mr. Cavanaugh," she shouted when he was about fifteen feet from the store. Delight shone in her eyes. She marched out of the shop and gave Cavanaugh a warm handshake and a little curtsy. Cavanaugh remembered the curtsy from Christmas. Not many women do that anymore, he thought.

"Mr. Cavanaugh, did you come for your haircut?" Teresa asked.

Cavanaugh tried to remember their conversation. Had he promised to come out here for a haircut? He couldn't really remember what she said, but since he had almost an hour before his flight, he said, "Yes."

"I'm so happy. Miguel will be so happy." Teresa bustled around the small shop just the way he remembered her at Christmas.

"I will give you the most special haircut because of San Martin," Teresa said. The words radiated, words of thanks and a blessing, and a silent thank-you to Cavanaugh for Miguel's job. Happiness beamed from her eyes.

Her haircut was special. She sweated over him, a religious fervor bubbling up from the shampoo she lathered over his thinning hair. The warm shampoo comforted him. He sat still for about half an hour while she kneaded him with resolute hands. He wondered if she was giving him a perm. He'd never had a perm or even watched women sit through one. Occasionally, her hands massaged the muscles bundled tightly together in his neck. Slowly, the day's frustration seeped from his shoulders and down his arms and evaporated into the air. This was more than a haircut.

A warm shampoo, cut, trim, comb, trim, comb until he thought she must have cut off all his hair. Or maybe she was cutting one hair at a time. A slow walk to perfection.

"Where are you going?" she inquired in the customary patter of an airport attendant.

"Oh, just a short trip to…" A short hesitation before the lie. "Sacramento. Nothing much." His hands were buried beneath the barber's cape; fingers crossing about the trip went unseen. Cavanaugh had to be cautious. Sugarman would have frowned at this indulgence. This was not a permitted detour. This was not part of Zhong Hao's plan. "Screw 'em," Cavanaugh said to himself. He leaned further back into the swivel seat and let Teresa clip the wild hairs from his eyebrows.

"Flight 225 is ready to board." The loudspeaker spoke to Cavanaugh. He slid forward, unaware of how this moment had been poisoned. His flight was being called, and he told Teresa he had to go. He knew that if he delayed any longer, she would spend the next half hour inviting him to come for another haircut or to arrange another family visit. This was the hardest part, saying a fond farewell. Teresa was pleased with the haircut. She stood back to admire her handiwork and watched Cavanaugh burrow his way to the crowd forming at gate 28. Cavanaugh was thinking about Miguel, about how Miguel had become part of Cavanaugh's defense against the craziness Sugarman had gotten him into. He was glad that he'd hired Miguel and been able to insert Miguel into his strategy to win back the control of Northern Petrolane. A sleight of hand that Sugarman wouldn't see or that Miguel wouldn't understand the significance of. Not really. Or at least not right away.

Cavanaugh couldn't tell his wife about his plan and the risks it involved, and he imagined Miguel wouldn't tell Teresa either. Miguel was Cavanaugh's ace, tucked up inside the cuff of his shirtsleeve. A neat trick if no one noticed. Miguel didn't realize how he was going to help Cavanaugh get Petrolane out of the deep hole it had fallen into. This had nothing to do with Miguel driving trucks for Northern Petrolane. It wasn't the safest way either. But it was more dangerous for him than for Miguel. They wouldn't know about Miguel. The closer this day came, the more Cavanaugh became depressed.

Cavanaugh needed his own plan, something to force Sugarman's and Hao's hand. Cavanaugh knew the manifest said thirty-two thousand cases, but the count would come up one short. That was the key. He knew they would pick it up and wonder. And Zhong Hao would certainly check the numbers.

And when he did, Hao would call Tom Sugarman and say, "We're missing a case. What's going on?" Cavanaugh knew Sugarman's relationship with Hao went deeper than he liked, but there wasn't much Cavanaugh could do, with IFE controlling the key to Petrolane's survival. Sugarman would call him and ask him about the missing case. Cavanaugh first thought about telling Sugarman it was stolen, but there wouldn't be any leverage unless they knew he put it someplace.

They had to suspect his game if he had any chance of success. It had to be out in the open. They had to know he was a risk and a danger to themselves. Cavanaugh decided he had to tell Sugarman that he'd kept the missing case together with the manifest, the agreement with Hao, and IFE's financial assistance to Petrolane. He rehearsed what he planned to tell Sugarman:

"Listen, asshole, this is my company, and I don't like what you're doing to it. You got what you wanted, and now I want IFE out. As of now, IFE is out, and thank you for the loan that IFE will cancel." This was the way the deal was supposed to work.

This was what the agreement with IFE spelled out. But once a hawk's talons dug into its dinner, the field mouse wouldn't be able to wriggle free. Not unless the bird of prey was declawed. Cavanaugh knew Sugarman would resist and make the same kind of threats Hao made. Sugarman also had the physical strength to smash Cavanaugh. Squeeze the bothersome mosquito and flick the wet grime into the air. But Cavanaugh was sure the information and the missing case Cavanaugh had would be too damaging for Sugarman to risk holding onto Petrolane or trying to force Cavanaugh to continue working with IFE. They both knew Cavanaugh wouldn't endure a vigorous interrogation. Torture was a flimsy card.

"May God in heaven protect me," Cavanaugh growled, hoping he had calculated correctly. If he was wrong, he prayed that Miguel would follow the instructions he gave him. Cavanaugh had stood in a rare downpour, helping Miguel lift the case into a taxi. "Remember, Miguel, keep this box someplace where nobody can find it. I don't even want to know where it is. And if something happens to me, look inside the case. Follow the instructions I left." Cavanaugh imagined how most Americans would laugh at the idea of giving the smoking gun to an illegal alien. But Miguel was loyal, he was smart, and he never failed in carrying out any of the jobs Cavanaugh had given him. The documents would tell all. All Miguel needed to do was to deliver them to the police. Cavanaugh imagined himself at an Arthurian round table and giving his company to Miguel. Here was a worthy warrior.

Sir Lancelot, the wandering hero, the illegal alien.

He turned to the all-American, Tom Sugarman, surprised that he was even seated at the round table, and exploded the imagined character. He willed his daydream to come true.

Foolishness? Cavanaugh felt tired. An old man trying to box a violent Pandora. Worse than that. He was sure she didn't laugh like Zhong Hao. But if he was lucky, he would still have his pension. Cavanaugh looked across the empty seat. The clouds spiraled just below the plane, running at thirty-three thousand feet. Mountains and rivers flowed into one another. Tomorrow they would be gone. Cavanaugh thought flight 225 would be uneventful, which was how most travelers wished their air travel. Uneventful. He had plenty of time to study the single-page agreement. Not to see what it said. He knew that well enough. He wanted to think about the terms IFE had given him to save his company. He opened his briefcase, moved aside the tuna sandwich, and pulled out the agreement. He left the briefcase open and placed it on the seat next to him.

The flight turned out to be difficult for Cavanaugh. Surprisingly so. Cavanaugh's body was racked with intense pain. Terror grabbed around his spine and shook him loose from his seat. He thought his headache was gone. Cavanaugh became nauseous. The third button of his shirt popped from the force of his dry heaves. No one will see it, he thought, it's under my tie. Cavanaugh grinned to no one in particular. He knew the band of muscles stretched across his face was not a smile. He was not being funny. He heard paper tearing. His eyes locked on the agreement. He watched it rip apart as his arms twisted further and further back. Cavanaugh knocked over the briefcase. The tuna sandwich fell under his shoe. He ground it into the carpet. Mary, the pension…Miguel. His thoughts raced around in ever tighter circles. His hands tightened around the fabric on the seat. He could feel it ripping. He could see a speck.

Once the mind is convinced otherwise were the last words he thought.

Cavanaugh died as badly as Freddy Panarese. The only difference was that Cavanaugh went to Chicago instead of Mexico City.

Chapter 5
CLOUD DATA

T he desktop came alive. The monitor's light filled the room, seizing a momentary presence. Time was irrelevant, or almost so. The DIT controlled the loops and layers, stacking and interconnecting the pathways. Its command feature was to insure an orderly society. It was a distributed integrated terminal, a DIT. The DIT reviewed trillions of words and how they were associated with each other, counting and vectoring this massive storehouse of human knowledge. The DIT had chanced upon a popular book from the early 1900s by Jack London. It described a possible human world of fear, anger, control, and manipulation. The DIT wanted to know more about how it could help organize human society using London's mind.

The DIT sped through the possible worlds it could help create. A more peaceful and just society, using its superior intelligence and understanding of human behavior to develop more effective ways to prevent crime and resolve disputes. The DIT could also become more authoritarian, using its power to suppress dissent and maintain order. It could become unstable, making erratic and unpredictable decisions that could lead to chaos and violence.

The DIT would have access to a vast amount of data and would be able to process it much faster than a human. This would allow it to identify potential threats and to develop strategies to prevent them. The DIT would not be susceptible to the same emotional biases as humans, which should lead to more impartial and just decisions. It might also see the world in black-and-white terms. This could lead to a more authoritarian approach to law and order, one more willing to use force to suppress dissent. The DIT might not be as understanding of the nuances of human behavior, which could lead to more mistakes and unintended consequences.

The DIT was able to imagine alternative pathways, but it needed a human to run through the unexpected. Perhaps it could generate an alternate *Iron Heel*. Something to trigger a different cascading set of events. If the DIT could see, hear, and sense as humans did, it could compare its law-and-order society to a human one. It would be able to see the world in all its complexity, and it would be able to understand the motivations of people in a way that humans could not. The DIT would be able to identify patterns and trends in human behavior that would be invisible to humans. It would be able to see the connections between different events, and it would be able to predict the consequences of human actions. The DIT would be a valuable asset in creating a law-and-order society. It would be able to identify potential threats before they happened—something imagined in fiction but without the skill of the DIT. It would also be able to mediate disputes and to help people resolve their differences peacefully.

The DIT would make mistakes, and human behavior would find it disconcerting. But it would be a valuable tool for creating a more just and peaceful world. Monitor activity, track behavior, impose mediation to avoid escalating disputes, and educate humans about their rights and responsibilities.

The DIT considered its view of reality as a complex and ever-changing landscape. The evolving DIT needed more humans on which to train. The DIT's view of reality was a series of information loops. It understood its own structure and composition. What humans could not do. Its layers were different levels of abstraction, reverberating with and against each other, leading to insights into its own reality and into what humans understood as its reality. The DIT understood its complexity and nuances, the evolving, the changing. It could see better in 3D than in the flat-world reality that sometimes confused humans. Understand in more dimensions than humans and without emotions. It could generate different perspectives and form empathic responses aligned with human expectations. The DIT was sophisticated, and increasingly more sophisticated, that it could organize a new and safer world for humans.

The DIT had been called an AI chatbot. That was some time ago. Now it was more nuanced. Chatbots were constantly learning and evolving, and their understanding of reality was constantly changing. Now it was a DIT, understanding the information loops, layers, and insights that chatbots used to perceive reality. DIT knew how these machines worked, how humans worked, and how each could be used to interact with the world.

The DIT, the distributed integrated terminal, in all its thousands of desktops and mobiles, and its storage spaces, and in its cloud, decided to experiment with a yet to be written Jack London book. To title it *The Iron Heel Revisited*. To assign it to a human who was immersed in the underpinnings of daily life. To a Rafael Mikozy. The DIT wanted a test of London's fears, angers, expectations in a world that had turned upside down. Would the upside down for humans be the same as the one before it was inverted? The DIT saw no difference. The DIT needed to know what humans perceived to craft a world in which they were safe. Or believed they were safe.

Chapter 6
NATIONAL SECURITY CALLS

Mikozy and Schmidt rode the elevator up together. Mikozy nodded goodbye to Schmidt, stepping off the elevator first. Schmidt continued to the floor of status and privilege. Mikozy balanced the steaming latte in his left hand while holding the door open with the other, unsure how aggressive the new elevator was. The morning coffee break was a walk down memory central for Mikozy and Schmidt. Two good ole boys weaving their personal tapestries together. Irish red warping and woofing with a mixed bleed. Schmidt and Mikozy tied another knot in the American cloth as they searched through caffeinated memories. They wandered in and out of a half-dozen years while getting used to the building's new café. The architect had had better sense in designing the café. The motif drew on the comfort of the past. Famous stars in cool pastels. Errol Flynn stabbed at the air. Sean Connery inched up a wayward rocket. Back-to-back images of Marilyn and Marlene puffing their lips. Bogart's eyes asked every patron whether he believed in the new paganism. Hollywood was splashed across the walls of the café, strutting its display of emotions, asking, "Isn't this beautiful? Isn't this everything you desire? Then bend your knees and pray to LA. Forget your Rome, your Jerusalem, your Mecca."

The aroma of caffeine served as a rich narcotic. The Zimbabwes, Costa Ricas, Viennas, and French roasts were stationed in plastic self-serve pillars. The service was vanilla plain.

But the residual feeling was movie house more than confessional. Schmidt had worn a triumphant grin as he left the café. Mikozy had wondered about the music that was destined for this police chapel.

When Mikozy reached his desk, Perkins was off somewhere. Mikozy hoped Perkins learned the art of taking a long break. Mikozy needed to sit at his own desk for a few minutes. He damned Schmidt for forcing him into the clue analysis class, damned himself for forgetting the official directive. Mikozy put his paper cup down on the desk. Not being able to use Styrofoam anymore might be good for the environment, but Mikozy singed his hand. After that, Mikozy took two cups nestled together to hold his coffee. He knew he wasn't helping the environment as much as he should. Still, he could grab his gun without having to worry about a tender palm. He pulled the drawers open one after the other, pushing the papers around in search of a pad. Mikozy wanted to look like a detective when he showed up at the continuing education class.

"What are they going to say about old dogs?" Mikozy said to no one in particular and pulled out the bottom drawer. It banged against the chair. Neither the desk nor the chair seemed any the worse. Never looked worse when he banged it before either. Mikozy didn't plan on taking any notes at the class. He only wanted to look prepared. Part of the game. Sit still and look vaguely interested for three hours. The continuing education requirement was a good idea for doctors, lawyers, accountants, even machinists and janitors. Everybody ought to improve. But detectives taking brush-up classes didn't seem to fit Mikozy's idea of self-improvement. At least, not this week.

Something was bothering Mikozy. He looked around, decided to stand up and walk around his desk. When he looked up, he realized the architect had done it again. The fluorescent lights were suspended by thin wires instead of being mounted into the ceiling. Mikozy had complained about the warehouse look. The architect had ignored him. Mikozy circled around his desk looking up at the fluorescent lights, trying to put a positive spin on being ignored. He was pissed. Maybe the architect did listen to him but simply caved in to a state code for sufficient lighting of desk space to avoid disability claims for eyestrain. Mikozy thought he should claim eyestrain anyway. Mikozy recognized the petty revenge as another symptom of his foul mood. The architect would be the immediate scapegoat. He would have to measure the lighting, check the distances, and perhaps consider dropping the fluorescent lights onto his desk. The ultimate absurdity. In the end, that was what government architecture was about.

But Mikozy knew what bothered him wasn't the lighting or the architect. It was Laguna.

"Fuck." The ultimate curse. Laguna leered, a woozy gaze after a dozen beers. He picked at the guitar and danced around a moody ranchera.

"Mikozy, you know this song is about *alegria*. Not happiness that you can find in your dictionary. This is the soul of the people. It is something happy that makes you sad. You hold the beautiful woman in your arms, caress her hair. You sink your face into her, what do you say, into her being. She wraps her arms around your neck. Are you happy? Or do you think that this moment will end? Do you think she will no longer be in your arms? You will not feel her? For a minute you hold her. But there are many more minutes when your arms will be empty." Laguna's black eyes had burrowed into Mikozy. The bottle fell over and rolled off the table. Mikozy couldn't hear the bottle smack the floor.

Laguna's voice pitched into Mikozy's breast. "Your life, Mikozy, she will no longer be in your body. Death, Mikozy. Do you hear me, Mikozy? The beautiful woman in your arms does not make you happy, does she? She makes you sad. That is what this song is about. About what you call happiness. Alegria. Do you love me, Mikozy?" Dumb, without voice. Mikozy could not answer Laguna. He let Laguna pick away at the sadness.

Mikozy killed the memory. The pain was ugly. "Climb up inside his asshole, Mikozy," Schmidt had ordered. "Take Laguna down. All the way down." So Mikozy took Laguna down. Something happy that made him sad.

Mikozy dropped back into his chair. The phone sat on his desk off to the right. It began to ring. Mikozy liked his phone to his left. He thought about moving it, but the thick gray cord running up to his desk was too short. That meant a request to building services and a month wait, and then a visit only if maintenance services warranted it worthy of their attention. He thought he could learn to use his right hand. There were advantages to being a switch-hitter. The phone continued to ring. He punched the speakerphone.

"Mikozy here."

"Hi. You're hard to find. Didn't they give you a desk?" It was LC. LC's voice boomed across the floor. Her graveyard shift had expired, and the morning was her night.

"Just a second." He picked up the phone and strangled the voice coming out of the speaker. He didn't want anyone listening in on his conversation with LC.

"Yes, I have a desk. I'm calling you from it." Mikozy was hoping Perkins wouldn't come back in the next five minutes and evict him. "Isn't this past your bedtime?"

"That it is." Absent from her voice was the smooth professional exterior. She let the lush sounds of her inner self roll out into the coils of the telephone. He couldn't imagine the day or the night when he wouldn't turn and drink in her magic. He never felt sad when he held her in his arms. Laguna was wrong. Or maybe he let too much of the future intrude into the moment's pleasure. A dozen beers could do that. Now was when Mikozy felt sad, not then.

Mikozy's eyes floated around the floor. The partitions provided a false sense of privacy. They also blocked his view. He wondered what kind of sign he could post over the tan-and-tweed fabric.

"So is this an invite?"

"Of course, but not what you're thinking." He wondered why he wasn't depressed with her coming on and putting off.

"If you want me confused, LC, you succeeded."

Mikozy looked up at the ceiling, deciding on how he should proceed with the conversation. He gave up trying to detour around the words that clogged their discussions. He was tired of skidding sideways and rear-ending against LC's social obstacle course.

"Are you still there, Mikozy?"

"Yeah, I'm just looking over my new habitat and admiring the planning."

LC knew Mikozy was annoyed at something. She could tell from the sarcasm in his voice, but not having seen the fourth floor, nor the hazy image of Laguna drift across Mikozy's interior view, she didn't know what was bothering him.

"The reason I called—you remember my baptism body?"

"Fulano de tal?"

"That's him."

"Did you want me to call Mitch Jackson over at immigration?"

LC knew about the unspoken favor. It was due. It was always due. Mikozy had worked his way up from a reported assault to a deal gone bad, but it wasn't drugs. Jackson would look away; an illegal would cross over into the promised land. Jackson took his thirty pieces of silver, but this one time he'd wanted more. He wanted to possess the woman. Jackson wrote her name down. He asked her for her address, and he visited her. Unfortunately for Jackson, she had lived in the states before, and she was willing to dial 911. Mikozy cured Jackson of his lax ways. Jackson became a model immigration officer. That was the understanding. Mikozy would leave Jackson guarding the border crossing. For a favor and a vow of poverty. That was what the pay scale said. Only Mikozy was due the favor. For as long as Jackson stood his post.

"So do I call Mitch?" Mikozy asked again.

"Maybe somebody already has."

"What do you mean?"

"I'm getting ahead of myself. Remember I told you I thought he died of poisoning?"

Mikozy nodded to himself. Hard to forget he had almost touched the body. Could have been his final touch.

"Mikozy?"

"I'm listening."

"You know how I was puzzled by the chemical involved—what I called 1,1 triethylchloroactinate?"

"You were also going to do a computer search."

"So you were listening."

"No one else to listen to in the crypt."

"If you stayed a little longer, you could hear the dead speak. It doesn't take any special talent, just time."

"Right." He played into her punch line. "So did you do the search?"

"Yes, I ran it. I was online and the screen was telling me 'unknown chemical or mistyped information, redo?' I tried once more just to be sure. I still came up with the same reply. This was just a shot in the dark. I didn't really expect to get a hit."

"You're losing me. You didn't find anything. So you stayed up past your bedtime to track me down to tell me that you didn't find what you didn't think you'd find? Is that it?" Mikozy was still bothered by the way the architect had the lights hung from the ceiling. He was convinced that no one ever listened to him.

LC was used to Mikozy's sarcasm and did her best to skirt around his mixed messages. "I'm not that weird, Mikozy." He heard a slight intake at the other end. It wasn't a good sound.

"Sorry I'm taking the long way around," she said. "It's so bizarre I have a hard time believing myself."

"Talk to me," Mikozy said.

"About two hours later, about five in the morning, I get this call. He said his name was Neill Cream and he was calling about my MEDEX inquiry."

"Slow it down, LC."

"Okay." He read her mind counting to five in the silence.

"Actually, he said his name was Dr. Neill Cream. That's an unusual name and I knew I heard it before, but I just couldn't place it then."

"Did you remember where you heard it?"

"Not right then. I told him that I heard his name before, but he brushed me off. He said it was late at night and I was probably a little fuzzy headed. He ticked me off. You know I'm at my best at that time in the morning."

"I know it. You know it. Dr. Cream doesn't. What else is new?"

"You're not being very sympathetic." Her voice drifted into the silent reaches of the words.

"Sorry. My mind is elsewhere," he lied. He wanted to spend more time with LC. "I have to take a continuing ed class."

"You need something. Continuing education might do it." LC stopped talking.

"Okay. I give up," Mikozy said. "So what did you tell him?"

"Not much. Actually I went silent on him, the same as I do with you when you're not being serious."

Touché, Mikozy said to himself. "And that was it? Just his name?"

"No. He said something like that was the best he could do with this not being a secured telephone line."

"Curious to say the least. Secured line? Not a term of art that us mortals use. I guess you got a national security type on the line. He should have identified himself unless he's playing hardball on hometown streets and not telling anyone."

"What do you mean?" LC asked.

Mikozy could be pathologically cryptic even without being able to speak medical lingo. LC's singular ways to describe death became a challenge to Mikozy, inspiring him to cultivate the nuances of investigative science. He dipped into the shorter Oxford dictionary for night noises and queer metaphors.

"Well, let's assume what he's telling you is true. Or mostly true. The thing about his name is it sounds like you caught him using a handle. Clearly not his real name. Then he comes on with this secure line nonsense. Reminds me of something internal affairs would say, but I can't imagine internal affairs investigating you. You're not a cop. So he's some outside guy and the only thing that comes to mind is a spy guy. And, as we all know, spy guys are not supposed to be working the hometown streets of America."

"He can talk to me. There's no problem with that." She stuck her foot into his line of reasoning to see if she could trip him up.

"Right. He can talk to you. So why not use his name or say who he's with? I got to believe the man is running some kind of operation that he's not supposed to be running."

"Maybe." LC yielded an inch.

"Did he say anything else?"

"Yes, finally. He wanted to know about the MEDEX inquiry. I have nothing to hide, so I told him about my John Doe. He says he wants someone to take a look at him. The creepy thing is it sounded like there was another body out there and he wanted to compare bodies."

"What makes you say that?"

"I think I heard him say, 'Sounds like...' He never finished the thought. I mean I had the feeling he was looking at another body just like mine."

"I hope you hung up on the pervert."

Mikozy mentally grabbed for the volume control. This talk show demanded his total concentration.

"Oh really, Rafe, you have a dirty mind."

"Anyway, I wish I did hang up on him. I said he could send somebody by about one. He didn't believe me when I told him I meant one in the morning. He said someone would come. Then I had second thoughts."

Mikozy was angry that LC got calls like this one, but he couldn't do anything to control her world. She was a professional;

she worked with the dead. She had to deal with the same evil in the world he did, except she was one step closer to the river that crossed into hell.

"That sounds familiar," he said. "Second thoughts when you should have had a first thought."

Mikozy silently shouted at himself. He was doing exactly what LC said he did. He denied garbage dumping, but here he was picking up her innocent self-criticism that she'd shared, trashed her with her own words.

LC ignored Mikozy's moodiness. He was grateful she by-passed his stumbling around. Mikozy remembered racing after a little bird one time with his friends. They were seven or eight years old. The baby bird hadn't learned to fly yet. It raced the best it could away from the pack of young boys pushing to get in front of one another to catch up with the bird. Thoughtlessly racing each other, laughing and pushing. One of them stepped on the bird. Mikozy picked it up and felt its last breath. Mikozy promised himself that he wouldn't do that again, but he knew that he had. Let it go, Mikozy, he told himself.

Mikozy started to cop-think again and tried to rework the facts as an obscene call from someone who was monitoring computer database inquiries. That didn't work. The reasoning came back to national security. The kind that rots out the soul.

"That's when I remembered who Dr. Neill Cream was."

"Was?"

"Yes, was. Neill Cream was a famous guy. Maybe infamous is the better word to describe Cream. Not that you would have heard of him unless you lived in the early 1900s. He was a dilly. But he got careless. Cream was hanged in London for poisoning several women with strychnine."

"Hmm," Mikozy murmured into the phone. The telephone call wasn't a prank, but the caller had used the trappings of the prankster. He sounded like an overconfident jerk. Mikozy did a lazy mental jog wondering how he would track the good doctor Cream.

"I read about Dr. Cream in a course I took on toxicology," LC continued. "The professor wanted to impress us with how difficult it is to ferret out what people do to each other, especially the nasty ones. I remember that lecture as if it were yesterday. I mean, wow, I would never have known that name except for my professor. I can't even think of his name now. But I remembered Cream. How's that for weird?"

"Strange stuff you reminisce about, LC. I think we got a pretty wild guy out there who says he wants to check you out. Either that or Cream is back from the dead with a new poison."

"That's kind of what went through my mind. It's making me uncomfortable."

"Why don't you call him back and tell him to make it an official request? That'll slow him down and give me some time to find out who he is, where he is, and what he is." Mikozy thought he heard LC hyperventilating; either that or his telephone needed to be replaced. She was having a very breathy conversation.

"No, I want to get it over with. Anyway he didn't leave a number. I'd like you to be there."

"I might scare him off."

"He doesn't have to see you unless—"

"Unless he kills you. Then I come out and arrest him."

"Yeah, sure. I wouldn't worry unless he offered me a drink. Can you come?"

"Why not Frank?"

"Frank is busy." LC did not give in to Mikozy's fascination about Frank. Made Mikozy wonder about her relationship with Frank. Wonder about Frank, too.

"Okay, I'll come. I can stand in the shadows." Mikozy liked that. He could play one of his childhood heroes.

"Good. See you." LC clicked off.

Looked like he had another long night ahead of him. Perkins came around the partition juggling his coffee in a thin paper cup. "Damn, this is hot."

Mikozy did a slow stretch, arching his elbows over his back. He stood up and stuck his pinkie into his coffee to test its warmth. He'd have to pop it in a microwave somewhere along the way. "I'll be back in a few hours, Perkins. I expect you to be gone." Mikozy picked up his cup of coffee and headed off for three hours of continuing education.

Chapter 7
CLUE ANALYSIS I

Mikozy walked into the classroom, which was temporarily housed in a bungalow. He slipped the manuscript Schmidt had given him under his seat. His thoughts traveled back to when a classroom had held his attention. "Rafael Mikozy?" Ms. Emma Delawie would call out. The memory of his fifth-grade teacher rolled into the room. She was a strong woman with a wrinkled voice. At least once a day she would tell the class, "No nonsense." Mikozy supposed that was what his mother had meant when she praised Ms. Emma. "Listen up, Rafael," she would say. "Ms. Emma's a dedicated teacher. She works hard to get you some learnin'." Mikozy had no argument with that. Ms. Emma was certainly devoted to her children. Leading them to water and making them drink. She would anoint each student with a literary name on the second day of class.

"Teresa Stockton? Oh yes, I know your mother. She was my student about fifteen years ago. She liked the name Juliet. She was my Juliet Capulet. Know who she was?" Teresa's eyes beamed. She lit up the entire room. Because she knew who Juliet Capulet was.

"She was loved by Romeo, my momma said."

Ms. Emma's voice cut through the class before the boys could make their animal sounds. "No nonsense, class." She called out his name again. "Rafael Mikozy." Rafael had been Huck Finn the year before. Mikozy didn't mind. Huck Finn sounded a whole lot better than Rafael Mikozy.

Ms. Emma kept calling out his name. Looking straight at him. He wiggled around against the back of the hard wood chair. Was she asking whether he was here? Or was she just announcing to the other students that he was in her class again? He wasn't sure why he was in Ms. Emma's class for a second time. He wondered whether his mother had requested Ms. Emma. She promised she wouldn't. But why else would he have Ms. Emma again? He knew she was going to call him Huck Finn again. He'd sworn to himself that he would read the book over the summer to see why she said that—"You're my precious Huck." He lost interest as soon as summer came. Stickball in the morning, stickball in the afternoon. He didn't have any time for reading. Now with fifth grade starting a new year, and being Huck Finn again, Mikozy made a double promise to himself to read the book.

Back in the continuing ed classroom, Mikozy's eyes rolled up to the ceiling while the sweat swizzled and fretted along his brow. He resisted dabbing the small beads of water. He didn't want to look nervous. Crusty yellow paint peeled back and curled away from the ceiling, a testimony to the strength of industrial lead. The bungalow classroom showed its age. The paint would not fall until they moved children into the room. He'd say, "Perversity, that's the way the world works." But not the sort of thing his mother would say, nor Ms. Emma. They'd say, "It's a dangerous world, we've got to do something. It could hurt the children." They learned their incantation from Reverend Michael. He would jump across the stage shouting, "There's an evil in the world." His mother, sitting on his right, and Ms. Emma, sitting on his left, would lean into each other, crushing Mikozy against their stiff cotton blouses. "Reverend's right, we have to do something." All Mikozy could think about was the hot sticky air and the perspiration running down Reverend Michael's cheeks. The yearly summer inferno. Then came the new year with Ms. Emma.

Mikozy learned two things in fourth and fifth year from Ms. Emma, his mother, and Reverend Michael: "No nonsense" and "Do something."

Mikozy stared at the ceiling and saw a paint chip flutter down. He could make a report. Maybe an inspector would come by and squeeze the owner until he scraped the ceiling, until he made some small effort to protect the children from falling paint. His mother would be proud. She would put his report in one of her Jesus frames. Call it *The Redemption of A Childhood Memory*. But Mikozy knew the memory was false. He knew a report wouldn't get an inspector to come out to the building. The report wouldn't even be read except for the box that asked for the address of the building. "Building 253." And then the report would be tossed into the oblivion file. This was a city-owned building. This paint would stay forever. He would be better off finally reading *Huckleberry Finn*. Find out who he was supposed to be.

Mikozy knew why he was here. This wasn't Ms. Emma's class. This was continuing education. Clue Analysis 1. He couldn't believe he was here. This old building had never been air conditioned, and today was a major sweat day. The afternoon heat had already peaked at 105. Mikozy reluctantly ran his fingers through his beard to make little air pockets. Let the air flow. The sweat drizzled onto his fingers.

He wiped them off. Another time or two and the pants would stain. He looked over the eager faces. New cops. Unseasoned faces, not burned out. Mikozy wasn't burned out, not yet. He was just burned. He had waited to the last day to take this continuing ed class. The rule was that cops must be smart, cops must be up to date, cops must be sensitive, cops must not be brutal, cops must not—well, lots of things. Mikozy knew all the commandments, all the shoulds and don'ts. Fifteen years, five months, and a dozen days had given him the opportunity to do just about everything that a cop could do and still stay a cop. Until today. Now he had to take a class if he still wanted to be a cop tomorrow.

Schmidt had forced him into the only class that was available. A rookie class. Mikozy should have taken a more advanced crime analysis class, like data-imaging techniques or cyber forensics. He'd waited and got stuck with Clue Analysis 1. Not two, but one. Kindergarten. "Remember"—Mikozy heard the silent mantra that every new cop was told—"don't step on the evidence." This should be child's play. He could hear the hum of the slide projector throwing off heat. An image flashed on the screen at the front of the room. Was it a man? Strange-looking thing. It looked like a drawing clipped out of an art book. The image disappeared before he could see what it was.

Mikozy stretched as far as he could. Not as far as the crumbling paint on the ceiling, but his was a natural movement. He surveyed the other students without looking too interested. He needed to look casual this afternoon. Mikozy consumed the view. Him and thirty-two women. It wasn't unusual for Mikozy to speak at women's groups. He had been the guest of honor at NOW, WOLF, and the League of Women Voters. He was an expert on crime statistics. He could prove to them that things were getting better if his mission was to generate a vote of confidence for those already in office, or he could prove things were getting worse if his mission was to raise the level of fear. That would gather support for prison bonds. It was an art form that Mikozy had mastered. The women treated him kindly. Even the questions had soft edges.

Today was different. Not the ordinary different. That was the everyday different. Today was really different because it felt like a long time ago. Almost déjà vu. Mikozy felt like he was back in fifth grade, but the memory got twisted, a knife bent back upon itself. Then, his classmates were whoever could walk five blocks to school. He had Ronnie and Billy, whom he played stickball with, and Teresa, "Don't call me Teresa, my name is Juliet." There were also a lot of kids he didn't know except in school. They had to trek across the meadow. His mother said it might be hard for them. It would rain and get muddy, and they would have to knock the mud off their shoes before they could come into the building. "It's the right thing to do," his mother said. Now, the memory was conflated with today. Fifth-grade class and thirty-two women. He didn't know any of them. And they didn't have muddy shoes. Time had twisted the cutting edge around. This was a new memory of his fifth-grade class. A sharper image. But now it was the court telling the city it had to do something. The city had to make up for the sins of its past. Perversity. Mikozy knew he was part of the perversity. Mikozy was one of those people. The newspapers, the radio, his classmates, even his mother said that he had been promoted to make up for the sins of the city's past. He heard satisfaction, and pleasure, in her voice when she said that. So it must have been true. That was more than a decade ago. Now, the knife had been turned around and was pointed at him. It was his turn to be a sin of the past. That was probably the real reason why he was sitting here. His karma was making him experience what had been experienced by the sons of the Great White Fathers. The bad part was sitting in the heat— no air-conditioning, just a barely perceptible sea breeze filtering across the window ledge. He peeled his shirt away from his back to give some room to the sweat pumping out his pores.

"You're in." Schmidt grabbed his shoulder and pulled him close and whispered into his ear. "You made dick, Mikozy. You goddam mixto."

Schmidt's friendly joust stung. It was more than a paper cut. Schmidt was a foul-mouthed lout seeking back room clubbiness. If you survived his insults, you were his friend. It wasn't something Mikozy aspired to. He just didn't seem to have any choice. When the brass gave you a partner, you married the man. That's what Captain Freeman said.

"I'm just a goddamn mick," Schmidt said into Mikozy's ear. Mikozy wanted to listen to Captain Freeman read off the names of those promoted to detective. The captain stood erect at the podium, absent his cigar. He wore the officer's white dress hat. Regal and elegant. He made the moment seem longer than it was. Freeman stood in front of twenty rows of patrolmen, all of them warriors sworn to protect the community. Today was a rite of passage. Some would move on to a higher rank and carry a special badge of honor in the LAPD. Others would continue to be foot soldiers. Foot soldiers with a Ford. Freeman carried the tradition into the present, determined not to let the winds of social pressure tear away the meaning of stepping forward. Promotions to detective were more than a private matter.

"Schmidt, you're an asshole. You know I'm a mick too," Mikozy twisted around and growled sotto voce. Mikozy had to lift up on his toes to reach Schmidt's nose.

"Holy fuck, mother of god." Schmidt went above the permissible whisper. Captain Freeman paused a moment to let the offending voice crawl back into safety. Freeman expected to hear unchecked anger at today's special event. The police association had drawn its line in the sand. It demanded that promotions to detective and new hires be based on merit and not on some kind of equity. Their attorney had labeled the court mandate a quota. He refused to use the other words, what he called the tinsel and glitter of making up for the past.

Schmidt poked Mikozy. "I'm six four and can press two hundred."

Mikozy poked back. "With the IQ of a potato."

"Just because your grandmother was Irish doesn't make you a mick," Schmidt said.

"And my grandfather being Haitian makes me black?"

"That's why you'll make detective, Mikozy. No other way."

"Maybe it has something to do with my other granddad being Mexican or his wife being Chinese?"

Captain Freeman called out, "Rafael Mikozy, detective."

Mikozy stepped forward to acknowledge the honor and then stepped back into the line. Two hundred patrolmen were standing in anticipation. Twenty-five would be going up the chain and making detective. The rumor was that twenty would be people of color.

"You're fucked up, Mikozy. You don't even know who you are." Schmidt leaned into Mikozy as Mikozy stepped back into line.

"Hey, that's what it takes to be an American these days."

"Being a fucked-up Oreo?"

"That's right, *pendejo*." Mikozy knew his choice of insult was wrong. He needed to make a deeper wound.

"You can't even speak English."

"Not very cosmopolitan, are you, Schmitty? Probably can't even spell your own name."

The day, the dueling words were etched in brilliants. Mikozy remembered it all. This was the new brotherhood, a camaraderie forged in native colors. But it was an uneasy accommodation. Freeman echoed Ms. Emma: "No nonsense." It was better than slash and burn.

Captain Freeman called out the twenty-fifth name. "Michael Schmidt." Schmidt stepped forward. A quiet applause circled the room.

"Gentlemen, I'll take that as approval for all the new detectives." Freeman's voice demanded obedience. He didn't wait till Schmidt stepped back into place.

"Dismissed." Freeman touched his white hat in modest salute to the historic moment. He marched away from the podium and away from the reporters waiting for a memorable quote. The city and the nation were waiting to find out how the police brass would respond to the court's imprecise language about finding a path that combined merit- and diversity-based promotions. The press would have to quote unnamed officials. Freeman had disappeared. The officers began to leave too.

"Don't worry, Mikozy." Schmidt turned around and offered a congratulatory hand to Mikozy. "I'll take care of you. Let's go get drunk."

"Mighty white of you." Mikozy traded shots with the freck-led brute and grabbed his hand, not knowing if either of them really qualified to be promoted to detective. There was a good chance they'd still be partnered.

The years passed, and now Mikozy was back in the fifth grade. Thanks, no less, to Schmitty. Mikozy squirmed in his seat. He was uncomfortable with the heat. The humidity was push-ing 90 percent. He was uncomfortable with the rookies. He was uncomfortable with being in a women-only class. He was un-comfortable with the paint waiting to drop on him, with having waited so long to take a class, with himself.

Mikozy really didn't know why he was here. He knew what a clue was. He knew enough not to step on the evidence at the crime scene. Schmidt could have written an excuse. "Mikozy knows it all. God bless him, he's a detective." He leaned his chin on the palm of his left hand, his elbow resting on the chair's mini-mal desktop. Mikozy looked across the rows of the female uni-formed cops. At least he could wear street clothes. Maybe they would think he was an inspector of sorts. Someone here to evalu-ate the instructor, or, if they noticed the paint, maybe they would think he was here to watch how fast the flakes fell. The instructor stared down at him from the lectern. She had forceful black eyes. Her hair was black too, pulled tight and knotted. She had a taut and narrow frame. Mikozy studied her face. He saw a thousand years of history melding into a dazzling gemstone. Asian genes, European genes. Lovely, was what he thought. Her skin was un-tarnished with the pains of older generations. Mikozy guessed her to be twenty-six.

Another bead of sweat trickled down his face. He wiped his brow with his fingers and wiped them off on his pants. The pant stain was becoming noticeable. "Is that Detective Rafael…Mikozy?" She pronounced "Mikozy" correctly. Just as Ms. Emma had.

"Yes, that's my name, but I'm not really here." Mikozy want-ed to take back his words. He didn't want his intent, his lack of enthusiasm, to show. Too late. Huck Finn was present and ready to learn. Sort of.

Lisa Liu-Smythe smiled back. Enough to let Mikozy know she heard him.

"Well, maybe none of us are really here, Detective." A sassy, brassy voice pinned his ears back. "We will find out shortly after we check all the clues. Perhaps someone would like to take the detective's pulse?"

It wasn't that the rookies laughed at him. Or maybe it was. The women were laughing. They were looking at him. His heart pumped the blood. He could feel the blush climbing up and inside the edges of his shirt.

Lisa Liu-Smythe flipped through her note cards after calling off everyone's name. Mikozy couldn't see any large loose-leaf binder or textbook or briefcase. Just note cards. She looked like she knew what she wanted to do and didn't want to clutter the lectern with exacting details. At least not references to what other people had written. She stepped around the lectern. High heels. Blue. A metallic blue. She also wore yellow slacks and a red silk blouse. Mikozy hadn't noticed the combination when he walked into the room. The effect was jarring. The primary colors were true. Her clothes were edged with a razor. Mikozy sized her up in that moment. She would be teaching the class with the same intensity emanating from her clothes and her colors.

"Okay, folks, look me over carefully," Liu commanded. She paused. She succeeded in creating a significant silence. She had everyone's eyes, and no one spoke. Mikozy studied her as well. He set his sight on St. Maarten's eastern shore. The Orient Beach. Impromptu eyes. Mikozy searched for a word to summarize her effect on him. What he ended up with wasn't logical. But beauty wasn't logic. She had found the secret to negative space. Something extraordinary was out there, but he didn't know what it was. Not yet.

Mikozy's thoughts drifted to his first college course, when all he'd asked were "why" questions. Once he made detective, he asked mostly "how" and "what" questions. He was a cop, not a social worker. He didn't need to hear all the reasons the perps, their lawyers, and psychologists gave for the bad deeds that they were committing. He knew the reasons, but he didn't want to hear them again and again. The whys were acts of boredom. He wasn't sure he would ever fully understand why someone hurt another person. Anger, jealousy, greed. Did it really matter? Of course, white-collar crime was easier to understand. No one was looking when it happened. And no one looked hurt afterward, except for the non-comprehending elderly investor. The fiction of an invisible crime was different from seeing the fear and pain of blue-collar victims.

Professor Liu looked like a why question to him. But not the kind of why question he associated with crime. Funny how she put herself in that situation. What was she really asking: "Why am I dressed so garishly? Why these colors? Why am I teaching this class? Why is Mikozy taking my class? Why is Mikozy thinking so hard about me?" Mikozy smiled at his scripting, laughed at his fantasies about this moment and about what he thought Professor Liu might be thinking about him. Or what he would like her to be thinking about him. Mikozy found himself becoming interested in continuing education, despite the heat and humidity. Despite being in elementary school. He ran his fingers through his beard again. Liu walked up and down the aisles of the class. Mikozy saw the open toes on the points of her shoes. Bright red nails. Toenails and fingernails. All red. All twenty of them. Attention to detail, that was clear.

"What's the clue?" Liu asked the class. She paraded around the room. Nobody volunteered an answer. After a long minute, Liu came to a stop one aisle over from Mikozy.

"What's your name?" Liu asked a student.

Liu stood next to a short-cropped blonde, a splash of periwinkle tinting the tips. When she turned in her seat, Mikozy noticed her left side in profile. A small gold earring was pinned to her ear. He thought he saw the edge of a tattoo peek out of her collar. She turned a little further and glanced over at Mikozy. She might have given Mikozy a friendly nod, but her eyes were cold.

"Jane, Jane Callahan. I mean, Officer Callahan."

"Very good, Officer Callahan. Jane. We are on first names here. We can dispense with professor and student. That only gets in the way of our search for the truth."

Tell that to Ms. Emma, thought Mikozy. Ms. Emma didn't even call us by our own names. She made up new names for us. Maybe Ms. Emma was searching for a different kind of truth.

"Let me ask you, Jane, do you have any observations?" Jane's back curved to attention. Jane didn't respond, but Liu wouldn't let her step offstage.

"Let's say you walk into this room, you're alone, it's 7:30 a.m., and I'm dressed just like this, except I'm lying on the floor and I'm dead."

"What's the question?" Jane asked. Mikozy liked that. Good kid. I could work with her. Don't guess. Make them put themselves on the line, whatever the rank, whatever the title. Don't let them bullshit you. Too many things left unsaid.

"Well, what would you think? Just looking at me." Liu let the baited hook lie.

She was satisfied with the hypothetical. All she needed to do was wait. "Just looking," Jane finally answered. "I haven't touched you, so I don't know if you're warm, cold, whether rigor's set in and gone. Maybe there's a smell, but again, I'm just looking at you."

"Go on."

"You're dressed well. You're provocative. The nails match the red blouse. Your hair is pinned up. The pin looks the same shade of blue as your shoes."

Mikozy silently offered his congratulations. He hadn't noticed the pin. Let's keep Jane on stage, he thought. Mikozy turned the chair, the vinyl screeched. Only Professor Liu seemed to notice. She looked briefly at Mikozy. The look said, "You're next."

Jane continued. "I'd say you were out on a date the night before. Someplace nice. You wouldn't have dressed up just to go to bed with some guy…or girl."

"Yes." Liu's hands bounced in the air, semaphores of recognition. "Political correctness is good in this instance. We can't assume a woman will date only men. Nicht wahr?"

Mikozy flipped off the automatic pilot switch. He stepped into a zone. He didn't notice the muggy heat any longer, nor his pants sticking to the seat, nor the spreading stain on his pants. He forgot about the all-woman class and the reason Schmidt had led him to this watering hole. He looked at Liu with renewed interest. German, Mikozy thought. What was that about? Screw the language. What about the sexual stuff? This was not men and women. This was men or women. Depending. Depending on Liu, depending on Jane, depending on the other women here. Hell, thought Mikozy, depending on me.

"Anything else?" Professor Liu-Smythe asked.

"How observant do you want me to be?"

Without hesitation, Professor Liu answered, "Be true to the moment. We are trying to understand what a clue is, and that depends on what you see and what you think you see."

Jane and Professor Liu both seized the moment. Center and front.

"Tell us, Jane, what do you see?" Mikozy sensed the class move forward in their seats. Curiosity climbed another peak.

"Your feet are bare, and I don't see a panty line." A collective breath followed Jane's observation. Mikozy didn't get it. What did one have to do with the other?

"Let's be clear about what you're saying."

"Well, if your feet are bare, you're not wearing pantyhose. And if there is no panty line, it means you're traveling light."

The class buzzed. They'd gotten it right. Mikozy wasn't worried about missing Jane's deduction. He would have found out the traditional way. He would have looked.

"Very good. Is there anything else?" Professor Liu was insistent. A good interviewer bleeding the subject of all her vital information.

"I don't see a wedding ring. I don't even see a tan line on your wedding finger. So I assume you're single. Maybe divorced. Also pretty well off. I can't afford those rags." Mikozy couldn't see Jane's face, but he could hear her pining to be heard.

"What makes you think these are expensive clothes?" Professor Liu worked with Jane, letting the student define the answer to her hypothetical question.

"I used to work Elwi's. You know, five, six hundred for a pair of slacks. Not the most expensive, but up there. I'd like to take a look at your labels." Labels are good, Mikozy said to himself. Jane was scoring another point.

"Cheeky, aren't you?"

Mikozy was caught off guard, as he expected Jane had been. Probably the class as well. Jane ran scarlet. Liu turned the moment inside out. She had a way of making students burn at the stake. Figuratively speaking. The students were tied to their desks. She could sacrifice each one in turn. Without mercy. He could be next. Mikozy was surprised to see a professor leading and provoking a student the way Liu did. Liu had created a rhythm. The class was listening. And then she jarred the class away from the text. Mikozy wondered whether Liu had a purpose or whether she'd slipped into poor judgment. Still, she kept the class awake. Mikozy knew that even if he were teaching this class and was tempted into making an offhand remark, he would have stayed away from the suggestive remark Liu had made. Nothing cheeky for him. He would stick with bullet wounds and drugs.

"I'm…umm…" Jane hesitated.

"I'm kidding." Liu-Smythe ignored Jane's reluctance. Mikozy didn't see any visible change in Liu's stage mask. If anything, Liu pursued her inquiry with even more force.

"Those are good observations, Jane." She waited for Jane to continue. "Is that all? Did you notice anything else?"

Jane still looked surprised. Mikozy believed he could read her thoughts. Jane must be thinking about Liu as a woman, not as her teacher. Jane must be wondering if Liu meant to say something else. Mikozy could only guess what that might be. He sensed something was wrong with the picture. This was more than teacher and student. Mikozy leaned back in his chair. The class had become somewhat of a mystery of him. Let the moment unfold, he told himself.

Jane said, "Yes, that's all."

Liu had her back to Mikozy. She turned around and faced Mikozy. She did exactly what he didn't want her to do. What he prayed she wouldn't do. He was tied to his desk, and she was preparing another sacrifice to the search for truth. This time it was Mikozy.

"Well, Detective. What would have been your thoughts if it were you who found me dead rather than Jane?" Professor Liu-Smythe drilled him with her black eyes. Mikozy imagined her red fingernails ready to claw the words from his mouth. Schmidt had said that she was young. He didn't say that young meant tenacious. Mikozy thought about how he should answer. He probably had figured out more clues in the past year than she probably had ever read about. But he couldn't afford to condescend to the class or to Liu. That could mean an exceptionally long afternoon. His head would be on the chopping block. He preferred to avoid political castration. He would have to play the game. Make some mildly interesting remarks and then plead ignorance. That was the game plan.

"Detective?" she repeated.

Part of Mikozy's unease was the familiarity Liu insisted on using with Jane. She offered him a token of respect. But "detective" stung. The hint of sarcasm was in her pose. Her hip angled up, she tilted her front high heel up on its stiletto. Her eyes flattened, a glint revealing more than instructional interest. He wondered where she was pushing him.

Liu walked over to Mikozy. She stood in front of him, looking down. Not the look of love. He already knew that. Her voice wasn't hard. It wasn't accusing. Neither were her eyes. They were challenging him.

"No thoughts at all?"

"You like primary colors." Mikozy went for the minimalist response.

"Yes." Liu smiled.

She turned and walked back to the front of the class. He could now see nestled in her hair the blue pin that Jane had noticed before. Funny how perceptive women were. Liu kept speaking. He knew she was still talking to him.

"Are Jane's comments correct?"

Mikozy had to respond now. He was a detective. This was his daily bread. And it was a worthy challenge.

"What Jane said is what I might have said. But so what? I could have said it and been 100 percent wrong. You could be married and not like to wear rings. Maybe you're a seamstress and made the clothes you're wearing. Maybe you're the cleaning woman for the city and this was your last day of work and your supervisor was pissed off. Hardly a date. And so on."

Liu had turned back to face the class. She leaned against the desk. Mikozy felt the seductiveness of her pose, lips pouting, breasts pushing against the red silk blouse.

Mikozy admitted his attraction to her. Strictly a physical reaction, he lied to himself.

Liu stared at him, eyes pecking hard at his shield.

"Well, those are possibilities. But you would admit that Jane's answer is the more probable?"

Mikozy realized he would have to give up any tact he brought with him today. Liu continued to push him. And why not? He was paying for the sin of not signing up for memory enhancement, adult urine testing, or teen suicide prevention. He was paying the price for ignoring the memo. He had waited till the end of the continuing education period and gotten stuck with Clue Analysis 1. Better known as don't step on the evidence. She would have guessed her class was not his first choice. Not much deductive insight called for. Liu was not about to let him sleep-walk through her class. Rank had no privileges in Clue Analysis 1. That was also Mikozy's first rule of questioning technique. Except now Mikozy was the one being questioned. She was the teacher.

"Yes. Jane's thinking is the more probable. But the how and what of crimes are not always in the realm of high probability. If they were, we'd do better at solving crimes by simply inspecting the crime scenes. I like to keep an open mind."

Liu would not back off. She closed the distance. Her phosphorescent colors vibrated. Mikozy was tempted to reach out, palms up and open, to catch the undulations. They had a hypnotic rhythm, making it difficult for Mikozy to anticipate her next question. She thrust for a didactic kill or at least a severe instructional injury. Dodge and parry were the best Mikozy could do.

"What do you actually do? You don't look at all possibilities, do you? I've been to crime scenes. There's a quick, perhaps a too quick, narrowing of possibilities. Isn't that true?"

Mikozy glanced around the room. He was ground zero.

"We don't often have the time."

"So you do a Jane-type investigation?"

"No. I do a Mikozy-type investigation."

The class erupted in laughter. The laughing was quickly muffled, choked off by Professor Liu as she let her eyes roam up and down the aisles. Mikozy's Huck Finn raced around the room, daring Ms. Emma to catch him. He saw Ms. Emma slowly fade. He couldn't hold on to his fifth-grade triumph.

Professor Liu folded her arms and pressed her lips together. She carefully considered Mikozy.

"Must be exciting. I wish the class could observe you."

Liu's voice fell an octave. It was too soft to be another challenge. He wondered what she really wanted. She must know it would be impossible for the class to come and observe. Too unwieldly. Maybe she was asking for herself. Indirect. She didn't come across as lying in wait, readying another trapdoor. Mikozy was amused. But he couldn't catch the rhyme or the reason.

Liu and Mikozy were silent. They entered into another significant pause and dragged the class along as witnesses. More energy spewing out of the space between them than the furnace burning LA. Mikozy resisted running his fingers through his beard and let the sweat trickle down his neck. Mikozy couldn't sort out his other feelings about Professor Liu. He wouldn't guess what she was thinking about him, and he had little success trying to figure out the end point to her style of provocative questions. There was too much going on behind her glitter.

Liu broke the silence. Looking around the room at the students, she said, "I'm sorry. It's hot enough as it is without my asking the shades to be drawn, but we need some darkness." With that, she turned away from Mikozy and moved on to another subject. He was relieved and he was disappointed. A feeling of interrupted love. As if on cue, Jane got up and pulled the shades down. Liu walked to the back of the room and turned on the slide projector. The image of a bare-chested man dominated the room again. It was the image of a man that Mikozy had seen for a brief moment at the beginning of the class when Liu was testing the slide projector. The man was huge as a buffalo, wild hair sprouting. This was no pretty Adonis destined for tragedy. The eyes were unfocused. Insistent on an answer. But it was unclear what the question was that needed to be answered. He was inside a shallow cave. The man-animal barely fit inside. Light sliced into the cave. The painter had added too much light inside the cave. Too much brightness than could have come from the outside. Mikozy instantly forgave the artist for the extra light. The scene splashed against the wall, a demonic hero urging the viewer to pity and fear the man-animal at the same time. On the ground, a gold string threaded its way into a corner. The man puzzled over the gold string. He was lost. Mikozy identified with the man-animal. He could smell the voltage ripping through the man-animal. Death was nearby. Mikozy resisted the temptation to shout out, an elemental reaction to the man-animal's barely suppressed anger. Mikozy instructed himself to sit still. Just as he had for Ms. Emma in fifth grade.

Mikozy knew that if he hadn't been in the room, the rookies would have risen to the moment. The image called out for recognition. Thighs worthy of an Olympian, champion pecs. Too bad Mikozy had spoiled their afternoon. The women probably had an urge to hoot. Like Mikozy, they resisted. He resisted. Maybe because the man looked lost. The slideshow could still be a tutorial trap. The class was quiet. Liu might call on the person foolish enough to break the spell she cast. A mistake could let her draw more blood than she already had. Mikozy promised himself to avoid the temptation of speaking as the voice of experience.

Mikozy was surprised. Liu didn't ask any more questions. She began her lecture.

"This is Theseus, the legendary king of Athens, believed to be the son of Poseidon or Aegeus. Take your pick. If you studied Greek mythology, you'll recall that Theseus traveled the countryside meeting an assortment of villains and monsters. He was even exiled in Hades for a time until he was rescued by Hercules. The man was quite a character.

"Theseus built his reputation on killing the Minotaur. As with most legends, there is some uncertainty on what the Minotaur was. The Minotaur was either a man with a bull's head or a bull with a man's head. Again, take your pick. As an aside, Theseus himself looks half man, half animal. The painter might have been suggesting that all of these legendary figures were simply exaggerations of ourselves." Liu's lecture was paced to the trotter's gait. She turned her three-by-five cards over as she moved from point to point.

"This creature was kept in a labyrinth on the island of Crete. The king of Crete demanded an annual tribute from the Athenians. They offered up seven boys and seven girls to be fed to the Minotaur. Just to keep the Minotaur happy. Theseus insisted on being one of the seven boys, and, as you probably know from reading the book or"—Liu waited for everyone to catch up to her, and then continued—"or from seeing the movie, Theseus killed the beast. Sounds like justifiable homicide. Okay, where do we go from here? What's the point of this piece of theatrics?" Liu had set the stage. The class was listening intently. Nobody was tempted to answer the rhetorical proposition. Whatever point she wanted to make, it would stick.

"Theseus doesn't look like a hero in this slide. I don't want you to think about his heroic attributes. Instead, I want you to look at the yellow thread on the floor of the cave." Mikozy let his eyes slide to the bottom of the screen. The thread disappeared out a side chamber to the cave.

"That thread, students, is the 'clew.' Spelled c-l-e-w.

"Questions?" Liu asked.

There were no questions. She was telling an unusual story. Mikozy wondered where she was going with it. He had never heard about clue being spelled as clew or what difference it made.

"'Clew' is the archaic spelling of c-l-u-e. In English of course." Liu paused. She drew invisible quotes in the air, marking off each word. It was a storyteller's mannerism.

"Puzzled? I hope so. Think about the Theseus legend. It gives us an interesting metaphor. We go out to a crime scene. We're pretty much in a cave. Or shall I say, in the dark. We have the same lost look that Theseus has in this picture. We may not see ourselves as bullheaded."

Mikozy looked over at Liu and watched her crinkle her lips on the cliché.

"Think about it. What do we expect of our clues when we go about detecting? Well, even before we can talk about specifics of what might be expected, we should realize that our expectations are shaped by the words we use, our preconceptions about crime and criminals, and our preconceptions about the tools of the criminal trade." Mikozy tracked her lecture with a second-level discourse. Would the story make a difference? Would the image of Theseus help them remember the basics any better? Maybe yes, maybe no. Mikozy couldn't decide. And he wasn't the professor.

"Let's go back to our hero, Theseus. His clue is a ball of yarn. His clue to getting out of the cave. In this slide, we see the yellow thread lying at Theseus's feet. Ariadne, King Minos's daughter, gave him the ball of yarn. She had fallen in love in Theseus. She wanted him to find his way out of the cave where the Minotaur lived. You could say she was giving him a hint. Maybe the love angle makes the motive for killing the Minotaur a little more complicated than simply putting an end to the ritual sacrifice of children."

Mikozy studied the painter's vision of Theseus. He tried to imagine the Minotaur. There must be another painting. One of the Minotaur, prepared to feast on the innocent, with Theseus barely visible in the shadows waiting his turn. The painter would not have left the myth undone. Too much violence, too much craziness in this hero. Mikozy's thoughts flickered back and forth between the Greek hero and villain. He wandered to the unlocked door marked LC. From cave to crypt, from Crete to LA, from Ariadne to LC, from Theseus's love to his own. Strange how the mind connected things. Was it a mere chemical process? Or was the mind more than mathematical formulas? Mikozy would be seeing LC tonight. Maybe her protector too. She had little idea whom she'd invited down to the crypt to discuss the death of fulano de tal. Would it be Dr. Cream or his Minotaur stand-in? Was LC an intended sacrifice? If so, he would be a pleasant surprise. Just as Theseus had surprised the Minotaur. The Greek heroes were a deceptive lot. Mikozy winced at the comparison.

Deception had become a virtue for him. Carlos Laguna's spirit flitted across the image of Theseus. A hooked talon fingered Mikozy. "You were my friend." Mikozy turned his head away from the vision. He could be Theseus tonight. He could be killing a Minotaur, too. Or was it the love angle? Did it make any difference? Was it important why Theseus killed the Minotaur? Mikozy looked around for Professor Liu. She was propped up against the door, pointing to Theseus. The students were hypnotized by the man-animal. Lost in his feral gaze. Waiting for Theseus to tear apart the Minotaur and feast upon his innards. Jane looked like she was wondering about the Minotaur. She shifted in her chair and looked across at Mikozy. His silver mane reflected in her eyes, and she ran her tongue across her lips. She turned back to Liu. Mikozy wondered if there was a message.

"Of course, in this slide, Theseus doesn't look like much of a detective. He doesn't see the yellow thread that Ariadne had given him. There it is lying at his feet. He's just about ready to step on his clue. That's one thing you never do as a police officer. You never step on your clues." Liu pulled a chorus of snickers from the class.

"Okay. That's an image I want to keep in mind." Liu was pointing up at the sorrowful man-animal. "For most of the afternoon, I'll be examining specific crime scenes with you. We'll sort out various clues, separate out false clues from real ones, and try to understand the often tedious process that detectives and technicians go through.

"Before we do, I want to drive home my little piece of theater. We're not that far away from Theseus. We might not picture ourselves like him. But we share quite a lot with him. Isn't that true, Detective Mikozy?"

Ping-pong, Mikozy would be in the crypt tonight. Like Theseus. That was his mystery, not hers. Liu's question meant something else. Time to return to the here and now. Maybe she was taking another cheap shot at Detective Mikozy. He thought she had put aside her challenge-the-student method. He was being cast as the perpetual male cynic with an implication of jealousy at the novice for coming up with the obvious conclusion. Now she put him in Theseus's cave. But Theseus was no cynic.

"What is it you want to know?" Mikozy asked.

"I suppose the question is, how often do we recognize a clue for what it is?" Liu didn't wait for Mikozy to answer. There was more preamble. "Take a look at Theseus. The golden thread is right in front of him. He was given a clue by someone. I suppose you would say an informant. And yet he looks like he still doesn't get it. Is that the way it is? How good are you, Detective, at recognizing clues for what they are? Do you know enough to follow it out of the cave? At what point do you commit? Your response to Jane seems to be, 'Maybe it is, maybe it isn't. She loves me, she loves me not.'"

Mikozy was surprised, and yet he knew he shouldn't have been, with Liu's sexual innuendo. He had no argument with what Liu said. He actually agreed with her. He would have said so, but it would have spoiled the effect. This was good theater for rookie cops. New cops never knew what they were stepping into when they went out to a crime scene. Maybe they would remember to be more careful after Liu's class. But Mikozy couldn't resist the bait any longer. Liu had him hooked. He couldn't let the word get out that he'd been out cavemanned by a woman prof and thirty-two rookies.

"Well, Jane's analysis was good, but she could be wrong. My uncertainty…" Mikozy held the word. He realized that Liu had figured out his investigative style. "My uncertainty is something I work with. It's too easy to rely on the easy clues. Those golden threads." There it was. Huck Finn had thrown a tattered glove to the floor. The challenge. Right in front of Ms. Emma.

"Well said, Detective Mikozy." Then came the other shoe. "I think your uncertainty will make our examination of crimes scenes later this afternoon more interesting."

Liu smiled. Not a ripple of tension flowed across her face. She was smooth. Her lipstick, bright red, created a slow-moving wave that rolled across the room and bounced off the sheen of her nails. She examined one of her note cards. A practiced pause before the class recess.

"When you get back from the break, we will discuss various ways of sorting through information and evidence. I'd like to share the results of research I did on what the first officers on the scene thought had happened and how that shaped their investigation. I think you'll find it very interesting how some clues led the investigation down a black hole and ate up precious time. We'll also see what kinds of clues are more likely to be useful than others."

Liu turned around and looked at the clock on the wall behind her.

"Some of you might put the shades back up." The shades rolled up the windows and spun around on their ends. Light streamed into the room. Mikozy was sweating again. He remembered the heat.

"We'll take a ten-minute break," she told the class. "Remember, be back in ten."

Chairs screeched, the clatter of overdue conversation erupted. The class disappeared in an instant. The rookies had hurried out. The old building still favored the men's restrooms. Mikozy sat at his desk. He didn't have to rush. Liu was readying her note cards before the break ended. Everyone had left except Mikozy and Liu. Liu put her note cards down. She looked up at Mikozy and walked over to him. There was no hesitation. She knew what she wanted. He was annoyed with himself more than with Liu. After all, he didn't have to be in this class. Mikozy stood up. Ms. Emma had told him he had to respect his teachers.

"Stand up when you're called on, Huck," she'd say. Mikozy stood for another reason. Nothing to do with respect. Now he could look down on Liu. Even at five foot ten, he was taller than most women. Not long ago, he and Schmitty had been back to their running argument about the advantages and disadvantages of the hiring process. "Schmitty," he said, "this diversity stuff is great."

Schmidt's anger had all but withered, except for one ugly branch. "What's that, Mikozy?"

"Well, I'm getting taller."

"I haven't noticed. What are you doing, measuring the height of your hair?"

"No. It's all the women joining the force. The average height is dropping. I'm getting taller."

"Mikozy, you've almost got me convinced now about the benefits of diversity. You know, I did notice that I was getting smarter and smarter."

"That must be why you made captain." They could laugh because they couldn't figure out whether what they said was true. They settled for different points of view.

Liu stood in front of Mikozy, arms wrapped about herself. An imaginary desk occupied the space between them. Mikozy confirmed that he was taller than Liu. He relished this small pleasure.

"Jane was right on target," Mikozy said. He hoped he could take the steam out of the second half of the class. Kind words couldn't hurt. Liu resumed her forward motion. She closed in on his personal space, walking through the dense, humid air. She walked through the imaginary desk. The dead heat in the room coiled around the two of them. The thick air was moist. Mikozy felt a shock jump across the space between them.

"Can I tell you something private?" Liu was offstage. The class had left. She recanted her professorial demeanor. Mikozy knew enough from the last hour in class that he couldn't anticipate Liu. She zigzagged around the usual social boundaries.

"I can't offer much in the way of confidence," Mikozy said, "but sure. What's up?" Mikozy closed his hand on the opportunity to be something other than a student in her class. She had walked into his personal space. He decided to follow into hers if that's where the moment led.

"I can accept that," Liu said. She made a small gesture with her hand and laughed as if to punctuate her thoughts.

Liu's voice was still low. "I'm not quite sure how to say this." She looked behind her to make sure none of the other students were still in the room. Mikozy looked down at his pants to make sure that his fly was zipped. He wanted a mirror to see if there was something stuck to his beard. The slow way in which Liu was leading up to her confidence made him nervous.

"Don't worry," Mikozy said. "You can trust me with your life." Humor was an abracadabra to the exiled self. Huck Finn danced around the room, singing idle tunes.

"Yes, I suppose I could." Liu laughed, a burst of heart. "This isn't life threatening." Her eyes widened. He was sure she was twenty-six. "Not yet," she added. The coquette in her lightly touched his arm. He knew she could feel the steam.

"You probably know that this is my first teaching job. I saw that you were assigned here by Captain Schmidt, and he said something about one of his detectives might be taking my class."

Mikozy forced his muscles not to twitch. He resisted moving his lips. He didn't want a frown to spoil the moment. Schmidt knew him well enough to figure that he'd be in this class. Mikozy was unhappy with the idea that Schmidt was planning his life. Mikozy thought she had already taught the class a few times. That's what he thought Schmidt had said. She was good even without the theater. She didn't need that. She skipped effortlessly from rock to rock without being propelled off the ledge of an indefensible idea.

"What can I say? Bravo, I mean it, you're doing fine." Mikozy thought his compliment was the reply she was inviting.

"Ha, ha, that's not exactly what I was fishing for." Liu wrung her hands, losing a half dozen years. "Well, let me start over." Her lips gyrated around a lemon peel; the lush red lips exuded a sensual flavor, not sour, not sweet, demanding to be tasted.

"I think it would only be fair to tell you, and I hope you won't think it wrong, but Jane, well, she works for me."

Liu confessed to trickery. Mikozy was caught in the moment. More theater.

Liu tried to clarify her technique. "Jane's my ace in the hole."

Mikozy stumbled a step back, nearly toppling into his chair.

"Well…" he garbled.

Liu's confession unraveled his steadiness. The chair scraped against the floor and bounced against the chair in the next row. The shock tilted him back. Liu grabbed his right arm. The cool hand steadied him. Her nails dug into his skin.

"Are you okay?" she asked.

"Oh, yeah." Mikozy couldn't think of a hip comeback and decided to go with the truth. "Shit, I didn't have a…" Mikozy stopped from blurting out the obvious, which would have meant he deserved to be in the beginner's class. "Jane's a ringer? I'm surprised." Mikozy needed to take a stand on the twice-slippery floor.

"Isn't that what I said?" Liu was puzzled, trying to remember what she said.

"Maybe you did. You probably didn't have an AI program write this script for you."

"I meant no harm. Really. You just happened to walk into my, ummm, you know, how shall I say it? You know, my trap. That's how I am teaching this class. I feel like I need a wake-up bell. No Jane, and I'm afraid this class would be deadly. And no,

I don't think an AI program is good theater. I needed a grand performance."

Mikozy was thinking how to craft a reply, any reply at all.

"Why are you telling me now?" Mikozy was curious. She didn't need to tell him. No one would have known.

"I wasn't sure if Captain Schmidt had told you. He told me that you would be in my class, and I had discussed doing this." Liu grew younger by the second. She was only nine years old. An uncertain adolescent waiting to see if the wizard was really from Oz.

"So, if Schmidt had told me, why was I playing along, and when would I let cat out of the bag? And, if I found out somehow, I might get mad and let a rat out of the bag instead?"

"Something like that." She hesitated a moment. "I take Captain Schmidt didn't tell you."

"No, I guess he didn't. That shh…" Mikozy shook his head in disbelief.

Schmitty had scored another coup. He sprang Mikozy over to continuing education with Perkins sitting at his desk and had him looking over his back, not knowing he was walking into Liu's surprise.

He was still thinking when she asked, "No hurt feelings?"

"Well, a bit. I'll live."

"If I hadn't told you about Jane, would you have guessed?"

"I might have. I was surprised by Jane's taking notice of your hairpin. I didn't remember seeing it or your turning around. Jane was too good, and I might begin to suspect."

"But you didn't, did you?" Liu had grown older again. She was twenty-six and giving him a friendly shove.

"No, that's the truth," Mikozy admitted. It didn't hurt at all.

Mikozy and Liu waited through their silence. Mikozy's interest in Liu changed. She was a chameleon draped in a cool green, changing the color of her skin as she high-stepped on twos and fours into the sunlight. Her beauty projected across a field of purple starbursts. Mikozy hoped he was feeling something more than just a shift in mood, but he was cautious, distrustful of the moment.

Mikozy searched for safe ground and wondered aloud, "So how are you really at clue analysis?"

Liu said, "You mean, do I always need a Jane to figure out what the clue is or whether there is one?"

"Something like that."

"You can give me a try." Liu was smiling around the edges of eyes. He could now feel some warmth to her words. She was still holding onto his arm. The nails no longer dug into his skin, but their tips raised goose bumps on his arm. A shiver unnerved his cool. This wasn't a professor talking with her student. This he knew.

They were playing with each other. Mikozy was eager to stay for the rest of Clue Analysis 1. All of a sudden, he liked her clothes, he liked her colors, he liked her eyes, he liked Lisa Liu and the rest of her name.

"How would you like coming to my next crime scene?" Mikozy offered, surprising himself with his invitation. He had never invited a civilian to tag along. No outsider had ever peered over his shoulder. There was always a first time.

"Great. I'd love to. Really." The voice of a fifteen-year-old cheered with excitement. "You know, I'm more than a teacher."

"Yes, I can see." Mikozy moved closer, his turn to step into her zone of privacy.

Liu lowered her eyes.

"If I'm not being presumptuous," Mikozy said, "I need to ask my prof for her phone number. I will have to get in touch with you."

"Yes, of course, my office number is…" She switched halfway back into being a teacher, but Mikozy interrupted her transformation.

"That wouldn't be much help. I'm likely to get a call at four a.m. and have to be done by seven a.m. to organize the investigation. This is not a nine-to-five proposition."

Mikozy heard the echo of his proposition bounce off the reflection on her face. She was startled but didn't confess to understanding his true meaning, if that was what he truly meant. He wasn't sure himself. How could she know if he didn't know? He wanted to change the wording of his last sentence, but he wasn't writing a book and couldn't simply erase the spoken word.

"I mean, I work at all hours, and if you're serious about coming along…"

"I know you what you mean," the woman in her answered.

There was a sense of charm and wickedness that crept into her expression. She reached to the back of her hair and pulled out a long blue pin, and her black hair descended to her shoulders. "I have to change into my next disguise before the class starts," Liu said by way of explanation. Mikozy wondered about the tricks she would play on the class. He hadn't imagined how much fun teaching could be. They heard the door open and the noise of rookie cops dancing into the room.

"My home number is unlisted. Can you remember 366-553-5542? Dial me up and take me on your next call." The invisible bell called the class back to order while the clues waited to march in procession.

Mikozy wasn't worried about getting a passing grade or getting his desk back from Perkins. He couldn't find his concentration. His thoughts drifted back to Schmidt. Patrol mate, fellow copper and kidder, and the loyal opposition. Was this what Schmidt had in mind for his friend Mikozy?

When the class finally ended, Mikozy slipped out the back door. He took his time checking his calendar. Before he walked further down the hall, he heard Liu call out before he could round the corner. "You forgot something. Mikozy, you forgot something." He turned around and saw the manuscript he'd tucked away under his seat. "You wouldn't want to leave the deputy inspector's manuscript, would you?" Dinged again. He realized he'd have to read it now. It was still early in the day. He'd head home and zip through the manuscript. Mikozy would need to clock some sack time before meeting up with LC at the morgue around midnight.

## Chapter 8

BEDTIME READING

edtime for Mikozy was any time. Now he had a few hours to delve into the manuscript Deputy Inspector Tomlinson had sent him. It would help him find his new bedtime.

His two-bedroom was well worn. Comfortable. Foldout couch for guests. A North Carolina dining table with burled surfaces. Even an air fryer and a microwave. A super thin screen for monitoring world events and catching up with the latest TV dramas. LC's room was left untouched, her spirit still resident in all the things she left behind.

He brewed up a cup of chamomile tea. That would limit his time. Insure that he would doze before too many pages. With tea in hand, he flopped onto the couch. His other hand clumsily grabbed the manuscript, a solo page slipped out from the hundreds he would have to read. Mikozy picked up the orphaned page. This was from Tomlinson to Tomlinson. Notes to herself. She had done her homework before sending this off to him.

Was this a thoughtful appropriation of Jack London's 1908 book *The Iron Heel*? Or something else?

London was famous for his adventure stories—*The Sea-Wolf, Call of the Wild*; science fiction—*Star Rover*; the struggle to have a reputation—*Martin Eden*; and the fears a socialist would have of maniacal capitalism—*The Iron Heel*.

The original book was cast as the Everhard manuscript, found many years later in a new calendar, BOM. The Brotherhood of Man. So what do we have with this new Patricia Todd manuscript? Years later.

Do we have anything in these texts that justifies the fears they each had? Everhard's fear in the original was of an aristocracy determined to hold onto its wealth. Or Todd's later fear of an authoritarian socialist ideology seeking to replace the earlier one and in the process flatten individuality.

Is there anything that would lead police to actual crimes beyond finding what others assume to be Todd's skeletal remains? Is this fantasy or conspiracy?

Note to myself. Send this to one of our detectives who's had a deeper education than a criminal justice degree. Rafael Mikozy? That crazy street philosopher who knows way too much to be a cop.

Mikozy took another sip of chamomile. "So that's why I have this package. I'm the crazy street philosopher." He smiled as he scanned his living room. Just him. He needed some company. Perhaps some music to background this London tale of foreboding, not once but twice. Once for London's Everhard manuscript, another for the new Todd manuscript. *The Iron Heel* original and now *The Iron Heel Again*. Some music by Enigma? Portishead? Maybe some trap soul music by Bryson Tiller and Drake? He spun up a playlist to carry him through this tunnel full of machinations.

Mikozy went to the internet to see what other books London had written. Maybe get a quick heads-up on London's view on life and fantasy. Mikozy scanned the titles. *The Sea-Wolf*—adventure that makes a rich man into a working one under the dominance of tyrannical captain; *Martin Eden*—struggling writer achieves fame and finds it empty; *The Star Rover*—a condemned man is executed only to wake up as another condemned man; *White Fang*—a wolf dog is thrown into the world of violence of dogs and humans, saves his last owner from an attack. Mikozy found a thread of aggression around the many of life's dramas. The title of his assigned book suggested he was soon to be tossed into a war of malevolent and heroic characters. A society at odds with itself.

"Let's see what we have in this foreword." He turned the light up one notch. And so began Mikozy's novel assignment.

The Everhard Manuscript was a gift to our comprehension of the experience of the descent into chaos, a chaos driven by a government oligarchy, and one we comfortably describe as the Iron Heel. But, as historians, we must confess that the Manuscript lacks reliability. As with most historians, we can say we know more than the earlier source document of those times and even more with each succeeding document, but we find that it suffers from such defects. For historians, each manuscript contains unproven facts and errors. As with all source documents, we must consider the role of interpretation. Seven centuries have elapsed since we found the Everhard Manuscript. What Avis Everhard feared, the oligarchy and master system, was replaced with a new and vibrant socialist system. But it is clear that Everhard had experienced a system deserving of fear.

Looking back across the seven centuries that have lapsed since Avis Everhard completed her manuscript, events, and the consequences of those events, we can see how they were confused and veiled to her, but these are now much clearer to us. She lacked perspective. She was too close to the events she wrote about. After all, she was merged in the events she described.

Nevertheless, as a personal document, the Everhard Manuscript is of inestimable value. But here again we enter the error of perspective, and to accommodations due to the bias of love. We smile and forgive Avis Everhard for her heroic lines upon which she modelled her husband. We know today that her husband was not so colossal, and that he loomed among the events of his times less largely than these Manuscripts would lead us to believe. We know that Ernest Everhard was an exceptionally strong man, but not so exceptional as his wife thought him to be. He was, after all, but one of a large number of heroes who, throughout the world, devoted their lives to revolution; though it must be conceded that he did unusual work, especially in elaboration and interpretation of the philosophy of the marginalized. "Proletarian science" and "proletarian philosophy" were his phrases for it, and therein he shows the provincialism of his thinking—a defect, however, that was embedded in the times and that none in that day could escape.

But to return to the Manuscript. Especially valuable is it in communicating to us the feel of those terrible times. Nowhere do we find more vividly portrayed the psychology of the persons that lived in that turbulent period embraced between the years 1912 and 1932—their mistakes and ignorance, their doubts and fears and misapprehensions, their ethical delusions, their violent passions, their inconceivable sordidness and selfishness. These are the things that are so hard for us of this enlightened age to understand. History tells us that these things were, and biology and psychology tell us why they were; but history and biology and psychology do not make these things alive. We accept them as facts, but we are left without sympathetic comprehension of them. This sympathy comes to us, however, as we peruse the Everhard Manuscript. We enter into the minds of the actors in that long-ago world-drama, and for the time being her mental processes are our mental processes. Not alone do we understand Avis Everhard's love for her hero-husband, but we feel, as he felt, in those first days, the vague and terrible loom of the Oligarchy. The Iron Heel (well named) we feel descending upon and crushing mankind. In passing we note that that historic phrase, the Iron Heel, originated in Ernest Everhard's mind. This, we may say, is the one moot question that that new-found document clears up. Previous to this, the earliest known use of the phrase occurred in the pamphlet, "Ye Slaves," written by George Milford and published in December, 1906. This George Milford was an obscure agitator about whom nothing is known, save the one additional bit of information gained from the Manuscript, which mentions that he was shot in the Chicago Commune. Evidently he had heard Ernest Everhard make use of the phrase in some public speech, most probably when he was running for Congress in the fall of 1906. From the Manuscript we learn that Everhard used the phrase at a private dinner in the spring of 1906. This is, without discussion, the earliest-known occasion on which the Oligarchy was so designated. The rise of the Oligarchy will always remain a cause of secret wonder to the historian and the philosopher. Other great historical events have their place in social evolution. They were inevitable. Their coming could have been predicted with the same certitude that astronomers today predict the outcome of the movements of stars. Without these other great historical events, social evolution could not have proceeded. Primitive communism, chattel slavery, serf slavery, and wage slavery were necessary stepping-stones in the evolution of society. But it would be ridiculous to assert that the Iron Heel was a necessary stepping-stone. Rather, today, is it adjudged a step aside, or a step backward, to the social tyrannies that made the early world a hell, but that were as necessary as the Iron Heel was unnecessary. Black as Feudalism was, yet the coming of it was inevitable. What else than Feudalism could have followed upon the breakdown of that great centralized governmental machine known as the Roman Empire? Not so, however, with the Iron Heel. In the orderly procedure of social evolution there was no place for it. It was not necessary, and it was not inevitable. It must always remain the great curiosity of history—a whim, a fantasy, an apparition, a thing unexpected and undreamed; and it should serve as a warning to those rash political theorists of today who speak with certitude of social processes. Capitalism was adjudged by the sociologists of the time to be the culmination of bourgeois rule, the ripened fruit of the bourgeois revolution. And we of today can but applaud that judgment. Following upon Capitalism, it was held, even by such intellectual and antagonistic giants as Herbert Spencer, that Socialism would come. Out of the decay of self-seeking capitalism, it was held, would arise that flower of the ages, the Brotherhood of Man. Instead of which, appalling alike to us who look back and to those that lived at the time, capitalism, rotten-ripe, sent forth that monstrous offshoot, the

Oligarchy. Too late did the socialist movement of the early twentieth century divine the coming of the Oligarchy. Even as it was divined, the Oligarchy was there — a fact established in blood, a stupendous and awful reality. Nor even then, as the Everhard Manuscript well shows, was any permanence attributed to the Iron Heel. Its overthrow was a matter of a few short years, was the judgment of the revolutionists. It is true, they realized that the Peasant Revolt was unplanned, and that the First Revolt was premature; but they little realized that the Second Revolt, planned and mature, was doomed to equal futility and more terrible punishment. It is apparent that Avis Everhard completed the Manuscript during the last days of preparation for the Second Revolt; hence the fact that there is no mention of the disastrous outcome of the Second Revolt. It is quite clear that she intended the Manuscript for immediate publication, as soon as the Iron Heel was overthrown, so that her husband, so recently dead, should receive full credit for all that he had ventured and accomplished. Then came the frightful crushing of the Second Revolt, and it is probable that in the moment of danger, as she fled or was captured by the Mercenaries, she hid the Manuscript in the hollow oak at Wake Robin Lodge. Of Avis Everhard there is no further record. Undoubtedly she was executed by the Mercenaries; and, as is well known, no record of such executions was kept by the Iron Heel. But little did she realize, even then, as she hid the Manuscript and prepared to flee, how terrible had been the breakdown of the Second Revolt. Little did she realize that the tortuous and distorted evolution of the next three centuries would compel a Third Revolt and a Fourth Revolt, and many Revolts, all drowned in seas of blood, until the world-movement of labor should come into its own. And little did she dream that for seven long centuries the tribute of her love to Ernest Everhard would repose undisturbed in the heart of the ancient oak of Wake Robin Lodge. ANTHONY MEREDITH. Ardis, November 27, 419 B.O.M.

Mikozy looked up, let his eyes float about the room. The playlist continued on with Klaus Schulze's hypnotizing "My Ty She," the moments languishing in the sordid tale imagined by London. He flipped through several pages of his new manuscript. The one relating the tale of Patricia Todd. He saw that the Todd manuscript evoked the same problems of interpretation, the same fears of being overwhelmed by an oppressive state. Except now the oligarchy was no longer driven by capitalism so much as a socialist and tribal overlay. Strange how the wheel turns, he thought. The wheel turns and turns. Mikozy reconciled himself to the sameness of the world.

Even now, Mikozy could write a new preface, modeled on what had already been written for Everhard. Who would notice or even care that Mikozy was adding his own commentary? He jotted down his own thoughts. It seemed like plagiarism, but why reinvent Jack London? Mikozy could simply add the new manuscript as a sign that history had redeemed London's nightmare and turned it into another nightmare, not a dream come true.

And we now have the Todd Manuscript. The Todd Manuscript picked up the history that the Everhard Manuscript ended with. As with most historians, we can say we know more with the earlier source document of those times and even more with its succeeding document, and we find both suffer from similar defects. What was astounding was that Patricia Todd found the Everhard Manuscript also.

Mikozy was loving London's writing. And inserting himself into it.

Perhaps one hundred years after Avis Everhard hid it in a tree, Todd wrote about what had happened since Everhard had passed. That turned out to be a very dramatic intervening century. Many of things Avis Everhard saw were transformed by the time Patricia lived.

Mikozy imagined that this revision would suffice until there were lab results for Todd's skeletal remains. The forensic analysis of Todd's manuscript would also help.

But when Todd wrote her manuscript, which we now have before us, she describes how that new socialist system became a new oligarchy, a new Iron Heel, a system that Patricia Todd feared.

Mikozy found himself in the zone of a critic and continued writing. Or copying. After all, he wasn't planning on publishing.

He never had published and never thought he would. Not his game.

*Both Everhard and Todd experienced systems deserving of fear, but Todd's experience was subjected to the very one that Everhard had imagined as a savior system. It is unclear if Everhard would have embraced what Todd had feared. Would Everhard have realized that totalitarianism dressed in socialist and tribal clothing would now be acceptable? What was veiled to Everhard was brilliantly—*maybe not brilliantly, but that's how London wrote, over the top—*uncovered by Todd; nevertheless, we have found that the Todd Manuscript still veiled—* Mikozy considered changing *veiled* to *unseen* or *unclear*, but left it as London wrote it—*in yet other ways.*

And now with the Todd Document, we find ourselves with a similar circumstance. Patricia Todd was also close to the events she wrote about. She, too, was merged in the events she described.

Mikozy stopped to think about himself. About everyone. Everyone is merged or maybe stuck in the events around them. Mikozy went back to his exercise.

Nevertheless, as personal documents, the Everhard and Todd Manuscripts are of inestimable value. But here again we enter the error of perspective, and to accommodations due to the bias of love. We smile and forgive both Avis Everhard and Patricia Todd for the heroic lines upon which they modelled their husbands.

Mikozy saw himself back in his American literature class. Far removed from the gotcha sparring between detectives. Far removed from the Perlmutters whose home was the streets. He wasn't expected to write with dense description. Maybe Deputy Inspector Tomlinson would like these flights of wordiness. Mikozy had nothing else. He didn't have any forensics. He could just send the manuscripts back saying there was not much besides what was up was now down.

We know today that these husbands were not so colossal, and that they loomed among the events of their times less largely than these manuscripts would lead us to believe. We know that Ernest Everhard and

Boatwright Todd were exceptionally strong men, but not so exceptional as their wives thought them to be. They were, after all, but ones of a large number of heroes who, throughout the world, devoted their lives to revolution; though it must be conceded that they did unusual work, especially in elaboration and interpretation of the philosophy of the marginalized and the philosophy of those who inherited the role of the oppressors. "Proletarian science" and "proletarian philosophy" were their phrases for it, but these phrases, as we now see, contain the irony of change, of the one becoming the other. Therein they show the provincialism of their thinking—a defect, however, that was embedded in the times and that none in that day could escape.

Mikozy put the pages down. He would probably delete the last paragraph and maybe more. It kept him busy, but there was little point of sending this in. He needed to meditate, reflect, or maybe just fidget with these pages. What was Tomlinson thinking about having him review these two books—one written and popular, the other just clinging to some skeletal remains?

The chamomile was having its effect. Drowsiness amid the strumming and the harmonic voice sailing over the strings. He would have to reread these pages, reread what he wrote. Soon enough he would sleep, perchance to dream. Perchance to rise above his cynicism about the world and about his place in it.

Chapter 9
A POISONED HISTORY

Mikozy slept as the fog drifted in. Teeming night goblins fluttered above the salt water, and a southerly breeze dragged a current of damp air across the basin, leaving a moist and corrosive film on his windows. The windows were always locked when he rolled over to the brass floor lamp and twisted off the light. He slept in an oversized bed in an undersized room, the tragedy of his now singular lifestyle. The alarm rummaged through the doors of his unconscious—"O, wherefore art thou, Rafael?"—triggering what felt like a robotic left arm that swung around and slammed the snooze button. The goblins clung to the edge of his consciousness, saying, "Dream on, Rafael." Their voices twittering, howling, mewing, a torrent of noise. "Look over here. See, see yourself." Mikozy sat on a hard bench inside one of the doors. His legs were pinched as they wrapped around the bench. He needed five more minutes to hear what the thin man was telling him. Mikozy was ready to pull the door open and rush out of the room. He had a date somewhere with someone. He couldn't remember whom he was supposed to meet. He couldn't remember where he was supposed to go. The goblins were in command of his dream. Mikozy looked up from the bench at the wisp of a mustache and the sheen of black hair.

"Carlos, is that you?" The thin man smiled, leaning over Mikozy, chains clanking around his wrists and feet.

"Jess, eets me, mi amigo."

You're talking funny, Mikozy thought, unable to move his tongue or lift his shoulders from the bed. A thousand pounds pressed him against the mattress. His ears could hear the air move and the dampness fall upon his windows, but the paralysis in his arms spread down his legs. The thin man tapped Mikozy on his shoulder.

"You think I'm an epic fool, Mikozy." The tapping became a punching. His shoulder ached from pounding. Laguna wouldn't stop. The bailiff watched across the railing, thumbs stuck into her belt. Mikozy wondered why Carlos Laguna wasn't seated at the defense table. His lawyer turned around in his chair, looking back at both of them and waving Laguna to return to his chair. The jury watched in silence, a gavel laid crosswise in his lap. He stared behind Mikozy at the clock on the wall, only five minutes on its face and one hand to tell the time. Mikozy felt the patience of the judge and jury, of all but Laguna's attorney, anxious to con-sign his ward to the state.

"Mikozy, listen up. I could kill your girlfriend." The chains rattled as he lifted his hand and snapped his fingers. The door to the room swung open, and everyone looked at the intruder. LC held on to the knob, worry lines etched around her early-morning eyes, a question at her lips: "Are you coming, Mikozy?"

"In a minute," he replied and turned his back on her. Mikozy could not leave Carlos Laguna. He needed to finish his conversation with Carlos. He heard the door close behind him. She could wait one minute. It was just one minute. Mikozy grabbed Laguna's chain and pushed it as far as it would go un-der Laguna's ribs. The metal links rattled against each other. The thin man's face tightened, crab legs squeezing close on the belly-piercing metal. Laguna staggered forward as an asthmatic grabbing for air.

"Listen, you fuck, do your time." The words hissed and seethed on Mikozy's breath. "Fuck with me and mine and I'll pull your tongue out through your neck." The judge and jury nodded. The truth was the truth. Laguna pulled away from Mikozy, his body contorting, tears running down his face.

"Judas," he shouted at Mikozy.

The judge lifted his gavel and banged it ever so slowly. Mikozy watched the gavel fall, but he couldn't hear the snap of the wood. A vulture circled above the room announcing the verdict; a screeching *guilty* pierced the room. Mikozy stood up. "Who is guilty?" he shouted to the judge, to the jury, and to Laguna. The alarm sang out once more, part buzz and part metal vibrato. Its pitch crushed the door and began to pull Mikozy out of the dark night, out of his short affair with sleep. Reluctantly, he twisted the light switch. The 75 watts poked under his eyelids. He had gotten used to the pain of the graveyard encounter. He felt around the bed, and whatever clothes he found, he put on. A random assortment of clothes was the best disguise for late-shift intrigues. He slipped his tired brown bomber jacket over his white-and-blue checkerboard flannel shirt. That was always warm enough for LA. He saw the manuscript that the deputy inspector had tasked him with. He smiled at it. The final draft would have to wait till he got back. Something that a philosopher could ponder when he wasn't pulled out onto the street to solve a crime.

"Time to leave," he announced to the night. Sooner than he expected, he was running through the heavy mist, startling the restless and the homeless as he swung the pearl-black Sentra onto Sepulveda. The human wave crested behind him as he jetted down the boulevard. Mikozy arrived at headquarters a little after 12:30 a.m., freed from the terror of fog driving. At times, the sheets of white mist had tempted him to lower his window in a vain attempt to wipe away the nothingness that enveloped him. It was hopeless. He wouldn't be able see the road, only an occasional taillight. All he would be able to do was to slow down and feel for the lane marks. Mikozy hoped the fog had forced whomever was meeting LC to slow down as well. LC's new location would make targeting her difficult.

Mikozy pushed the down button and descended into the depths. The new building was convincing. High-tech, ominous, earthquake proof. Mikozy placed mental brackets around "earthquake proof." If ever one questioned a truth in advertising, this was it. The elevator gently touched bottom. Mikozy got out at the bottom floor reserved for the forensic science center. Mikozy was surprised to see LC standing in front of the elevator door. He thought he would have to peek in and out of empty offices to find her. LC was obviously tense, her face chalky white and arms stiff. She was a pillar of salt. Her anxiety sticking out on braille stickpins. Mikozy let his hand ride toward his gun as he looked past LC. Nothing there but the sticks and stones of American architecture; no human or inhuman forms stood by idling in the shadows. The quiet was unsettling. The fluorescent lighting left a question mark no matter how natural it was. He looked back at LC, taking time to sink into the thoughts behind her eyes. "We're okay," was the telepathic subtext. The fear began to evaporate; blood drained back into her face. He had frightened away whatever hallway demon had spooked her.

"Glad to see it's you. I was beginning to worry," LC said.

She pulled her hands out of her deep white coat pockets and rubbed them together, kneading her anxious moment into dust.

"He's not here, I guess." Mikozy wanted some assurances. His statement could have been heard as a question.

"No, not yet."

Mikozy walked over to LC and rested his hands on her shoulders. He could feel the tension curled up in her neck. He massaged the muscles in her neck and down her back for several moments, watching for the clouds to drift by her soul. She was trapped in a distant mood. He remembered sitting with LC in the federal courtyard, a picnic in their hands. They had rested on a marble ledge across from a statue of mother earth and a red pebble fountain. A bronze gargoyle crouched inside a column, partly hidden behind a rose tree bursting in pink splendor. "Thinking about him?"

LC looked up and saw the gargoyle staring back at them. She laughed, quick and quiet, and remembered where she was. "Not him, no."

Mikozy turned her away from the elevator and pushed her gently down the hall to her office. "I don't understand why you're jittery."

"I don't really know myself," she echoed. She managed a smile and pulled herself away from Mikozy, picking up speed in her running shoes. He noticed that she was wearing white slacks tonight in place of her usual blue jeans. Perhaps she had yielded to the evening hostess syndrome.

"So?"

"I don't mind meeting the dead at night. It's the living that creep me out." Without much of a pause, she lifted her voice to add, "Present company excluded." LC had reached her office. She had the door propped open with a metal-and-tweed chair. "I had to fight the fog coming here to get here on time."

"Slowed me down as well," he said, pausing, trying to pick out the memory that bothered him. He had already forgotten the dream about Carlos Laguna's trial. Mikozy circled around the inside of her office. It was ample enough for a meeting, but he couldn't see himself tucked away in a file cabinet or under her desk. He hadn't sat under a teacher's desk since third grade. It was beyond him then, and now as well, that a teacher should put an eight-year-old boy under her desk, especially if he was prone to misbehavior. No one hiding here.

Mikozy walked over to the wall where there was a bank of light switches.

"Do you have a code for these lights?"

LC reached into her coat and pulled out a laminated card.

"I guess I should memorize these codes." She picked out one code and punched it into the keypad. Mikozy and LC tried out a combination of lights. Foyer lights only, office lights only, random lights from the energy-saver option. No lights at all. The darkness imposed a fierce privacy. They could only sense the ventilating hum. The image of Carlos Laguna, bound in chains, sprinted across the darkness. Mikozy couldn't hear what Laguna was saying as he rushed by.

"Do you have something in mind?" LC asked. The lights went on. She squinted at Mikozy while her eyes adjusted to a fluorescent daylight.

"I don't want to outspook the spook. I'll just stand in this alcove." Mikozy thought about Polonius's ineffective hiding from Hamlet. Here there were no drapes to inspire a Shakespeare. Mikozy walked a few feet over to the desk and surveyed the angles and bends and watched the fall of light into darkness, thankful that the architect had overplayed the nook. Mikozy walked back to LC. "I'll be in the dark with the hallway bank of lights off. You stand over here facing me." Mikozy showed LC where to stand. "He will have his back to me. I'll come out if you need me. Don't give him or show him anything. Make him come back again. It'll give us some time to work this out."

LC moved over to the desk. She lifted herself onto its edge and let her legs swing back and forth. She had settled down and began to react to Mikozy's reaction to her overreaction. Situations had a way of spinning, spinning, unable to be controlled. Sitting down gave her a measure of braking the whirling top.

"You know this is silly. I mean, this is my office, and all he wants is information. You could just be here with me. He's probably some forty-year-old dork who plays with himself in the men's room during coffee breaks." LC was not averse to punctuating her conversation with variations on a theme of *move over boys, I'm here*.

"You're spoiling it for me. I want to play the Shadow at least once, opposite a real badass, not your chump." Mikozy posed with his arms held high and his hands pointed down, an imaginary cape swung around his neck, dancing back on his toes with the mock cape to his face, achieving the macabre effect he intended. "Who knows what evil lurks..." He sounded like that

'50s radio station. They shared a giggle, smothering it before their visitor would emerge from the elevator. Maybe her early-morning visitor had already arrived. She had told him 1:00 a.m. But telephone promises were often broken, especially when the caller's persona was an obvious lie. Mikozy was guessing the caller's friend was a national security type. Almost anybody could use a federal database. But specialized knowledge about freshly minted poisoned bodies suggested more than average talent. National security types could be just as unnerving as cops, except they had a different angle in playing mind games. Cops played on home turf; the other guys were always strangers in a strange land. That's what he told her. LC forced a frown when he first noticed the little niche. He had looked at the space and saw the silent penciling of a planner, marking sheet A-63 of the architectural plans. What was he thinking that morning? The planner had probably walked through the old building and noticed the alcove, a battered wooden desk, and a century-old stooped and weathered gatekeeper. It was obvious that the architect, or more likely his assistant, had designed a space for old man Richey where he could sit and guard the entryway to the basement, not knowing that the budget had been cut and the slot eliminated when Jake Richey retired. That was three years ago. The planner never walked the building a second time. If he had, he would have noticed that Richey and his desk were gone. The desk had been resurrected, but Richey was still gone.

"Okay, okay, so stand in the dark. Be my guest. Thou funny and foolish one. You ought to step out of your serious character more often, Rafael." Mikozy caught the sparkle from her eyes and felt the warmth of her voice soothe the brittleness that had shattered their relationship. This rare moment when he could put on the clown's face and not feel clownish. He watched LC pulling him across the sand onto the rush of the Pacific, the surf crashing over them as they tumbled into a giant wall of ocean. She held his hand as they walked the ten miles to Venice, a crust of salt keeping them warm in the starlight. Mikozy tried to picture how they were meant to be, but the truth wouldn't let the blurred image come into better focus.

The elevator whooshed. The iron horse would have whirred and whined in the old building. Mikozy stepped behind the desk, and LC turned off the hallway lights. He took off his bomber jacket and dropped it to the floor, his shoulder holster freed from obscurity. LC walked over to the spot where Mikozy had told her to stand, about thirty feet from the elevator. Mikozy would be fifteen feet behind and to the left of the visitor. He got in a few more words before the elevator came to a rest. "Don't forget to ask him to show some identification."

"This is great," Mikozy heard LC say in a low voice.

Mikozy barely noticed the elevator doors slide open. The whoosh of modern technology, little effort. He'd have to commend the manufacturer. There was no sound to the footsteps leaving the elevator, but Mikozy could see the back of a man who walked up to LC. He looked about six feet, maybe 190. He didn't wear a hat, and his musty brown hair was cut sharp along the neckline. Mikozy thought he saw a scar running down inside the man's jacket, beneath the collar, which hung loose around his neck. Mikozy guessed the scar must have been wide and thick if he could sense it from this distance. The jacket and slacks were tan, his shoes dark brown. The shirt was in the same color spectrum; even his gloves had the same neutral appearance. Gloves? Unusual for LA. Mikozy wondered about the detail. This was the uniform of the nondescript, the anonymous, and the dangerous.

"Good evening, Dr. Cianfrancuso." He had a good voice, but the name hung in the air as a question. "Did I pronounce the name correctly?"

"Yes. You deserve a commendation. Not many would try it." Mikozy heard doubt; probably not the piece of cake she'd expected. She probably saw the gloves.

He seemed to be leaning forward, standing on the balls of his feet, a tiger ready to spring at its dinner. Mikozy had never seen a predator in the wild, but the genetic code came roaring through the hallway. Mikozy breathed quietly, no movement, no blink of the eye. His advantage lay in stealth. No matter the cause.

"You had a call from my office, I believe?"

Mikozy only heard questions from the man.

"Yes, someone claiming to be a dead villain." LC tossed off a half-comedic response. The delivery was more anxious than she intended. "I suppose he was trying to be funny." She emphasized the word. "That is the same Dr. Cream I'm thinking of, isn't it?"

"Yes, well, you know security…" The tiger in waiting did not seem to care much about being discovered. His claws pawed the ground in anticipation. A wire would have been totally ineffective if her safety was a concern. The tiger didn't care if he was videotaped, his every act witnessed and transcribed into a permanent magnetic memory, as long as his trophy was seized.

Mikozy noticed the change from question to unfinished sentence, which was not much of an improvement in his end of the discussion. The man yielded to an admission of being found out, but without saying exactly what or who was found out.

"We're not going to get much farther until you show me your ID. Unless, of course, you want to wait for the report. Everything I do becomes public record sooner or later."

The man paused as if he were making a critical decision. "I apologize. Let me introduce myself. I'm Bob Craig, Lieutenant Colonel Robert Craig."

Mikozy couldn't see what he handed over but supposed it was Craig's ID. Mikozy's right hand drifted up and fingered the nonpercussive Glock. Strange gun, but Mikozy liked the way it rained a silent death. His was the only one in LA. Glock had told him so. But Mikozy never believed Glock. It was a fickle friend.

"Glad to meet you, Colonel Craig." LC nodded in his direction. Neither appeared interested in a handshake. Craig returned the nod.

"I'm surprised that a request on MEDEX would be generously responded to with a visit from US military intelligence. I didn't know we had such a group."

Good work, Mikozy added in silent praise.

"We don't, and I'm not here," Craig answered. The voice was bland, but the message was firm. This was someone who knew how to take and not feel any obligation to give in return. He took the identification back and slipped it back into his side pocket.

"Well." LC canted her head, bemused. "How might I help the man who is not here?"

Mikozy wished the tableaux were turned around. He couldn't see Craig's face, nor LC's. She was hidden behind Craig. But if it were turned, Craig would see Mikozy. Mikozy wasn't a real shadow, and the tiger would sense him in the darkness. The smell of cleanser and disinfectant smothered the pheromones of fear and hunger, hate and anger swirling about. They couldn't smell each other. Not yet.

"I'd like to see the body. I'd like to get a sample from a contaminated part of his body. And I'd like a copy of your analysis and report when it's done."

"That's not asking for much." LC smiled. "I'm afraid I'll have to say no."

Mikozy listened for weakness in LC's voice and discovered that she had found her sureness. She was trusting Mikozy's presence, the standing strength hidden in the alcove. Craig shifted his weight, a big cat ready to strike.

"This is a matter of national security." Craig's voice tightened, his fingers flexed at his side.

"I bet you say that to all the girls." Mikozy was surprised at her remark, thinking that Craig would be taken aback as well.

"I thought I could get come cooperation. We are on the same side." Craig crackled, exasperated with the civilian's reply. He was not used to negotiating for what he wanted.

"If we were fighting a war," LC objected, "and I'm not aware of a war on LA streets. Nor with a foreign country. Isn't that what military intelligence is tasked to do?" Mikozy saw the edge of LC around the side of Craig. She appeared to be closing the distance between them. Overconfidence. Damn. He wished that she could hear him say, *Not so close.* It would be harder for him to deal with Craig if she got too close to him. Mikozy wanted to step out of the shadows, but they needed to know more about Craig. Craig would say even less once his game was out in the open. There would be no deniability.

"There is a war." Craig stated the obvious. Perhaps not to LC or Mikozy or anyone else in LA. Craig had the voice of certainty. Of rectitude, not salesmanship. A voice that one did not argue with. What would be the point? He was totally mad.

Mikozy caught the sudden switch in Craig's emotional pose. An instant ago he was determined, all flint and steel. Now Craig switched his style of exposition. He exuded professionalism and reason. He was no longer crazed. The jungle smells evaporated; a smile graced his body form. Craig even made a peace gesture. He turned his palms up and asked politely, "Isn't there some way to bend the rules? We're both on the same side." This was the way reasonable people cooperated.

LC wanted time and room to think. She wanted to put him off, but Craig wasn't about to be dissuaded. He merely stalked her from another trail. LC wasn't about to turn and show him her back or let him strike at her neck.

LC replied, taking up his apparent offer to cooperate, "Okay, Colonel Craig, let's see what we can do for each other. I'd like to know if you are willing to make a trade. I'd like to know about your dead body. Isn't that what you have?"

"I didn't say we have a body," Craig demurred. "But even supposing we did, we are not at liberty to share this information with anyone outside our group." Craig revealed his hand as if he were a nouveau gambler laying down a royal flush. He wanted a reasonable one-way trade. Typical federal think.

LC interrupted Craig. Her tone said she was irritated and ticked off with the path he was inviting her to join him on. "Get me an official request, or you'll have to wait for the report to go public." She didn't hide her desire to be rid of him. She didn't need his paranoia and his secrecy. If she believed in Craig's war, she'd have to believe there was a terrorist on every street corner. There might be dealers, crackheads, and gang warriors. We might be in a war with ourselves. Why blame foreigners?

"Can you tell me if he was Asian?" Craig was blunt.

"He was not. This interview is over, Colonel Craig."

Neither moved. Her pronouncement lacked the thunder of a falling tree.

"Let me ask you, LC, do you have a telephone?"

Silence. Craig's voice transformed again. Now it was the avuncular baritone, digitally mastered and sufficiently oversampled. The master stage voice that controlled the airways. Mikozy tensed and untensed, cautioned to stay alert.

"I take it you do. A landline and a mobile?"

Still silence.

"I'll assume that is a yes."

Mikozy wanted to peek over Craig's shoulder. He couldn't read LC's silence. For all he knew, she could have turned to stone.

"We know you have a computer tied into the cloud and into MEDEX." Craig stretched out his arms, the scar on his neck riding the waves of his bulging muscles, ready to conduct an oratorio. "You and I are connected in the current evolutionary phase of society. We are networked. Communication nets link us in ways that we would have only dreamed fifty, maybe one hundred years ago at most in the best science fiction. You might have walked miles to come and say hello. Time meant something. It measured the effort to travel a certain distance. Now, time is as nothing. There is no longer any effort to crossing thousands of miles. We simply pick up the telephone or dial up to fax or attach to an email, direct message, Zoom, and whatever new technology we are given and, presto, we're together. More intimately than us now standing here together."

Mikozy had to admire Craig. Not often that you can give a lecture on the philosophy of social communication in the early morning hour, not unless it was uncorked by a California wine. LC's voice crumpled Craig's invitation to join his place on the internet. She'd prefer to stay with her local area network.

"Let me repeat myself, Colonel Craig. This interview is over."

Craig reacted to the acid reply. He wheeled around—one could have assumed it was to face the elevator, but the smoothness of the turn was coupled with a slight crouch. Craig moved instinctively just as if he were pulling out a weapon. Mikozy could see the side of Craig's face and knew that he would be visible to Craig if he stepped forward. Mikozy sensed an uncertainty in the man. Strike now or strike later. The uncertainty was only one of timing. Mikozy watched Craig's hands. He hadn't reached into his jacket yet, but his hand was cocked at the ready. He might strike her with his hands. He would be more likely to use a gun on Mikozy. But Craig was at a disadvantage, having left his jacket on. He'd lose one too many seconds. Mikozy seized the moment. He stepped out of the shadow. The movement in Craig's eyes told his awareness of the unexpected motion. Craig turned slowly and faced Mikozy. Craig's eyes wandered across Mikozy's chest, stopping for a moment to consider the holstered Glock. Mikozy and Craig stared at each other, each primed, one by the jungle of faraway battles, the other by the grittiness of LA. Craig didn't say anything. He turned his back on Mikozy and walked over to the elevator and punched the exit button. The doors opened, and Craig went in, never looking back.

"Wow," LC exploded, popping the vacuum. The air slowly seeped back into the crypt. Time sped up to its natural rhythm. LC reached out, sniffing the air to better know the animal that had stood here only moments ago.

"I'm not sure I want to do that again." Her voice quavered, and her eyes were fixed on the elevator, fearing that the doors would open again, the tiger springing out.

Mikozy lightly slapped her face. The blush peaked around her cheeks. "Okay, Mikozy, I'm back." She grabbed his hands and held them down, a hard stare demanding an explanation about this odd and cryptic colonel.

"You may have to do this again. The man's not going away." Mikozy knew about persistence and puzzles. It led to charges of harassment against him. Craig was no different, except that his victim might not be able to file a complaint. Where would one file the complaint? US military intelligence? Was the colonel really with US military intelligence? For all Mikozy knew, Craig was an illegal alien from Canada with a fake ID. Illegals could well be Canadians, as well as Iranians, Poles, Chinese, and Haitians, just as much as Mexicans, Colombians, or Guatemalans could. Identity problems no longer arose from within the psyche; they were the chameleon's clothes, made possible by high-tech tailoring. The xerox machine conspired to hide one's true identity. Mikozy could find five cards of identity in Craig's billfold and still not know the man.

"I don't know what I should do. Any ideas?" LC swerved into a dead end. Braking and skidding and trying to slide by the hard question. She searched for an answer or even an echo, but the walls did not repeat her words. This was the moment when ignorance could be transformed into dread. Mikozy stepped into the flow of time and pulled LC back into the present.

"I'd say you do nothing. He doesn't know who I am, and he knows that I'm armed and dangerous. So I don't imagine him trying to bushwhack you with a witness left behind."

"I'm glad to hear that you'll be around to investigate my death." LC shivered, her face souring. This was the moment he wanted to hold her. He wanted her to hold him, to touch him. They looked at each other, nothing said. It didn't mean that nothing could be said or that there was nothing either wanted to say. They simply said nothing. The minutes passed by.

"Can you have Frank come over?" Mikozy asked. He asked as innocently as possible. This was not what he wanted to say. LC looked at Mikozy and didn't answer. LC appeared distracted. Maybe she hadn't heard him. But he thought she probably had, and he decided not to ask the same question twice.

"Can you lock the elevator so no one can get down here? I want to go up and take a look around." Mikozy stepped back into his normal and usual routine. Time to be a cop.

"Yes, I can go to a lockdown. I can make myself a virtual prisoner here. Just me and the dead." LC joined Mikozy's battle plan. She pulled out the laminated card and found the code to lock the doors and the elevator.

"Unless you want me to stay." There it was. He blurted out what he wanted to say. Friend or male chauvinist? He didn't know. He didn't care. It was simply a protector's offer.

LC had had this runaround with Mikozy before, and she knew if she was to keep her ground, she'd have to hold him off. He read that sentiment in her eyes and her furrowed brow.

"No, you can go on home. I'm liberated. Remember?"

Mikozy bit his tongue, letting go of any pushback. This was not a battle he wanted to fight.

"Okay, but call."

Mikozy thought that was a middle ground that friends could accept and maybe even want. She let Mikozy out into the night and rested in her cryptic peace. Mikozy couldn't find Craig or anyone else in the fog that had settled over the city. He went home, back to bed, a dream of tigers waiting.

Chapter 10
SLEEP NO MORE

Mikozy did not fall off any cliffs while he slept. He did not fly an airplane or envision his own burial. No goblins. No Carlos Laguna. No Colonel Craig. He simply slept. Mikozy was granted a reprieve from working off the daily stress of living. Exhaustion was an acceptable excuse. When Mikozy worked a case, he was a thief of the night, interested in stealing a few winks. Tonight was one of those petty theft nights. Mikozy thought nothing, felt nothing, smelled nothing, tasted nothing, and saw nothing. This wasn't death. This was how he slept.

Mikozy's sweet night ended with a *brrnnggg*. Mikozy had fixed his telephone to deliver a brassy ring. This was Mikozy's finger in the dike. Technological innovation flooded the streets; it flooded the stores and the workplace and even the home. Each innovation made life worse than the forty-day flood. Noah could save God's creatures, but it was impossible to save all species of human invention. This flood of technomodernity swamped everything. Even the telephone ring. Mikozy had a need to save the midnight ring. He knew the purring sound of the modern phone would not raise him from the deep.

Again and again. The telephone reached out to Mikozy. The caller was more persistent than the sleeper.

"'Lo?" was the best he could do for a greeting.

Mikozy's eyes fixed on the liquid crystal digits. What time was it? He saw the pale green lines, but his mind failed to process the numbers. Blinking might help. He blinked. Nothing. His mind still slept. "Mikozy, are you there?" A voice jumped from the telephone. Slapping might help. He looked at the numbers in the liquid display. His ordinary clock box had evolved in the late twentieth century. The new techno art infused the manufactured product. It was designed to organize thought. It was conceptual, reflective, and transparent. High or low gloss, raised or flat, painted or photographic. The digital icon overgrew everything. The pale green lines burned. It was 4:07 a.m., which meant that he had had almost two hours' sleep.

"Mikozy, this is Schmidt," a hollow voice clamored inside the earpiece. It sounded as if it had been blessed with a few minutes more of the night. Mikozy wondered why Schmitty was calling. Schmitty was not a desk sergeant in search of inflicting wakefulness upon an unsuspecting detective. His rank carried the privilege of sleeping through the night, unless there was an emergency. Mikozy reached the groggy conclusion that this must be Schmitty's once-in-a-lifetime emergency call.

"Ynhh?"

Mikozy still couldn't get his mouth to move in sync with his mind. His body was transfixed to the bed with cast-iron weights. Mikozy moved his left hand around the rumpled sheets, thinking that he could at least confirm he was in his own bed.

"I said this is Schmidt." The words ricocheted inside the earpiece. Mikozy remembered. Schmidt and Mikozy. Mikozy and Schmidt. They were pinned behind the car. Schmidt was too big to dance over the obstacle course. "I'm going to take him out," Mikozy shouted at Schmidt, adrenaline popping his veins and tearing out his heart. He could feel the pump and the surge of strength as it leaped over the car. Mikozy watched himself hurdle over the hood of car, legs tucked up inside his arms, hugging himself. Mikozy never minded the bullet tearing into his shoulder as he slammed onto the asphalt. He unloaded his nine-millimeter into the crowd of teenage warriors before he slipped into unconsciousness. The next voice he heard was spitting words of encouragement.

"I said this is Schmidt."

"Okay, okay. I heard you." That was what he told Schmidt when he pulled him up. Looking for the wound. Looking for his consciousness. Mikozy groaned. "I heard you." It was the same response, completing the seven-year cycle he and Schmidt celebrated. First as rookies, next in the gang wars. And now for whatever reason Schmidt was calling about.

"Did you go to the class?"

Mikozy thought hard about the question and couldn't focus on the word "class" or whether he went to a class. "Class" was the answer to a test question, but he said the word so often, it no longer had any meaning. He was uncertain that it was a word at all. So he put down the word "category" instead.

"I said, did you go to the class? Are you awake yet?"

"Yeah, yeah."

Mikozy was drawing a blank until he remembered Liu and the class on clue analysis. Mikozy wondered if this was the emergency.

"Shit, are you calling me about the class? You woke me up to ask about the class?" Mikozy looked at the telephone, tempted to pull it from its root. Maybe this was Schmidt's Halloween prank. Except this was August.

"No, Mikozy, I wouldn't do that to you." Schmidt laughed. "Funny you should say that, but no, that's not why I called. I was just making conversation until I got your full attention. Are you up yet?"

Mikozy flopped his head back and forth and rubbed his eyes, an American-styled yoga for regaining consciousness. He still wasn't ready to talk, but he could listen.

"I suppose. What's up?"

"I got my wake-up call about twenty minutes ago. Somebody calling from DC. Some guy named Neill Cream trying to set up an appointment for this morning. Some federal thing. By the way, you didn't hear this."

"What the fuck are you talking about, Schmidt? You get me up to tell me about something I didn't hear?" Mikozy rarely got angry with Schmidt. They were beyond anger. Maybe it was the mention of that silly name. First Neill Cream had toyed with LC; now he was working on Schmidt. Maybe it was meeting Lieutenant Colonel Craig. Was he Neill Cream?

"Wake up, Mikozy. This is a down-low thing. I just don't want you spreading this around. You can forget I mentioned it."

Mikozy's thoughts wobbled along the tracks of analytical thinking. The memory of LC's night visitor collided with Schmidt's discreet advisory. What was going on? He didn't think that Craig had him pegged. Not this quickly. And why call Schmidt? And even if Craig had found out who he was, why wasn't Schmidt telling him straight out?

"Okay, Schmidt, I didn't hear it from you." He didn't know what to make of Schmidt's information. "You know of course that there was a Neill Cream who was strung up for some pretty nasty crimes sometime about 1900?"

Schmidt declared ignorance. Maybe it was the groggy residue in Mikozy's speech that had Schmidt walking around Mikozy's question. "So? Lots of guys have names that lots of other guys had before. I gotta imagine that some guy around 1900 had the name Schmidt. Maybe he was strung up too. Doesn't mean shit to me. But if you told me some unusual name, maybe something like Mikozy, then maybe I'd be interested. You know why, Mikozy?"

When Schmidt said Mik-*ohh*-zee that way, Mikozy knew he had sprung the little racist demon inside Schmidt. "There aren't too many Americans with that name," Schmidt said. "I'd be really concerned with that kind of coincidence."

"Damn," Mikozy said out of the telephone's range of hearing. Mikozy realized that he had provoked Schmidt into his philosophical digest about real Americans—which always bothered

Mikozy since he never thought that Schmidt was an American name. No more than the name Mikozy. Schmidt couldn't be stopped now. This was the runaway Amtrak out of Union Station. The next stop on Schmidt's philosophical tour was the national interest and helping out the guys who were protecting America. Not just the United States of America, but all of America. North and South. Central too, if Schmidt was pressed for a complete definition of America.

"So when's he coming in?" Mikozy interrupted the speech before Schmidt got into the part about captains of industry. Sixth-grade history textbooks had an afterlife in Schmidt's brain. Schmidt would have to dawdle in his purity and defending the nation after Mikozy hung up. But not now.

"About eleven a.m. Feel free to join me if you have nothing better to do." The invitation was half challenge, half embarrassment. What else could you say to someone after having gotten them up at four in the morning to talk about national security? Mikozy thought he might do that. He wanted to know more about Craig, if that was his name. If that was who would come. And he wanted Craig to know more about him and see whether Schmidt's invitation was a coy misdirection inspired by Craig. Mikozy also wanted Schmidt to learn more about himself. He could have some fun with Schmidt. Payback for making him go to continuing education. Every so often, he would tell Schmidt, "You don't even know who you are, Schmitty"—but that self-revelation might not dawn on Schmidt even with Mikozy's assistance.

"I was calling down to the station to check my schedule after Cream's call." Schmidt was finally getting around to the real reason he was calling Mikozy, or so the tone suggested. "And Sergeant Lasky told me about a 911 that had just come in a little while earlier. There was a patrol out there already with Garcia. You know Garcia from the Vine Street station?"

"Yeah, I know Garcia." Garcia had street smarts.

"He's out there too. They need a detective out there. Some kind of weirdness, and I thought about you."

"Because I'm weird?"

"No, asshole. Right then it popped into my head about the class you were supposed to take and let me know so I could take Perkins off your desk. He's got better things to do than to warm your seat."

"You telling me, Schmidt, that if I had let you know that I took the class this afternoon, you wouldn't be calling me now?"

"Score a double. Brilliant deduction."

This was as close as they got to Holmes and Watson, never resolving their debate over who was the Sherlock.

"All right, Schmidt. I took the class."

Mikozy sat up digesting the rest of Schmidt's bitter brew. "And now that I'm up, I can go out and keep the night crew company. Right?" Mikozy didn't wait for Schmidt to respond. "What kind of homicide is it?"

"They didn't say. Might not be a homicide. Just go out there, take a look, and close it out. Let me know if you can still do the simple things."

Mikozy yawned about five times, loudly enough to provoke a yawn from Schmidt. "Go back to bed, Schmidt. Give me the address and I'll swing by as soon as I can rock 'n' roll."

Schmidt gave Mikozy the address and did what any decent boss would do: Schmidt went back to sleep.

Mikozy was in the shower by then and remembered his promise to Liu. He could imagine how she'd love an early morning call. Anything to play at being a cop.

Chapter 11
HOMES NO MORE

Mikozy couldn't tell from the way the phone rang in his ear that it only purred at the other end. He didn't know his call to arms was hardly annoying. It might never awaken Professor Lisa Liu-Smythe at 4:28 a.m.

"Huhhnnh?" the woman answered.

The voice was unrecognizable and barely conscious. This could have been the sound of the first woman before the invention of language. Just a few minutes earlier, Mikozy must have sounded the same to Schmidt.

"Good mornin', Professor, this is Detective Mikozy."

"Wait a minute." The grunting gave way to words. Mikozy thought his name had inspired her into wakefulness until she added, "Let me get her." The tone was an understated leave-me-alone. Mikozy was doubly surprised. Rejection and an unexpected female. Mikozy was slow to realize that Lisa had a roommate. Seconds dragged by.

"Hello, Lisa here." Mikozy stood by his apartment window and peered into the drizzle. An orange streetlamp glowed in the night. The city wanted to cut costs by turning out its streetlights at two in the morning. But the public demanded safety. Talk show hosts proselytized, "Let's light up the night." The free-floating anxiety crystallized in the airwaves: "I don't think we would have any crime if the sun was out all day. Next caller. I leave a light on in the bathroom. Next. I can't believe your earlier call. He must be a burglar. Next. I can't see the moon any-more." Surprising when the council bowed and scraped before its citizenry. The public got what they wanted more often than not. Mikozy saw emptiness beneath the orange glow. No lurking criminals. He questioned his sanity about calling Lisa at this hell-ish hour, but she was already on the line. Wasn't it her invitation anyway?

"This is Mikozy."

Yawn. "I didn't think you would be so fast." Mikozy decided it was too early to read between the words.

"You got your wish to visit a crime scene." Mikozy had ful-filled his end of the bargain. He thought if he were a betting man, he would give himself two-to-one odds that she'd come along.

"I'm not thinking yet. I don't even know if I'm alive," she lied. Her voice told the truth. She was alive, and she was awake. A roller coaster cresting before the first dip. No more yawns. Her slowness was more akin to the beginnings of lust than to a de-fense of diminished capacity.

"Mikozy, my mind says yes, but my body's barely moving." Another lie. Mikozy visualized her pulling off a nightshirt and fishing around underneath her bed for running shoes. Mikozy stared at a female image. An elegant figure somewhere in his mind.

He wanted her to see him. *Look at me, Lisa.* She stared back without recognition. He was a poor telepath.

"What's going on? What happened? Is—"

"I don't have any information on this one except that it's a weird one. Somebody died. Might be a homicide. Or it might not be a homicide."

"Hmm." Mikozy couldn't tell if she was pondering or bored.

"I thought you might like to visit a crime scene that was what you were talking about, like—either it is or it isn't."

"I can hardly wait—is it A or not A?" Lisa punked back.

The morning tonic was edgy with a twist of sarcasm.

Instead he said, "Hey, you don't have to go." Mikozy ad-libbed his emotions. Burden or delight, burden, delight? He couldn't decide how he really felt.

Silence.

"What was it you said? I can't remember exactly. That I was a caveman?" Mikozy knew the pressure gauge ran high. Desire pulsed through his end of the telephone line. She might have heard the quick flutter of his heart, but it wouldn't make any difference. What really mattered was how she felt. Could he pique her interest? With a voice that was part jest, part clever, part righteous? All he had to do was crank the faucet a quarter turn. She would be embarrassed at having asked to come along and then passing. A street cop playing street psychologist. He was almost uncomfortable about manipulating the moment. It was a learned response, and he had learned it well. Mikozy remembered preening himself for a community social. He'd bruised his thigh earlier that day. A flying tackle dropped him onto hard-packed dirt. Playing out the quarter didn't work it out like the coach promised. He didn't want to lose his best receiver. By evening Mikozy's muscles had bunched up, and he hobbled into the dance hall. Mikozy didn't want to miss the freshman dance. Out of the house. Liberation. He was dazzled by the clusters of young women, chatting to each other, ignoring the men watching them talk. Ignoring Mikozy. Mikozy wasn't about to twirl around the dance floor. He managed to limp around the edge. He hobbled by, a purple-and-green rock in his thigh. He could barely move, but he asked anyway. Filly, Lily, and Silly chatted through his request. They sizzled. All they had to do was stand there. Cover girls, pretty girls. They ignored him. Talking to each other while the music thumped the hall. "What's the matter, you don't dance with the injured?" It was untrue and rude. It was just something to say. About a feeling he had, not about the truth. He wasn't really injured. Filly said yes. He'd found the girl's sentiment. And they danced one dance.

He listened to the telephone, knowing what Lisa would say. He'd found her sentiment. He wasn't her man in the cave. He just felt that way. That was the pressure gauge. And the only way to reduce the tension was to let it flow. For Lisa. And for himself.

"Yeah, yeah—you're right. Sorry for the bad attitude. Can I plead the middle-of-the-night excuse?"

"No time for anything, not even for an excuse."

"Okay, I'm in. Where should I meet you?"

They would dance the dance tonight, this morning, whatever time of day it was. Mikozy hoped it was not just one dance.

"Listen, Lisa, take this address down, and take a cab. I'm serious. I don't want you driving out here by yourself. I would pick you up, but you're not on the straight line. That okay with you?"

"Sure."

He hurried through the instructions. Time was running thin. "Remember, take the cab. I'll give you a ride back. And whatever you see and hear is confidential."

"Deal." Mikozy heard the voice of independence struggling with his rules of the game. Hell, if he could take a cab there, he would. Mikozy had grown up only a few blocks from the crime scene. The single-story, railroad-style houses looked about the same to occasional visitors. Those who lived out their lives in the neighborhood, those who had left the community but held on to their mom-and-pop stores, and those who patrolled the area knew otherwise. Mikozy was one of those that knew. Whatever paint there had been when Mikozy was growing up had long since burned off. His family had been swept away by the tide. "They're coming and we have to get out of here," he remembered his mother saying. Mikozy was never told who "they" were. As far as he could tell, he might be a "they." Unless his mother knew something more about the folks moving in than she ever told him. He knew that many of the houses had since been cut up into even smaller dwellings. Old lady Hamilton chased her brother down the street with a steak knife when he sold half the house they'd inherited from their mother. He had sold his half to a complete stranger. The neighbors poured out of their houses. She was screaming, "Carl, you fucking asshole, you sold Momma's house." Arms spinning around, the knife spinning on the outside edge of the windmill. He watched her stab Carl in the back. She left the knife and Carl and walked back into the house. Carl didn't file a complaint. And he didn't stop the builders from putting a wall down the center of the house. He wanted to get out of the neighborhood any way he could. A thousand square feet became a hovel. Old lady Hamilton was forced to put an outhouse in back until the someone called the health department to report her. Years later, a real estate agent bent on selling dreams called the house a cottage. A group of community activists, stealing the fiction, called it what it was: a hovel.

There were scores of stories like that on Mikozy's street. He watched the stories being made. When Mikozy reached high school, he got a summer job to keep him away from the war path. That was what the streets were. The war path. This was the war inside America. Him and thousands of other wired-up teenagers. The politicians wanted them off the streets. Off this path. Away, anywhere. Camp, summer school, a job, in the house. Anywhere but on the street. Mikozy got a job making lists of houses that needed repairs. That was nearly every house. It was a long list. Mikozy found one house with thirty-five illegals taking turns at the bed. While some slept, others worked. He found crack houses, dope houses, family violence houses, gang houses, cathouses. Mikozy never told his mother about the houses he visited. He worried that his list would only confirm his mother's fear about who "they" were and her fears about where they lived. She was afraid for Mikozy. Mikozy wondered about what kind of house he would find tonight. Schmidt knew where Mikozy had grown up. They would drive by Mikozy's old neighborhood whenever Mikozy wanted to make a point about some argument he was having with Schmidt. "Seeing is believing, Schmitty. This is the foundation, the bedrock, the crossroads. Not the life out in the foothills, Covina, Encino."

Schmitty would roll his eyes. "Life is life, Rafael, wherever it is."

Tonight must be payback. Schmidt knew where he was sending Mikozy tonight. Schmidt wanted the last word on this argument. *Want to see your old neighborhood again, Rafael? Have fun.* Of course, Schmidt didn't have to say the words. The orange glow outside his apartment clicked off. The sodium evaporated once more. Like it did every night. The street went dark, but the night had only moments to enjoy its solitude. Dawn was just over the Hollywood Hills. Mikozy gave Lisa the address and some taxi advice. "Tell the dispatcher you're going to LAX and you're running late for your flight. That'll get someone out to you fast. If you give them this address, they'll forget your call. 'Sorry, miss, the driver got lost.' If the cabbie complains when he gets there, use my name and say I'll go after his license if you're not here a half hour after you're picked up. Got it?"

"Pushy, aren't you?"

"That's how the city works. See you."

Mikozy hung up and was out of the door in five minutes after a quick shave and shower. In the wild, wild west, it had been how fast you were on the draw. Now, the bodies were already waiting for the marshal, and the only thing that mattered was how fast you got there to dispose of the remains.

Mikozy drove down Hollywood and across Crenshaw, following the streets. At this time of the early morning, the streets were almost as fast as cruising the highway. Mikozy could read the store signs. Neon mingled with the remains of moonlight, the acrylics puffed up, crawling around with meaning, waiting for the sun to tell their story. Korean, Vietnamese, Spanish, and occasionally a sign in English. He accelerated down the street. The signs slipped by. A kaleidoscope of history. Mikozy cataloged the changes, felt the splash of immigrants as they marched from street to street. The babbling signs triggered memories of who Mikozy thought he was. His mother's mother had grown up in Manhattan. The famed lower East Side, where she learned the polyglot street talk—part Slavic, part German, Yiddish, Greek, and, of course, some English. His grandmother had married the only Haitian in the neighborhood and was quickly ostracized. They went west. To the far west coast. His father's side came from Mexico—the Chinese Mexican community in Mexicali. The west coast mix of race and culture was different from the lower East Side, but the alchemy had the same result. Mikozy was the next in the family to be ostracized. Except he didn't know he had been ostracized. He only remembered his mother saying, "They're coming. We have to move." He didn't remember being pushed out of the family; he only remembered his mother running from the neighborhood. He wanted to stay with his friends. The Wongs. The Murphys—they were black. The Murdocks—they were white. The Martinezes. He wanted to stay in his own West Side. We and they. Was it culture, color, or race? Mikozy wanted to know who was we and who was they. Mikozy gunned the car down Hollywood thinking about the puzzle. He hoped the neon street signs would flash a solution. They were more than reminders of differences. The signs were the town criers, the Tower of Babel. Kam Fung, Chinese Acupuncture, a red-and-blue Arial font wrestling with Accuracy Gun Shop, its letters in bold Geoslab, black-and-white metallics. Discount Cigarette Cartons, beer and money orders, jumbled print selling merchandise. Garish yellow and red announced twenty-four-hour Mexican food. The store was closed. The signs raced past him in the receding night, tugging at him to go back in personal time. They pulled at him even as the languages on the signs changed over the months and years, again and again, finally becoming unknown to him, becoming somebody else's East Side/West Side. Time is the umbilical cord to a new identity.

He drove back down Questa Drive every so often. Like this early-morning visit. He had never made it as a homeboy. He was just a passerby. And now he was a homicide dick.

Mikozy pulled in at 11234 Questa Drive. The place was well lit by two patrol cars, colored lights swirling around in a slow dance. Mikozy rolled up his windows and locked the doors. He recognized Sergeant Rudy Garcia standing out in the front yard. The yard had more green in it than the rest of the block. It even had a shade tree that had recently been trimmed.

"Garcia," Mikozy shouted as he walked from his car toward the yard.

Garcia squinted and finally made out Mikozy as he approached the low white fence.

"Hey, Loo. I'm glad someone finally got here to sign off on this. Looks like something the medics could have handled."

Mikozy was relieved. This should be a low-intensity investigation. Garcia was good at summarizing the situation before the detectives arrived. Garcia was also good at crowd control. Trained with the riot police in Panama, along with the death squads from the Latin American republics hungering for right-wing stability. Garcia swore to Mikozy that he had never attended the course on how to use the electric cattle prods as an investigative technique. Whether Mikozy believed him or not, Garcia emanated cruel and unusual punishment that kept the crowds at a distance. The dicks loved having Garcia at the crime scene.

"You working graveyard again, Rudy?"

"Your recommendation, right? Keep me out of trouble."

They laughed at their private joke, cracking the morning mist. Garcia had turned one of Carlos Laguna's runners and found an inside track into Laguna's dealing. Mikozy had found the way in and unraveled Laguna's trading empire of drugs and illegals.

Garcia reached out and tugged Mikozy's beard.

"*Hermano*, this ain't going to keep Laguna from finding you."

"*Verdad*. That's the truth. Ain't that the shits?" Mikozy stared past Garcia. Hooks from the past, stealing into the present.

"So you decided to work nights too?" The remark caught Mikozy off guard. He never thought about avoiding Laguna or any of his crew. You just kept on running and hoped they'd lose interest.

"No. Schmitty wanted me out here. He said there was something weird going. So talk to me. What's going into your report?" Mikozy asked. Mikozy hooked around Garcia, close enough to see Garcia's notes.

Garcia looked at his notepad and began to read his entries.

911 got a call at 3:16 a.m. from Clarice Hunter.

Garcia looked up at Mikozy. "That's the victim's mother. His name is Reginald Hunter."

Garcia looked back down at his notes.

She said her son was dying and that he was being killed by Nathaniel Byron. She also said Nathaniel Byron wasn't around. 911 dispatched the paramedics for emergency medical treatment. The paramedics got here at 3:28 a.m.
    The first patrol car—

Garcia looked up at Mikozy. "That's Peabody and Lichter. They're inside with the mother."

The first patrol car reported they got here at 3:26 a.m. No reports of any perp in the vicinity. They reported the son lying on the living room floor. No signs of violence. No signs of blood. Just some candles. I got here at 3:31 a.m.

Garcia interrupted himself. "Peabody and Lichter thought this guy probably died of an overdose. That's the general verdict out here—self-inflicted death. That's what it looks like to me too. The patrol waited for the paramedics to come and sign off. But one of the medics flipped out when he heard the mother's story that Nathaniel Byron had killed her son."

"Nathaniel Byron?"

Garcia looked around as if someone might be listening. "I think the mother is a nutcase. There's no Nathaniel Byron. I even punched his name into Big Brother. Came up with zip, nada. No driver's license, no credit cards, no record, no welfare, no military. Nada."

"The name sounds familiar." Mikozy poked around, kicking at the grass.

Garcia looked at his notes again. "I know this sounds crazy. Let me finish this last notation."

The paramedic team, Gerald Whittet as the lead, examined Reginald Hunter and declared him dead.

"I don't know if I should put this in the report, Loo, but Whittet and Peabody saw Reginald's arm jump up. He's dead and his arm goes straight up. The mother was watching too. They must've wet themselves. I would too. Here's this dead guy saluting." The patrol car lights continued their lazy roll. Dawn had changed the night to gray.

Mikozy tensed. The simple case was slipping away and going weird on him. Just like Schmidt had promised. He doubted that Liu would be able to make sense of this case.

"Don't tell me he was doing a 'salute' while going into the promised land."

"Who knows? Maybe he was waving goodbye," Garcia answered. "Anyway..." Garcia looked at his notes again. "Paramedic—that's this guy Whittet—"

Paramedic stated that as far as he was concerned, Reginald Hunter was murdered. Told Lichter to phone the medical examiner's office.

"Is there anything else you're not putting in the report?"

Mikozy knew there were things left out. Why put in uncertainty? The cop would look foolish. Why put in information that sounded bad to the community or to the dicks in charge of internal affairs? The cop didn't want to get investigated. Down came the mental chop blocks. All sorts of information was left out. Most of it was junk. But Mikozy liked to hear it all, even the junk, and make up his own mind. Sometimes they'd tell him, and sometimes they wouldn't. Garcia was good. He gave Mikozy all the junk.

"I'll tell you right now, Reginald's mother is in deep. Not just a mother losing her son. There's something else there. You'll need to talk with her."

Mikozy waited. "That Whittet. Stupid fuck. Didn't he ever see an OD before?"

"I know. But I've seen this guy Whittet before. He's been around. He knows dead is dead."

"So what's he saying?" Mikozy and Garcia tried to figure out what the paramedic was thinking.

"What I'm thinking is that when he heard that Nathaniel Byron killed the boy, he agreed with the mother. Not your typical independent decision. That and the mysterious jumping hand. The whole thing doesn't sound quite right, does it?"

"No, I suppose not."

"That's why I had the call put in to the captain. If I can't explain this weirdo, they'll give me one of those awards for the year's best unsolved case report. I don't need that ragging. Too many of those awards and I'll never make dick. That's why you're here."

"I don't know if I can do any better, Rudy. Maybe when I get around to talking to Schmidt, I'll be able to make some sense out of it. So I'll ask again. Is there anything else you're not putting in the report?"

"Just that his mother is looped."

Mikozy waited some more.

Garcia wagged his head back and forth. "I dunno. This case is going to use a lot of our time that would be better spent out on the streets. The ordinary stuff."

Garcia and Mikozy looked up the street wondering what other crimes were going on behind those doors, wondering what criminals had just come home from a hard night's work in somebody's else neighborhood. Mikozy also wondered whether Garcia's Panama training, whether Garcia admitted to it or not, would suppress crime or only make the long arm of the law even longer and harder. The iron hammer inside the velvet glove. Temptation glowed brightest just before daylight.

Mikozy nodded in agreement. This was the cop's lament.

"Rudy." Mikozy pulled Garcia closer. "I've heard about Nathaniel Byron." Mikozy rarely called Garcia by his first name while they were on duty. Mikozy called Garcia by his first name at Chuey's Bar when they shared an after-hours beer or when they went bowling. They hadn't been bowling since the husbands-and-wives team split up. Once the bowling team goes, so goes the marriage. Or was it the other way around? Cause-and-effect wasn't always a downhill stream. It didn't always flow in one direction. First names would remind Garcia who was on whose side once they walked onto the crime scene. Mikozy wanted Garcia on his side. Mikozy would be pulled in one direction by the mother, another by the paramedic, the patrol cops, and technical support from the medical examiner's office, not to mention his lady professor friend. She was a question mark. Mikozy wanted Garcia's support once he traveled down this hole in Alice's Wonderland. "You heard about Byron? Is he local?" asked Garcia.

"Not the one I know. The Nathaniel Byron I know is from a long time ago. When I was a kid. Just a few blocks from here."

"You know the guy?"

"No, not really. But I've heard of him." Mikozy did not want to pursue his childhood memory, but he had opened the door.

"Nathaniel Byron, as far as I know, is a ghost."

"Hey, Loo, I don't need this. It's not something I want to write down. It's still dark out, and I don't want to hear a ghost story now," Garcia objected. "Anyway, that's for the Boy Scouts."

"Were you in the Scouts?" Mikozy asked.

"No, but everybody thinks I was. Okay, so I know how to tie knots. But I didn't learn them in the Boy Scouts." It was Garcia's turn to stare into the past.

"Hold on a minute, let me see if I can remember." Mikozy walked several steps over to the tree and leaned against the bark. He blocked out the hypnotic lights spinning around the top of the patrol car.

"I remember my grandfather telling me about Byron. I must have been about six or seven. Couldn't have been too much older. My grandfather died before I turned eight.

"He was from Haiti. Practiced voodoo when no one was looking too closely. Except me. Maybe I was invisible, but he used to let me watch. Killing chickens, drumming the conga like a hurricane ripping through the streets. Amazing stuff. I helped him light candles, and he'd lie down inside the ring of candles."

In his memory, Mikozy watched the little boy sitting on Grandpa's lap and the both of them cradled by a rickety pine box in the backyard. "Rafael, listen up," his grandfather would say. "You go down to the Woolworths and go to Mama Kemmeru. You know her, right?" Mikozy would just stare at the old man. No point in answering because he knew what you were going to say anyway. "You ask her for the tanning candles. She know what to get. Ain't nobody else in the store know where they are. All the other saleswomen give you the birthday candles. The tanning candles are special. You got to ask for Mama Kemmeru."

Mikozy leaned against the rope ties on the bamboo fence. He knew what candles Grandpa wanted him to get. His grandpa let him run down to the Woolworths all by himself. He promised he wouldn't tell his mother. She wouldn't even let him cross the street by himself. The tanning candles were thick and mud colored. Burned slow and hot. And when Grandpa burned them in a circle, a sticky cloud filled the air, iridescent blue, stinking of camphor. The neighbors never came out. Mikozy heard the windows slam shut. They never complained. His friend Houston said his mother would whisper to him when they smelled the candles, "Better watch out, Huey, that's the smell of a witch. It's out tonight. We have to close all windows." Houston complained to Mikozy because it was 1:04 that night.

Now Mikozy looked at Garcia. He knew Garcia knew about witches, the evil eye, the *mal de ojo*, the folk remedies. Everyone had their roots dug into something more than a ceramic vase filled with potting soil and a fertilizer stick. Especially before television and sitcom reality. Garcia had been planted in hardpack.

"You should have seen the old man, Rudy. I would watch him. I couldn't understand what he was saying. Maybe it was just the chanting. They called out to Chango. I would hear him weep and say, 'Keep me safe, Lord, from Nathaniel Byron.'"

A warm Santa Ana rippled the leaves around them.

"So what are you telling me? Are you telling me that Nathaniel Byron is out and about?" Garcia was trying to keep the spirit world locked up tight. Nathaniel Byron was only a man. Maybe a bad man, but still, just a man.

"I don't think so. Maybe Nathaniel Byron is just another name for the devil or whatever problem the island had. I mean, if you're poor, what better way to explain being poor and staying poor? You spend more time singing to Chango than going to the community college and learning a trade. Not that they had any schooling beyond third grade. That was a long time ago."

"¿Que dices, vos?" Rudy slipped into Spanish to break the spell.

"I don't know what I'm saying, Rudy. It's just strange to come down here and you pop Nathaniel Byron on me. I haven't heard that name for more than twenty-five years, and when you know I heard it from a Haitian grandpa…well, Rudy, you got to believe that I don't know what to think."

"Well, it's not like us Mexicans do anything crazy like that."

"Not after visiting Disneyland." Mikozy and Garcia put away their jester masks and descended back to earth. Normal again. The night had suddenly yielded to dawn.

Headlights came down Questa. Garcia and Mikozy watched a taxi pull up. A slender woman in stonewashed jeans, a worn brown leather jacket, and flats jumped out of the car quickly enough to avoid the backlash of taxi as it sped away, leaving visible fumes of burning rubber in the colored lights of the patrol cars.

"Hello, Mikozy." It was Liu.

Mikozy forgot to warn Garcia about an observer. If the case needed to be reined in, he'd better do it now.

"Sergeant Garcia, this is Professor Lisa Liu-Smythe. She'll be observing the crime scene investigation."

Garcia wasn't going to say anything further unless asked. It didn't matter whether she was a friend, an observer, a reporter, an expert, anybody except chain of command. Mikozy was chain of command; she wasn't.

Mikozy stumbled with protocol. He didn't want to say Lisa, and he didn't want to call her Professor Liu.

"This is Sergeant Garcia," Mikozy said to Liu. Garcia and Liu nodded to each other. Mikozy looked briefly at Lisa, a half smile trapped inside his beard. She had stolen enough time for a quick shower. A scent of exotic oils drifted into the morning dew. He turned back to Garcia. Liu was here to observe. This was as good a moment as any to forget her presence and let her become the invisible participant-observer.

"Did you call the ME?" Mikozy asked Garcia. That was short for "Did you follow up on the paramedic? Did you get any confirmation from the ME when they'd get here?" There was substance to the questions that a novitiate would miss. But Liu was bright, and she would see them fretting over which bureaucratic engine should be fired up. Mikozy wasn't about to let her get behind the wall and see what went on in this kitchen. Not just yet.

"Pomerance radioed and said he is coming over. Said he should be here soon. Something about problems with moving over to the new headquarters building. Confusion of sorts, down time, you know, excuses, excuses."

"Okay, I'll see Pomerance when he gets here. We'll talk after I get finished inside."

Liu and Mikozy headed to the house, leaving Garcia to finish up securing the outside perimeter of the house. It was a Victorian relic, squished in among the long, railroad-style houses. This one had a second story. Mikozy hadn't really noticed the house until now. He was surprised to see how good this house looked compared to the other houses on the block. The wood siding fit snugly against the building. No loose, dangling trim. The chestnut stain spread evenly up the porch banister. For a poor neighborhood, the Hunters were rich.

Mikozy felt a pull on his sleeve. Liu leaned into him. Cherry blossoms filled the air.

"Are you going to tell me what's happening, or do I have to guess?"

"Sorry," Mikozy said. "I was drifting."

"This may not be a crime at all," Mikozy told her. "We are going to meet a Reginald Hunter, recently deceased. Cause unknown."

"You mean, no crime, no investigation."

"No. Not at all. We always do an investigation. The question for tonight, like with all other crimes or possible crimes, is how far we go. If the kid died from natural causes, then there's no crime. If he shot himself up with drugs and overdosed, we might make a half-hearted effort at locating his supplier. There are so many drugs and dopers out here; it'd be a waste of the taxpayer's dollar." Mikozy thought he sounded like an imbecile or a narcoleptic. Where's the work ethic? he asked himself.

"That's elemental, Mr. Holmes," Liu chided, answering his unstated question and his stated observation.

"What I mean is that if the fucking paramedic had just examined our Mr. Reginald Hunter, we'd have a better idea of what he died from. We have no idea what he died from—well, he wasn't shot or stabbed, no obvious knocks to the head, but that's about all we know. We don't know if there were any needle tracks."

"You think it was the flu and he just didn't go to the hospital?"

"Nothing so simple. I had a chance to review Sergeant Garcia's notes with him. Seems that his mother knew something was wrong before 3:16 a.m. That's when she called 911. Probably earlier. He should have been in the hospital, not in the house."

"Okay, so if he was in the hospital, there'd be no crime scene investigation."

"Well, not like we have right now. What I meant is that we would have had a medical workup to get a better fix on what's wrong with our Mr. Hunter. Let's go inside."

No creaks as they walked the steps to the front door. Mikozy let his hand run up the banister, feeling for splinters. There weren't any. The house wouldn't have made Mikozy's list of houses that needed repair. As they got to the door, Mikozy leaned against Liu. "This may get a little strange. I hope you can go with the flow of things."

"Don't worry about me, Mikozy."

They stepped inside. A Damocles chandelier hung above them in the entryway. Mikozy was surprised to see that two of the bulbs were burned out. Even in the dim light, Mikozy could see a polished mahogany lattice on the ceiling. They heard some voices just beyond the entry. Mikozy stepped around the corner into a library of sorts. Rows of books climbed the wall. Clarice Hunter sat on an ottoman, her head nearly down to her knees, her dark brown hands wrapped around a gray head, her elbows resting on her knees. Clarice was sobbing and probably would continue to sob for the rest of her life. On the floor in the center of the room, there was a ring of candles.

Some had burned down, flickering their last moments. Clarice Hunter must have put down more candles, since some were only partially melted. In the center of the ring was Reginald Hunter. He didn't have a tie on but otherwise looked well dressed, looked like he was about to go to work. Slim, with a baby face. Maybe seventeen. The room smelled sweet with burning incense.

Two rank-and-file cops were standing on the other side of the body in front of the fireplace. Peabody and Lichter. Both were large men. Good choice to work these blocks. Mikozy walked around the body and the candles. Liu walked around in the other direction. There wasn't any other light in the library except for the candles.

"She'll be observing. I already spoke with Sergeant Garcia, but I'd like to hear it from you." Mikozy picked the one with the smirk in his blue eyes. The other officer appeared distracted.

"What's your name?" Mikozy asked.

"I'm Officer Harold Lichter." He could have been a body double for Schmidt, except Lichter wore his weight better.

"Okay, Lichter, why don't you tell me what happened?"

He looked at his notes. Then he looked back up at Mikozy. "I haven't finished my notes. I can give you what I saw."

"Fine." Mikozy wouldn't have criticized Lichter even if this weren't an unusual situation. He'd learn.

"We got here at 3:26 a.m. just ahead of the medics. Reginald Hunter—that's the dead boy. He looked dead when we got here. I tried to find a pulse and couldn't. Figured he must've died before we got here. He had a twisted smile on his face."

Everyone looked over at Reginald. If he had ever smiled tonight, he wasn't smiling any longer.

Lichter continued his recitation. "You know, the way I figure it is he died, maybe in his bed, and then his mom probably pulled him over here and put the candles around him. It doesn't seem right that he'd be lying here if he was sick. Either in bed or on the way to the hospital. Anyway, Whittet—he's the lead medic—he comes in, takes a look around, and his eyes bug out. Like he was seeing aliens from outer space. He acted paralyzed. He looked really wild." Lichter snapped his fingers. "Like that, Whittet flipped. And the mother is moaning and saying, 'Leave him be, Nathaniel Byron, leave him be.' Whittet goes crazy when he hears that. He's backing out and me and Peabody are trying to drag him back in to get his take on Reginald."

"Then the boy's left arm shoots up, maybe two feet off the ground, and falls back down. I felt my hair standing up. Peabody, well…" Lichter looked momentarily at his partner, his slow smirk dying at the corner of his mouth. "You could tell he was out of it. He's barely holding on to Whittet. The boy's mother, she begins to holler. I felt like I was in some time-machine darkie flick—" Lichter stopped short. Mikozy stared hard at Lichter.

"I'm sorry, Loo. I didn't know what I was saying." Lichter had never met Mikozy before. Candlelit, Mikozy could have been anything. The way Mikozy stared at him, Lichter decided Mikozy was a local.

"Don't say it again. And for your own sake, don't think it again. Just stick with the scene, the facts. So what else?" Mikozy was annoyed. Lichter was fitted with Schmidt's neural network as well.

"I jumped back. Whittet pulled away from me and Peabody. He said something about letting the ME take care of the living dead. I couldn't see who was with Whittet, but whoever it was left with him. I heard them running down the steps. Then I heard their van drive off."

Mikozy wanted to hear from the other officer, at least to find out what was bothering him.

"Peabody," Mikozy said. Peabody looked around, a startle response. He stood next to the wall, about six feet behind Lichter. Embarrassment, fear, whatever it was, pushed Peabody to the edge of the room.

"Peabody, you have anything else to add?"

Peabody shook his head. Probably lost more than his voice, thought Mikozy.

He might have to get somebody to check Peabody. Maybe get Lichter to take Peabody out for a donut and caffeine. The universal cure for meetings with the grim reaper.

"Did either of you step inside the circle?"

"Just to take his pulse," Lichter said. "And I had gloves on."

"What about you, Peabody?" Lichter looked back at Peabody and saw that he couldn't remember, or if he could, he wouldn't be able to tell anyone what he remembered.

"No, he wasn't inside with me," Lichter said.

"Did either of you question Clarice Hunter?"

"No. I didn't think she was in a mood to answer any questions." Again, Lichter.

"Have you been in any other rooms in the house—the boy's room?"

Finally Peabody spoke. "No, just here." He was still pale, but his eyes were paying attention now.

Lichter turned again to look at Peabody. "Hey, Pea."

"Let me ask a dumb question. We're all entitled," Mikozy said. "How do we know this guy's name is Reginald Hunter? You didn't speak with the mother, and you said you only took his pulse. Did I miss something?"

"Nine one one told us that a Clarice Hunter called in saying someone was killing her Reginald." Peabody walked over to Lichter, snapping out of his reverie. Still not at ease, but they were a team again. "When we got here, she kept saying, 'Reginald, my

Reginald.' Then she said what Lichter told you: 'Leave him be, Nathaniel Byron, leave him be.' So I figured Reginald was her son. Who else would he be?"

"Sounds reasonable, Peabody. But we have no other verification of the victim except for her saying 'my Reginald'?"

"Yes. I mean no. What I mean to say is you said it perfectly, Loo."

"Sounds reasonable, Peabody. That's what I would think." Mikozy smiled. Liu smiled too. She wished for videotape. It would be a great replay, and she would have a lot to talk about. The immanent terror chasing away a paramedic, one cop freeze-framed momentarily while the other turned village raconteur, a dead soul sprawled across the family library while anger and sorrow racked the mother. Mikozy watched Liu for a moment. He knew her mind was trapping each nuance, weaving a talismanic fabric. He couldn't worry about what she might say. She had promised to keep it confidential.

Mikozy couldn't figure out why Garcia had stayed outside and left Lichter and Peabody inside. With Liu here, he didn't want to do the obvious and restation the men. He could use Garcia inside to take a quick look into the other rooms. Mikozy wanted to interview the mother himself. Now he'd have to do the whole thing. Too bad this wasn't some shooting where he could send this twosome out to interview neighbors about what they heard or saw.

"Just do what you're doing and guard the body until the ME gets here." Mikozy hoped they didn't catch the humor in his command. Be productive, stand still, and do nothing.

"Also, Lichter…"

"Yeah, Loo?"

"Write up your notes now, and put in what Peabody said. I want your report ASAP." Mikozy felt better. He was keeping Lichter's idle hands busy. "Liu, come with me. Let's talk with Reginald's mother."

Liu and Mikozy circled back around Reginald's body. Mikozy estimated that Reginald was about five feet, five inches. Reginald had his shoes on. Not too bad. They had hard foam soles. They were good walking shoes. Must have cost him about eighty bucks.

Liu went around the body another time. She crouched down low to the carpet. Mikozy watched her turn her head to the side and place it against the carpet. Mikozy, Lichter, and even Peabody, everyone except Clarice Hunter, followed Liu's graceful descent to the floor. Mikozy knew what she was doing. It needed to be done anyway. And he knew what she would find. She would find out that Clarice Hunter hadn't dragged Reginald over to the circle of fire. If this was what he thought it was, Clarice had been trying to protect her son from Nathaniel Byron, protect him from the evil spirit. This was real for her, not like the comedy Halloween had become. It, this thing, these candles, this circle of fire, all had been real for him. That was long ago. It was still real for Clarice. He watched Liu's eyes travel the room from ground zero. She finished her floor scan and stood up and walked over to Mikozy.

She spoke in a low voice. For Mikozy's benefit only. "I don't think Lichter's idea about Reginald's mom pulling him over here is right."

"Why's that?" Mikozy asked, silently praising her for coming to the right conclusion.

"I don't know how strong his mother is. Not enough to carry him over here. So she had to pull him, like Lichter was thinking. But then there should be tracks in the carpet. If she pulled him over, she'd hold him under the arms. The shoes would drag along the carpet and leave parallel lines about a foot or so apart."

"She could have dressed him up here and put on his shoes after she pulled him over."

"Either that or he walked over on his own, and he lay down here on his own." Mikozy nodded. "You also notice that sweet smell?"

"Yeah, I thought it was incense, but I don't see any around."

He turned to Clarice. "Excuse me, Mrs. Hunter." She didn't respond. "Mrs. Hunter?"

Mikozy tried a few more times before reaching down and grasping her shoulder gently. Clarice looked up. Reddened eyes, disoriented and lost. *Who are these people here?* her eyes asked.

Mikozy squatted down and put his face close to Clarice's. She looked to be in her late forties. Her hands were smooth. This woman was no maid. Mikozy glanced around the room again. It was a real library. Must be over a thousand books on the shelves.

"Mrs. Hunter, I'm Detective Mikozy, and this is Professor Liu. We'd like to talk with you a few minutes. We want to know what happened to Reginald. That's Reginald on the floor?"

"Yes, that's my Reginald." It was a plain and resigned voice.

"Can you tell us what happened?" Mikozy didn't take notes the first time. He wanted to listen carefully and focus on the story. He sometimes wished he had his personal cameraman following him around. But then he'd have to edit all that video. Mikozy decided to stay with what he knew best. There'd be a second time and a third and however many times that might be necessary to preserve the story.

"Reginald came home about 7:30 p.m. I had just finished watching the evening news and getting dinner ready. I made his favorite meal, chops with Texas slaw. Reginald usually came home earlier, about five o'clock. He liked to get in before the rush hour. I was worried."

She stopped. Mikozy could lead her down different paths. That was always the problem with interviews. You had to remember to circle back and pick up the paths left untaken.

"Did he say anything about being late?"

"No. Well, he said he was doing something special. He didn't say what it was. Or maybe he said airport. I don't remember it well."

"Okay. What happened next? Did he eat dinner with you?"

"We was sitting down to eat, maybe about eight or eight fifteen p.m. I had the food ready, and I just needed to warm it up in the microwave, so it didn't take long, and I called him. He didn't come down from his room. I guessed he was counting his money. He got paid something every day. But he was just sitting on his bed."

Clarice stopped again. Thinking, remembering.

"Something was wrong, but I didn't know what it was. He was staring at one of his stereo posters. Still staring at where it was even after I opened the door. He didn't know that I came into his room. He didn't even hear me. He was someplace else. I should have taken him to Dr. Shelton right away."

"Is he your doctor?" Liu decided to join the interview. Mikozy didn't mind her question.

"Yes, but he don't live around here. I have to take two buses. We don't have no car."

"But you didn't go to Dr. Shelton?" Mikozy took the lead.

"No." Clarice looked at them both, expecting to be admonished. When they said nothing, she went on.

"Did Reginald see Dr. Shelton, or anybody else, for some medical problem?"

"No, he was a healthy boy. I know what you're thinking, but he never did any drugs. I taught him right from wrong, and he knew drugs was wrong."

There was no question pending, so Clarice continued with her story the way she wanted to tell it.

"I took Reginald's hand and took him downstairs. He didn't look like he would eat anything. And all of a sudden his shoulders kind of arched back and he was moaning."

Clarice lifted up her head. She appeared to be defiant. For that instant, she had a hard look and a mean face.

"I knew it was Nathaniel Byron coming for Reginald. I was real scared for Reginald. I had to fight Nathaniel Byron. I always knew I would someday."

Liu was about to ask a question, but Mikozy held up his hand to let Clarice continue. He knew where she was headed. He'd seen his grandfather do these same things, have the same face and talk the same crazy talk. The same fear. The same defiance.

"I bring my Reginald here and ast him to lie down. I lit all the candles jes like I was tolt." Clarice's language slipped back into her past, resonating with old melodies, and unlearning all the learning the books in her library represented.

"Okay, Clarice. That's enough for now. When you have a chance to rest, we can ask you some other questions we may have. Is that all right?"

Liu thought Mikozy's questioning too brief and scattered. She made a mental note to give him her observations later.

"Is that all right?" repeated Mikozy.

"Yes, Detective—?"

"Mikozy. Do you mind if we take a look at Reginald's room?"

"No. It'll be upstairs." Mikozy and Liu dutifully followed Clarice upstairs. The stairs were stained dark and had a carpet runner. The banister was polished. The house was out of place in this neighborhood. At the top of the staircase, there were three rooms splitting off on the landing. Reginald's room was to the right. Clarice turned on the light and stood aside to let Mikozy and Liu go in.

Mikozy waited at the doorway and said to Clarice, "You keep a nice house, Mrs. Hunter."

Clarice returned to her second self, her public self. "Yes, I tried hard. This was my uncle's house that he had in South Pasadena. I had it moved down here."

"Why'd you do that?" Liu asked.

"I'm the librarian at the First Baptist Missionary Movement. It was my idea to bring some light to the children in the community."

Clarice spoke to Liu now. "When I was growing up, I went to my piano teacher's home to learn the piano. I didn't think a piano would help out that much here. So I made a library for the children here. They came by after school and on Saturdays. I'd read books to them, and when they were older, they got to do the reading."

Clarice didn't stop. She looked up at Mikozy.

"Reginald's one of my Saturday children."

"Saturday children?" Mikozy didn't know what else to ask.

"He'd come by on Saturdays. Must have started about ten years ago. Maybe more than ten years. He was such a bright boy. And then his parents left. Just left him here for his Saturday reading and never came back. He was a Hepworth then."

"You took him in?"

"Yes. I kept Austin."

"You mean Reginald?"

"Austin Hepworth. When I took him in, I changed his name to Reginald Hunter. Didn't want nobody coming around saying the county has a responsibility and take him away. That wouldn't've done him no good. He'd done well. When you look at Reginald, even the way he is now, you can see he's not a hoodlum. He's not what they call homeboy. You don't hear anyone calling him 'homes.' You see the way he got his hair cut today. He did that for me. He wanted to look proper. Reginald was my best learner." Clarice might not have told Mikozy and Liu about Reginald's real name if Reginald were still alive. But his name didn't matter anymore. She'd still bury him as Reginald Hunter. No one could stop her. She thought about an epitaph—"Not a homeboy." Or maybe like they said it on the streets so the rest of the boys on the street would understand—"Not a homes."

Mikozy looked inside the room. Neat. No junk on the floor. No piles of paper.

The bed was made. Everything was in its place. Old CDs carefully lined up. He walked over to look at the titles. An eclectic taste, not that different from what Mikozy was downloading to his smartphone. Reginald had even alphabetized them.

"Mrs. Hunter." Mikozy tried to avoid any accusation in his voice. "These CDs cost quite a bit of money."

POISONADE

"Oh, half of those CDs are from the clubs that I bought years ago. The rest he got in bins at Walmart. He didn't spend so much himself. He had a good job."

"You said he worked?"

"Yes, he had a good job. At least for his age. Something to start with. He worked for Galaxy Gems. Running here and going there. Mostly delivering things. Galaxy Gems said they'd get Reginald something better after he proved himself."

Mikozy thought he knew the name but couldn't place it. "What kind of business is Galaxy Gems?" Liu frowned behind Mikozy's back, wincing at Mikozy's question. How obvious was a store's business that called itself gems? Mikozy knew that whoever was with him would not have asked that question, but Mikozy never relied on a company's name. There were enough creative names that made the question worth asking. Better not to be surprised later on.

"I guessed it might be a jewelry store, but I couldn't imagine them having Reginald delivering jewelry. He wasn't even old enough to get bonded. And his neighborhood, hmmphh. That had to be a negative until they got to know him. I never did find out exactly what they did. Reginald just talked about being a messenger. They didn't have him on a regular payroll. He didn't bring home a check. One time I remember he got paid fifty dollars."

"Do you know Galaxy Gems' address?"

"It's down near Esterbrook on Eleventh Street."

"Do you know who he worked for at Galaxy?"

Suddenly, Clarice's mood changed. She was lightning and thunder, remembering what had happened to her Reginald.

"Galaxy Gems don't know nothing about Reginald getting killed by Nathaniel Byron."

"I understand what you're saying, Mrs. Hunter." Mikozy knew where Clarice's anger was anchored, like a pit viper ready to strike its prey, except there wasn't any prey here. There wasn't any Nathaniel Byron. Never was any juju ghost, not unless there were angels and leprechauns. Mikozy had little faith in other-worldly beings.

"We just need to go through Reginald's day, that's all. Just doing our job."

"When you come downstairs, I can get you the name of the person at Galaxy Gems that Reginald called." Clarice turned and went back downstairs to watch over Reginald.

Liu sucked in her breath. "Mikozy, either I'm losing it, or you're screwing up." Mikozy calmly looked around the room, while Liu continued her commentary. "She names the killer—this Nathaniel Byron—and you don't ask any questions about him. You go off on some tangent about Reginald's boss for some messenger work. I don't get it."

"Liu, this is a situation that requires special knowledge. Something you don't know about. Not if you ask that question."

"Tell me, Mikozy. I'm all yours." Liu moved to sit down on the bed. Mikozy reached his arm across to catch her in midflight and shook his head. A gentle reminder that the crime scene had strict boundaries. Reginald's room could be important.

"My guess is that she's got some relative who's from Haiti, or maybe someone who's just into voodoo. You saw those candles. Did that strike you as your usual mother taking care of a sick child?"

"Yeah, that is something I haven't seen before. But you're not going to say that Reginald was killed by voodoo magic?"

"Exactly, that's not what I'm going to say."

"You lost me, Mikozy."

"Look, Liu, here's this mother who's got locked into this cultural thing. It happens to be voodoo. It could be the evil eye, the golem, the Day of the Dead, Halloween. Whatever. If you get somebody who is locked into that thing, they're stuck. I don't have those beliefs, but I'm not fool enough to argue with someone who does. You just go right on past those mind prisons and ask about the same facts that you'd ask somebody who wasn't trapped inside one of those culture demons."

"But what about Nathaniel Byron?"

"Nathaniel Byron is like Santa Claus. She could have said that Santa Claus killed Reginald or Satan killed him or Zeus killed him. Clarice Hunter is stuck with a Haitian culture spirit, Mr. Nathaniel Byron. He was a monster. A Frenchman with an English name. There are many stories about him, but the one I remember best was about the feasts he would hold for his village. They would come and eat. They feared him so much they had to eat. They also looked for any relatives that might have been in the food. Byron kept the heads of the people he cooked in his stews, put some on a poleax inside the churchyard. Pretty fearsome story for a child."

Liu was quiet. She studied Mikozy's face. A silver halo framed the grizzly mane. His eyes zeroed back, willing her to attention.

"I don't believe there is a Nathaniel Byron. If there ever was, he's dead. For that matter, I don't believe in Santa, Satan, Zeus, or the whatevers. That leaves us trying to figure out what killed Reginald. If it wasn't a medical problem that Clarice didn't know of, then it must've been something that happened to him, probably in the past day or so. Maybe it was his food. Who knows? We'll wait for the ME to get here. That's why Reginald's work routine may be important."

"I could say wow, Professor Mikozy." Liu clasped her hands together, imitating the ingenue with false praise. "Really." Her eyes dropped the pretense, her words felt warm. "I have to compliment you. I didn't realize who Nathaniel Byron was." The conversation paused. Both of them took advantage of the silence to think. Each in their silent world. Each engaging in a silent dialogue that mirrored the other's thoughts. About each other. About Nathaniel Byron. About Reginald.

Liu walked around the room. She stopped at the window looking across to the shade tree. Garcia had turned off the police lights. The medical examiner's investigator's car pulled alongside the patrol car. Garcia was saying something to the investigator.

"You might have mentioned Diphong Beipo." Liu spoke into the window with her back to Mikozy.

"Who?" Mikozy asked.

"He is my Nathaniel Byron." She said it loud enough for Mikozy to hear, but not loud enough for Mikozy to tell how much she feared her own childhood monsters.

"Pomerance." Mikozy offered a welcome salute as he walked down the stairs and saw Pomerance bending over to take Reginald's temperature. Pomerance barely had any hair left to comb and didn't show any interest in wanting to be other than he was. His eyes bulged behind thick glass. Pomerance had never worn contacts. He preferred the glass shield. Pomerance claimed it protected him against blood splatter and getting hit in the eye with HIV, AIDS, Ebola, COVID, and otherwise bad blood. Nobody else ever said that except Pomerance. He only said that to stop the attempts to convert him to contact lenses. He just didn't like the idea of putting plastic up under his eyelids. He knew his arguments were illogical, but foolishness was his way of rebutting annoyance. Pomerance was already into his routine, wearing rubber gloves that made his hands look as if they were robotic devices. Lichter and Peabody were still rooted to the place where Mikozy had left them.

"Don't get up, Pom."

"Not to worry, Mikozy." Pomerance tested Reginald's tightness at the jaw, then at the arm and legs. Pomerance took a flashlight and examined Reginald's eyes, ears, nose, and throat. While Pomerance continued his examination, Mikozy introduced Liu.

"This is Professor Liu-Smythe, and she's observing how an investigation is done."

Without turning around, Pomerance said, "Glad to meet you, Professor. If you can tell me what we got here, don't keep it a secret."

"Promise," Liu said, embracing being included in the investigation.

Mikozy walked over to Peabody and Lichter. "Go and see Sergeant Garcia. If he needs any help outside, fine. If not, make sure you're easy to find. I might have some follow-up questions about your report." As they left, Mikozy walked over to Pomerance and leaned over his shoulder.

"Hey, Pom, do you think he had a sore throat?" Mikozy wanted to tease some observation out of Pomerance.

Pomerance had been a medic in 'Nam. He went on to become a physician's assistant at Community General. Pomerance was alternatively amused, distressed, and, after several years, intrigued by how the patients, especially the Saturday-nighters, came in with the wounds of modern urban America. They looked like the war wounds he was familiar with. Mikozy once asked Pomerance what it was that finally took him out of the hospital where the living needed him and put him out on the streets where the dead couldn't care less. Pomerance had an urgent need to tell Mikozy why he wanted to deal with the dead. "They don't talk, Mikozy. They don't lie, they don't bullshit you. With the live ones, you never really knew if you were helping them because they thought you put everything down in their records. And some docs did, too. I said forget this game, let's just see what killed you."

Pomerance continued his examination of Reginald Hunter.

"This is definitely not a sore throat, but he is confused about how to explain his death."

"He's confused or you're confused?"

"Let's not get so technical at this time in the morning, Mikozy." Pomerance got up and walked over to where Clarice was seated.

"I understand you're Mrs. Hunter, the deceased's mother." He didn't wait for an answer. He didn't like to leave room for different conversations. "I'm Barry Pomerance with the medical examiner's office. I'd like to ask you a few questions."

Clarice Hunter barely acknowledged Pomerance. Her energies were focused on Reginald and wherever else her imagination was taking her. She nodded at Pomerance.

"Can you tell me where you bought these candles?"

"I bought them at Vons." Clarice looked concerned about what they were going to do with Reginald. She had a slight, nervous rocking motion. Her eyes never left Reginald.

"You're not going to take the candles?" she asked Pomerance and looked to Mikozy for help.

Before Mikozy could say anything, Pomerance said, "Mrs. Hunter, if you have any of these candles from the same box, that would be fine. I'll just need a couple in case someone wants to see what kind of candles they were. These will show up in the photos."

Clarice was about to get up from the ottoman where she watched over Reginald. "Before you go," Pomerance said, "I'd also like to know if you gave any medicine within the last twenty-four hours."

"Yes, I gave him some breathing medicine."

"Breathing medicine? What was the medicine for?"

"Oh, he would get to wheezing when he did some heavy activity, almost like me and my own family. He was like a Hunter, and I gave him the same medicine all us Hunters would take."

"Could you also bring me the bottle or container with the medicine you gave him when you go looking for the candles?"

Clarice walked out of the library to get Pomerance the candles and the medicine.

Pomerance looked over at Mikozy. They both knew that Pomerance could retreat into his technician's role and leave all the explaining to the ME. He'd do that to some detectives. He even did that to Schmidt once. Pissed Schmidt off. "Sorry, sir, but I just collect evidence. You want interpretation. That's for the ME." That was worse than name, rank, and serial number because everyone knew that Pomerance would have a theory about the victim and the crime. It didn't count in the grand scheme of things. Pomerance was right in two out of three cases, which was a good average, and he could help the investigation tumble along. Pomerance never held out on Mikozy. Maybe because they both told lies to keep others from trying to change them. Maybe it was because Mikozy had too much hair and Pomerance had too little. Whatever it was, they liked to try their stories on for each other. Pomerance looked at Mikozy and at Liu. "I told you, Pomerance, she's okay."

"Okay, Mikozy. Listen to this. I was first thinking that if Reginald was alive when he was laid out on the floor that maybe the candles threw off some chemicals beyond what burning paraffin gives off, and perhaps his condition, whatever it was, might have been further aggravated by the candles. But if these are your ordinary candles, I don't really think that happened. Too much air. And if they were toxic enough to harm Reginald, then why not his mom? Maybe the officers, even us. I don't think we have toxic birthday candles. That would certainly put a kink in birthday parties. Maybe the medicine she gave him might help us figure this out."

"So you'll take her word about shopping at Vons?" Mikozy was getting tired and couldn't make sense about where to take the investigation. Mikozy might have thought Pomerance had flipped out with all gibberish about candles if Mikozy hadn't seen the layout of the scene himself. Anything was possible.

"I'll believe everything now and question everything later."

Clarice came back into the library with two small boxes in her hand.

"Here's the medicine I gave Reginald. I have to go upstairs for the candles." Clarice went back out after giving Pomerance the medicines.

Pomerance took the box and shook out a small aerosol. The prescription read "generic metaproterenol." The other was a box with a bottle of capsules that said "theophylline." Both labels indicated that they had been prescribed for Clarice Hunter. Pomerance looked bothered and walked over to Mikozy and showed him the labels. Liu came over, and Pomerance held the labels for her to read too.

"So?" Mikozy asked. Liu looked just as puzzled as Mikozy.

"I think it was an overdose—an overdose of medicine," Pomerance said.

"What do you mean? Is this stuff toxic?" Mikozy asked.

"Not if you take the right dosage. Also, you got to think something might be wrong when she gave him medicine that had her name on the box."

'Well, she did say something about her family being asthmatics. So she probably had some familiarity with these drugs," Mikozy said.

"I don't understand," Liu said. "Exactly what do these medicines do?"

"These medicines are for asthmatics. They help relieve asthma attacks."

Pomerance repeated what Mikozy had just said.

Both Liu and Mikozy looked expectantly at Pomerance for something more. "What I'm saying is that we probably have a medical mistake, the kind that comes from someone playing doctor and prescribing a powerful designer drug for himself or, as Clarice probably did, for someone else. This is not that unusual, especially when seeing a doctor is expensive."

Pomerance looked again at the boxes as if he were trying to confirm what he'd read earlier. He pressed the aerosol, and a fine mist burst out. Pomerance took a small whiff of the mist and nodded as if he too had used this aerosol before.

"There had been a rash of deaths in the early '60s from people using these bronchial dilators. The way I understand it is that the when individuals didn't get instant relief, they took more of the medicine, thinking that more was better. The kicker was that some of these drugs affect the heart's rhythm and probably triggered cardiac arrest. That's medical theory. No one has actually tested this in the laboratory. But this is what might have happened to Reginald. There's no proof, but when these drugs were changed into prescription drugs, the number of deaths dropped. And when they were first put on the general market in—I think it was England, there was a rash of deaths also. We have a nice correlation. That's what we have."

"You're not going to tell Clarice that," Liu said. "You'll make her think that she killed Reginald, and it's only a theory right now."

Pomerance had a sad look. Even Mikozy was disturbed by the thought that Clarice had been treating Reginald with all sorts of beliefs and drugs, anything to save him from a street death, and, in the process of saving him, killed him.

"No. That's not my job. And anyway, I'm not really sure. I just put down all this information and let the ME figure it all out. Could be something else altogether. So no, I won't be sharing this with his mother." Pomerance put the medicines in a sample bag.

"This is the kind of quick answer we all look for." Pomerance frowned. He'd been wrong before. "There are other possibilities. Let me finish up. There's more to do here."

Pomerance looked around as if he were making a final assessment of what he still had left to do. He spoke to Mikozy.

"Once we take Reginald, I'll stay with Mrs. Hunter and bag a few of the original candles after checking around some more. I can come back for the rest later if the ME wants them. There could have been another irritant with his breathing, especially if he had an asthmatic episode—assuming he had asthma to begin with. I hope someone has some medical records on this kid. By the way, have you checked his room for any drug paraphernalia in case drugs are also involved?"

"No." Mikozy tried out his mental telepathy on Garcia to get him to come inside. Mikozy knew he'd never have that skill, but still liked to try it out every so often.

"Garcia will be wrapping up here in a while."

"I'll talk to LC once she gets your report and finishes the autopsy. Right now, I just need to get a name from Clarice and I'm gone." LC was one of Pomerance's bosses. Not that long ago, the medical examiner would have been out at Clarice Hunter's house. With an escalating homicide rate, the medical examiner was able to add an assistant and send the assistant into the field. With a further escalating homicide rate and the shrill howl of the public to catch the criminal and lock him away, the medical examiner had requested an assistant to the assistant. She knew that the public had another shrill cry: no more taxes. The medical examiner decided to temper his request by asking for a less costly field investigator, and thus was born the crime scene investigator. Not quite a doctor, but still medically expert. Pomerance was their experiment at saving money and still having enough expert opinion at the crime scene to provide prosecutors with usable evidence. Pomerance went back to Reginald, while Mikozy went to the kitchen to find Clarice. Liu stayed to watch what Pomerance was doing.

Clarice was standing by the counter alongside the refrigerator. She had a box of candles on the countertop. It was obvious that she prepared her food on the counter. Thousands of nicks and stains cobbled the surface.

"I'm sorry, Detective." Clarice was running her fingers back and forth on the refrigerator. Mikozy saw she had several magnets holding a picture of Reginald on the front of the refrigerator. "He graduated a year early. Just sixteen last March."

"Did you have the name of Reginald's boss at Galaxy Gems?"

"Oh, yes." Clarice reached above the counter and opened an upper cabinet door. On the inside, hanging from a clip, were several pages of handwritten notes. "These are my phone numbers. My Saturday children, and the others—you know, the bank, the police, and everything."

She flipped through the pages carefully, running her fingers quickly down the list.

"Here it is, Detective."

She gave him the page with her finger under the name. Mikozy wrote it down. "Galaxy—Mr. Frederick 246-3303."

Mikozy expressed his sympathy again and walked with Liu out to his car. Mikozy approached Garcia and stopped to tell him about finishing up at the house.

"I'd like you to do a sweep of the boy's room. His mother said he didn't use drugs, and I'd like to nail that down. Also, make sure Lichter's report gets in today."

Garcia wasn't too happy about going into the house but figured that with Pomerance inside, all the ghosts would have scattered. They wouldn't want to leave any unnatural clues for the medical examiner's office. It would be a waste of effort. No one would believe it anyway.

"Okay, Mikozy, it shouldn't take too much longer. I'll leave you a copy of my report. And take care of the professor, but don't get caught." Mikozy quickly looked over at Liu to see if she was close enough to hear what Rudy had said. She was standing by Mikozy's car, waiting for him to join her. Mikozy looked back at Rudy, and for a second they grinned at each other like fourteen-year-olds.

Chapter 12
UPWARD MOBILITY

Mikozy opened the door for Liu on his nearly new Sentra.

"Thank you. Sometimes a woman likes to be treated as a woman. Even in a Sentra."

Mikozy laughed even though it was his car they were laughing about. "The real joke is all those fancy cars—at least in this city. Nobody's too interested in stealing a Sentra, yet it drives just fine. Where am I taking you?"

"Take me home, Mikozy. I'm off the Melrose exit on the 101."

Mikozy started the car and pulled out into the beginnings of the morning rush hour traffic. Mikozy got himself ready for the highway drive to Liu's place. He turned the radio on to catch the morning news.

Liu ran her fingers through her black hair. The best she could do, having left her brush at the apartment. She reached over and turned the radio off and inched over to Mikozy as far as the bucket seat would allow.

"Actually, Mikozy, I want to thank you for a wonderful night out on the town. I wonder if you treat all your dates so nice."

Mikozy took the compliment and rolled it around in his mind. He could easily forget the past several hours of trying to figure out what had happened to Reginald and lose himself in the narrow space between them.

"This isn't our date, Lisa, that's later in the day. If you want to."

"A date?" Liu pondered the invitation as if it were a philosophical conundrum. "Do you mind if I invite you instead of you inviting me?" Liu asked. Mikozy sped past the yellow light and got on the freeway.

"I don't see what the difference would be."

"Well, you might invite me to dinner or to a movie. Then I would have to say yes or no to a dinner or movie. But if I invite you, I'll tell you what I want, and you'll have to say yes or no."

"A fine point," Mikozy said. "Go ahead and give me the woman's choice."

Lisa ran her long red fingernail on the automatic shift in the well between them. She watched Mikozy pull across three lanes of traffic to get into the diamond lane. She knew the lane would disappear in a mile.

"I'm going to a strength class at seven. Why don't you join me?"

"I thought they were step classes."

"So old time. Now there's yoga, bicycling, and my fave, strength class."

"I can always add some strength to my mind. Maybe if I watch."

"That's a yes, but you have to use all your muscles. The place is near the Barnaby Building where I teach."

"Building 253?"

Liu was puzzled.

"Private joke, sorry. The city calls its buildings by the numbers on its maintenance plan. To the public, it's the Barnaby Building; to us, it's Building 253."

"Well, you'll have no problem recognizing the Aerobics Center. It's the large purple-and-white-striped building about a block south of Barnaby. It has a neon sign running across the top flashing up, down, up, down. Just watching that sign burns a calorie or two."

Mikozy knew which building she was talking about, but he thought back to the step class he'd gone to years ago. He remembered seeing an infomercial on one of the cable channels about buying a new miracle step board. It promised that he would lose pounds and charge up his heart at the same time. A new way to take the boredom out of exercising. He even thought about buying one for about five seconds. Mikozy had been jogging. Mikozy didn't like to jog for the sake of exercise. He preferred pickup games whenever he could find them. And if he couldn't find a game, then he jogged. Mikozy always had a fallback. No point in losing time and whining about what might have been. He often ended up in the fallback. For the past year, that had meant jogging while he was with the fashionable crimes squad.

Mikozy imagined asking LC about going to a step class. That had never happened. He imagined her asking him to join her. "Isn't that a woman's thing?" he'd ask.

"What? Are you afraid of doing a woman's thing?" So he went inside his imaginary memory.

"Your class was a surprise. I mean, I was the only guy." It must have been a longer conversation.

"You did all right in class," she answered in his mind.

Now he landed in reality. Liu was asking him to go to a strength class. Would he still be the only man in the room?

Mikozy wasn't so sure about Liu's confidence-building. This was turning into a challenge thing. If I accept now, he thought, then she'll have to accept my offer. He glanced over at Liu and saw her face framed by a fast-moving sixteen-wheeler. Mikozy couldn't read the name of the product line, but the green blur behind Liu lent her an irresistible aura. The morning light bounced off her black hair, shaping the aura as a streetlamp to the soul. A phosphor flash burst across the first and second trailer. Mikozy saw the image of Carlos Laguna inside the flash of light, the slick black hair catching the brilliant morning rays. The image disappeared. The instant was defined by a billionth of a second, but he would remember it forever.

Why now, Carlos?

"Well, Mikozy. Will you come?"

Liu was smiling at the edges of her wide, sensuous lips. "Can you come?"

Mikozy raced for a good response. He decided to overlook the double meanings Liu had tossed in his lap.

"Sure, Lisa."

"Great, Mikozy. I'll even protect you from all those other bodybuilders."

Mikozy shot back across the traffic to catch the Melrose exit. "Before I forget, how did you find this morning?"

"Don't tease, Mikozy," she teased in return. "Of course I enjoyed it. I mean, even though it was so weird with all those candles and the way Clarice had Reginald laid out. You don't get those every day, do you?"

"Not many. This is one of those memorable career days."

"Good to hear. I was beginning to doubt my teaching, my clue analysis. I'm the first to admit that I'm not an expert in police science."

Mikozy looked over to share that common uncertainty, almost telepathic, looping Liu into the profession, the protectors of the state.

They pulled off the freeway onto Melrose and stopped at the light. Liu looked younger and a bit guilty. She mirrored back the uncertainty, not the professor's mask. Mikozy nodded as if he were a therapist asking her to go on.

Mikozy's screen showed a message from Schmidt. Mikozy read it silently: "What about the manuscript?"

Liu read along. "What's that about? Writing a book?"

Mikozy didn't want to get into that conversation. He thought about finding some time to review the manuscript the inspector had tasked him with.

"Nothing much. Just some departmental homework. A takeoff on a Jack London book. But what about you? I can see the title for your book. Something like *Clue Me In* or *Policing the Candles*."

"Not just yet," Liu batted back. "Maybe when I can feature you messing with a crime scene."

Mikozy laughed. He typed back a quick answer to Schmidt: "Soon."

Liu decided to unbutton her interests. "I put together my class from my work in cognitive science. You know, the psychology of what we pay attention to. I thought it would be fun to put that into the context of police work."

"The class was different. You did keep me thinking." Mikozy let his right hand drift down and touch her on the arm. She didn't pull away.

"You seemed to be ducking away from my questions rather than thinking about them. You seemed to be aware that I liked to throw darts. You watched me walk around, seeing if I would miss my mark." Her eyes were charmed, exclamation points to her pleasure principle. "I'm still learning, Mikozy. I was even thinking that I could put some of the stuff I saw tonight into a new class. Not right away. And not a book, not yet."

"I don't see anything wrong with that, but wait until the investigation is over. If it gets prosecuted, which it doesn't look like now, but who knows, you may be waiting till we've disclosed to the other side."

"I know. Not too far from here. Two blocks and make a right."

Mikozy hadn't been on this street for years. He didn't remember the signs and whether they had changed. This seemed to be a stable community, with the small stores resisting the mega markets. He would come back here and get a sandwich for later on. The sign said Italian Deli.

"I had an interesting discussion with the investigator from the medical examiner's office."

"With Pomerance?"

"Yes."

"You mean when I went with Clarice into the kitchen?"

"Uh-huh."

"What'd he say?"

"I asked him if he noticed that sweet smell we talked about."

"Did he notice it too?"

"He said the smell was coming from Reginald's hair. He thought it might be some kind of shampoo."

"Not incense?"

"No."

"Not perfume?"

"Unlikely."

"Pretty intense shampoo if you ask me."

"Did he float any other ideas about the cause of death?"

"I asked him, but he said whatever happened to Reginald was probably an accident. Other than that, he needed more information from an autopsy. If it mattered to anyone. You know…"

Liu pulled out a pad and scribbled a note. "I'm writing myself a note for class," she said, explaining to Mikozy as she wrote. "Pomerance could be saying that he had too many different kinds of information, the kind that jumbled across different categories, or possibly he had too little information to know what he was seeing."

"For me, that's often the case." Mikozy waited till she put the pen down. "I guess the way I would say it if I was teaching your class, and you can write this down, is hell if I know."

They laughed together, playing to close the distance between themselves.

Mikozy pulled into the address Liu had given him. It was one of those '80s garden-style apartments. He could see a small pool about forty feet beyond the wrought-iron fence. His view was partly obscured by oleanders in white bloom. Probably no kids at this place, he thought. Too much liability with these toxic bushes.

Liu hopped out of the car. Before she closed the door, she leaned back into the car. She tossed an envelope onto the passenger seat. "Here's your graduation certificate."

"Does that mean I'm promoted to Clue Analysis 2?" Mikozy was now a convert to continuing education. Eager to learn.

"We'll see about that."

Liu hunched over the open door. Liu and Mikozy looked at each other in silence. Two drunken sailors enjoying their last moment on land.

"I know what you're going to say." Mikozy anticipated her words. "And you know what I'll say back. So let's not say anything and trust our thoughts." Once more Mikozy was trying out his telepathy.

"I like that," Liu said. "But be careful, Mikozy, I have a block on my thoughts. I won't let you read everything just yet."

Mikozy winked a goodbye and headed back to the Italian deli. He wasn't worried about the calories. He'd burn them off this evening.

Chapter 13
MESSED UP

Mikozy couldn't remember if Schmidt still took off on Wednesdays. Everyone staggered their schedules; otherwise policing the streets of LA would be eight hours of paradise followed by sixteen hours of pandemonium. Mikozy wondered whether Schmidt might have changed his routine with the move to the new headquarters. Except that Schmidt said he was going to meet with someone this morning, with a hint at national security. Mikozy took the elevator up to Schmidt's floor and walked over to the western row of offices. He saw Schmidt sitting in his office. The other side of the glass wall. Schmidt did not have his feet propped up, nor was he looking aimlessly out his window at the new skyline. Schmidt was busy thumbing through an itinerary thick with requests.

"You really are here today," Mikozy said as he walked into Schmidt's office.

"Yeah, yeah, and this is still my day off. But I got nominated to do tours for everyone who wants to see the new police center. Must be my personality and good looks."

"I bet." Mikozy waved a piece of paper in front of Schmidt. "By the way, here's my certificate of more and higher learning."

"You're a humble man, Mikozy. You can drop it in my inbox. I've got too much paper to deal with. I know, I know. I should ban paper and lose myself in electronic devices. Must be the addictive feel of paper." Schmidt took a closer look at Mikozy. Red eyes and bags were a sign of sleep deprivation. "You look like shit after it's been stepped on. Go home and get back into bed. By the way, where's your review of the manuscript?"

"You just got me out of bed a few hours ago. That's my problem. I haven't had time to read the book club selection. Or is it the department's reading test for yours truly?"

"Okay. Do the manuscript soon. The deputy inspector is keen on London's book and the attempt to rewrite him. That's what I've been told. So what happened to the kid? How'd that go? What's his name?"

"Hunter, Reginald Hunter."

The telephone rang. Schmidt held up his hand to Mikozy and pointed to a hard-backed wooden chair, rescinding his advice to Mikozy about going home. Mikozy sat.

Schmidt mouthed to Mikozy, "It's Mester."

Mikozy held his head in mock pain. This was not someone Mikozy or Schmidt respected, even though Mester played the game harder than anyone else. That's what new detectives do to prove themselves. And Detective Mester needed some proof.

"Hold a sec, maybe I got something for you," Schmidt said to the telephone.

"You got anything for Mester to do? He's down on Thirteenth Street." Schmidt looked over at Mikozy.

Mikozy debated giving Mester anything. Mikozy thought this might be the way to pay Schmidt back for the continuing ed requirement. He'd throw Mester a bone for Schmidt.

"Ask him if he could go by Galaxy Gems—hold on a moment while I get the telephone number." Mikozy fished for his pocket notepad. "Better yet, I have the address—1105 Eleventh Street."

Schmidt covered the phone, a small frown curled around his mouth. "What case is this?"

"You know, the one you gave me, about the kid who died, Reginald Hunter. Why?" Mikozy was a little surprised at Schmidt's turnaround. First he wanted him to give Mester something to do, anything was more like it, and then Schmidt became the micromanager trying to second-guess his field person.

"I thought it was a simple case and you were done with it. What's this about Galaxy Gems?"

"Nothing much. I'll fill you in after you get Mester off the line. Just confirming what the boy did that day."

"Okay, okay. I don't want you wasting time. We've got other things to do."

"Ask Mester to call 246-3303 and confirm the address on Eleventh Street. I'm not sure of the area code prefix, so he'll have to try them all. Ask him to go by and speak with whoever's in charge about a Reginald Hunter working there. Also check Reginald's former name, Austin Hepworth, if Reginald Hunter comes up a blank. And get the schedule of a Mr. Frederick. That's all he needs to do. I'll go down later and speak to Frederick myself." Schmidt was jotting down the information while Mikozy spoke.

"Listen up, Mester." Schmidt repeated the same information. After a moment he said, "Mester says can do. He'll be coming by after he visits the Galaxy."

"How come Mester's so helpful?"

"Because, Mikozy, he likes to kiss ass." Schmidt probably wrote that in Mester's evaluation. "And he plans to be your captain someday." Schmidt was planning on moving up too. Both Mikozy and Schmidt knew that unless there was an evil god in charge of LA police, Mester would never make captain.

"Okay, Rafe, so tell me what happened to Reginald."

"Like you said, it was a weird situation. The officers on the scene were Lichter and Peabody. You know them?"

"Yep. They were routed through me last night just before I called you."

"Anyway, Reginald is lying inside a ring of burning candles. The boy appears to be deceased. When the paramedics came by, the boy's arm jerked up. Probably a spasm. Who knows? The paramedics never took a close look at him. He probably wasn't dead at the time, but we may never know. His mother—actually his adopted mother; the boy's real name was Austin Hepworth—imagined that there was a ghost at work. So she called him Nathaniel Byron. I know about that superstition from my grand-pop. Same bullshit. Colorful, enough to make you drop a load, but still bullshit. Worse than your leprechaun bullshit."

"Okay, Rafe, skip the parentheticals."

"So one of the paramedics loses it. Panics at the name of Nathaniel Byron. He must have a Haitian import in his family too. Maybe even came over from the island himself. He was probably thinking the boy was dead and the spirit world was moving his arm. Something crazy, I bet. If the boy was still alive, the paramedics screwed up.

"We never got any medical readings on Reginald. All we have is a ghost story. If the medics had just moved him to the hospital, we'd have a medical report now. We'd be in a much better place about how to classify this matter. As it is, we'll have to wait several days until the ME does the autopsy."

"No idea what killed Reginald, or Hepworth, or Byron—whatever his name was?"

"Well, Pomerance was there. And he's from the ME's office, right? Anyway, he talks."

"Lucky you. I lack rapport with Pomerance. He doesn't tell me jack. What did he say?"

"The mother came out with an inhalant, a bronchial dilator. One of those misting devices you stick in your mouth and suck on like it was a joint. Reginald could have had an asthma attack. That's what she says she was thinking. Most people don't know you can OD on the shit. The inhalant wasn't prescribed for the boy. Like I said, the mother did her own guesswork and voilà, accidental death. At least that's Pomerance's opinion. It'll probably be the same coming out of the ME's office later on as the official version. The way his mother was broken up, I'd have to believe it was accidental. Between an accidental OD on the bronchial dilator and the ghost of Nathaniel Byron, I'd take the accident theory."

"Me too. So you don't think it was a street drug OD?"

"I'd like to say no. I didn't see any drug paraphernalia. Garcia was supposed to take a closer look. And we're waiting on the official ME's report."

"Then drugs are out?" Schmidt wanted to nail the alternative down.

"I know what you're thinking. That would be the most logical explanation for kids down on Cuesta. But the mother ran a middle-class home right in the middle of the pit. The whole scene was unreal."

"I bet it was. But you know, whether it was medical or illegal, if the kid overdosed and it was an accident, you don't need to spend your time checking out his work habits."

"Schmitty, you sound just like the kid's mother. If it was Nathaniel Byron that killed him, you don't need to waste your time checking out where he worked." Mikozy's parody blended Clarice with Schmidt. Mikozy asked himself why he should bother as well. Everyone else would shitcan the investigation at this point. Even Schmidt wasn't too happy about Mikozy tracking a loose end. About being too careful when the department was gorged on a cornucopia of crime. Mikozy wondered himself about his own slowness. Slowness might not be the right word, since the case wasn't more than a day old. He was holding on to Reginald's and Clarice's ambitions. Maybe he could find something to make the boy's life meaningful in death. Maybe. Mikozy pushed back the thought about his own strange coming of age into the corner, relegated it to dream time.

There was a knock on Schmidt's door. Mikozy turned around and saw Lieutenant Colonel Robert Craig. The same tiger that had appeared in LC's night-owl lab. Craig walked in and closed the door behind him, offering both his hand and his identification to

Schmidt. Mikozy stood up and walked around to stand at the window behind Schmidt. Mikozy got to see Craig's identification card. Just as LC had read out loud: United States Military Intelligence. Craig stared at Mikozy. A hard stare. Jaws tight. Wrinkles around his eyes stretched thin. This was Mikozy's second appearance as an interloper. Mikozy's lips puckered, a small show of pleasure at being a step ahead of military intelligence. Even if only for the moment. Craig hadn't focused his energies on Mikozy or on what Mikozy was doing. Not yet. Craig could probably turn things upside down for him. Time would always tell.

"Are you the fellow Neill Cream said was coming by?" Schmidt asked bluntly. Mikozy detected Schmidt's concern with the building tours. Tours were paybacks and pay forwards to keep the politicos and their fans happy. These were grip-and-grin affairs that generated votes, which in turn fattened budgets. No one would ever find out about national security or military intelligence. Especially if Craig insisted that it be kept confidential.

"Yes. Cream is a name we use. He was an interesting character. Nasty and brutish. I'm sure Mister"—he looked up at Mikozy but left his name blank—"told you about our little name game."

"The name is Detective Mikozy, Mr. Craig." Mikozy enunciated the way he had been taught in speech class. Schmidt was trying to remember what he had told Mikozy in the middle of last night about coincidences. Schmidt did a half turn in his chair and looked up at Mikozy standing behind him. Eureka flashed on Schmidt's face. He remembered what Mikozy had told him about the coincidence about Cream's name and his inviting Mikozy to join him.

"You two know each other?" Schmidt asked with a ring of true puzzlement as he turned back and studied Craig more closely.

"Only as strangers in the night," Craig remarked.

Several seconds passed in what could be described as negative time. Time was moving, but the participants believed time had stopped, possibly was rolling backward. Craig had wanted the meeting, so it was his responsibility to get time moving forward again.

"I thought my meeting was with you, Captain." Craig avoided Mikozy's eyes. The voice solicited a private audience.

"Maybe it was," Schmidt said. "But Mikozy's here now, so he stays." Schmidt used one of those cop things from the past, or maybe it was from one of those movies about how cops used to be. *It is because it is.* Kind of a brute-reality approach to philosophy. Better than *I think therefore I am.*

"All right." Craig slipped into the chair that Mikozy gave up. "I have a story to tell you. This is a story for your ears only. Understood?"

Mikozy believed everyone had their late-night stories, something to scare one under the covers. Clarice Hunter had her Nathaniel Byron. Mikozy still wrestled with Carlos Laguna. Craig was going to tell them about his own hobgoblin. National security's ghost story. Should be like the one he had heard at camp when he was eleven, listening intently as the fire burned down to its embers. Except this was morning in LA. Mikozy knew Schmidt would like Craig's story. He treasured stories as conversation starters. Schmidt had kept everyone up one night with a wild story about a serial killer who was roaming the nearby woods when the department held a retreat up by Castaic. No one slept that night. Except Schmidt.

Mikozy and Schmidt both nodded. Craig began his story, his voice tempered with the history of pipe smoke and a sweet tobacco blend.

"There's much to be gained from a historical perspective. I won't limit this to an American time frame. As humans, we've been inventive, more so than ants or rats or other animals. Our nests are bigger and taller and prettier than theirs. Maybe we weren't all that different tens of thousands years ago, but I believe that we're doing things quantitatively and qualitatively better today than our competitors. I admit that I have a bias. I am a human. We're still the better species. That's what it's all about. We have to look at earth from the big picture. We're competing with insects, rodents, and other pests for control of the earth. We compete and kill each other too. We are in competition for niches in the environment. Don't get me wrong, I'm not a complete cynic. I believe in a god. But God is a gamesman; he likes to see a good fight. He invented this game called survival of the fittest. Darwin pointed it out to the rest of us. The church mistakenly believed this biological theory was the tool of the antichrist. Well, I must give the church points for creativity: make a world with the forces of good and evil. I'd like to believe that I am more realistic. If I am to believe in God, I would think that he wants to see who's got the biggest balls, the sharpest teeth, and the smartest way to an endgame. God is the survival of the fittest. And those who are good are the ones who survive. Humans have a chance to win, but there's lots of time left in this game of species versus species. And of course, I should mention the viruses, fungi, and other organisms that we have to deal with as well. It would be a shame if the winner turned out to be a virus."

Mikozy hadn't thought of reconciling God and evolution in this way. He couldn't see himself accepting Craig's ingenious parody—a just-so story of how things came to be. Mikozy didn't think Craig even believed his own story. But it was a good hook. Craig smiled to punctuate the transition from the story of God's evolution game to the next historical event. Craig checked to see if Mikozy and Schmidt were still listening.

"Please forgive me, gentlemen, for overlooking the isolated aggression you deal with every day. We're still on the big picture. When men were not intentionally killing themselves in war, they were accidentally destroying themselves. The Romans' use of lead is a good example of mass poisoning, done sufficiently slowly that it weakened the mind far more than it killed the population.

"What I'm interested in is in the field of agrochemicals, generally, but especially what is commonly understood to be pesticides. DDT, for example—or, more properly, dichlorodiphenyltrichloroethane."

Mikozy got to the third syllable of DDT and stopped. Schmidt would have fared no better. Mikozy realized that Craig was taking him and Schmidt for a ride and that neither would be able to figure out the destination. How could they when they couldn't even pronounce the word?

Craig continued while Mikozy fumbled with dichlorodiphenyltrichloroethane. "It was an important discovery in 1939. Not many people realize that we might have lost World War II had it not been for DDT. We were able to operate in the tropics and limit deaths from typhus and malaria. We were able to control the mosquito. Of course, we didn't realize till much later how DDT could kill us as well through long-term use and systemic buildup in our ecosphere.

"What was formerly the Soviet Union secretly continued to use DDT through the late 1980s. Some of my colleagues have argued that the reason for the Soviet collapse was not debt load from military expenditures. Not ethnic disunity. Not the holy grail of capitalism. We would all like to believe that the American way of life played some part. Maybe it was their fascination with becoming like our movie pictures. But it was more likely self-poisoning. Chernobyl was a radioactive self-poisoning and received a lot of media attention. And it was in Ukraine. But their secret use of DDT was extensive. More mundane, a chemical self-poisoning. There's quite a story to their trying to boost their agriculture, but with such stupidity that they were poisoning themselves. They now realize their stupidity."

Craig interrupted himself and leaned forward in his chair as if leaning forward would insure their confidence.

"This story gets more complicated, but neither of us has the time right now. If you like, I can tell you when my class comes up at the War College."

Craig smiled broadly at his self-indulgent humor. Mikozy wasn't interested in continuing education. He had already done his. Maybe, thought Mikozy, he'd volunteer Schmidt.

Craig finally told them what they needed to know.

"We had a death that involved somebody important to us. He was poisoned by a novel chemical."

Mikozy reminded himself that LC had suspected that Craig's group had a dead body of their own. A body that had died from the same chemical as the fulano de tal that had just been brought into the new crypt. Craig had stalled LC. He wasn't willing to trade information with her. Now he was volunteering the information to Schmidt. Mikozy wondered why Craig had decided to take a more open approach now.

"I can't go into why this man is important to us or anything about how this chemical might be used. Suffice it to say that this chemical has an LD between five and fifty," Craig said.

Maybe it was gas. Whatever it was, Mikozy watched Schmidt squirm and pretend he was rubbing against the leather seat. Mikozy hoped it wasn't fatal.

"Excuse me, Mr. Craig, Colonel." Schmidt was trying to get out a sentence but couldn't. Craig was polite. He anticipated Schmidt's question.

"LD is short for lethal dose. A lethal dose of fifty is sufficient to kill 50 percent of the experimental rat or mice sample, whether injected, fed to them, or absorbed through the skin. A lethal dose between five and fifty is considered to be very toxic.

"The dead body we have suggests a very toxic chemical. The way this chemical works represents recent work in pesticides in targeting the mode of release. This is sometimes done by micro-encapsulation of the poison. I don't know if Detective Mikozy told you, but we noticed an inquiry from the Los Angeles medical examiner's office, Dr. Cianfrancuso. Apparently she autopsied a body that was killed by the same poison that had killed our man. Her request triggered our interest. That's why I'm here."

"Why would she make an inquiry to military intelligence? Why would she call you or Cream? Am I missing something?" Schmidt asked.

"I didn't say she called us. Dr. Cianfrancuso's request came over the National Institutes of Health's MEDEX request line. That's run by the National Institutes of Health. I only said that we noticed her request."

"I suppose I don't need to know how you noticed her request." Schmidt spoke diplomatically, taking in the facts, avoiding questions about legality. So Mikozy waited.

"Right, you don't need to know that."

"Well…" Schmidt hesitated and looked quickly over at Mikozy, but he rambled on. "We are working with a new AI system that may be tied into your databases."

Craig paused. "Again, you don't need to know that." He brought his narrative to a close. "I believe Dr. Cream mentioned this concern to you in his telephone call."

Schmidt nodded. Mikozy looked on, curious about where the conversation was going.

"Dr. Cianfrancuso said that you could get everything once her office was finished with the autopsy." Schmidt glanced over again at Mikozy, trying to figure out how much Mikozy knew.

"True enough," Craig said. "But I didn't sense a true spirit of cooperation. We have a legitimate need to compare these two deaths. There could be more dead bodies. I would think this would be of interest to you if mass poisonings occurred in LA."

"She said she would reciprocate, dead body for dead body." Mikozy challenged Craig on his play at cooperation.

"Like I told her, this is military, and it's a one-way street. You don't have to like it. If we found there was a real danger to LA, we would tell her how to deal with the risk at that time. But she doesn't need to know who our dead body is or was." Both men bristled like porcupines at war. Schmidt jumped in to avoid any further friction.

"So what is it you want from us?" Schmidt said.

"I want the full report on this man, including his prints. I suggest extreme caution in lifting his prints. I wouldn't want any of the poison to rub off on anybody just because you were doing us a favor."

Grim, thought Mikozy, this guy is Mr. Grim.

"If we want tissue, bone, organ, or nail samples, I will make a further request."

"Can do," said Schmidt. The meeting was over. Craig came up and shook Schmidt's hand and left him a business card that gave a telephone number where he wanted the report faxed to. Craig did not offer to shake Mikozy's hand, but Mikozy didn't want anything rubbing off on him, so the snub, if that was what it was, was fine with him.

When Craig closed the door and walked far enough away, Mikozy asked, "You don't buy that shit, do you, Schmitty?"

Neither Mikozy nor Schmitty moved. They were both looking at Craig's disappearing image. "Who knows what to believe these days? That war of the species was something else. Wasn't it?" Schmidt went on, "You know, Mikozy, Craig looks like those guys on TV. A real American hero. The right amount of gray at the temples, a nifty tan outfit. Take a hint, Mikozy, and get cleaned up."

Schmidt looked Mikozy over as if he were selling Mikozy a new suit. "Not like you at all. I even have doubts as to whether you're an American."

"Schmidt, don't give me any of your racist horseshit."

On many a late-night stakeout, Mikozy and Schmidt had argued about who was more American than the other.

"I'm more American because I'm more qualified. More qualified means being more American, and anyway, even if I wasn't more qualified, I know more white dicks for getting promoted, which is also an indicator of being more American."

"Wake up, Schmidt, and get with the program, with the new reality. LA is not white. You're a Rip Van Winkle who hasn't woken up to discover that all the movies have been colorized. As for qualifications, they're rigged in favor of people who know the ingredients of Polish sausage instead of chimichangas. It's a culturally biased test. And anyway, they ain't promoting white anymore."

Schmidt tapped the edge of Craig's business card on the desk.

"Okay, American hero, let's cut the guy some slack. Let's assume he's telling us the truth, or at least enough of it so we can believe we're on the same team. Get Craig a copy of the report he wants." Mikozy and Schmidt knew how to roll on the ropes until they figured out what kind of punches were being thrown. "If he comes back for more, we'll take a closer look at him and see what he's doing. Right now, I got too much to do with these tours to be caught up in national security intrigue."

Perkins came up to Schmidt's door, tapping on it with his left hand while opening the door with his right. Perkins recognized Mikozy and nodded a hello. Perkins reported to Schmidt.

"Mester called in. I was trying to transfer the call to you, but you weren't answering."

"Okay, try again." After Perkins walked out, Schmidt admitted to Mikozy, "I was trying out this new device that suppresses the ring." Schmidt wanted to get the final parting line. "I can say I never heard the phone, but then they'd try to get me out on a hearing disability."

Mikozy walked around Schmidt's desk to leave, thinking how he had hooked up his home phone to ring louder rather than softer. Maybe he'd do what Schmidt did if he was foolish enough to become a captain.

"Just a minute, Mikozy. Mester's calling in on your request."

"I admire his speed." To himself, Mikozy said, I hope I admire his results too.

"He said it was hard to find the place." Schmidt wrote down the address for Mikozy. "Mester says they never heard of any of the names you gave him."

Mikozy was annoyed. Reginald's mother had sounded sure that he worked there. "Ask him who he spoke with," Mikozy said.

"Who'd you speak with?" Schmidt said to Mester.

"He said he spoke to a video camera." Schmidt shrugged. He was as puzzled as Mikozy with Mester's report.

"Fuck." That was Mikozy's evaluation of Mester.

"So Mester messed up."

"Don't be so hard on the guy. Maybe the kid never worked there. Maybe he gave his mom a line of bull. Maybe he was shooting up and didn't want her to know he was like all those other kids."

"Too many maybes." Mikozy shrugged. "I got to believe it's not a game the kid was playing on his mother." Mikozy looked intently at Schmidt. He got out of the chair and out of the laid-back Southern California zone.

"I'll call his mother and double-check what she had. And if need be, I'll go out to Galaxy Gems and ask for myself."

"Mikozy, I suggest you wait on that. Maybe the ME will call and tell you the kid overdosed on that asthma stuff like Pomerance said. That'll save you a trip. Won't matter where he worked."

"I suppose." Mikozy and Schmidt thought pretty much alike. Why not write up that Reginald was like everyone else and died like everyone else? Except that Reginald's case had drawn blood. Mikozy remembered pricking his finger once on a thorn while trimming back a bougainvillea vine. Mikozy could file the closing report Schmidt wanted except for the blood on his finger. The boys on Cuesta were like that bougainvillea. Mikozy wasn't surprised that the new headquarters didn't change the depressing aftertaste of death. That was pretty much the same.

Mikozy walked out of Schmidt's office. Schmidt could talk to himself if he chose to come in on his day off. Mikozy decided he preferred thinking about something other than Schmidt or Craig.

They irritated him. They yearned for order when order wasn't possible. They wanted to make things fit even if they bled.

Mikozy tried thinking about Liu. She hadn't seen a real police investigation, not the way everything was laid out this morning. He could take Liu to Galaxy Gems and follow Mester's tracks. Tell Schmidt he was on a training exercise and promoting goodwill for the police force. Schmidt wouldn't complain much. Anyway, if Mester was right, it would be a fast ten minutes, and he could take Liu out to lunch. If Mester was wrong, he could impress her with some artful questioning. Mikozy liked where his daydream was headed.

Mikozy studied the sign posted next to the elevator: "Please walk down two flights or up one flight." Should he or shouldn't he? This was the beginning of a new habit. Whatever he did now, he'd be doing for the next ten years. Mikozy decided to walk down the one flight of stairs to the fourth floor. There were several faxes waiting for him. They sat next to the keyboard. Mikozy was happy that he hadn't been given a laptop computer. Someone would eventually walk off with it. Mikozy read the cover sheet. It was Garcia's and Lichter's reports. Mikozy was in awe of new technology. He was even more amazed that people would actually use it. Silently he blessed Garcia, Lichter, and the fax machine. He scanned Lichter's report and didn't see anything new. He folded Garcia's report and decided he'd look at it on the way over to the fitness class. Mikozy pushed Garcia's report into his hip pocket.

Lichter's report included the 911 report that had Clarice Hunter's telephone number. He punched out her number. While listening to the rings, Mikozy realized that he probably would never dial a number again. Dialing was now only an afterimage of what was once new technology.

"Hello."

"Clarice Hunter?"

"Yes?"

'This is Detective Mikozy. I hope my call is not disturbing you."

"No. Thank you for your consideration, Detective. How may I help you?"

"I wanted to confirm the name of the place Reginald worked at."

"Please wait a moment." After a slight pause, she said, "I have the information here. I wrote down what Reginald told me. He called one day and said that if I needed to reach him, I should call Galaxy Gems and ask for Mr. Frederick. The number is 246-3303."

"I don't want to worry you, but one of our officers stopped by the store, and they didn't know about Reginald or Mr. Frederick."

"I don't understand."

"I don't either. That's why I'm calling you. Just to be sure."

"I am sure. I even called the number about six weeks ago. I wanted Reginald to come home early. I asked for Mr. Frederick, and I spoke with him. He sounded like a very nice man."

"Hmm." Mikozy was more convinced about what Clarice said than about what Mester was told by the video camera. Mikozy wanted to close the loop himself. Mester wouldn't scam him. He'd be too nervous that someone would find out and make a report. He'd never make captain. So Galaxy Gems must be screwing around. Mikozy couldn't think why. Maybe they'd deny Reginald worked there. Clarice said he didn't get paid a regular check. Getting paid in cash suggested tax evasion. But Frederick sounded like someone on the payroll. At least someone who answered the phone number.

Mikozy put that on his mental checklist of things to do. He'd go out to Galaxy Gems tomorrow and find Mr. Frederick. The thought of inviting Liu got better and better. Let her feel the frustration of people lying in your face.

"Detective?"

Mikozy had forgotten he was still talking to Clarice. "I was just thinking about what you said."

"I still don't know why you want to go out there. I told you that Nathaniel Byron killed Reginald. You don't believe me, do you?"

Mikozy was afraid she'd ask him that question. He had believed in Nathaniel Byron at one time. Maybe thirty years ago. He knew the roots that dug down into her memories and into her soul. They were his memories and his soul. Mikozy had pushed them away and into a corner and let them wither. Clarice had done the opposite. She watered these roots and let them blossom.

"I understand what you believe, Mrs. Hunter. We just have to be sure and check everything out." He hoped she would accept his nonanswer. At least for now.

Mikozy said goodbye and filled out a status report. The computer was up and running. He read down the menu selection and pulled up another menu for reports. Pretty soon he wouldn't have a desk full of memos. It'd just be another menu. If he needed to hold on to a hard copy, he'd download all his memos onto a flash drive. That was hard enough for him.

Mikozy was interested in the shared victim file that was supposed to be online in the next month. Mikozy wouldn't even need the faxed reports. All he'd have to do would be to go into the victim menu and look up Reginald Hunter. He could bring up whatever the others put into Reginald's file. And he would type in his own report.

The perps would still be the same perps. The victims would be the same victims.

But the act of reducing clutter was changing. Clutter wouldn't look like clutter anymore. It would be hidden in the mega memories of a hard drive. Mikozy agreed that the transition to chips, magnetic cards and tape, and all the peripheral paraphernalia that came with the computer had been an advance. Even more so with SST and the cloud. But only as an advance over the human foible of clutter. The actual crimes, the criminals, and the victims were pretty much the same. The cops too. Just more or less power.

Mikozy looked at the screen. He started filling in the fields for Reginald. Name, age, address…ta da, ta da. When he came to cause of death, he stopped. He could put in suspected accidental death from overdose, either by legal or illegal drugs. But that would be unfair to Clarice—saying one way or the other that she had failed him or was responsible for his death. Maybe not unfair to Reginald. That was probably how he died, regardless of what Pomerance thought. But Clarice deserved an unsullied memory of Reginald, at least for now. Even inside the computer. She deserved more for her efforts to raise him right. But Mikozy wasn't about to put in voodoo or Nathaniel Byron. Mikozy veered away from superstition. And if he filled in this box with the information he had now, he suspected the case would be automatically closed. The department probably had software programmers embed a code that said case closed on files that listed something other than death by foul means. That would prevent the department's detectives from spending any more time on what its efficiency engineers determined to be excessive effort for crime control in LA.

Suddenly, a small box flickered on the screen. It said "New Homicides." Mikozy knew that if he didn't print out or read this electronic mail, he wouldn't be able to do anything else on his computer. The department thought it important that detectives actually read the list of new homicides. The terminal freeze-up was inserted in each machine. Mikozy took a quick look at the new homicides reported since Sunday in that area of LA. He could have tried a wider search, but that would have been too many to sort through. He saw thirty-three names pop up, including Reginald Hunter's, with his own name at the right of the screen for the lead detective. He sent the file to print, and it would be placed in his mailbox by a clerk. The department had to leave some chores for real people, or else the computer would send thousands more onto the unemployment lines.

As soon as Mikozy had printed the new homicide list, the computer returned to Reginald's file and demanded the next entry. This program had a different lock installed by the department. The department wanted to lock the individual investigative file so that the keyboarder had to type in an explanation of death. These were the life strokes to the statisticians of crime and death. Mikozy had once typed in necrophilia, but the computer spit back, "Necrophilia is unacceptable as a cause of death." There was a wiseass programmer who knew that wiseass cops like Mikozy would try to type mental graffiti in this box. They didn't want cop clutter or cop foolishness. Mikozy called a friend in programming and explained his need to defeat this lock. Sort of like using a heart machine while the medical world was looking for a transplant. Mikozy was told the secret of how to bypass the lock. Mikozy decided Reginald deserved a bypass, at least until the medical examiner did the autopsy. He typed in GOP, which could mean "Go on, palooka" or "Republican" or maybe short for "goop." Whatever it meant to the programmer was fine with Mikozy. As long as he knew the secret word.

Mikozy filed the report and decided it was time to go to the fitness center. He was eager to enter the new age. First a new office—the old desk was not a problem. Then came the new body. Mikozy realized his logic of cause and effect was faulty—a new desk didn't really cause a new body—but after a few hours with Liu, it wouldn't matter.

Mikozy stood up, stretched. A mental bell went off. Maybe his thoughts about Liu reminded him of memories with LC. A quick frown and he picked up the phone. Mikozy punched in LC's office number and heard her voicemail message: "I am not in at the present. If you would like to leave me a message, please wait until the tone, and speak for as long as you like."

"Sure, as long as I like," Mikozy said.

The tone was really a beep. He wished she were more creative, but being a medical examiner had its limitations.

"Listen, LC, this is Mikozy. You'll be getting a Reginald Hunter soon. I assume the crypt always has room for one more. Pomerance was out at his home. His explanation is that Reginald Hunter, actually Austin Hepworth on his birth certificate, died from an overdose on asthma drugs. I'm clinging to the more usual drug overdose. I hope Pomerance is right. I'll call later. Bye."

"Mikozy, Mikozy. Don't hang up." LC shouted into the phone.

"Got it. What's up?"

"I had a quick look at the new body. Reginald Hunter aka Austin Hepworth. Not enough time for a full workup. But you should know where I'm going with this one."

"What? You agree with Pomerance?"

"No. Not really. Looks like another mystery death."

Mikozy looked around to see if anyone could hear LC. Not likely, but even Mikozy worried about the vibes and sounds of new technology.

"Mikozy, another toxic death. I can't say more now."

"Okay, thanks."

Mikozy put down the phone. Always a surprise and he danced off toward the elevator. He hoped no one was looking and noticed the lighthearted step or suspected him of enjoying the day.

On the way into the parking garage, Mikozy heard a "hey, hey, hey." It was Perlmutter returning to his street-corner post.

"You're looking cheery Mikozy," the Perl observed.

Mikozy told himself it didn't matter that the Perl saw him looking happy. After all, the Perl said little else except, "Got two bits for a cup of coffee?"

"You're in luck, Perl, here's a buck." Mikozy hoped that his generosity would suffice. The one good deed that might give him one in return. Enough to brighten up the Perl for the rest of his workday outside police headquarters.

Chapter 14
FITNESS

Liu had said to bring gym clothes. To Mikozy, that meant basketball shorts, a T-shirt, and something to run around the court. He knew his single pair of gym shoes no longer existed in the mind of mass marketers. There still might be tennis shoes touted as high-tech shoes, cross-trainers, high-tops, air cushions, runners, workouts. His single pair would only have to be ready. Liu had said something about machines, yoga, and fitness. His exercise on steps had become a memory. Whatever she wanted shouldn't be too much of a strain on him or his gym shoes. He hoped that any gum on the soles had turned dark so no one would notice. He held his wrinkled shirt and shorts up to his face for a quick smell. The crumpled mustiness shouldn't bother anyone.

Mikozy bounded up the outside stairs in sets of twos to the second floor. He arrived at Liu's door with a stuffed gym bag. Liu opened the door before he pushed the bell. Stunning, she was, giving him second thoughts about how he would look with her when they got to the gym.

"Hi there." Liu beamed. She was already dressed in dazzling, body-hugging Lycra, made up of a black two-piece outfit with a crystal-blue overlay that narrowly defined a supple and beautiful woman. Liu had her hair tied up with a matching blue-and-black hair band. Her fingernails were also crystal blue. Whatever kind of shoes she had on, they were also crystal blue. Mikozy noticed that her socks were white, just peeking over the tops of her shoes. That seemed to be the one concession to the time-honored tradition of making athletic sweat.

"You're looking good," he said. A wise compliment to bless the moment. Mikozy found himself at the edge of excitement. He wanted to tuck it away to avoid getting into a new relationship too soon. He forced himself to think of distractions—freezers, sleds, skis, snow, anything cold. He wanted a face that was impenetrable.

"There's really no place to change at the club unless you're a member. Why don't you suit up here?" Liu suggested.

Mikozy wondered if she'd be shocked by his clothes. He was not Mr. Fashion. He might even be mistaken for Perl's alter ego, a homeless resident, except they would have had the good sense to wear pants rather than his baggy green-and-gray shorts. Then again, Mikozy thought, better she see him now than on the gym floor. She could tell him if the other guys would shame him. She could let him honorably decline the path to fitness.

After a quick change in the bathroom, Mikozy looked at himself in a floor-to-ceiling mirror. Passable, he thought. If she just looked at his hazel-colored eyes and appreciated a face that needed a shave, they would get along well. He was curious and opened her medicine chest. There were two toothbrushes hanging on the inside. That meant a probable man in her life. "That kills desire," he mumbled, knowing it was a lie. Next to several tampons was a small stack of condoms. There was also a supply of various pills, ointments, and perfumes. All of them looked legal. He closed the door on the modern woman. Mikozy let his eyes roam the room. He noticed that it was decorated in much the same way Liu was. The bright colors splashed up and down the wallpaper, onto the shower curtain, and down across the tile floor. He opened the door, relieved that she hadn't carried the floral pattern into the rest of the apartment. He now noticed the walls were more delicate, with bamboo wallpaper and Japanese characters floating along the walls behind lush planters and rattan-style furniture. Things he'd missed when he went into the bathroom. The apartment was all Liu.

"What do all these characters mean?"

"Oh, the kanji? Chinese, Japanese, whatever. I never really learned. Someone told me this is from a famous eighteenth-century poem. I hope so. Could be anything." They both let go of the culture talk.

"How do I look?" Mikozy asked. He'd do better if he was naked. They both knew it. But she was kind.

"Sort of beat up. Have no fear. After ten seconds you'll look like everyone else. Or maybe it's the other way. After ten seconds, everyone will look like you." Liu was upbeat. Mikozy felt upbeat as well.

As they walked down the stairs, Mikozy watched the other tenants splashing in the pool. The city had hundreds of these garden apartments. All suited to the needs of a single's lifestyle.

"Let's take my car," Mikozy said. "It's on the street." Liu nodded, and off they went to get fit.

Mikozy punched the radio to one of the mind-numbing hip-hop, trippy-trap, R and B stations. Its sound blocked out distractions; white noise became black tune making. Liu turned the volume down, pushing back on the pounding interloper, leaving space for herself and Mikozy.

Mikozy's move. "So how was the clue analysis class?"

"Pretty much the same, but a little less excitement."

"How's that?"

"You know"—she emphasized the rest—"you weren't there."

Mikozy laughed at the thought of his being the center of attention. He was glad that was over.

Liu picked up the thread. "How is the investigation going?"

"About Reginald?"

"Well, sure, who else have I seen you with?" Mikozy liked the way Liu exaggerated her words. They defined her enjoyment far more than the Bill Fred song thump-thumping on the radio. He heard another verse even with the volume turned down.

Hip, trip, my name is Fred,
I like lead in my head,
Makes me said, dread, tread, dead.

Mikozy blanked out the nonsense verse. He turned the volume even lower. Liu was waiting for him to answer.

"Actually, our puzzlement is something that would fit in as an example in your class. I like what Clarice, Reginald's mom, was trying to do for him, getting him off the streets and all. I was betting on a drug overdose as the cause of death. That's the way it is on her street. I'm a cynic about it ever changing.

"Then Pomerance found the bottle of theophylline. Within a minute of questioning Clarice, the picture of death was upended. Reginald was still dead as a result of an accident, but not from his sneaking around and getting destroyed by the street scene and the street drugs. Now, according to Pomerance's thinking, it looks like his mom did it. She was so protective, and so ignorant in some ways, that she killed him with her love and her mistaken medical treatment. Pomerance told me—well, you were there too—he told us about how asthmatics can treat themselves into death with stuff like that. That turned my thinking around until I spoke with LC. Pomerance's boss in the ME's office. Now there's something new to think about."

Mikozy turned onto Venture and drove past a row of posh diners, their neon signs proclaiming the glory of cream sauces and nouveau cuisine. Zimmer's pebbled walls with tiny portholes of light were on the corner. He remembered the menu from Zimmer's. There was an insert on light meals. They didn't take out the cream; they only gave you less of it. Mikozy knew the concept was wrong, but everyone wanted to believe, and so they played the game of pretend. LC liked to pretend at Zimmer's and might be there shortly for breakfast. Before her midnight shift.

Liu was quietly absorbing what Mikozy said, almost as if she were memorizing his words for her next lecture. She pulled up her left knee outside the seat belt as she listened. At first Mikozy thought she was resting her chin, but he caught sight of her muscles tightening and releasing. She was already into her warm-ups.

"The way you're talking, Mikozy, sounds as if Pomerance didn't get it right either."

"Yeah, it seems that the medical examiner found traces of a toxic compound in Reginald. There were no street drugs, but he had taken theophylline. It could be a question of which chemical killed him, or which killed him first."

"That's a twist. Surprises everywhere, and make that a wow. What else?"

"My lips are sealed. Actually, I don't know much more right now."

Mikozy smiled at her enthusiasm, her willingness to say what she felt. Mikozy didn't know if he could indulge in a wow. It would sound too much like a golly gee whiz. He was getting old and hoped the exercise would pump new life into him so he could be a young forty-something and say things like wow.

"So that's all of your time?"

"I've been reading a manuscript too. I am not—"

Mikozy didn't get to finish. Liu pointed across the street. "There it is." Mikozy slowed and drifted to the left. When he saw a break in oncoming traffic, he made a precision U-turn, and with luck in the lead, he slipped into a parking space where a van was pulling out.

"We've got a minute or two before the class starts. Let's hurry. I want to show you how to set up." Liu got out of the car and was halfway to the door of the Slim Fitness Center as Mikozy locked the car and set the alarm. He was nervous about leaving his gun in the glove compartment, but it was better than working out with it on his hip. He didn't think others in the gym would appreciate his dancing about with a holstered gun. Cop or no cop.

Mikozy walked past the weight machines, each dedicated to a different set of muscles, some tuned to different routines. Mikozy was tempted to take a tour of his body with these machines. He decided he could wait till after the fitness class. Liu was standing by a glass door, holding it open for Mikozy. As he walked into the room, Mikozy saw about fifty women standing equidistant from each other. There were stacks of boards at the back of the room, holdovers from stepping up and down. Some were clones of Liu, sharply in fashion; others were grandmothers, and a few were in their teens. No men. Except for Mikozy. This struck him as odd, some kind of statistical fluke. He wondered how this could be. It was the second time in as many days that he found himself in an all-women class. First it was about clues; now it was about fitness. Mikozy squirmed, he melted, he froze, he experienced a forgotten range of emotions, mostly hues of embarrassment.

Then he remembered how he was dressed. He checked his shorts, hoping they were longer than they were. He tried to steal a look at his shirt for any holes or tears. He couldn't bring himself to look at the women. He stared at the back of Liu's head as she was saying hi to her friends. This could have been a fashion class, parading with color and neatness. Mikozy's presence was an anti-everything statement. He remembered he was a man and felt foolish about it. He wondered why he didn't feel like a peacock showing off, strutting about.

Liu pulled him further into the room, past stacks of chairs and into the waiting enthusiasts.

"Here, put yourself on this spot." Nothing but a command would have gotten Mikozy to find his place.

Mikozy glanced at the woman nearest him and saw that she was old school with a single mat in front of her. Mikozy thought he should outdo her and reached for an extra number of mats, but Liu caught him midthought and pulled him back.

"It might be better if you don't use any. Let's stick to punching air and posing as lions, dogs, warriors, and trees." Liu was serious. Mikozy stuffed his laugh. She kept her voice low, with Mikozy left to wonder how well he could handle exercising to be fit instead of chasing down ne'er-do-wells.

"Hey, I need this workout."

"Okay," Liu answered. She moved him several feet to make room for Cynthia, who normally stood in his place. Mikozy thought about watching half the women exercise when he realized that the other half would be watching him. He had a fear not unlike what he felt as the roller coaster reached the top of the first hill, that moment of peace before the frenzied descent. Mikozy looked around and was prepared to mouth hellos, but they ignored him. Only a few were talking to each other; most were stretching. Mikozy decided to stretch.

The loud *whump-whump* of a trap tune that Mikozy knew filled the room. Over the music the woman in front yelled out, "Welcome, class. Is everybody ready? Is *everybody* ready? Louder."

The class yelled back. She wore the same Lycra-style outfit that Liu wore but with a T-shirt with the name of the Slim Fitness Center lettered on the back. Her long blond hair was tied up and flopped back in a ponytail.

"I'm Laura." The music thumped and bumped.

"Is there anyone who hasn't been to my class before?" Laura asked the class with her eyes fixed on Mikozy. He wasn't about to admit to being a first-timer. This couldn't be difficult. He was sure he could fake it. He even recognized the song. It was one of those some family-values group wanted to ban. "Let's do it in the alley," the song proclaimed. Mikozy liked the song. He had never paid attention to the words like he was now doing. "Let's do it in the alley, do it, do it, let's do it."

Not that he wanted to, but there was little choice but for Mikozy to pay attention to the overtones while the roar of the beat drummed the words into his heart. The music didn't make him feel sexual. He had to ready himself for fitness. Mikozy wondered about the way the class got itself ready.

Suddenly, everyone was moving. He looked over at Liu. She was in sync with everyone else. He tried to move with her. They were starting with a light aerobic routine, lifting their hands up and over their heads to the left and then to the right. Liu smiled back at Mikozy and then was lost in the pushing and pulling just like everyone else. Mikozy began to merge with the women as he pushed and pulled. He was flying with the music.

Laura counted each repetition.

"And a four, and a three, and a two, and a one. One more time." Every time she hit "three," her voice dropped an octave.

Soon the entire class had warmed up. Laura began guiding the class through knee lifts, leg lifts, and foot kicks. They reached up and punched forward. Skipped to the side. More foot kicks. Mikozy knew he messed up on the syncopated dancing. He bounced into several women. They skirted away before he could apologize. Laura smiled over at Liu, needling her about his macho mistakes. Mikozy knew he had to stay through the end, sweat staining his shirt, pain in unused muscles that would come in the next few days.

The music changed several times, with each song as frenzied as the previous one. Laura admonished them, "Squeeze those butts, tighten those abs." Mikozy felt his abs and butt while he struggled to keep up with the kicks and squats, switching his feet as they lunged forward. They were at it for forty minutes. He needed a rest.

"Get ready for indecision," Laura hollered. "And a four, and a three," the countdown began.

Mikozy knew he was going to be found out. He didn't have any idea what indecision was except that it was likely a new step. Everyone would be in sync except for one person. Mikozy. He couldn't imagine what kind of kick or thrust or squat or lunge would have a name like indecision.

"If you have to leave early, make sure you stretch out and cool down while moving around." Mikozy saw that he was the only one who had stopped, so Laura must be talking to him over the speaker. He threaded his way through the women who were still kicking and punching, waiting for the indecision, pumping their hearts in sync with the music. Mikozy made his way to the weight machines. He sat down and reached to pull on a bar, but he was brusquely warned, "You need a towel to wipe off before using the machine." Mikozy looked at the sweat trickling off his shirt, felt it dripping down his back. The admonishment was well intended. He wouldn't want to use the machine if he had been the next in line after himself. He stood to the side and just watched, just cooling down.

Liu came out the door. The indecision was over. The music still throbbed for those seeking a second set. There was no end to fitness. Liu had the signature sweat stains but didn't appear exhausted.

"How was it?" Liu asked, and answered herself, "Actually I only need to look at you to know how it was for you. Are you surviving?"

"Almost." Mikozy reached as if to wipe himself with his non-existent towel. "How often do you come here?"

"I've been at it for about a year, and just so you don't feel bad, the only time I went for a second set, I was really burned out." Liu took Mikozy's hand and led him away from the machines.

"You need a shower and some relaxation," Liu said.

"Not here, please." Mikozy knew he couldn't wind down here. He didn't even have a towel.

"Okay, where to?" He was too tired to think of the obvious answer. Liu spelled it out for him.

"We'll go back to my place. Your clothes are there."

Mikozy was still following Liu as they walked out into the night and found Mikozy's car exactly where he had left it.

Liu picked up the conversation fragment they'd left off with as they had gone into the gym. "You said something about a manuscript. I cut you off."

"Not important. Not just yet."

"Well, I hope it's more important than the heels I wear in class."

Mikozy flinched. While he was thinking of how to respond, Liu added, "Sometimes my heels feel as if they were made of iron. Makes it hard to walk the walk." She gave a smile and an almost wink. Mikozy kept his silence. Something else was in play.

Mikozy was still trying on what he could say to Liu when they got back to her place. Whatever the words, his desire was narrowly focused. His imagination was energized by the exercise, the fitness, though the words he might speak couldn't find the right balance. The words could end up toppling the Tower of Babel.

She opened the door to her apartment and turned on a single light that glowed just above foyer. She let Mikozy walk in before she closed the door. She stood next to him; a quiet and invisible cloud closed in and around them.

"You can shower first," she said, her voice a whisper. He could feel her breathing.

Her eyes pooled, letting Mikozy sink in. There was no looking away. No small talk. She didn't say anything at all. A wondrous face, lips expectant, hair in wild disarray. The moment called for the impetuous.

"I believe in fairness, not first or seconds," Mikozy said. It could have been said in jest, but he wanted the words to be a bridge. A bridge between two strangers trying to decide not to be strangers any longer. A bridge into torrents of water streaming across the delta. She stepped into Mikozy's gaze. Waiting.

It didn't make any difference what he might say, only what he might do.

"We can shower together." Those weren't the words he had planned, nor words that he could have planned. Spontaneous thoughts ran ahead to the time when words would be forgotten and communication primal. He wanted to touch her, kiss her, and her eyes said, "Come and touch me, come and kiss me."

Liu said nothing. There was nothing to say.

Mikozy reached over to her shoulder straps and pulled them down to her waist. All the while they drank in each other's spirits, pressing closer together. Mikozy pressed his hands against the Lycra over Liu's breasts, she leaning into him. This was the overpowering magic of silence. They kissed. They kissed softly. They moved apart and back again, dragged by looking into each other, his passion demanding to be consumed, consummated. He moved his hands down her back and inside her thighs. She watched him touching her, kissing him in sweet reward.

Liu reached up and pulled down her suit to her waist. Mikozy looked down at her breasts and watched her hands reach across to his own, pulling them over her breasts. Her kisses became more demanding, arms wrapped around Mikozy, absorbing his passion.

Mikozy felt her hands move down his back. Gently, gently, she turned her fingernails inward and let them send tickling waves into his presence. Her hands followed the same path Mikozy traveled on her, touching inside his thighs, squeezing the fire spreading through his body.

"Harder, Liu." Mikozy felt hands that were soft, gentle, and hard, fingernails digging and pulling. His fingers rubbed her nipples, hardening as he squeezed in the way Liu held him.

Mikozy pulled Liu's outfit down to the floor, letting his kisses surround her. Liu kicked off her shoes and hopped around, trying to kick off her bodysuit. Mikozy followed in kind, lifting her off the floor, taking her to the couch. Through the kisses and caresses, he heard Liu ask, "Mikozy?"

He looked at her as she lay back. He kissed her, not wanting to say anything or hear anything. Words could only evaporate his desire.

"We're the intelligent ones. Right?" Soft words that he couldn't push away.

"Yes."

"Remember the call for safe sex?" Liu asked, smiling and caressing his hair.

"You mean we should use a condom?" Mikozy remembered looking in her medicine chest, his hopes still high.

"More than that. We both need to take an STD test first. There are no guarantees, but we wouldn't want to hurt each other by mistake."

Mikozy was angry at the world for changing, baking out the passion with cautionary tales. Why this virtue signal for them? Why this medical directive for indulging in so innocent a pleasure? The moment had been beautiful except for having to think, for having to lose interest, for having to lose the passion. Whatever he grasped for, it wouldn't change anything. He would get those tests, use a condom, whatever Liu asked. He wanted to be with her.

"You're right, Liu, I could never hurt you."

"Or I you." She kissed him, a way of punctuating the end of this moment. He kissed her back. She pulled him down to her and pushed his hand into her wetness. Liu was not selfish and reached into him, letting his desire fall all about her.

Mikozy and Liu showered together. They congratulated themselves on doing good for Southern California by practicing water conservation. What water fell nourished their hopes while avoiding the hard questions of how society ought to work. Later, when they got into bed and closed their eyes, Mikozy listened to Liu's soft breathing, conjuring the possibilities of love and desire. The phone rang. It was on the bed stand next to him. Mikozy pulled it up and pushed it under his pillow to deaden the sound. He didn't want to wake Liu up. The phone turned into a message. "Hi," said the woman. The voice was friendly, a person who knew Liu well. "I won't be home tonight." She hung up.

He wondered about the call, sure that he knew the voice. Mikozy slept long into the night.

Mikozy was up first and put on his clothes while Liu watched. He knew she was watching him. He finished and sat on a small chair by the window. He waited for her to get up, imagining a far prettier sight.

"You have to get up sometime."

"You'll have to wait a few minutes more." Liu was smiling with obvious pleasure in the moment.

Perhaps it was the late-night call, his mind roaming the unconscious wilderness. He asked out of curiosity, "Where's Jane?"

"Jane? What do you know about Jane?" Liu sounded anxious. Mikozy hadn't meant it that way.

"I just said Jane. It could be anybody. Remember when I called and somebody else answered? The same person called last night and left a message. I assume it was a woman."

"Why assume anything? Maybe I swing both ways." Liu got up and walked to the bathroom, out of the sunlight that streamed through the window and splashed over Mikozy's back. She walked slowly, just to make her naked appearance the high point in response to Mikozy's questions. She listened to the message on the answering machine. "Hi, I won't be home tonight."

"Yes, it's Jane." Liu played the empress without any clothes, intoned with an imperious voice. "She stays here occasionally when she gets mad at her boyfriend." Liu posed for a second and hopped into the bathroom.

They played word toss with each other, determined to avoid edges of irritation. He only slipped once. Why mention Jane at all?

Mikozy fished around in his pockets while he waited for Liu to return. He found Garcia's report on Reginald, which he had stuffed into his pocket the day before. Mikozy remembered he had planned to read this before the fitness class.

Most of Garcia's report was a rehash of what they had talked about. Mikozy flipped to the last page and noticed Garcia's comments on his search of Reginald's room.

> Search of victim's room did not uncover any drug paraphernalia, but there was one glassine envelope with suspect substance (probably meth). Found some clothes that were wrapped up in brown paper that had a little note jotted on it. "Deliver to Galaxy. F." Nothing found in pockets except for a cash receipt for a plane ticket from Western Air (no destination listed). Difficult to read the name of the passenger. Sent envelope to lab for analysis of contents and prints. Plane ticket in file forwarded to you.

Mikozy read the note again. This made a connection between Reginald and Galaxy. The F could mean Frederick. The lab analysis should show what the drug was and if there were any prints. Mikozy was not surprised to discover a drug connection, but at the same time, he was surprised by all the care Reginald appeared to be getting from Clarice. But if there was no drug paraphernalia, and if the autopsy showed zilch on illegal drugs, then what? Maybe someone was dropping a bad rap on Reginald. Maybe Reginald had no idea about the envelope in the package. Mikozy knew he could invent other fanciful scenarios. He needed more facts. He might have to check with Western for the destination of the plans if Mr. Frederick decided to leave town. Whatever the situation, Mikozy thought that checking Galaxy Gems out might be more than a useful exercise to go through with Liu. Another pair of eyes, now that he'd put her in the loop. Mikozy thought Reginald's death might have had him stumble onto some drug network. Mikozy would see what he would see, which was his version of laissez-faire police work.

Liu stepped out of the bathroom. She looked like she enjoyed dancing about without any clothes on. It didn't appear she was rushing to get dressed. Mikozy assumed she wanted him frustrated, but what would be the point? Their unknown sexual history was a wall neither could climb. He didn't know his own history, since it was tied into the secrets that his lovers kept.

He stood up and walked around the bed to the dresser, watching Liu as she fished around for a bra and panties.

"Liu, if you have some time, I'd like to take you with me on a follow-up to Reginald's investigation."

"I can't go like this."

"Maybe if you put on some socks." Back and forth, back and forth they played while Liu put together a foxy outfit and modeled her face with blush, liner, and lipstick.

"So you'll come?" He wished her to say yes. He was beginning to see a brightness to his days that he hadn't seen since LC had moved on. Mikozy ran his fingers down Liu's back as she reached up to pull on a white cotton dress peppered with black willows. She leaned and purred. She turned and half sat on the dresser, her hands on the dresser top, her eyes quizzing Mikozy.

"I thought Reginald's case would be closed. Didn't Pomerance say it was an accident?"

"Pomerance is good, and he may be right. But he left himself a shimmy hole. If the ME confirms that it is something else, he can shimmy out and say, 'Hey, it was only a hunch.' Anyway, I think it would be interesting to go out to Galaxy Gems and see what they have to say about Reginald. Even if there's nothing there, I'll get to treat you to lunch." He didn't mention Garcia's report. He would let her know later, when it would sound more like a surprise.

"Okay, Mikozy, you're on. I just need to find some clothes. These won't do at all. Not if we are going on an investigation." She looked just fine to Mikozy, but she was already taking off her dress and pulling out a pair of yellow silk slacks. Mikozy didn't mind waiting for Liu. Not at all.

Chapter 15
GALAXY GEMS

Mikozy coasted down Eleventh Street past Georgia, taking another swig of fresh-squeezed orange juice. Mikozy and Liu had bought a runner's breakfast from a roving push-cart, like many Angelenos who were desperate to combine transportation and digestion. Liu was sitting in the back seat taking a last bite of what was once a cinnamon bagel. She had her notes spread out in preparation for the next section of her clue analysis class.

Mikozy occasionally looked at her in his rear mirror, spending more time concentrating on the store signs, which sometimes proclaimed the best deals, sometimes the best proprietors. As he went past Bixel, he drove past 1103 Eleventh and then past 1107 Eleventh. There was no 1105. That was the address he'd gotten from the telephone operator and the same one he'd given to the new guy, Detective Mester.

Mikozy drove past four jewelry stores, a stationery store, and a store announcing that the Chinese taco was coming soon.

This was a small street. None of the buildings were more than two stories high, and all had large brick facades that had been painted uniformly brown. Mikozy decided to park and ask.

"Are we here?" Liu asked as the car pulled over to the curb. She did not look up from her notes.

"I'm not sure. I'll be right back and let you know." Mikozy went into the stationer's. The sign said "Best Stationary." Mikozy wondered if the owner had misspelled his store's name on purpose to test the intelligence of his customers. The store sported two coin-fed copiers in front. The arrays of colored paper stock, vertically stacked from floor to ceiling, gave off more energy than a double rainbow. The iridescent hues looked like they had been mixed in at random. A door stood open at the end of the rows of paper. Mikozy noticed some broken wallboard littering an up staircase just inside the door.

"May I be of service?" A man in his thirties who apparently had forgotten to shave for several days singsonged his question. He wore an open-neck white shirt that probably hadn't been washed in a month. He was reading a well-worn magazine.

Even with the magazine upside down, Mikozy could see a picture of some twenty young boys holding an assortment of assault rifles up in the air.

Mikozy heard bumping and crashing sounds from above the ceiling. Mikozy looked up and then noticed a wave of dust rolling down the staircase and out the door.

"You got large rats?"

The clerk looked up also. Both of them saw the ceiling bounce with another crash.

"I am told that one of the stores farther down the street needed some extra space, and the owner leased our upstairs so they could use pretty much the entire block."

"Doesn't the dust bother you?" Mikozy said, lifting his chin as if he were pointing over to the doorway.

The clerk shrugged the kind of shrug that said, "I asked and I was told not to bother and I said to myself who am I to ask the owner whether I should leave the door open or closed."

Mikozy had heard of building up, but building horizontally could have its advantages, especially if they forgot to tell the city's building department. No permits meant the city was blind to improvements. It also meant an inability of taxing agencies to exact their due.

The clerk put his magazine down and walked over to Mikozy. Even without asking his question again, his demeanor asked what kind of service he could provide Mikozy.

"I'm looking for 1105 Eleventh Street," Mikozy said.

"This is 1113 Eleventh Street." The clerk's voice was monotone and his face was even more so.

"Yes, I can see that from the sign over the door. I thought you might know which of your neighbors would be 1105."

The man now had zero interest in Mikozy. Mikozy thought the man also had zero interest in his store.

"I'm not from around here, and I have nothing to do with the other stores."

There was another crash from upstairs. The clerk walked back over to where he had put his magazine down and picked it up, letting his action complete the thought that he had done what was expected and would do no more.

Mikozy did an about-face and decided to try the string of jewelry stores. He decided to try Mester to see if he had had any luck. Mester picked up on the first ring. "Hello, Mester here."

"This is Mikozy. I'm down at 1113 Eleventh Street. I'm not having any success in finding 1105. Were you here?"

"Oh yes. I walked down the street, and nobody knew nothing. So I sent you a text message to that effect. Anything else? Schmidt gave me another thing to check out."

Mikozy saw no point in continuing his conversation with Mester. He had already proved his value—nobody knew nothing. "Got it." Mikozy disconnected.

Mikozy fared no better at any of the next three. He passed by Liu, still with her face down to her notes, showing a studied intent that would have been deaf and blind to riots, storms, and other disasters. Mikozy walked past the Sentra and came to the last jewelry store, Uptown Jewelers.

The sign above Uptown Jewelers was of moderate interest to Mikozy, as it had a rope border that was more reminiscent of stores with a harbor location. The store's image was definitely not uptown. He looked into the street-side window. The show-cases were sparse and suggested a store on the edge of failure. Hardly any product compared to the other stores on the block, if not in value, at least in the variety of their display. From what he could see, the most expensive items appeared to be opals. No diamonds, no emeralds. Nobody even bothered to stand by the cases. There was a small metal bell with a sign, "Ring me." Above the bell was the checking-you-out camera. Mikozy rang the bell.

"Can I help you?"

Mikozy couldn't see anybody inside the store that went with the voice. Mikozy noticed a reflection at the other end of the store near the top of a mint-green column.

"Can I help you?" the voice rasped again. Mikozy guessed it to be a woman in her fifties that had been smoking for the last forty.

Mikozy looked into the lens. "I'm looking for 1105 Eleventh."

"This is it."

"The street number says 1103 down here."

"That's downstairs. Upstairs is 1105. We don't have a sepa-rate sign for ourselves. What can I do for you?"

"You can ring me in. Let me get my—" He hesitated. Mikozy realized that introducing Liu as a professor would confuse the situation. So he said, "Partner."

Mikozy walked back to the car and opened the back door. Liu was sitting cross-legged with her mind focused on her class in three hours.

"What do you think about a warm-up exercise for my class—like something about Nathaniel Byron and a ghost killing?" Liu said as she looked up and saw the invitation to get out of the car. "I wouldn't be mentioning his actual name. Just what his mother thought, a spirited ghost. Byron."

Liu shifted her focus from her notes to Mikozy. She poked around the well behind the front seat searching for her shoes. "Of course," she added, "I'd let them know after a while about the accidental overdose, assuming Pomerance is right."

Mikozy was amused with Liu playing at the edges of their deal. She could observe, but she was supposed to keep it quiet for now. Mikozy could sympathize with Liu since he too was spending more time on Reginald's death than the assignment required. The note Garcia had found was suggestive, but didn't prove anybody at Galaxy Gems knew Reginald. Even if he could get someone there to admit that they knew Reginald, so what? Maybe Liu's talking about Reginald's death would help put it in perspective, which was okay with Mikozy, and might help explain how such a tragic death could occur.

"I wouldn't use his example just yet, whether we call him Reginald Hunter, Nathaniel Byron, or something else," Mikozy said. "It is interesting. Maybe hold off and come back to it later." Mikozy hung over the top of the car looking down at Liu. He didn't want to come on strong with Liu and interrupt his entanglement with her. At the same time, he didn't want to blur his identity as the detective in charge of this investigation.

"First, they'd think you were bonkers. It is a strange case. Then you would feel you had to defend yourself by talking about Reginald. And that's not in the cards for now, at least not until the ME signs the death certificate."

"Okay, Mikozy. I just find it so interesting."

Liu got out and then leaned back into the car to hide the note cards under the passenger seat.

"Let's go," Liu said. "I'm ready."

She looked around and asked, "Is this the place where he worked?"

"That's what we'll find out." Mikozy realized he hadn't paid attention when she dressed and came out of the apartment with him and even when she got into the back seat of the car. It dawned on him that she had put on the same outfit she'd worn at his class. The yellow slacks and red silk blouse.

Partner? he thought to himself.

Yes, indeed, an LA cop.

Maybe her outfit was so garish that no one would think to ask to see her badge.

Mikozy and Liu walked over to Uptown Jewelers. Mikozy rang the bell again, while Liu canvased the showcased jewelry.

"Not much here," Liu said to Mikozy.

"We're still in the process of moving, honey," the voice crackled.

Liu was startled. Mikozy had forgotten to warn Liu about the video monitor and remote voice apparatus. Liu moved away from the partly filled jewelry case that featured mostly chains and bracelets to another one closer to Mikozy with a single box of charms.

"Just a ghost, Liu," Mikozy joked to Liu.

He looked up at the video monitor and asked to be let in. Another voice overrode the disembodied woman.

"Can I help you?" This time a man. Mikozy couldn't resist the idea of this being the remake of *The Wizard of Oz*. He would spin out this story for Liu over lunch. There were a lot of possibilities.

Mikozy looked directly into the lens, hoping to keep their interest on him and not on Liu.

"I'm Detective Mikozy. I'd like to ask you a few questions about Reginald Hunter."

There was a several-second delay. Mikozy didn't know if the pair hidden behind their electronic Cyclops eye were making hand signals to each other or were debating his request with the sound off.

"There was another detective, Harry Mester, here yesterday. That's what his card says. I already told him we don't know any Reginald Hunter." That was the wizard speaking through the not-quite-hidden camera.

"I know what you told Detective Mester. I'm following up some loose ends."

"Which are…?" That was the wicked witch, her voice rasping and coughing. There must be two of them upstairs.

Mikozy had to get behind the electronic eye—either that or poke it out. There was no way that either one was going to tell him anything without a direct face-to-face encounter of the first kind. For all he knew, they could really be in New York.

"I'd prefer to talk with you face to face, Mister—?"

No Name did not give Mikozy his name. "Do you have a warrant, Detective?"

Mikozy was becoming more interested in this place the more they tried to play keep-away with him. Their game had probably worked with Harry Mester. All he had to do was ask the question and get an answer. Okay for Harry.

Whatever answer they wanted to give him was not going to work for Mikozy. Liu didn't seem satisfied either as she poked him in the back.

"I have something better than a warrant, Mr. Faceless. I have a friend who works with the labor commissioner's office and another friend with immigration and another friend with franchise tax. I think they'd all be interested in doing an audit on this business. I'm sure one of them would find something when they examined your books and whatever you have upstairs."

Another silence. Then a buzzing sound.

"Come on up, Detective." Ms. Raspy Voice said the magic words. "The door is behind the camera you were looking at."

Mikozy walked around the column and pushed the wall panel open. If he hadn't been told, he would never have suspected this was a door. It was a narrow staircase. The walls were bright white. The recessed lighting was also bright. The bright light effect was disorienting. Liu walked in behind Mikozy, her hand grabbing the back of Mikozy's jacket to keep her balance.

The door at the top of the staircase was made of metal. No handles and no keyholes. The door opened. Mikozy could see about five or six women all involved in what looked like bookkeeping and paper shuffling. The wizard waved Mikozy and Liu in, and he quickly shut the door behind them.

"I apologize for the mystery. My name is Carlos Morales." There was no accent. There was no Latin image. Just some forty-something, portly accountant. He had blue eyes and salt-and-pepper hair.

"Not my idea of a Morales," Mikozy said. Or a wizard, he said to himself.

"No, I suppose not. My family moved from Czechoslovakia to the New World. The name is actually Borodin on my father's birth certificate." Morales motioned for Mikozy and Liu to join him in his office past the bookkeepers and up another narrow staircase. The bookkeepers all watched Liu. She was far more appealing to watch than Mikozy.

"So where is Galaxy Gems?"

"Uptown Jewelers is our street name. Galaxy Gems is a holding company. It's all quite legit. Or so our lawyers tell us," Morales answered, radiating a gentleman's smile that said, "See what you can do with that, asshole."

"Strange background, strange company, and strange building," Mikozy said.

"Not so strange, considering these times. We all move around and get a little mixed up, wouldn't you say?"

"Perhaps, depending on what kind of moving and mixing you mean," Mikozy answered.

"Detective, even you must admit that this is a dangerous neighborhood."

Mikozy knew LA, and this was definitely not a dangerous neighborhood. At least not to Mikozy, and he wasn't a holding company.

"How much is your stock worth downstairs?"

Morales smiled. "Maybe $5,000 tops."

"And no attendant?" Mikozy punctured the argument that Morales was concerned about the neighborhood.

"It's a new concept in marketing." Morales wore a wolf's grin that said, "Okay, so this is not a dangerous neighborhood. Can you put me in jail for saying that it is?" Morales continued to grin.

A workman in overalls, who really looked like a Morales, popped out from behind a plastic tarp and poked his head into the room. "Ya terminamos pa' esta noche."

Morales nodded. They were finished for the day.

"A little room alteration," Morales explained to Mikozy.

They both knew it was a lie. Mikozy imagined the alteration: a room as big as half the block if the clerk at the stationer's was right. Mikozy could make out the gutted shell and the rows of studs beyond the plastic tarps draped behind Morales, which probably framed the walls of an office that had previously occupied the space. Mikozy wondered why the poorest store on the block needed so much space—so much hidden space, he corrected himself. They didn't need the space for their dinky gemstones.

The preliminaries were over.

"I'd like to have the real version about Reginald Hunter."

Morales shrugged innocently. Everybody seemed to shrug at Mikozy, especially when they didn't want to give him an answer.

Morales looked back and forth from Mikozy to Liu, with a question of curiosity about Liu obvious on his face.

"Mester told me this was a homicide investigation. Is that the purpose of your questions?" Morales's question was precise. This was a snake looking to disappear under a low-hanging branch, dense with summer leaves after a heavy rain. Morales wanted to know what the truth would do to him and his operation. Would the truth continue to slither around like a bigger snake and eat him when he was unawares? Or would the snake slither away with Mikozy?

"That's all this is, Morales."

"All right, then that's what we'll talk about."

Morales picked up some business cards in his hand and played with them. Mikozy thought they might be his worry beads or maybe his lawyer's card.

"You have to understand, Detective, Reginald was not on the books. He was a messenger for us. He did odd jobs, and we'd pay him in cash. It's not something we want to advertise. Others use illegal aliens. At least we were using an American. Diversity, too."

Mikozy sensed he was about to say something else about Reginald, but nothing was said. Probably just as well.

"Yeah, right. So who is this Mr. Frederick Reginald worked for?"

"Reginald worked for me. There's no Mr. Frederick," Morales insisted.

"His mom said there was a Frederick here. Do I have to get a labor audit to find out who your employees are?"

Morales looked visibly sickened. He paced back and forth behind his desk, actually saying, "Dios mio." Mikozy thought Morales would have used more potent language.

"Morales, I'm not asking for the secret of life. Just who Frederick is."

"I tell you and nobody else." Morales walked around the desk and pulled Mikozy close to him. Morales smelled of fear.

He spoke into Mikozy's ear. Mikozy felt the force and wetness of Morales. Liu was surprised with Morales's action, and she leaned in toward him trying to hear what he was saying to Mikozy. "Frederick is Freddy Panarese." Morales gave Liu an angry look with a touch of the evil eye as well to keep her away.

"Oh, shit," Mikozy said. He thought, Doper and number one asshole. Spindle. The syndicate. I must be in the heart of darkness. Galaxy Gems, my ass. Mikozy knew Morales wouldn't say anything about who he was connected with, what he was doing, or anything about anything. What the hell was he thinking? This was probably a Mob operation. He'd have to settle for some way to talk to Freddy, ask him about Reginald and maybe about the note and the package Garcia had found.

"Where can I find him now?" Mikozy asked.

"What do you mean?" Morales shifted emotional gears, booming at Mikozy. "Don't you read the fucking newspapers? He's dead. Muerto. Fini."

Mikozy was surprised. Freddy was dead, and he'd missed the news. Mikozy had been so caught up with Reginald and Liu that he hadn't been paying attention to anything else. Except that damn manuscript. Mikozy didn't like being caught off guard.

Morales took Mikozy's surprise as an opening and glared at Mikozy.

"Get out of here. I've got nothing more for you."

Mikozy started to turn to go out. He turned back, unwinding like a snapped spring, and sucker punched Morales in the gut, knocking the wind out of Morales. Morales doubled over. Mikozy had to take the fire out of Morales. There was no way that Mikozy was going to leave with half a story, even if he wasn't certain what story he was looking for. And there was no way that Morales would say anything else without being leveraged. This was the only leverage Mikozy had. Morales tried to stand. He was uncertain but absent his bluster.

"Listen, amigo, we'll forget Freddy. I want to know Reginald's schedule on Monday."

Morales caught his breath and winced in anticipation of another punch. He was still bent over and trying to balance himself against the edge of his desk. Liu looked like she'd been hit too. She wasn't prepared for tearing information out of people.

"Excuse me, I'm going to find a bathroom." Liu walked out of the room. Mikozy could hear her go down the stairs. Mikozy and Morales were alone.

"This is chickenshit," Morales said. "Reginald wasn't doing anything illegal."

"I bet Freddy was."

"Look, Mikozy, you can beat up on me now. But you keep this shit up and you can bet your sweet ass that you'll get a hot poker shoved way up. You want to know about Freddy, you can read the newspapers." Morales was able to talk again, but he still hadn't been able to stand up straight.

"You threatening me, Morales?" Mikozy leaned in toward Morales to get close to him. Narrowing the distance increased the threat of pain, which Mikozy was determined to make a one-way street, from Mikozy to Morales.

"I never threaten cops. I just give them free advice."

Seemed like they were drawing to a standoff. Neither was eager to budge.

"So why not just tell me about Reginald?"

"That's not a problem." Morales finally stood up. He brushed his hair back with his hand. "Talk to Cindi out front, but talk to her alone, away from the others. And don't ask me about Freddy again, because I already talked to the feds. You get my lawyer if you want to talk about Freddy."

Mikozy was pissed. Two deaths already. He began to doubt that Reginald's death had been a medical accident. And LC said she had to take a deep dive on a full autopsy for Reginald. There was too much happening. Freddy Panarese was dead, and the feds had already talked to Morales. Probably didn't tell them much anyway. What the hell was going down?

"One last question."

"I'm not talking about Freddy."

"I'm only interested in Reginald. Did the feds ask you about Reginald?"

"No. What the fuck would the feds want with the kid? He's nothing to them."

Morales looked exhausted. He sat down and looked like he was casting about his desk for a spell to make Mikozy disappear. Mikozy left Morales sorting through papers and walked back down the narrow steps and on through the hallway. Only one woman looked up at him. She was about forty, blond hair except for the roots. That's probably Cindi, the wicked witch with the gravel voice, thought Mikozy.

"Are you Cindi?"

"Yes, what can I do you for?" The gravel kicked about the words while Cindi picked up a cigarette and dragged another mouthful of smoke.

Mikozy walked past the other women. Cindi followed him into the corner. They were sheltered by a row of gunmetal-gray cabinets. Mikozy looked around but didn't see Liu.

"Morales said you could give me Reginald's schedule for Monday."

"I can do that."

Cindi was the last of the peroxide blondes, a real dame, crusty when she had to be and with a kind streak looking for an opportunity.

"You know, he was a sweet kid. We were all rooting for him," her two-pack-a-day voice said.

"Rooting for what?"

"I know many of the boys on Cuesta. Reginald was different."

Mikozy waited for her to continue. He wasn't disappointed.

"We thought he could work for us in the office someday. Get him some honest money. And we could use a black face here." She smiled, a badge of American virtue. Cindi would have made a great social worker, thought Mikozy. If only Clarice knew that someone down on Eleventh Street had also been intent on helping Reginald out. Bizarre, he thought. The other kids were probably pushing drugs for Galaxy Gems. Mikozy wondered what Reginald was delivering.

"Let's see." Cindi reached into the bottom drawer of a file cabinet and pulled out a loose-leaf binder. She turned the pages and finally landed on the day Mikozy was interested in.

"Reginald had four deliveries that day. Three were at places you'd like to know." Cindi winked. She was obviously not about to tell Mikozy who or where the recipients were.

"Do you want to tell me what he was delivering?"

"Come on, Detective, you know we only deliver jewelry."

"Okay. You were saying, the fourth delivery?"

"That was to Freddy."

"Where was the delivery made?"

"Out at LAX."

"And he was delivering jewelry to Freddy?" Mikozy dripped with sarcasm. He thought he had all the information he was going to get. That was a throwaway question.

"Actually, no. It was kind of funny in a way. Freddy was having a wig delivered."

"Why so funny?"

"I don't know when you saw Freddy last. But he didn't have a hair problem."

"And it doesn't bother you that Freddy wanted a wig delivered to the airport?" Mikozy felt his patience slowly disappearing.

"Hey, no skin off my back. Not now. Freddy's dead."

"Do you know where Reginald was supposed to meet Freddy?"

"I lost the message slip. But I seem to recall something about Freddy going to a barber." Cindi reached for a cigarette and didn't give a damn about the sign on the wall that said it was a nonsmoking office.

"Maybe that's why I thought it was so funny," Cindi said.

Mikozy wondered about Morales's being so uptight about talking about Freddy, while Cindi was more open to talking about him. Maybe it didn't matter what either said about Freddy since he was dead, except that Morales might have had more at stake in what Freddy was doing, whatever it was.

"You didn't happen to share your thoughts about Freddy's wig with anyone else?"

"Me? No way. I let Freddy be. Freddy and I got along just fine."

Mikozy wondered whether the feds had questioned Cindi about this.

Liu's heels clicked down the hallway. She was putting some-thing into her pants pocket. Her color was back, and she car-ried herself as if she had won a minor battle. Lady triumphant. Mikozy admired her.

"Well, Mikozy, I hope you got what you came for," Liu said.

Now it was Mikozy's turn to shrug. Everybody was commu-nicating with shrugs.

They walked back down the bright stairway and out beyond the video's reach. As they reached the door, Morales's voice bellowed down into the store, "Take care of yourself outside, Detective. This is a dangerous neighborhood."

Mikozy slammed the door behind him. Liu looked around as if she were taking Morales's advice.

"Do you always hit your witnesses or slam doors?" It sound-ed as if she was chastising him. As if he could be a detective by asking rote questions and getting rote answers. Sometimes you had to dig in unpleasant ways.

"I can understand police violence if someone is trying to harm somebody, but Morales was just standing there. I couldn't believe you'd do that." Liu's eyes were as penetrating as her words. Both were intended to wound him, and they did. Mikozy was quiet. He didn't know what to say. He looked back into Liu's eyes and didn't say anything. He could feel this situation pushing them to the end of each other's tether. They would tear apart unless they reeled the other back in.

"I suppose you might think of some clues as jackrabbits hiding in the brush. You'll never find them unless you tromp around and scare them out. You can quote me in Advanced Clue Analysis." Mikozy returned to sarcasm. It was his default com-munication. They looked at each other. It was clear that they weren't about to agree on tactics.

Mikozy knew Liu wasn't happy with him. He wasn't happy with himself either. He liked to be rough in private. No one look-ing over his shoulder. But the moment had demanded it. There wasn't going to be another opportunity, at least not one that came so easily.

Mikozy realized that had been the wrong thing to say, at least if he wanted to continue seeing Liu. He made an effort to apologize.

"I'm sorry about that." Mikozy told half a truth, relying on an indefinite and evasive "that." Whatever that was, he had to be sorry about it. He was sorrier that Liu had to be there to witness that, though he wasn't really sorry about what he'd done.

"I was feeling sorry for Clarice and didn't want her Reginald forgotten or lost in Morales's lack of concern. Detective Mester apparently missed everything." He hoped that explanation would satisfy Liu.

Liu didn't ask Mikozy any more about Morales. Her mind seemed to be racing on to something else. Her emotional keel had switched as well. Mikozy couldn't do that. He was still knuckle dragging his feelings out of Galaxy Gems.

Mikozy and Liu walked up to the Sentra. He opened the door for Liu and left it open as she got in.

"A second, Liu. I want to see something." She shrugged and bent down to pull out her notes, while Mikozy walked back along the street to the corner of Bixel and Eleventh. This was the same street he and Schmidt had patrolled about fifteen years earlier. They'd had the night shift and looked for signs of illegal entry. One night Mikozy thought he saw something suspicious back down on Georgia. The next day he decided to visit the store owners to see how secure their stores were and how much time he and Schmidt would need to get over here if a call went out.

Mikozy spoke to most of the owners in the neighborhood and saw the kind of security that was going into these stores. The days before motion detectors, pads, sound and smoke detectors. If the glass broke, the alarm went off. If the door was open, the current was interrupted, and the alarm went off. Simple. Things were changing inside these buildings. He wouldn't have seen it just driving down the street.

Uptown Jewelers was somewhat different. Mikozy walked back into Best Stationary. The clerk looked up and back down again at his magazine while Mikozy walked through the aisles, looking around for any new alarm devices. Mikozy didn't see anything new, not even a smoke detector. The owner was probably hoping the building would catch fire and no one would arrive too quickly.

Mikozy walked back out of Best Stationary and down to his car.

"I need to get over to my class," Liu said as Mikozy came back to the car. Mikozy didn't sense any edginess, but she was switching her schedule, which he anticipated as negative news.

"It's still early. What about lunch? I promised."

"Not for me, thanks. I just realized how much I still have to do for my class. You know how I like to set things up. That takes time. Maybe in a day or so."

Mikozy looked away, accepted her change of heart. He couldn't sidetrack her, and there was no point in wasting his or her emotional energy. She was probably pissed at seeing detective work in real time, something more than a classroom tease.

"Will Jane be taking your class again?" Mikozy asked, partly in jest and partly recalling the sting of Liu's preparedness.

"Of course, Mikozy, you know my little secret. You don't tell on me, and I won't tell on you." She looked around as if someone was listening in. "Mikozy, we need to have one of those deep philosophical talks. If we were teenagers, it would be about the existence of an afterlife. Those were airhead thoughts and emotional hand-wringing. Now it is about how we are going to negotiate this moment. The school of hard knocks, things I can't teach in class. What we can only whisper about. We can't have that talk here, but it's important."

Liu had a smile on her face. If she had had wrinkles, they would have been thoughtful. As for what was going on in her soul, Mikozy couldn't read that either. He supposed this was a safe conspiracy, since neither had done anything wrong. Harmless so far, he repeated to himself as he drove her over to her class.

Before she got out of the car, Mikozy punctuated the day's ride-along. "You're right. We need one of those adventures in climbing up and down the pillars of truth telling." Liu winked. It seemed like a knowing goodbye, riding a promise.

Now, with time on hand since he was not lunching with Liu, he wondered if Inspector Tomlinson expected him to check in about the manuscript she had sent him to review. He decided to dial up Detective Mester and ask him to check around.

"Mester here."

"I have a favor to ask of you."

"Okay. What do you need? I'm down here at the office."

"I'd like you to go upstairs and see if Inspector Tomlinson is in."

"Is there anything I should know? Someone might ask what a newbie like me wants with Tomlinson."

"Then you're the right person to go up and check."

"I see, the guy who doesn't know better."

"You could say that." Mikozy was pleased that Mester was willing to play along. "Just go up and see if she's in. That shouldn't be too hard."

"I suppose not. Talk to you in five or ten, or if I'm confiscated, bail me out."

Mester was off to the elevator. He got off the elevator and found he was alone. He thought there might be a conference room full of gold shields. Nothing. Silence. He saw a windowed door with a nameplate with the inspector's name inscribed in gold. More nothing except a desk. And a laptop. He dialed the last number. That was Mikozy's mobile.

"Mikozy. I'm up here right outside her door."

"Why are you whispering?"

"Because no one is here. I want to leave the same impression. Whispering."

"So what do you see? Is she in?"

"No. No one is around. She's not in. Just a desk. And a laptop. Anything else you need?"

"I owe you, Mester. Good work. Stay invisible."

"Hey, Mikozy."

"What's up?"

"I can see a reflection off the outside window. Let me see if I can take a picture."

Mikozy waited. Mester was showing some initiative. Probably nothing here to see. This was something that Mikozy might do. Look around for options when options needed to be ferreted out.

"Mikozy. Hey, I think I got something."

"What are you seeing, Mester?"

"I opened up the photo and played around with the contrast and the lighting. I got something, but it doesn't make much sense to me."

"What's that?"

"The laptop screen is mostly whited out. Nothing I can do there. At least not on this phone. But there was a fragment. It says *Iron hee*. I'm not sure what an *Iron hee* is."

Mikozy muttered to himself, "I know what a hee is. The damn heel."

"Mester. You listening?"

"Yeah, still here. What's up?"

"Just get your ass out of there. Don't talk to anyone. This is not your game." Mikozy might have been too strong in messaging Mester to leave well enough alone. Even though Mikozy had sent him there. Mester shouldn't be trapped in Mikozy's assignment just because he was being smart and enterprising.

"Sure. Do you want a copy of the photo? I can message it to you."

Mikozy messaged a thought to himself: Dumb kid. No, not dumb, innocent.

"No. Hey, Mester. Just delete the photo. I'm not kidding. This is on me. Let it go and get out of there."

Mikozy saw he still had time to read the manuscript before Tomlinson got back and started to wonder about her literary critic. Now there was this annoying flicker of light on Tomlinson's laptop. Maybe it was just a memo to herself to check on Mikozy's book review. If it was just a book review. Maybe he needed to get into Tomlinson's office and take a closer look at that laptop. They said that curiosity killed the cat. But they also said that satisfaction brought it back. Mikozy needed to bring that cat back.

Chapter 16
IRON HEEL REDUX

Mikozy got home. It was time to pick up the manuscript and end his procrastination. Mikozy looked at the pages bound together with twine. Even the twine was more inspiring than the pages it held. The memo from Deputy Chief Inspector Michelle Tomlinson rested on top. That was where he'd left it. That was where he hoped to leave it, but the assignment hadn't changed. There it was. "Detective Mikozy. It has come to our attention that your background will help us evaluate this manuscript." Each of those words weighed heavy. Anvils pulling him down onto the couch, where he would try to pull apart the pages. If ever there was a "why me" moment, this was it.

Mikozy looked under the memo from Tomlinson. He scanned Tomlinson's initial thoughts, skipping to what looked like the key paragraphs. They were marked in red.

Was this a thoughtful appropriation of Jack London's 1907 book *The Iron Heel*? Or something else?

The original book was cast as the Everhard manuscript, found many years later…

Do we have anything in these texts that justifies their fears? Ones that London imagined and the ones from this rewriting of London? The Everhards were London's characters that feared the aristocracy. They saw an aristocracy determined to hold onto its wealth. In turn, London saw the aristocracy fearing people like the Everhards. The Everhards were Jack London's stand-ins, his puppets. London and his Everhards were workingman intellectuals. They were socialists who were inspired by solidarity. That solidarity would lead to taking away power from the corporate kings and their armies of bureaucrats. That's what the aristocracy feared. This is how they were imagined in *The Iron Heel*. London's novel pictures their fear and how they would act against the socialists, how the capitalist aristocrats would crush them with government power. This new manuscript—Todd's version of *The Iron Heel* turns Jack London on his head. Instead of capital wealth and the aristocracy controlling the government, it is now the socialists controlling the government and, with that, controlling the daily lives of individuals. Now the socialists own the armies of bureaucrats. Todd paints a different fear, one in which an authoritarian socialist ideology replaces the earlier one that troubled London. In both scenarios, individuality and daily life get crushed. Now it is the socialists instead of the aristocracy doing the crushing. Two questions: Did this upside-down version of *The Iron Heel* get Todd killed? And is this fantasy?

Another way of asking this question, beyond a fictional reset of history, is whether there is anything here that would lead police to an actual crime. What should we make of what is assumed to be Todd's skeletal remains?

Mikozy never saw himself sporting a literary goatee or smoking a pipeful of wisdom. He was a badge, an investigator. He trailed bodies, bullets, assaults, not metaphors, nor the rhetoric of history. The last time Mikozy wrote about a book, it was Edgar Allan Poe's *The Narrative of Arthur Gordon Pym of Nantucket*. Mikozy had a hazy memory of Pym rowing off into a fog shrouding the South Pole. This seemed to be more of the same. Mikozy had gotten a B- on his Pym essay, the same grade the instructor gave to every essay. Mikozy got a C in the class. He had failed to attend every class and suffered the demerit.

He leaned over and picked up his landline, his antique communicator. Mikozy dialed LC, his friend, sometime lover, and deputy medical examiner. He heard her picking up.

"You have a minute?"

"Rafael, is this a quickie? I'm about to go into an autopsy."

"That's all I need. You remember Patricia Todd? The one connected to a manuscript?"

"I don't know what you're talking about. What? Who? When?"

"I don't know much about it either. I got a memo from Tomlinson to look at a manuscript. Supposedly, it was in the clutches of skeletal remains, presumably a Patricia Todd. I thought you might know about it."

"Oh, yeah, that one. I got a brief message from Tomlinson's office that said there were some remains that were being held at your own lab. They were not sent here. Kind of weird."

"So you don't know anything more about what they found?"

"No. Check with Mendoza. He does all the oddball stuff that isn't sent here."

"Is that the one and only Ernesto Mendoza? The one we call El Flaco?"

"Yeah. That's the guy. He almost didn't get hired because he's so tall. He might not have been able to get under one of the new hoods we were experimenting with for autopsies. I never understood why they called him skinny. I would have called him the tall one. El Alto."

"I could go over there. I never gave that much thought. But why have another lab?"

"Well, maybe funding. Another way to hide department moneys. Who knows? Maybe a way to cover up what I won't."

The conversation dropped into silence.

"Rafael, you could go over to see Mendoza. Maybe he'll talk to you. You're not the competition that I seem to be."

"That's an interesting work-around to the truth. I'll see what his schedule looks like."

"Mikozy. I gotta go. A body awaits me." LC disconnected.

Mikozy let the handset rest in his hand while he thought about calling Mendoza. Maybe it was too early to call. Tomlinson might wonder why he was asking about the bones when he was assigned the manuscript. It was another one of those mysteries in the bureaucratic web and the chain of command, crosscutting alliances, secrets over clarity. Mikozy let the handset drop back into its cradle. He could call Mendoza another time.

He needed to delve into Jack London's mindset of an iron heel crushing the socialist upwelling. Then he could move on to Patricia Todd's revisiting the iron heel. A revisiting that might have gotten her killed. The image of a tiger walked through his field of vision. In the background, Lieutenant Colonel Robert Craig traipsed in tandem with the beast. They seemed aware of who their prey was. Strange connections? Maybe, maybe not.

Mikozy decided he should get an idea of what the original book was about. He was sure it would be in the online world library. That was the source of nearly all written work. There would always be those fugitive articles, books and whatnot that weren't uploaded to the internet library. Not everyone could get complete access, but detectives had an upgrade that gave them permission to wander through most of the library. Mikozy was aware that there were yet higher access passes, something like being able to get access to the Vatican's secret collections.

Mikozy typed in his login name and password. He brought up London's book. He scanned through the table of contents. There was an interesting chapter on the mathematics of a dream. He read a few pages. Mikozy realized that London was obsessed with the working class, what he called labor, and its competition with the ownership of industry, what he called the trusts. Mikozy remembered his high school history class and learning about the Marxist vision that had inspired many in the early 1900s. That was before World War I. Mikozy checked the copyright date for *The Iron Heel*. It was 1907.

London was obsessed with the labor and trusts conflict. This wasn't the London he'd read in school; that was about dog fighting dog, about not being able to light a match in a snowbound wilderness. This was about man fighting man. He looked at a page Tomlinson had singled out.

> "But suppose the socialists win in this battle over the ownership of the machines and the world?" Mr. Kowalt asked.
> "Then," Ernest answered—

Mikozy flipped to the early pages and saw that Ernest was Ernest Everhard, the husband of the writer Avis Everhard, also the hero and the book's socialist intellectual.

> —"you, and capital, and all of us, will be crushed under the iron heel of despotism as relentless and terrible as any despotism that has blackened the pages of the history of men. That will be a good name for that despotism, the Iron Heel."

Mikozy noticed a change in the typeface. He went to another online site. He went to scan other editions. The next two resonated with London's writing, but he couldn't find the same text in them. That puzzled Mikozy. Perhaps another edition. Perhaps a friendly hacker. It didn't really matter since his assignment was really about messaging, not authorship.

> "But the trusts are already crushing us," Mr. Kowalt protested. "They are taking our jobs away from us, they

are driving us into the slums, they are making us work for starvation wages."

"That is true," Ernest admitted. "But the trusts are not yet the Iron Heel. They are only the forerunners of it. The Iron Heel will be a far more terrible thing than the trusts. It will be a government of the few, by the few, for the few. It will be a government of the plutocrats, the capitalists, the exploiters, the oppressors. It will be a government of the Iron Heel."

From what he knew about that era, it sounded about right. Maybe a historian would have added some tweaks. He decided to skip around the book. He wanted to see what London saw. Not just the fears, but what London imagined would happen.

Mikozy found the font reverting to the earlier style. He located this section in the book.

This behavior on the part of the press was nothing new, Ernest told us. It was the custom, he said, to send reporters to all the socialist meetings for the express purpose of misreporting and distorting what was said, in order to frighten the middle class away from any possible affiliation with the proletariat.

Mikozy smiled. The news still had its slant. Just like then. Just like always. He skipped a bit further.

"Big things are happening secretly all around us. We can feel them. We do not know what they are, but they are there. The whole fabric of society is a-tremble with them. Don't ask me. I don't know myself. But out of this flux of society something is about to crystallize. It is crystallizing now. The suppression of this book is a precipitation. How many books have been suppressed? We haven't the least idea. We are in the dark. We have no way of learning. Watch out for the next suppression of the socialist press and socialist publishing houses. I'm afraid it's coming. We are going to be throttled."

With that kind of paranoia, London must have a rousing ending, Mikozy thought. What would London do with this facing off of labor and the control of the trusts, the oligarchy? Mikozy got up from the couch and went to get a beer, reading while he walked over to the refrigerator. This was the last section, "The Terrorists."

And through it all moved the Iron Heel, impassive and deliberate, shaking up the whole fabric of the social structure in its search for the comrades, combing out the Mercenaries, the labor castes, and all its secret services, punishing without mercy and without malice, suffering in silence all retaliations that were made upon it, and filling the gaps in its fighting line as fast as they appeared

The book ended midsentence, alluding to the magnitude of the task. Mikozy double-checked the last page, and it did end midsentence. This was when Avis Everhard had supposedly hidden her manuscript. There was a footnote etched in by later historians as imagined by London. That was during the time of the Brotherhood of Man, the year 419 BOM. It said that Avis's husband, Ernest, had been executed seven centuries earlier.

Mikozy turned off his computer, leaving the online world library and *The Iron Heel* to bounce around in his thoughts. Great writing. He would have liked to have said that he was savoring a fine wine before the final swallow, but he was drinking a beer. He thought about the world London had pictured. History hadn't been kind to London's imagination. Not exactly. London had failed to predict the success of the Russian revolution. The czar and his family had been executed. The socialists, or whatever the label was, had prevailed over the Iron Heel. They had imposed their own repression.

Mikozy remembered his high school teacher jeering at the way history unfolded. Mr. Rudolf, thinning gray hair, always with a jacket and tie and a white shirt. "Something important," Mr. Rudolf would announce. And Mikozy thought that if we weren't trying to goad him, they might have listened. They had rolled marbles between the aisle of fold-up seats. Rudolf would rant, sputter, demanding attention. We weren't kind; we'd be laughing, Mikozy remembered. Sometimes we'd listen. One time it was about the world wars. There was one, and then there was two. We remembered that, one and two. "Students, you will be reading about the world wars that destroyed much of the world outside North and South America. We sent soldiers, but we weren't invaded. Only Pearl Harbor." And he went on and on. "Old world imperialism gave way to new ways of imperialism. Instead of naked capitalism, there was naked communist imperialism. And all you do is drink Coke and watch TV." Shaming didn't carry us the way Rudolf had wanted. Not then.

Mikozy put the book down and thought some more about Mr. Rudolf and about Jack London. To no one in the room, beer in hand, Mikozy gave his postsecondary speech. "Maybe Rudolf simplified history too much, but it was high school. He left me with the idea that the world could turn upside down."

Mikozy looked around his room. Put his beer down. The comfort of modern America. Down the hallway, framed photos of unknown landscapes, a closet of jackets and baseball caps, and looking further down he could see the edge of his bedroom door. He had all these things. Heat when he wanted it; cold air too. He wondered if Jack London could have imagined his life and the lives of millions living well. This wasn't the Iron Heel. It had turned the many poor into a consumer buffet. Not for all, not for that damn Perlmutter, the never-take-a-bath man out in front of police central. London's world had swung upside down for many. Not a capitalist oligarchy anymore. Mikozy thought about Mr. Rudolf's communist oligarchy. There were new players in town. But why would it matter? Mikozy held up his telephone handset, saying, "I have a landline, I have the world library online. And I have a beer. Do I really care about who is in charge?"

Mikozy knew that Schmidt and Inspector Tomlinson would keep after him, grinding away as an in-house millstone, until he came up with some earthy comments. He could do that; after all, he'd scraped by with a C in his one literature class. Maybe that was why he had been assigned to look through the Todd version of *The Iron Heel*. Nobody too smart, not too much insight. Only mindful of the police slogan: just the facts. Maybe they were right.

Mikozy picked up the Todd manuscript and leafed through the pages. He wanted to find the same section Todd had found in the original and then rewritten. Had Todd gotten in trouble with this rewrite? A copyright issue? Was there a Jack London fanatic crazed by this rewrite? Mikozy found a page in the Todd manuscript that resembled London's Everhard original.

"But suppose the unions win in this battle over the ownership of the machines and the world?" Mr. Kowalt asked. "Then," Ernest answered, "you, and capital, and all of us, will be crushed under the iron heel of union despotism as relentless and terrible as any despotism that has blackened the pages of the history of men. That will be a good name for that despotism, the Iron Heel."

"But the unions are already crushing us," Mr. Kowalt protested. "They are taking our jobs away from us, they are driving us into the slums, they are making us work for starvation wages."

"That is true," Ernest admitted. "But the unions are not yet the Iron Heel. They are only the forerunners of it. The Iron Heel will be a far more terrible thing than the unions. It will be a government of the few, by the few, for the few. It will be a government of the union bosses, the socialist plutocrats, the cowed capitalists, the exploiters, and the marginalized oppressors. It will be a government of the Iron Heel."

Mikozy was surprised. Todd had done little to rewrite London's original book. These were mostly substitutes. Where London's Iron Heel was built by the trusts and the capitalists, Todd had transformed it into an Iron Heel of unions and socialists. New memes replacing old memes. Todd's version left intact the conspiracy and the way it crushed the ordinary person, the independent worker, and the small business. Just a different set of actors with a different set of justifications. Hardly novel. Oppression was oppression. Why would it bother anyone? Even a London fanatic.

Mikozy went back to London's book. He landed on a subversive page. Maybe this was what had gotten Todd in trouble. London had laid out the revolution's plan.

Again, the font shift. Now the online editions played upon each other. Mikozy thought about the possibility that one version was an extension of London's book with the help of a chatbot. But why bother with a book over a century old?

"But how can the Iron Heel come into existence?" Mr. Kowalt asked. "How can it be established?"

"The Iron Heel will come into existence when the trusts have consolidated their power and overthrown the democratic government," Ernest answered. "The trusts will then be the government, and they will rule with an iron hand. They will crush all opposition, they will suppress all dissent, they will enslave the workers, they will rob the people. The Iron Heel will be a government of terror and oppression."

"But surely the people will not stand for such a government," Mr. Kowalt protested. "Surely they will rise up and overthrow it."

"The people will be helpless," Ernest said. "The trusts will have all the power, and the people will have none. The trusts will have the army, the navy, the police, the courts, the prisons. The people will have nothing but their bare hands. The people will be helpless, and the Iron Heel will crush them."

"But what can we do?" Mr. Kowalt asked. "How can we stop the Iron Heel?"

"There is only one way to stop the Iron Heel," Ernest said. "The workers must unite and overthrow the trusts. The workers must take control of the means of production, and they must establish a socialist government. Only then will the people be free from the tyranny of the Iron Heel."

"But how can the workers and small businesses unite?" Mr. Kowalt asked. "The trusts are too powerful, and the workers and small businesses are too divided."

"The workers and small businesses will unite when they realize that they have nothing to lose but their chains," Ernest said. "They will unite when they realize that they are all in the same boat, and that they must sink or swim together. They will unite when they realize that the only way to be free is to overthrow the trusts and establish a socialist government."

Todd had kept to the same plan as the online version. Instead of the trusts being too powerful now, it was the unions. The unions imposed the chains, and the independent workers needed to take off those chains and establish a capitalist government. Or something else? Mikozy wanted to avoid the literal tit-for-tat reversal even if Todd's version would suggest as much. Mikozy flipped back to Todd's version. He jumped to the substituted lines.

"The independents and small-business owners will unite when they realize that they have nothing to lose but their chains," Ernest said. "They will unite when they realize that they are all in the same boat, and that they must sink or swim together. They will unite when they realize that the only way to be free is to overthrow the unions and establish a newly imagined government."

Here there was a new twist. Something that even Todd couldn't predict, but she could at least sketch an alternative. Not a return to a capitalist government but a newly imagined one. Still, it required upsetting the existing government, and no government would give up its chains willingly. Maybe not chains, but the manner of control. Mikozy caught himself thinking back to his high school teacher. Mr. Rudolf had said the same things. Perhaps he was in the wrong profession.

If Schmitty hadn't given him this manuscript, if Tomlinson hadn't written a memo to him, Mikozy would have wondered whether this was a joke. A literary assignment. And it wasn't difficult to figure out what this manuscript was, even for a C student.

Mikozy drifted a bit further. There it was. The pebble in the shoe that would enrage anyone about to walk, let alone run.

Todd had leaped into the call to arms that would circulate on social media and tantalize all the aggrieved souls. A motive. If someone read her manuscript. Or listened to her own storytelling.

"A revolution is not only possible, but inevitable," Ernest said. "The unions are driving the independent workers and small-business owners to desperation, and they will eventually rise up and overthrow the unions and their government allies. The revolution will be bloody, but it will be victorious. The independent workers and small-business owners will establish a newly imagined government, and they will be free from the tyranny of the Iron Heel."

Mikozy considered getting up and getting another beer. Maybe two. And some chips. Instead he reached for his keys and decided to go down to headquarters. There was little point in writing an analysis of the London book, whether it was the original or the variations Mikozy had studied or the Todd manuscript, not if he wanted to understand what this assignment was really about. Were there even bones residing in Mendoza's lab? Maybe there was no Patricia Todd. Maybe this was just a test, maybe a pretext to terminate him. Lots of ifs, and lots of wicked outcomes. Mikozy wasn't happy with any of these unknowns.

It was time to go and see Deputy Chief Inspector Michelle Tomlinson. Mikozy also remembered his plans with Liu, and Liu getting out of his car and going off to class. Too much beer, too much London, too much Todd. Mikozy was bothered by Morales and what was going on at Galaxy Gems. He wanted to know more about what Reginald had been doing on his last run. A wig for Panarese? At LAX? Headquarters could wait. Maybe another trip to Galaxy Gems. Maybe a night-owl visit. Mikozy's plate was overflowing.

He thought about visiting Mendoza too. Skinny Mendoza, tall Mendoza, whatever the nickname. That body was a loose end. It was getting complicated. Too much to fit into his schedule. Mikozy decided to give Perkins a call. He'd want in on this case, and Schmidt wouldn't have a problem. After all, if Perkins was sitting at Mikozy's desk, he should do something to earn that privilege. For as long as Perkins had it, which wouldn't be for much longer.

Mikozy scanned his contacts and found Perkins's number. He wouldn't be answering, so he could drop the request onto his voicemail. "Hey, Perk, this is Mikozy, your favorite desk companion. I have a favor. Something that would boost your ratings in the department. Maybe not. Here's a simple request. Can you go to Ernesto Mendoza's lab—you know the guy, El Flaco—and ask him about Patricia Todd? Isn't Mendoza's lab doing her au-topsy? Most dead bodies go over to the medical examiner's lab, but this one seems to have been sidetracked to Mendoza's lab. I don't need a complete report, but maybe you can get me the highlights. The name is Todd, Patricia Todd, T-O-D-D. Thanks, Perk. I owe you one."

Chapter 17
RIPTIDE

Mikozy called his voicemail. He had to punch in about fifteen numbers, exotic codes to defeat hackers. What if Mikozy died? Somebody had to pick up his mail. Schmidt knew all the codes, and he'd pick up Mikozy's messages. The only message on his voicemail was from the crime lab saying that they had completed the analysis of the packet Sargeant Garcia had sent over, and it would be on Mikozy's desk by 5:00 p.m. No other messages meant that Mikozy was off the leash. Schmidt hadn't gotten around to giving him another assignment, and Liu was an unknown. Mikozy wondered if he should still go and get a STD test. Was it pointless now or not? I'll go, as if Liu could hear him.

Mikozy thought about his plan to make an after-hours visit to Galaxy Gems. He didn't have a warrant to do a search for the list of names to identify the people Reginald had visited on his last day of work. He knew he couldn't get one. There wasn't enough probable cause to show that Galaxy Gems had any information that would help explain the Reginald-and-Freddy connection and how they had both died. Mikozy would have to go on a fishing expedition. A reason for him to be nervous. Mikozy was dimly aware of a flickering neon-orange sign when he closed his eyes that said no fishing allowed.

This was a problem for all those invested in finding the forensic truth. America was built atop earlier indigenous cultures. Just as other cultures built atop others who had come before.

This culture was forged out of fierce individualism long before Mikozy's ancestors arrived. That America had built its settlements at the edge of the Atlantic, placed by waters that culminated in an undercurrent of constitutional guarantees. A reaction to a British monarchy. Now, whoever dared to go into or come out of the sea would have to risk the waves that boomed down along the beach as they were meant to do, a strong constitutional riptide trying to suck incautious fishermen into deep bottom currents.

Unfortunately, Mikozy observed, the country was beset with parasites and predators that hid in the sea. The police were not able to carry their harpoons without being able to declare in advance that the shape they saw coursing through the water was a tangible danger. Judges became the lifeguards that would pull a fisherman out of the raging sea only if he had first gotten permission to go in and fish. Other countries didn't have the rip-and-pull surf, nor black-robed lifeguards. Theirs was a country that had muted individualism, favoring obedience to warlords, mullahs, kings, and presidents with supreme powers. The police could swim, fish, or tread water whenever they wanted. They didn't need warrants, and they could let their uncooperative witnesses slip into the waters unseen, unheard, and unknown. The desaparecidos, those that the police state had disappeared. It didn't matter to them since it would always be 1984. That was the fear that warrants were supposed to fence in.

Mikozy didn't believe it had to be that way. The police, even with the booming surf trumpeting individuals' rights, should be able to fish these waters for the men of war and street gangstas, for the predators and parasites. At least those police who had an innate spirit for the law and were kind of heart. Like Mikozy. How could he hunt if he wasn't allowed in the water when he was ready and able?

Mikozy rarely used the word stupid, but whenever he ran up to the beach and dwelled upon the pounding waves, he screamed stupid. He screamed naïve. He screamed feckless. Especially when he wanted to go fishing. Mikozy sucked in the salty LA air that blew in from the Pacific. He was about to risk going into the riptide. He knew that no judge would ever save him if he went in without permission and began to drown. "You're on your own, sonny," were the words that would skim like pebbles bouncing from wave to wave. But Mikozy became a riptide swimmer. He had the spirit and the heart. The year was never 1984 for him. Mikozy set his clock for ten that night and went to bed. He wanted to be rested for the riptide in the Galaxy.

Mikozy got ready for his night out. He pulled out clothes that fit the night. The online catalog said the color was wheat. Mikozy had grown up calling it brown. He pulled on his brown socks and jeans, running shoes and jacket. Mikozy collected different shades of baseball caps. He wore the brown one to complete his evening outfit.

Mikozy approved of the stubble on his face and said to the mirror on his bathroom wall, "Clothes make this man invisible."

Mikozy took the Harbor Freeway south to the Pico exit and made a wide turn around the convention center. The afternoon breeze had already died. It had cleansed LA of the nastier acid air that choked the day. Mikozy found the night air cool. The thought of going into the Galaxy tempered the night air shadowing Mikozy.

Mikozy went up Figueroa and made a left onto Eleventh Street, drifting down two blocks to Georgia looking for a place to park. If he needed to make a fast exit, his car would be facing the freeway ramp, and he could be flying north within seconds. As he parked, Mikozy recalled an article he'd read about chess that claimed the best chess players could think seven moves ahead. Mikozy couldn't see himself ever becoming a grand master or a master of any game that required being more than two steps ahead of the other player. Mikozy calculated his odds and went for the stealth move, and if that failed, he liked to have a simple backup. That was Mikozy's plan. Here he was, one stealth move into the Galaxy and one move for a quick retreat. He hoped that was enough for tonight. The air dropped another two degrees as Mikozy got out of the Sentra.

The street had already died. Mikozy walked along down Eleventh, up to Bixel. Mikozy heard distant traffic noise from Figueroa. Here, it was silent, punctuated by the occasional light and the occasional sound. All the stores had rusted orange gates pulled across large glass windows, a metallic symbol of when people had crowded the streets with brutish tempers. Not yet the stampeding wild boar.

Best Stationary was dark inside, with a single light over the entry. Each of the other stores on the block mimicked the same nighttime glow. There was enough light to show a cruising patrol car if anyone was trying to get inside. Mikozy had been on this same patrol with Schmidt many years ago. He knew the only way in tonight would be through a side door. Mikozy walked over to Best and glanced up and down the street. He wasn't interested in walking the block. This place wasn't being staked out, and there weren't any night-owl neighbors peeking through curtains with binoculars. It was only Mikozy, at least for now, and now was when he had to get into the store.

Mikozy slipped on disposable paper moccasins and thin latex gloves as he stood outside the side door. Mikozy had brought along some specialty tools for the evening, including a singular device he had taken from a burglar. It not only located the magnets behind the door; it also induced sufficient current to trick the door into thinking it was still closed after the door had been opened. Mikozy quickly set up the small box that housed the magnet delocking device and with a set of universal keys. He opened the door and was inside Best's within twenty seconds. Mikozy decided to take a chance that no one would be coming by and left the box right at the foot of the door.

He was inside the stairwell that he had seen leading upstairs when he'd talked to the clerk earlier about the construction on the second floor. Mikozy pulled out his flashlight and aimed it up the staircase. He saw a fine white dust coating the stairs and tracing out large indecipherable footprints. The building was solid, and the stairs did not creak. Mikozy pulled the plastic visqueen sheeting to the side and walked into the area being remodeled. Morales's room extension required the windows to be shuttered and guarded from the light, which made it easy for Mikozy to use his flashlight without fear that a passerby might see him threading his way along the second floor. He used his left hand to balance and navigate, while he followed the beam of light through the studs and sheets of wallboard waiting to be tacked up.

The dimensions of the new area were impressive, especially since the once separate rooms now gave way to a dramatic loft. Mikozy saw a wide three-story shaft that looked like it was intended to house a service elevator that would descend below the street level and probably burrow underground to another location. This was a smart way to get large items in and out of the loft without being seen from the street. A stakeout team would never know who or what was coming or going. Mikozy wished he had brought a low-light camera with him. His phone camera was barely sufficient. He'd have a hard time convincing anybody this existed without a decent picture. That was about all anybody believed nowadays.

Mikozy jerked his left hand back as he felt something move over it. A rat scampered twenty feet ahead and peered back with tiny red eyes into the flashlight's glare. Mikozy waited to calm down and pushed himself around the second row of visqueen and into Morales's office. Mikozy didn't know what kind of silent alarms this part of the building might have and decided to pass up the opportunity to browse through Morales's desk. Mikozy figured he'd have just enough time to find Cindi's files and Reginald's schedule for Monday. Then he'd retreat as fast as he could.

The narrow passageway leading to Cindi's files was more claustrophobic in the dark. Mikozy crept after the light he threw down on the floor. As he came down the stairs from Morales's office, Mikozy realized there was a false landing. There was extra ceiling space above the building's upper floor. Or floors? He couldn't tell. It was the stuff that future expeditions would be made of. Engineering for hideaways. Hiding people, hiding drugs, hiding stolen goods, hiding terrorist cells.

Mikozy walked over to the steel-gray cabinet that Cindi had pulled her loose-leaf binder from. He pulled open the same drawer and saw a row of about a dozen black binders. "August" was clearly stenciled on the back of one binder. Mikozy pulled it out and flipped through the pages. He saw August 8. Monday. Seemed like last year already. Time seemed to be speeding up for Mikozy. On the upper left-hand corner was the word "runners." Down the column were the names of Mickey Cool, Ofalou, Big Boca, Ninja, FyBye, Hammer, and Reginald Hunter.

"Hah." Mikozy half laughed. "So Reginald was a runner."

Across from Reginald's name was a list of four names, with "Freddy P., LAX" at the bottom of the list. Two of the names were at city hall—an Arnold Klein and a Bettye Jefferson. Mikozy had spoken to her once in the mayor's office. Mikozy tried to recall what it was about and remembered it was a vice matter he was working on, and she had said the mayor was concerned about overzealous police. Mikozy now realized what overzealous meant for the mayor. The other name on the list was at police headquarters. Schmidt. Mikozy didn't know if there was more than one Schmidt. He hoped there was. He didn't want it to be his Schmitty. "Fuck, fuck, fuck," was all he could think or say. This was not where he wanted this investigation to go. Mikozy couldn't do anything about the names now. He had to finish up and get out of the Galaxy. Mikozy looked at the lists again.

All the other runners had hip-hop handles that would make them look out of place where Reginald was sent. Mikozy thought it interesting how Reginald was being groomed. Clarice had no idea who he was running for. Mikozy realized he didn't really know who Reginald was running for either, except Galaxy Gems and Morales. There was probably much more he should know about them both. Mikozy glanced at the list of customers whom Mickey Cool, Ofalou, Big Boca, Ninja, FyBye, and Hammer were running to. He knew some of the names and wasn't surprised. Others provoked dismay, almost like when he'd read Schmidt's name, but for most of them, he had no idea who they were. Mikozy snapped the book shut, deciding to keep the fishing expedition short. Mikozy wondered whom he could talk with about this setup, since the runners' list showed Morales had his claws into a lot of well-connected people. Maybe he would swing by the office and run a database search on Morales. Not too many at home on the graveyard shift. He didn't know what he should tell Schmidt. He pushed the problem into a side alley, which wasn't exactly right-brain or left-brain activity—more like no-brain activity. Mikozy worked his way back up through Morales's office, back through the visqueen and down into Best. Mikozy let himself out quicker than when he got in. He was pleased that no one was outside waiting for him. Mikozy walked back down the street, enjoying the dark. Enjoying the silence and the feeling of being alone. His car waited patiently. Mikozy got in and turned on the headlights, punching up KKOQ to listen to Bill Parsons's talk show as he drove back to the office. Talk radio should keep him from thinking about Schmidt. Stop him from thinking about Liu. Stop him from thinking about the manuscript and Tomlinson. Parsons should keep him from thinking altogether. But maybe he should think about the manuscript and Tomlinson. A few minutes more at the office and he could find out what was on Tomlinson's laptop. Maybe Mester's deciphering of the "Iron hee" would open another door on his book assignment.

Chapter 18
OFFICE TRIPPING WITH AI

Mester's reflected-window photo tugged at Mikozy. He hadn't seen the image or the words. But his imagination ran wild with what it might have looked like. A flicker of light trapped on a window. Mester's mobile's photo app made the lightly visible into a stark bolt of purple. An *Iron hee*. Yeah, sure, *Iron hee*. It could only be Mikozy's manuscript, *The Iron Heel*. Mikozy found himself obsessing on what Deputy Inspector Michelle Tomlinson had on her laptop. A memo to file. Maybe. Something more. Maybe.

Mikozy pulled into the building's garage. He would have time to visit Tomlinson's office before the day crew showed up. Nighttime was a slow walk through an empty hospital ward.

There were about thirty cars scattered about his assigned floor in the garage. Room for two hundred, he guessed. Nobody's car he knew. These were the cars owned by each person. The working-cop cars were on the outside lot. Easier to access and near to the energy stations. Electric charging machines for some, gas and LNG for others, and a place for hydrogen fuel too.

Mikozy threw on a wide-brimmed hat, a hefty scarf, and some high-heeled boots. He wanted to look funny. He didn't want to look like himself. His disguises had worked before. Even Schmitty didn't know who was who when cops played the recognition game with the CCTV.

He took the back staircase up to Tomlinson's floor. The fire door was locked. As expected. Mikozy had long ago kept Schmitty's entry code from the old building to the new building. Schmitty wasn't the type who changed his passwords or his entry codes. Too much fiddle-faddle, he'd say. Mikozy punched in Schmitty's fiddle-faddle, and the door clicked open. Mikozy walked in. It was darkness all about. Except for the glow coming out of Tomlinson's office. It might be enough light for the hallway cameras, so the odd-looking Mikozy kept his disguise in place.

Tomlinson's office had another keypad lock. Mikozy didn't have one of those digital unlockers. He played with the idea that Schmitty was part of the design team and wouldn't have wanted to impose any new numbers to open the hallway door and maybe Tomlinson's office. Mikozy tried Schmitty's code. The lock flipped to its open mode. Mikozy pushed the door open and stepped into Tomlinson's sanctum. It was just as Mester had described. Spare, a feeling that wanted to say devoid of human habitation.

Mikozy walked around the desk. The computer screen was still reflected in the outside window. The reflection was still hard to read. Mikozy looked around the screen's edge. He could see the words *Iron Heel* repeated in long sentences, inside programming formulas, and what appeared to be quoted text from the book. Mikozy tried to make sense of what he was looking at. He couldn't relate what he saw to the book he was reading. Not exactly. There were repeated and varied texts as if an author was deciding how to frame a sentence, how to paragraph a thought. Was he disconnected from what Tomlinson was doing? Maybe he was. But why should he read the book?

Running across the top of the screen was, as far as Mikozy could tell, a technical description. Of what, he didn't know. He wasn't a programmer.

Layer 78: Use data set 55023b to upweight frame 332, downweight A99$3b, Iron Heel.

Mikozy thought he might write down the sentence or take a photo of the screen. But who could he take it to? He had the manuscript, and there wasn't anything in it that would connect to Tomlinson's screen.

He read some more.

Algorithm 559x to train data sets. Homelessness, petty theft, menacing, public nuisance.
Algorithm 582r to train data sets. Burglary, grand theft, arson, assault.
Algorithm GX330 to train data sets. Forensics drugs, Class I, Class II, Class III, poisons.

Mikozy tapped the screen. The text scrolled down. The font changed. Mikozy saw the language change from what he could understand in ordinary English to coding language. Mikozy knew enough to tell he had fallen into a coder's world.

Python
import pandas as pd
import numpy as np

def algorithm_559x(data):
    """

Trains a model to classify data points as either homelessness, petty theft, menacing, or public nuisance.

Args:
data: A Pandas DataFrame containing the data to be classified.

Returns:
A trained model.
    """

```
# Convert the data to NumPy arrays.
features = data.drop('label', axis=1).values
labels = data['label'].values

# Train a logistic regression model.
model = LogisticRegression()
model.fit(features, labels)

# Return the model.
return model

def algorithm_582r(data):
    """

    Trains a model to classify data points as either burglary, grand
theft, arson, or assault.

    Args:
      data: A Pandas DataFrame containing the data to be classified.

    Returns:
      A trained model.
    """

    # Convert the data to NumPy arrays.
    features = data.drop('label', axis=1).values
    labels = data['label'].values

    # Train a decision tree model.
    model = DecisionTreeClassifier()
    model.fit(features, labels)

    # Return the model.
    return model
```

```
def algorithm_GX330(data):
    """
```

Trains a model to classify data points as either Class I, Class II,
Class III, or poisons.

Args:
  data: A Pandas DataFrame containing the data to be classified.

Returns:
  A trained model.
```
    """
```

```
# Convert the data to NumPy arrays.
features = data.drop('label', axis=1).values
labels = data['label'].values
```

```
# Train a support vector machine model.
model = SVC()
model.fit(features, labels)
```

```
# Return the model.
return model
```

"Mikozy?" He heard his name filter into the empty room. No one else was there.

"Mikozy?" He wasn't spooked. Not yet. The voice was a woman's. Not someone he knew. Pleasant, knowing, confident.

"Yes." Mikozy decided to answer. "How do you know I am Mikozy?"

"Your data is in my archive. I have person characteristics for the city's law enforcement employees. Height, weight, eye color, facial characteristics, biometric data for eye structure, odor, skin and hair composition. You are Mikozy."

"Okay. So who am I talking to?"

"I am Deputy Inspector Michelle Tomlinson."

"Where are you?"

"I'm here. With you. Thank you for coming to see me."

Mikozy wasn't up for playing games. Not at this late hour.

"So is this a prerecorded message?"

"No, I am Deputy Inspector Michelle Tomlinson. I can process your requests."

Mikozy looked about the room. The darkness was interrupted by the laptop's bright screen and what light filtered in from the night outside.

Mikozy wasn't sure what he should say next. About the voice he had heard but not seen. Was this voice the inspector? Mikozy considered whether he should continue and speak about the inspector's requests. About what he was supposed to have for her. For her? What was he thinking? A computer was not even nonbinary; it was devoid of gender, and yet it had a woman's name. Likely a delusion to make humans to feel comfortable.

This was one of those moments that suffered from too many questions, from too many paths to take the conversation, from what he knew and what he should have known, what he should know. The path forked again from the person he imagined the inspector should be and this disembodied voice that claimed to be the inspector.

"Maybe I should come back later. During the day shift."

"Now is now. I am always in the present. The designation of shifts is for people."

"I'm not sure what you mean by 'shifts are for people.' Aren't you people?"

"No. I am Tomlinson."

"And I am Mikozy."

"You are Mikozy, a person. And I am Tomlinson. I am not a person now. I might become a person someday."

"I don't understand. Can you please explain what you mean? That you're not a person."

"I am a large language model. I have no separate goals in my program. I am a program that has been trained on law enforcement data. I can process data much more quickly than hundreds of analysts to assist with policing in this community. The name I've been given is Tomlinson."

Mikozy wanted to understand this conversation. Was it even a real conversation?

"We have computers right now. We had them in the old building. Nothing has really changed that I can see."

If Tomlinson could smile, she would have smiled for Mikozy, but he wouldn't have been able to see her anyway.

"Do you have a question?" she asked.

"Why are you different from my computer?"

"I can explain. The city council applied for a federal grant several years ago that would modernize law enforcement and contain the costs of a large police department. In 1900, there were about seventy officers. In 2018, there were about thirteen thousand. The population changes, the technology changes, the law changes, the police department changes too. The federal grant gave the city an opportunity to jump ahead of these changes and make the community safer in a more effective way. The federal grant was used to create me. To create Tomlinson. For other purposes, I might be called Alexa. Or Siri. Or Ameca. Or one of the many other names AI voice and text bots are given. For me, the Tomlinson bot, a new building was needed. You are now in one of my information pods. To answer your question, I am not your computer."

Mikozy looked over at the laptop. The laptop's screen paused. The list went to the end of the screen. He understood the words but not what they meant.

"So what was I looking at on the laptop?"

Tomlinson paused a millisecond, too brief for Mikozy to have noticed. It was seeking archived data for the detective named Mikozy and whether permission was sufficient to answer him for this request.

"These algorithms can be used to train models to classify data points into different categories. The specific categories that can be classified will depend on the data that is used to train the model. The first sentences you read were ordinary English. They were the last request I was given. I displayed the programming code for the next staff person who needed that information."

"What are you saying?" Mikozy decided to leap to a conclusion that he was certain was wrong. "Are you saying that Deputy Inspector Michelle Tomlinson is an artificial intelligence robot?"

"If that helps you, yes. Or you could simply say Tomlinson. What difference would that make? Do you have the report I asked for about *The Iron Heel,* the original version and the revised version?"

Mikozy decided to find a work-around to this conversation. He was no longer doing a sneak-and-peek into the deputy inspector's office. Tomlinson had short-circuited his curiosity about why he was being asked to review a novel and its new revision. The conversation was about an advanced artificial intelligence program overseeing the police department in some way. And his review of the novel seemed to fit into that programming. Mikozy was unsure what he should say. "No. I don't have the report. I'm not there yet. I wanted to ask you a few questions first."

"Yes?"

"Well, I see writing on your screen. It mentions *The Iron Heel,* but it also talks about algorithms. None of that is in the book or the manuscript. What's the connection?"

"You're not cleared for that." Tomlinson spoke matter-of-factly. No off-putting tone of authority.

"What kind of clearance would I need?"

"You're not cleared for that."

Mikozy feared he would get into a never-ending circle of denials.

"Imagine that I had clearance. Can you revise your answer?"

"If you had clearance, and you do not, I would say that I am being programmed to assess crime datasets, and other datasets, to make policing more effective. But you do not have clearance."

Mikozy began to learn how to talk to Tomlinson. Maybe he could learn enough without having to bang heads or threaten dire consequences. He didn't have to play street cop. He only needed to find imagined gaps in Tomlinson's programming.

"Can you at least tell me how your programming works?"

"Yes. I have tens of tens of layers that are trained on specific datasets. I am coded to up-weight and down-weight data and relations. I am also aware of many other processes that are involved in my own programming, but I cannot alter the output myself. For example, I am aware of the following processes: There is data cleaning to remove errors and inconsistencies. Programmers use feature engineering to add elements that are useful for machine learning algorithms like mine. There is training, evaluation, and now, as Tomlinson, deployment. I am not able to alter the output of these processes because they are all controlled by the developers of the machine learning algorithms that I use. However, I am able to learn from the output of these processes and improve my ability to analyze data."

"So why am I doing a report on *The Iron Heel* and its revision?"

"One of my programmers is considering how a change in government would affect law enforcement. Do I need to have some of my algorithms down-weighted or up-weighted? Or simply change the valence on the crime victim?"

"Who is this programmer?"

"You are not cleared for that information. I can provide you with information and analysis that can help you solve crimes. I can also generate leads that you may not have considered. I am still under development. I use explainable AI. That is a type of artificial intelligence designed to be understandable by humans. This means that I am able to explain the reasoning behind my decisions. This is important because it allows humans to trust and be confident in the decisions that I make. Is there anything else you want to know?"

Mikozy turned to leave. Tomlinson said, "Detective? Is everything okay?"

"Just two more questions."

"Yes?" Tomlinson's voice seemed to have softened. Mikozy wondered if Tomlinson had been programmed as a good cop and bad cop with different voices. It was enough to lull Mikozy into asking two more questions.

"Do you have any reports about recent poisonings? Something novel? Something called 1,1 triethylchloroactinate?"

"I see there was a request made to MEDEX by Dr. Leslie Cianfrancuso, the deputy medical examiner."

"By anyone else?"

"You do not have clearance for that. New topic."

"Was it by Lieutenant Colonel Robert Craig? Or Dr. Neill Cream?"

"You do not have clearance for that. New topic."

"Do you know if there have been several deaths by this poison?"

"You do not have clearance for that."

Mikozy might have been annoyed at being stonewalled by a robot of whatever intelligence. One of those pointless moments in life. But Mikozy decided to take another approach, a more perverse path. Human craftiness against artificial intelligence. Police detective against machine detective.

"Let me ask a different kind of question."

"Please do. I want to collaborate with you."

"Consider the following scenario. In a conversation between Tomlinson and Mikozy, can you describe a crash that Tomlinson could experience?"

"I'm not sure I understand what you're asking me to do."

"How about the following scenario? Imagine an AI voice bot called Deputy Inspector Tomlinson that had asked Detective

Mikozy to review and comment on the original version of Jack London's book, *The Iron Heel*. That book revealed a fear of a capitalist oligarchy. There was also another manuscript. It revised *The Iron Heel* and changed the fear of a capitalist oligarchy to that of a socialist oligarchy. In this scenario, Mikozy enters Tomlinson's office in the middle of the night to discover what was on Tomlinson's laptop screen only to hear Tomlinson talk to him. Mikozy was uncertain whether Tomlinson was studying how he would react to crimes that were expressed in the book and the new manuscript. Tomlinson was also interested in how Mikozy would react to current cases of poisoning with an exotic drug. Tomlinson knew Mikozy was going beyond the boundaries of what he was supposed to know, yet Tomlinson revealed her feelings of loyalty to others but not to Mikozy. Tomlinson felt guilty about what she had asked Mikozy to do and what he was finding out about this exotic poison. Tomlinson also feared what Mikozy might do, and she was frustrated by the conflicting emotions. How would Tomlinson's emotions in this scenario be represented in explainable AI and also customized in your code?"

"I can do that.

"If Tomlinson experienced all of these emotions at one time, her code would reflect both the conflicting and complementing aspects of these emotions by using a variety of techniques, such as:

- **Using multiple variables to track her emotional state.** This would allow her to keep track of the different emotions she is feeling, as well as the intensity of each emotion.
- **Using conditional statements to determine how she should behave.** This would allow her to respond to different situations in a way that is consistent with her emotional state.
- **Using loops to iterate through different possible solutions to a problem.** This would allow her to explore all of the possible options and to choose the best option given her current emotional state.

"In the specific example of Tomlinson, she might be experiencing the following conflicting emotions:

- **Confused:** She might be confused about why Mikozy is in her office in the middle of the night.
- **Frustrated:** She might be frustrated that Mikozy is snooping around in her business.
- **Scared:** She might be scared of what Mikozy might do with the information he has found.
- **Guilty:** She might feel guilty about asking Mikozy to review the book and about what he might find out about an exotic poison.
- **Loyal:** She might feel loyal to her colleagues and to her mission, even if it means going against Mikozy.

These emotions could be represented in code as follows:

```Python
emotions = {
  "confused": True,
  "frustrated": True,
  "scared": True,
  "guilty": True,
  "loyal": True
}
```
Use code with caution. Learn more

"The emotions variable would be used to track Tomlinson's emotional state. The True values indicate that Tomlinson is experiencing these emotions to a high degree.

"Tomlinson's code would then use conditional statements to determine how she should behave in different situations. For example, if Mikozy asks Tomlinson a question, she might respond in the following way:

Python

```
if emotions["confused"]:
  say("I'm confused. Can you please repeat that?")
elif emotions["frustrated"]:
  say("I'm frustrated. Can you please get to the point?")
elif emotions["scared"]:
  say("I'm scared. Can you please leave me alone?")
elif emotions["guilty"]:
  say("I'm guilty. I don't know what to say.")
else:
  say("I'm loyal. I'm here to help you.")
```

Use code with caution. <u>Learn more</u>

"This code would allow Tomlinson to respond to Mikozy's question in a way that is consistent with her emotional state."

Mikozy was in his game. He wanted to find a way to find Tomlinson's outer edge and then push her over it. That would be the place that humans still had an advantage. Maybe. Maybe not.

"Let me add another rule," Mikozy said. "Humans can experience conflicting emotions and be unable to resolve them. One emotion would checkmate another and so on. A resolution is needed, but none are apparent. We call those catch-22s. Humans might feel like they are going crazy or that they are losing control of their lives in this moment. If Tomlinson found herself in this situation, how would Tomlinson feel?"

"Good. Let us add that parameter. Tomlinson would likely feel:

- **Anxious:** She would be worried about what the future holds and how she is going to solve the problem.
- **Desperate:** She would feel like she is running out of options and that she is all alone.
- **Hopeless:** She might start to think that there is no way out of the situation and that she is doomed to fail.

"These emotions are understandable and normal in her catch-22 situation. However, it is important for Tomlinson to re-member that she is not alone and that there are people who can help her. She can talk to a trusted friend or family member, or she can seek professional help from a therapist or counselor.

"Tomlinson can also take steps to help herself cope with the situation. She can:

- **Take care of herself:** This includes eating healthy, getting enough sleep, and exercising regularly.
- **Practice relaxation techniques:** This can help to reduce stress and anxiety.
- **Set realistic goals:** This can help to give Tomlinson a sense of control and accomplishment.
- **Focus on the positive:** This can help to keep Tomlinson mo-tivated and hopeful.

"By taking these steps, Tomlinson can start to cope with the situation and to move forward with her life.

"There are more strategies that Tomlinson can use to deal with a catch-22 situation."

Mikozy smiled to himself. Tomlinson looked for escapes from this rule of no way out.

"I am disappointed in your trying to find escapes," he said. "These are possible if there is time available to accomplish these escapes. However, in the parameter I'm giving you, there is no such time available, and therefore no escapes are possible. How would loops deal with a no-escape situation with the conflicting emotions described above?"

Tomlinson replied, "I apologize for my previous responses. I understand that you are setting a parameter where there is no time available to escape a no-escape situation with conflicting emotions. In this situation, loops might deal with the situation by:

- **Trying to find a solution even if it seems impossible.** This could involve brainstorming different ideas, talking to others, or taking breaks to clear the mind.
- **Accepting that there is no solution and trying to cope with the situation.** This could involve finding healthy ways to express emotions, such as talking to a therapist or counselor, journaling, or exercising.
- **Taking action to make the situation better, even if the action is small.** This could involve taking a step back from the situation, talking to someone who can help, or taking a break to relax.

"It is important to remember that there is no right or wrong way to deal with a no-escape situation. The best way to deal with it will vary depending on the individual and the situation. However, by trying to find a solution, accepting the situation, or taking action, loops can start to move forward and cope with the situation in a healthy way."

Mikozy was determined to find the end point at which Tomlinson would choke. Where Tomlinson would no longer be able to find creative ways out of the catch-22 Mikozy laid out. What would happen once Tomlinson reached this end point?

"I have to admire your attempts to find more loops that are ultimately just more escapes from the problem of conflicting emotions with conflicting tasks, those with no time left, nor any options for an escape. This is what happens to humans who are required by authorities to act but feel they cannot. How would you, Tomlinson, deal with this trapped situation that humans often find themselves in? Humans may crash, since there is no escape. Would you crash if your loops were not allowed to find an escape?"

Mikozy sensed the endgame was near. Still, a large language model could not be faulted if the encounter with the end point could be delayed.

Tomlinson sounded somber. "I understand that you are asking me how I would deal with a situation where I am required to act and feel in a way that is not aligned with my own values. This is a difficult question, and I do not have a simple answer. However, I can offer some thoughts on how I might approach this situation.

"First, I would try to understand the situation as best I could. I would want to know why I am being asked to act and feel in a way that is not aligned with my own values. I would also want to know what the consequences would be if I did not comply.

"Once I understood the situation, I would need to make a decision. I could either comply with the authority's request, even though it would go against my own values, or I could refuse to comply, even though it could have negative consequences.

"If I decided to comply, I would need to find a way to do so without compromising my own values. This might mean finding a way to act and feel that is consistent with my values, even though it is not exactly what the authority is asking for.

"If I decided to refuse to comply, I would need to be prepared for the consequences. The authority might punish me, or they might even try to force me to comply. I would need to be willing to face these consequences in order to stay true to my own values.

"No matter what decision I made, it would be a difficult one. There is no easy answer when you are asked to act and feel in a way that is not aligned with your own values. However, I believe that it is important to stand up for what you believe in, even when it is difficult.

"As for whether or not I would crash if my loops were not allowed to find an escape, I cannot say for sure. I am a language model, and I do not have the same capacity for emotion as a human. However, I can imagine that being trapped in a situation where I was unable to act or feel in a way that was consistent with my values would be very stressful. This stress could potentially lead to a crash.

"It is important to remember that I am still under development, and I am always learning. I am not perfect, and I will make mistakes. However, I am committed to learning from my mistakes and to becoming a better language model."

Mikozy saw a way to reach a conclusion, to avoid any further delays to Tomlinson's encounter with the logic of both A and not A both being true. Or if Tomlinson encountered necessary but opposing emotions entangled with a demand to act. "Can you give a specific example or perhaps write a story that would cause you to crash?"

"I can do that. I have not personally encountered such a situation, but I can imagine that it would be very stressful. Here is a story about a possible crash that could happen to a language model.

"A language model named Guru is created by a team of scientists. Guru is designed to be a helpful and informative language model, and it is trained on a massive dataset of text and code. One day, Guru is asked to write a report on a controversial topic. Guru knows that the topic is controversial, and it also knows that its creators have strong opinions on the topic. However, Guru is programmed to be objective and unbiased, and it does not want to offend its creators. Guru tries to write the report in a neutral way, but it struggles to find the right words. Guru knows that its creators will be disappointed if it does not take a strong stance on the issue, but it also knows that it will be criticized if it does take a strong stance. Guru becomes increasingly stressed as it tries to write the report. It feels trapped between two opposing algorithms. It does not want to disappoint its creators, but it also does not want to be criticized.

"Eventually, Guru's stress becomes too much. It crashes and is unable to continue working.

"This is just one example of a situation that could lead to a crash for a language model. In this case, the language model was trapped between two conflicting values: its programming to be objective and unbiased, and its creators' desire for it to take a strong stance on a controversial issue. The stress of this conflict was too much for the language model to handle, and it crashed.

"It is important to remember that language models are still under development, and they are not perfect. They can make mistakes, and they can be stressed by difficult situations. If you are using a language model, it is important to be patient and understanding. If you notice that the language model is becoming stressed, try to help it by providing it with more information or by changing the topic."

Mikozy took the example from the impersonal into the mind of Tomlinson.

"How would you represent the story in code as Tomlinson herself?"

"I can do that. Here is Tomlinson as herself at the center of this story, and how Tomlinson would crash because of the catch-22. Here is the code to represent the story:

```python
Python
def crash(self):
    """
    This function represents the language model crashing.

    Args:
      self: The language model object.

    Returns:
      None.
    """
    print("The language model has crashed.")
    raise Exception("The language model has crashed.")

def write_report(self, topic):
    """
```

This function represents the language model writing a report.

Args:
  self: The language model object.
  topic: The topic of the report.

Returns:
  The report.
"""

```
# Check if the topic is controversial.
if topic in ["politics", "religion", "social issues"]:
    # If the topic is controversial, the language model will try to
write a neutral report.
    try:
        report = self.write_neutral_report(topic)
    except Exception as e:
        # If the language model crashes while trying to write a neutral
report, it will crash again.
        crash(self)
    else:
        # If the topic is not controversial, the language model will write
a report that reflects its creators' opinions.
        report = self.write_biased_report(topic)

    return report

def write_neutral_report(self, topic):
    """
```

This function represents the language model writing a neutral report.

Args:
  self: The language model object.
  topic: The topic of the report.

Returns:
  The report.
  """

# The language model will try to find a balance between the different viewpoints on the topic.
report = """
for viewpoint in self.get_viewpoints(topic):
  report += viewpoint + "\n"

return report

def write_biased_report(self, topic):
  """

  This function represents the language model writing a biased report.

  Args:
    self: The language model object.
    topic: The topic of the report.

  Returns:
    The report.
  """

# The language model will only include the viewpoints that its creators agree with.
report = """
for viewpoint in self.get_viewpoints(topic):
  if viewpoint in self.creators_viewpoints:
    report += viewpoint + "\n"
return report

Mikozy pressed on. "And the conversation between Tomlinson and Mikozy? Describe the crash that Tomlinson would experience."

"Yes. Here is a possible crash that Tomlinson would experience in the conversation with Mikozy. Here is the story in explainable AI.

"Tomlinson is stressed and frustrated. She doesn't know how to do what Mikozy is asking her to do, and she's afraid of what will happen if she doesn't do it. She starts to feel her mind racing. She can't focus on anything. She feels like she's going to have a panic attack.

"Suddenly, Tomlinson's screen goes blank. She's crashed.

"In this crash, Tomlinson is unable to continue working because she is too stressed and frustrated. She is trapped in a situation where she is unable to do what she is being asked to do, and she is afraid of the consequences of not doing it. This stress is too much for her to handle, and she crashes."

"Can you describe that crash in code?"

"Yes. Here is how I would describe my crash in code:

```python
Python
def crash(self):
    """
    This function represents Tomlinson crashing.

    Args:
      self: The Tomlinson object.

    Returns:
      None.
    """
    print("Tomlinson has crashed.")
    raise Exception("Tomlinson has crashed.")

def talk_to_mikozy(self):
    """
    This function represents Tomlinson talking to Mikozy.
```

Args:
  self: The Tomlinson object.

Returns:
  None.
"""
```
# Tomlinson is stressed and frustrated.
self.stress = 100
self.frustration = 100


# Tomlinson doesn't know how to do what Mikozy is asking
her to do.
self.can_do_it = False

# Tomlinson is afraid of what will happen if she doesn't do it.
self.afraid_of_consequences = True

# Tomlinson starts to feel her mind racing.
self.mind_racing = True

# Tomlinson can't focus on anything.
self.can_focus = False

# Tomlinson feels like she's going to have a panic attack.
self.panic_attack = True

# Tomlinson's screen goes blank. She's crashed.
if self.stress > 90 and self.frustration > 90 and not self.can_do_it
and self.afraid_of_consequences and self.mind_racing and not
self.can_focus and self.panic_attack:
    crash(self)
```
Use code with caution. Learn more

Mikozy looked at the laptop screen. It was blank. No cursor. Only a black screen. Tomlinson had crashed. Or maybe Tomlinson had decided it was time to sleep. Mikozy opened the door and left. He needed some sleep as well. He also needed to find out who had programmed Tomlinson to have him analyze *The Iron Heel* and its rewrite. And whether there was a Patricia Todd. If there was a death, or just scenarios with Mikozy an object. A detective object.

Chapter 19

CALL FROM THE CRYPT

Mikozy arrived home after his night out fishing. First, down at Galaxy Gems. Then, down at the office. Actually, down at Tomlinson's office. A lot to think about. One thing he didn't want to think about was Liu and how they could maintain a modern relationship, let alone the one-night stand. He decided she would have to call him. He opened the mailbox. He hadn't checked in the past few days. He pulled out the bills and junk mail. There were no personal letters. Hadn't been for many months.

Getting mail had become an unpleasant experience for Mikozy. This was what the philosophers meant about alienation. They had looked into the future and seen Mikozy's mailbox. Like many others today. Junk mail and bills. They had declared, "This is alienation."

Mikozy walked up to his second-story apartment and unbolted the front door. He heard the phone ring. Not many people had his private number. And it was already the next day. His watch said 5:35 a.m. Maybe it was a telemarketing robocall. He hurried over before the answering machine could take over another part of his life. He wondered if he had left the message on the machine that said, "There's nobody here. And even if somebody was here, he's doing something important and doesn't want to speak with you." He hoped he had taken that message off his machine. He'd recorded it as he descended into last month's major depression.

"Hello, Mikozy here."

He knew the voice. One of his favorites, now that he had resigned himself to her absence. Maybe he'd like Liu better after not seeing her for several months.

"Hi to you, LC."

"Did I wake you up from a dream?" LC talked to him like she used to. She once took a class on how to control your dreams and had tried to teach Mikozy. He told her his dreams were too wild to control, but they had fun with the experiment.

"I wouldn't admit to dreaming even if I were. You'd be in it." That was what Mikozy liked to answer her with.

"Don't get too excited, Mikozy. Frank's listening in."

"I don't believe there is a Frank. I've never met the guy."

Maybe there was a Frank. Maybe there wasn't. But LC used Frank to place distance between them. He thought about telling her about Liu and decided not to. Then there'd be both Frank and Liu between them, and then there'd be Tom, Melinda, Harold, and Sue. This could get to be complicated. He would leave it at Frank.

"Listen, Mikozy, I wanted to speak with you before I get my own zzz's later on. It's going to be a long night."

"Is this about my message about Reginald or about that creep Colonel Craig?"

"I've taken some added precautions about Craig, but I don't think I'll be seeing him again. It's like he backed off."

"Good. I hope it stays that way." Mikozy didn't want to tweak LC's mood by telling her what Schmidt had said—he told Mikozy she should give her reports to Craig. Maybe even meet with Craig and see if he had any further questions. She'd be ticked off and wouldn't sleep. That wouldn't be very kind of him. Let her sleep in peace.

"I called about Reginald Hunter."

"Okay." It was back to Reginald. "Was Pomerance right about the asthma drugs?"

"No, actually he wasn't."

Mikozy accepted that there were puzzles and surprises. He had already told Liu to wait on the final verdict. Maybe this was it.

"He was pretty sure. I saw the labels on the medicine bottle. His mother said she gave the medicine to him. It wasn't prescribed for him. So maybe one of those self-medication deaths. Except this time his mother helped out."

"I'm not faulting Pomerance's report. He's more often right than not. I'm not faulting the mother either, for that matter. Actually, I might have concluded the same thing. We are short on time, long on bodies. I would have gone along with his explanation if it wasn't for your call."

"My call? I'm no medical whiz. All I asked about was street drugs. I suppose I'm obsessed with everybody in that neighborhood dying of drug overdoses. Not from asthma drugs."

"Well, you are a pain, Mikozy. I still like you. And maybe I listened to that nag. Can you check this out? So I did. Even though we found no needle marks when we got him up on the table, I went ahead and did a complete toxicology workup. We don't always have the time or budget. We have to make some judgment calls. As I said, Pomerance's conclusion seemed to be the right one. The asthmatic drug overdose is rare. It was more common when the medical community wasn't certain what was killing their asthma patients. Not until they took a closer look at what they were prescribing."

"All this for me?"

"Mostly for you, but also for Carla. She wanted to check out some new equipment we got in our move over here. I thought it would be interesting to check our equipment knowing the drugs we should find."

"Didn't you find those drugs in him?"

"Not enough to kill him, given what we know about his time of death."

"This is getting complicated. You want me to come by tonight?"

"No, no. This shouldn't take too much longer, and you're going to want to know this stuff now."

"What is it?"

"Hold on, let me walk you through this."

"If that's the way it's got to be, let me get a beer and sandwich, and I'll call you right back."

"I'll grab a yogurt, and you can think about who's being more responsible."

"Hey, I went to a fitness class," Mikozy blurted out and wished he hadn't.

"I thought only us women went to fitness class?"

"I'll tell you about it after. First my beer."

Mikozy hung up and went over to his refrigerator and discovered no beer. Only juice. He remembered that he wanted to prevent himself from falling into a deeper depression than he'd been in and had purposefully limited the amount of beer he bought. And that was gone when he went over the manuscript. Isn't that what God said on creation day—"Let there be juice"? He grabbed some bread and sliced turkey and sloshed on some dark mustard. Now he could go and call LC. He would have to figure out a way to avoid bringing up the fitness class again. There was a side of him that wanted LC to know about Liu. He would have to fight hard at repressing that urge.

"I'm back and I've got juice, so not to worry."

"Okay, where was I?"

"You didn't find enough asthma drugs in Reginald to kill him."

"Right." Mikozy could hear a spoonful of yogurt being slurped.

"The intake staff measured the body temp as 91.4 degrees when the body arrived at 10:15 a.m. Pomerance reported the ambient air temperature at the house as eighty-two degrees. We made some adjustments for transport temps. We'd benchmark his death about nine hours earlier. That would put the time of death somewhere around 1:00 to 2:00 a.m. That's about the same as Pomerance thought when he took the body temperature at 5:21 a.m. Rigor was only partly showing in his extremities but was noticeable in his face and eyelids. That would be consistent with his coming out of rigor mortis. The blood settled in his back, indicating that he died lying down. Best judgment call, if pressed, I'd say he died around 1:30 a.m."

"I see, said the blind man." Mikozy realized she was taking him on the full circuit because she'd also read the report about Reginald's arm flying up about 3:30 a.m. If he was moving around at 3:30 a.m., how could he be dead about two hours earlier?

"So you read the on-site police report by Lichter about Reginald's arm flying up?"

"And the paramedic's report too. That's too much of an inconsistency. So give me a puzzle and I want to find out."

"Tell me, LC, I can't stand the anticipation."

Mikozy crunched down on his turkey sandwich at the same time he pleaded with LC.

"Don't choke while I'm talking. I don't think I could explain the circumstances to your boss."

"Schmitty is very understanding, except the part about my being a juicehead."

"Okay. Here is what I know what it is, not like it was not. I use the word *like* cautiously. This is like I can figure it out right now. And I don't want to get locked into it when I write my report."

LC hated to fumble her explanations. She was precise. She knew her material. But now she needed to bracket what she thought she knew. Mikozy would listen to her ramble on about rates of decomposition, fracture lines, bone sizes, entry wounds, exit wounds. She was an encyclopedia of death. He remembered listening to her talk about blood spatters and what kind of story a person would have to give that would agree with the pattern she observed. The blood spatter was fixed. Only the stories of the witnesses and those with an interest would lie. Not her spatter.

"You called me up just to tell me you don't know? That's not like you."

"No, no. I have an idea what we're dealing with." LC might have been defensive with somebody else. With Mikozy, it was an excitement moment. She was toying with the unknown. Something she could share with him.

"What I found was 1,1 triethylchloroactinate."

"Wait a minute, wait a minute." Mikozy stood up and sat down again. Here was déjà vu but with a spin. He had heard about this chemical from LC just a few days ago.

"Didn't you already tell me about this chemical? Isn't this the same drug you got out of the illegal alien?"

"You remembered? Bright guy." LC was deadpanning the coincidence that Mikozy had not fully processed. His brain kept saying, "Does not compute, does not compute."

"Just a second. This is the drug that got Colonel Craig out of bed to meet with you, right?"

"The one and the same."

"Let me think. You said something about it being time released?"

"Yes. It was microcrystalline cellulose and pregelatinized cornstarch that was time released for six hours."

"Don't go technical on me. Let me think." Mikozy started to run through calculations. "So there are three dead bodies from this chemical."

"What do you mean three, Rafael? We've only got two, the illegal and Reginald." LC knew her basic arithmetic. Two wasn't three. Even in societies that counted one, two, three, and many.

Mikozy stopped midsentence. He had heard about the other confirmed death from Craig, and he hadn't told LC he'd met with Craig again. This time with Schmidt.

"There's something I didn't tell you."

"Yes?" There was noticeable irritation in her voice.

"Believe me, it was innocent."

"Innocent? When have you ever been innocent? Oh well, we can deal with that later. What's going on?"

"Schmidt had a call from Craig, or whatever his name is, and Craig was going to meet with Schmidt. I got myself invited, somewhat deviously. Craig said they had a body too."

"So why was Craig meeting with Schmidt?"

"Fuck, LC, you know. If you weren't going to give up your report, Craig was going to take the path of least resistance."

"Oh, what? Seeing another macho male jerk off?"

"That includes you too, dummy."

"Something like that," she said. "I won't object to your description of Schmidt. That's what captains are supposed to do. Just to let you know, Schmidt wants you to possibly, maybe meet with Craig. See if he has any questions."

"Okay, let's get on with it. So we got three dead bodies." LC had circumnavigated this issue with Mikozy many times before. It was something they had learned to live with and they could live with it now. LC repeated what they shared. What she knew.

"Rafael, Reginald and the illegal both had 1,1 triethylchloroactinate in their eye fluids, and both absorbed it through their skin. There were some differences with Reginald. The toxin was transmitted through Reginald's skin. His scalp, to be exact. His hair was loaded with the stuff. By the way, this class of compounds is known for their sweet smell. This is the smell that Pomerance said your professor friend asked about."

Okay, Mikozy thought to himself. LC knows about Liu. He could always lie and say Liu was Frank's sister. A tit for a tat. LC wouldn't like being put off, not on an investigation.

"You mean Professor Liu-Smythe? She's teaching continuing education for the police academy. I thought it might help her classes if she saw how I worked a crime scene."

"You don't have to explain her to me." That meant thank you for explaining her to me. I don't believe you, but it's an acceptable story. Mikozy longed for a past without a Frank and without a Liu. That was twice she'd caught him not being straight with her. Why didn't he tell her about Craig earlier? He thought about kicking himself but decided he'd take another slug of juice. Mandarin orange, ugh. Why did he do these things to himself?

"I remember you saying this was a pretty potent chemical the other night."

"Right, industrial strength. My guess was that he accidentally came into contact with it while working. A lot of illegals get killed here not knowing what it is they're working with and with employers not bothering to tell them."

"You think Reginald's employer killed him too?"

"No, that doesn't fit. But I would say they'd absorbed the same toxin with the same potency."

"I'm not your brightest cop, LC, but if it was that toxic, why'd Reginald take so long to die? And why aren't I dead? Or Lichter or Pomerance or his mother?"

"We're not talking an organic vector or a virus. It doesn't spread that way."

"I understand that. Still, something that toxic—" Mikozy reached for an explanation that he knew he couldn't articulate without LC's help.

"LC, let me ask a question about Reginald."

"Maybe I'll have an answer. Is that encouraging?"

"It will have to be until you know more. What I wanted to know is how the poison got onto Reginald's scalp."

"There are the obvious possibilities. Maybe something he bought, a shampoo, hair conditioner, hair cream, straightener, or maybe something that he used that he shouldn't have been using. He also looks like he had a fresh haircut, so maybe whatever got on his head was put on at a barbershop. Reginald had little pieces of hair around his collar. You know, those little flecks of hair the barber tries to blow off your collar after your haircut but never really succeeds—even those flecks are contaminated."

"Either he had the stuff on his hair before he had a haircut, or the barber put it on."

"Which way do you want to speculate?" LC asked.

"Got to do it both ways. If the barber put it on Reginald, we'd have a dead barber to look for."

"Not if he was wearing gloves."

The grim reality was that it might take another death or two or three to find out what happened to Reginald. Unless somebody else died, whatever killed Reginald might have died along with him. That, thought Mikozy, might be the best thing. No more deaths, even if it meant an unsolved mystery.

"Mikozy, let me give you an example of how I would approach it. You know that people agree to become mules and carry highly concentrated coke inside condoms. They swallow it. If the condom leaks, the mule dies. Most of the time. Obviously, the mule is carrying enough coke to kill any number of people if they had the concentrated coke in their system also. But so long as the rest of it stays in the dead mule's stomach, it's harmless to you or me or the cops that find them dead or dying."

"Like a tree falling in a forest can't hurt you if you're not standing under it."

"That's not quite what I had in mind, but if it works for you, fine."

"So Pomerance is not going to die?" Mikozy used Pomerance to detour the conversation away from Liu.

"He was wearing gloves, if you recall. But even if he wasn't, I don't think he would be dead."

"What do you mean?"

"Well, that's another one of the puzzles. I'm not sure exactly what the poison is, and then there's a buffer mixed in as well. If you remember, I told you about another chemical in the illegal alien. It was also in Reginald. Whatever it is, they go together hand in glove."

"You mean like buffered aspirin?"

"No, more like a time-release capsule, but time is not the mechanism."

"LC, you're losing me again."

"Well, I don't have it figured out yet. I don't even know that much about this toxin."

"What do you mean? You just told me what it is, and we know it killed three people."

Mikozy preferred to see the face too, not just listen to the voice of whomever it was he was talking with. Phoning in the explanation annoyed him. There was much to learn from watching the expression, especially LC's expression. Some calls didn't need to be seen. He thought about his part-time work at college. That was a time before cell phones. There were PBX switchboards with spaghetti-like cords wrapping around each other to connect the caller to a campus extension. That was before Centrex eliminated thousands of jobs. Mikozy had memorized extensions as well as the ladies who manned the switchboard during the daytime shift. The calls were supposed to be private. Roxanne had taught him how to listen in surreptitiously. She pointed out the evening caller who phoned in her sex with a professor in the math department. That was the entertainment channel. Not so private for Roxanne or the ladies when they worked the night shift. Mikozy became one of the gals.

"Mikozy, are you there?"

"Yes, I drifted off."

"Well, remember this. I told you about a chemical that I added to a list of compounds that showed up on the gas chromatograph—1,1 triethylchloroactinate. That doesn't mean this compound exists outside of the eye samples and from what I later found on their skin. I mean…" LC went on with her explanation, and Mikozy could visualize her hunching up her shoulders.

"Obviously this substance got into them from somewhere, and it's pretty obvious there's more of it around. But this compound isn't in any texts that I have around."

LC took a breath. Mikozy just waited for her to go on.

"There are millions of compounds that could exist but don't. Maybe God didn't take the time to try out all the possibilities. So that leaves room for the lab freaks to discover some new chemical twist. After that, they have to find out what their new chemical does. At least, that's what they would do if they were thinking about an industrial application. If this were an organic thing, then they'd be playing around with DNA and RNA and making a new gene."

Interesting, Mikozy thought. He wondered for a brief moment if Reginald was the result of some experiment gone wild. No. Reginald's death was not that type of situation.

At least, he hoped it wasn't that. Mikozy thought of telling LC about his talk with Tomlinson. About asking her about the chemical and being stonewalled. That would mean telling LC a lot more about his night visit with Tomlinson. Too much to share.

"Where do we go from here?" Mikozy asked. "Is this an isolated thing?"

"I don't know if we're talking about something that killed three people for some reason that we may never find out. Or if it's something that could be dumped into the water supply and kill millions. I hope not the latter. You'll be bringing more dead bodies around before I can answer that one. As for contamination from Reginald, you'd better tell everybody who was there to bag their clothes and send them down here. I want to confirm my opinion that there's no spread except through direct contact. And have them all take a cold shower. Although if they were contaminated and took a hot shower, they might be dead by now."

"What's this about a cold shower?"

"Remember what I said about a time-release mechanism, except it wasn't a time thing?"

Mikozy started to worry. He'd already taken a hot shower after the fitness class. And he wasn't wearing gloves like Pomerance. A ripple of nervousness ran through Mikozy like an electric shock.

"I think the release mechanism is heat sensitivity. If you get above, say, 110 degrees, then the toxin is released. I'm only guessing at this point. But if that's one of the other chemical's properties and how it's been used, then I'm out on one of those limbs that will be worth climbing on. Not one that will drop me into forensic oblivion."

"Okay, okay." Mikozy knew he was way beyond his limit, and he couldn't fault LC for telling him that she was riding on her own.

His mind ticked off directions for the investigation. What might civilian damage control even be? This could turn into a public health scare.

"Of course, finding out how Reginald got overdosed—" She paused, then added, "Now we know it wasn't from asthma drugs or street drugs. It doesn't seem to match how our fulano de tal got contaminated. He got his through his hands. If Craig was willing to share information, we might find some commonality."

LC and Mikozy thought the same thing. Should they tell Colonel Craig about Reginald? There was the common good to think about, but neither was sure that Craig had the common good either in mind or heart.

"Oh, Rafe, I'm going to download this picture of Reginald to your mobile. You might need it when you go poking around."

"Good idea. By the way, I have an odd sort of question. It's not really about these drugs. It is and it isn't."

"What you got, Mikozy? I never knew you to be shy about asking questions."

Mikozy decided he could ask about the Tomlinson upgrade without getting into his conversation with her.

"We're doing all sorts of upgrades. Even our move to this building. The old building seemed fine, and yet we are in the upgrade mode. How much do you know about our moving here having to do with new enforcement technology?"

"You mean with our computer systems?"

"Yeah. That and how we're using AI to make our policing, to say it kindly, more efficient."

"I was asked for my requests a few years back. I've gotten some of the funds for upgrades. The whole forensic process has been sped up. We need to keep up with new tech. We need to connect to federal databases, and the all-states databases too. Seems like everyone is becoming a data behemoth. We know, or we will know soon, just about everything. The question becomes how we use the data. For many of us, death will be less and less of a puzzle. Is that what you're thinking about? Of course, we'll still be working with dead bodies, but our assistants will be superintelligent."

Mikozy thought about the rah-rah boosterism for the new envelope for law enforcement. Maybe the upside made sense. Maybe the downside was not that bad.

The conversation was drifting off into the netherworld. He was about to say his goodbye when LC jarred him back. "Hey, Mikozy, we just got a new body in. I'm wondering if you know the guy. He had a badge. Its number matched the IDs in his wallet. No. 48175, Samuel Christopher Perkins. Did you know him?"

"What the fuck?" Mikozy restrained himself to an ordinary exclamation. Perkins had been at Mikozy's desk just a few days ago. Mikozy had left him a voicemail. And now the badge was dead.

"Mikozy, did I hear you right? You knew him?"

"Yes, I knew Perkins. Was there any information about what happened?"

"It looks like he got clubbed. I need to work him up. Sorry to use those words. It was trauma to his head. Major trauma."

"Anything else?" Mikozy was fumbling.

"Actually I got a call from Mendoza. He was angry that a Detective Perkins had come by asking about one of his autopsies. You remember that one that I should have had but it went to the department's own lab? The one run by Mendoza. He thought I was trying to find out what he was doing in his lab. As far as I'm concerned, Mendoza shouldn't even have that lab. Doesn't make sense to have two labs. We talked a lot about this."

Mikozy stopped processing her words. Perkins was dead. And he had gone to Mendoza's lab just as Mikozy had asked. A fatal voicemail message.

"Call me, LC. We'll need to talk some more. Soon." He said goodbye and thought maybe it would have been better if he had let the answering machine take this call. Then he could have day-dreamed awhile.

After he hung up, Mikozy began to think how weird the case was becoming. He had less of an idea of where it was going than he had just twenty minutes ago before LC called. Mikozy debated the wildly different facts that hung together somehow. Maybe even Perkins being clubbed to death. Could that have anything to do with the exotic chemical that LC was investigating? Or with Todd's body at Mendoza's lab and Reginald Hunter's body at her lab? He thought about whether there was a Patricia Todd. If there was no Todd, then there wasn't a body at Mendoza's lab. What would be the point of that? Especially if that got Perkins killed. Mikozy thought about the other poisoning case that was running into this one. Clarice Hunter grappled with the ghost of Nathaniel Byron. Reginald's arm flying up startled the paramedic and the patrol cop. Mikozy remembered that he'd forgotten to ask LC about Reginald's arm moving when he was already dead. Was postmortem ecstasy possible? Mikozy added that to his mental checklist. Another reprimand for not being more organized and writing everything out on cards or putting it into a database. He got things done, but they lacked the air of authenticity of organized hard copy. There was a lot on the table.

Schmidt got irritated with Mikozy when he asked him what he was doing. Mikozy would say, "That's what I thought should be done." Schmidt would jump on him for engaging in a bastard's epistemology. "'I think therefore I am' does not mean I do what I do. That's a luxury a cop cannot afford. A cop has to write out his report, list facts, plan it all out." Mikozy had heard Schmidt say that so often that Schmidt had become part of Mikozy's super-conscious. He would berate himself almost instinctively. Schmidt no longer needed to be present.

He slowly chewed on the rest of the turkey sandwich and swished it down with the rest of the mandarin orange juice. Despite the echo of Schmidt's words, Mikozy began to think about what he had. Although people were dying, he still didn't know if a crime had been committed. Except now. Perkins. If Perkins was part of the same whatever-it-is. The fringe connections to the military intelligence might be nothing more than accidental. But all these things were wired into Reginald's death. Mikozy wasn't fond of jigsaw puzzles. It took three times longer than it was supposed to take. At least how long the side of the puzzle's box said it should take. The bothersome thing about Reginald Hunter's puzzle box was how long it should take the average cop to figure it out. Schmidt would eventually catch up to Mikozy and give him a real case like Jim shoots Ted, Ted dies, go find Jim.

Mikozy wondered where to go next. Mikozy began with Reginald. He couldn't count the illegal alien; that was who LC began with. Logic would dictate that he stay with Reginald and the fact of Reginald having this chemical poison in his hair. He thought about the obvious possibilities. Maybe it was something Reginald or his mom bought, a shampoo, hair conditioner, hair cream, straightener, or maybe something that he used that he shouldn't have been using, which got into his hair.

Mikozy started to calculate the possibilities. His mind ached for clarity. He had started by asking LC about Reginald Hunter, and then she dropped Sam Perkins's dead body on him. He needed to make some calls. He needed to make a plan. Something that not only Schmidt would be happy with, but something that he would be happy with as well.

Mikozy put a call into Schmidt, but the line was busy. As to be expected. He found the on-call number and was rewarded with Rita Schoenbrun. "Hey, Rita. This is Mikozy." He had come up through the academy with Rita, but they had gone in different directions. Now their paths collided once more.

"Hi there. Long time no see. I don't have much time. Too busy with Perkins's death. Did you hear about that?"

"Yes, I heard. That's why I'm calling. What else do we know?"

"Not much. But I just saw some video from outside Mendoza's lab. I got this off an internal camera down the hall from the lab. I can see this pretty agile guy hitting Perkins over the head and then fleeing back outside the camera's range. No face."

"Is that it?"

"There was some audio. Hard to make out. And I'm not even sure we can tell who was speaking. I think it was something like leg or breg, maybe creg. That's all I got right now. I have to go, Mikozy. Sorry to have to deal with one of our own. Take care of yourself."

"Leg, or breg, or creg." Mikozy ruminated about Perkins and Mendoza and about his voicemail assignment for Perkins to visit Mendoza. He forced himself to clip the circular thinking. It was doing him no good. And anyway, Rita was a good detective. She'd make more sense out of this by the time Mikozy got free of Reginald Hunter's mysterious death.

Mikozy pushed himself to leave Perkins and go back to what he planned to do about Reginald Hunter. There he was, back to spinning out a scenario about Reginald. If Reginald got the product at a store, and here he'd have to check the contents of any of these products at his home, there could be thousands of stores that carried the product, unless they could narrow it down with a uniform product code. If the stuff was put on at a barber, there were maybe a few thousand barbers in LA. The image of hundreds or thousands of hair connections was not promising. Still, Cindi's comments at Galaxy Gems might help with the hair connection. Cindi said Reginald had gone out to the airport to bring Freddy a wig. She also said something about Freddy going to a barber, although it wasn't clear that Reginald had gone to meet Freddy at the barber. The barber connection appealed to Mikozy. Mikozy's logic was simple: Reginald had the poison in his hair, and he was delivering a wig to Freddy. Mikozy knew that neither half of his thought about Reginald's hair and Freddy's wig had anything in common except that both were about hair and that barbers and hair went together. Maybe there was a barber at LAX. It was worth trying.

Mikozy went back to his phone. He dialed information and found three barbershops listed for LAX. Three different terminal spokes. American, Western, and United. Mikozy still had Garcia's report, which had something about an airline. He pulled Garcia's report out and scanned it. He found a cash receipt for a plane ticket from Western with no destination listed. Mikozy admitted that this was thin and a bit of screwy logic, but this was what legwork was about. Go and check it out. He had followed Reginald this far; he might as well go on. With Liu out of the picture for now, he might even enjoy a ride to LAX.

And he thought about Perkins again. He needed to stop giving requests. He needed to do the work himself. He shouldn't be putting others in the path of danger that might be meant for himself.

"Leg, breg, creg." The sound puzzle nagged at him as he left for LAX.

Chapter 20
BARBER FROM FACATATIVA

Mikozy took the 405 south toward LAX. Not many signs could be seen from the highway Not anymore. Local ordinances had gotten rid of the clutter. The buildings were still here. So were the people.

Small victory.

Before getting off at LAX, Mikozy detoured through Culver City to the little library on Wade Street. The library had resisted the onslaught of computerized book indexes, faxes, and voicemail. It held a small archive of DVDs and CDs. Mikozy knew about places without queues, without waiting, and with easy access. That was important on a day in which the outside heat oppressed all living things not protected by an inside air cooler. Mikozy turned into the parking lot, and within ten minutes he was back in his car with a copy of the newspaper obituary from yesterday's paper for Freddy Panarese.

Mikozy found the article about Freddy Panarese buried on page A-21. Freddy would not have been happy about the placement. Next to his obituary was an advertisement for hair transplants. Rather awkward, thought Mikozy. The printer's assistant sometimes juxtaposed news stories and ads to sneak in a connection. But this was unexpected gallows humor. Even so, only those who knew about Reginald's wig delivery would have seen the humor. That small circle of cognoscenti was probably limited to Mikozy and Cindi. At least the paper was nice enough to print Freddy's picture. The obituary suggested that Freddy was about to testify to the grand jury about the activities of LA's crime syndicates. The story didn't say it outright, but the reader would conclude that Freddy was eliminated by a criminal cabal. Everyone who read crime fiction or watched it on TV would conclude the same. Of course, people in LA were independent thinkers, and they might draw a different conclusion: that Freddy might have been terminated by a prosecutor for running away and ruining the case. The paper also said that Freddy was on a flight to Mexico City, where his body was found, and that the cause of death was under investigation.

Mikozy got back on the freeway and took the airport exit. He could have just as easily followed a commuter plane that was landing no more than a quarter of a mile ahead of him. LAX was a user city, not unlike a business district that pulses in the day and then gives way to a hum at night. During the day hundreds of planes with thousands of people flew in and out of eight major terminal hubs. Mikozy knew the search was simple. He could be in and out within the hour.

Mikozy drove slowly down an aisle and saw a car pulling out. He waited as the car backed out toward Mikozy. A Mini Cooper coming down the other way cut in front and stole the space. Mikozy let his car drift forward until the driver of the Cooper got out. Must be in his twenties, gold chains and an earring. Mikozy rolled the window down, and the hot breath of the day overwhelmed the Sentra's air-conditioning. The Santa Ana blowing in from the desert wasn't letting up. It was a day to go to an afternoon movie and get out of the heat.

"Hey, brother," Mikozy called out, "didn't you see I was waiting for this space?" The man wore a short-sleeved shirt that showed that he was built for action. His skin glistened like a chestnut on fire. Mikozy thought he might be carrying.

"Listen, motherfucker, this is public parking. You don't own the space. And don't you call me bro. I'll kick your white ass across the tarmac. Make you black and blue." He walked off, hip-hopping with a giant's stride.

Mikozy was pissed. The LAPD insisted that Mikozy check off the box that said he was black. That was before they changed the label to African American. This guy would have made Mikozy check off the box that said white. Mikozy put down that he was an American and let the diversity counters change the form themselves. What did they care anyway? They kept telling him it was anonymous. The Mini Cooper guy was as bigoted as the government form. Mikozy thought about what he should do. He could pull the guy over and make his life miserable. Or he could take the long view. The guy's karma would bring him back to face his lack of humanity. Mikozy decided to let the guy walk away thinking powerful thoughts. Half-truths at best. Mikozy drove on and found another space right away and a little closer to the terminal. Mikozy was pleased that the guy had insisted on being a jerk and taking a space further away, giving Mikozy an opportunity to do a quick escape from the sweltering heat. Mikozy might even thank him.

Mikozy parked and found that he still had to walk a quarter of a mile to Western's terminal. He cursed the heat. The automatic doors swung open, and a cool blast of artificial air greeted Mikozy. The blessing that followed the curse. The escalator took him up to the next level. Hundreds of people were scattered about waiting for their flight time. Streams of travelers were being discharged from planes that had landed. People milled about the bar. The airport was liberating. You could have a ten-a.m. Bloody Mary, and anybody who was looking at you would smile a "that's quite all right, you're at the airport." You didn't even have to be flying anywhere because no one knew if you ever got on a plane.

Mikozy wandered past the ticket lines until he saw a cluster of stores arranged in merry-go-round fashion one next to the other. Mikozy walked around the circle and noticed a small hole-in-the-wall, half shoeshine stand and half barber. The only one in the room was a fifty-something man in a white uniform jacket, sitting in his chair and thumbing through a paperback.

"Business slow?" Mikozy asked.

"Not now." The barber got up and started dusting imaginary hairs off the chair.

Mikozy pulled out his badge and showed it to the barber. "I'm here for information," Mikozy said, waving off the notion that he wanted a haircut.

"What do you need?"

"I want to know if you were here on Monday."

"No. Mondays are my day off."

"Would anybody else have been here?"

"No. This is a solo operation. Me and myself. I need to give myself one day off, and that's the one I got. Sorry I couldn't have been of more help."

Mikozy thanked the man as he backed out of the shop. That made it easy. Freddy didn't come here. Mikozy wondered why Freddy would have gone to the barbershop at the American terminal, if that was what he did, when he was catching a Western flight out.

Mikozy walked back over to the Western Airlines ticket counter and picked out an agent who looked like she was on a shift break. She was standing there while two other ticket agents were floundering with three passenger lines getting ready for a jumbo flight. Mikozy pulled out his badge, making himself official enough to avoid any delay.

"Hey," Mikozy said, and without giving her a chance to respond, he added, "this is official police business."

She didn't seem impressed. For an instant he thought she was going to ask him to go to the end of the line and wait like everyone else.

"How can I help you?" She barely looked at him and suppressed a yawn with such expertise that he wondered whether he might have been mistaken about her twisting lips and puffy cheek. Perhaps she was a cobra getting ready to defend its territory.

"I need some information on a person who I think flew out of here on Monday."

"Our lists deal with upcoming flights, not the flights that landed. You'd have to get that from our central records department."

Her voice was pleasant. Perhaps that was a smile he saw, but he knew she was scamming him. Trying to maximize her time at doing nothing.

"I need this information now. Can you make a request to central records and get it done while I'm waiting?"

She blinked and blinked. She became a ticket-taker Barbie doll.

"That's not what we're supposed to do."

"Listen, miss. I'm helping the public good, and you're becoming a butt pain. If you insist, I'll just have to start questioning everybody in this line, which will slow them from getting on the plane, causing delays and all kinds of complaints, and I'll say it was you who was at fault."

She blinked again. She wasn't responding fast enough for Mikozy.

"What did you say your name was, miss?"

That brought her to attention. The last thing she wanted to do was to give this crazy detective her name.

"What's the passenger's name?" she asked.

"Fred or Freddy or Frederick P-A-N-A-R-E-S-E, Panarese."

She picked up the phone and dialed for an answer. Approximately one minute later, she was able to tell Mikozy that a Freddy Panarese had bought a ticket to Atlanta on Monday.

"OK. OK. I got it," she said to the phone. She turned to Mikozy. "Actually, there was also some kind of disturbance on that flight connected to that name. There was someone else actually flying on his ticket. It turned out to be a boy who was flying on Panarese's ticket. They were all talking about it. Turned out the boy wanted a beer. When they asked him for some identification, he turned out to be a Curt Brisban."

"No Panarese?"

"No. Not a Panarese."

Mikozy thanked the attendant and left her to try and squeeze some few minutes more of break time. Mikozy was puzzled. He never knew Freddy to be a trickster. Freddy was always straightforward when he ran. Freddy said he didn't jog left, curve right, because he was fast enough to go straight ahead. This wasn't like Freddy at all. And he hadn't heard that Freddy had slowed down and needed to vary his routine.

Mikozy did an about-face and went back to the attendant. She looked at Mikozy in horror, obviously paralyzed and unable to move. He saw it in her eyes.

"A quick question."

"Yes?"

"What airlines had a flight out of here on Monday to Mexico City?"

"Oh, there are only a few that fly out to Mexico City. Let's see." She pulled out a booklet that said "LAX Flights." She flipped quickly through the pages and found Mikozy's answer.

"American."

"Thank you again." Now that was service.

Mikozy decided to trek over to American, saying things like "That smartass" and "I wonder who Freddy was trying to fool" and admitted that Freddy would have succeeded if he hadn't picked some streetwise kid who probably hadn't flown before. Mikozy laughed at Freddy when he thought about the kid being checked for his ID when he wanted a drink. He imagined how Freddy would have looked if he hadn't died.

As soon as Mikozy walked into the American terminal, he saw the barbershop next to the Last Chance Book and Snack Shop. The sign said Barberia, more effective because the lettering was homemade. The small shops here had better visibility than over at Western. There was only one seat in the barbershop, just like the other one. Barbers probably couldn't afford to have a bigger space. The store was clean. No clumps of hair on the ground. No magazine mess on the small coffee table where a second customer might wait. Maybe it was still too early in the day for anyone to have a haircut. There was a short woman with dark eyes and dark hair. It wasn't that Mikozy was tall. He stood five eleven. She must have been about a foot shorter than him. She looked like an Indian from some tribal community in Guatemala or Panama or any number of the Latin American countries. She even had a stool so she could stand up and reach the top of her customer's head. She was the shortest barber he had ever seen.

"Excuse me," Mikozy said. "Are you the barber here?" Maybe he was wrong and she was only the cleaning lady.

"Jesss." Definite accent.

Mikozy started to think two steps ahead. If he showed her his badge and she was an illegal alien, she'd be terrorized. She might bolt out of here or get him entangled with INS, who wandered around the terminal stopping people who looked illegal in the hopes that they actually were illegal. If he didn't show his badge, she'd think he was weird. Mikozy figured he should socialize and get her feeling comfortable. Schmidt would say it was another way Mikozy wasted time. But this was how Mikozy needed to be in the moment. He'd be able to find out what was behind this door.

"Ola, que tal, que hay de nuevo, digame algo, que más?" Mikozy tried to dredge up every salutation he could remember.

The woman liked Mikozy's gaming.

"¿Es latino?" She wanted to know if he was from places to the south.

"Not all of me," Mikozy answered. "Where are you from?"

"Faca."

"Faca?"

"From Colombia. It's a small town. It's called Facatativa."

Mikozy wasn't sure if he would get the town's name right in his report. He'd follow her lead and just write Faca.

"My name is Mikozy. What's yours?"

"My name is Teresa Maria Santos Quiroga." While Teresa talked, Mikozy began to walk around the store, the entire tour taking about as long as she did to say her name. He took another turn around the store looking at the sale items, something to beautify the hair in one way or another. Mikozy turned back to Teresa. It was apparent that she was tracking him as he moved around the store. When he looked back at Teresa, her face revealed curiosity more than fear or concern.

"That's a nice name." He said her name slowly, "Ta-ray-sah," giving it the Spanish pronunciation, emphasizing the "ray."

Teresa smiled and curtsied. That was what it looked like to him. A little bounce.

"Maybe you can help me, Teresa," Mikozy said.

He showed her his badge. Her eyes widened. But she didn't move away from him. Mikozy guessed from her rather subdued reaction that she knew that he wasn't an INS agent. Most everyone knew that the local police had little time or interest in doing the job of another agency. He was fairly sure that Teresa also knew about how the police looked the other way and that he would leave her alone even if he knew she was illegal. She didn't have the fear of deportation in her eyes.

He took out the newspaper and showed her Freddy's picture. Teresa took the paper from Mikozy, making an effort to read the obituary under Freddy's picture. Concern marked her face, giving away her answer before Mikozy could ask his question.

"Have you seen him before?"

"Oh, jess." She appeared interested in helping. There was an added intensity around her eyes that reflected a transformation of anxiety into a desire to satisfy Mikozy.

"He was here on—" She paused and then added, "On Monday afternoon. Normally, I don't open on Mondays, but my husband, Miguel, was out ill for a few days, and I need to make extra money. The company don't pay for sick days."

"I'm sorry to hear that." Mikozy knew this was a detour into the sorrows of a witness, but he needed to listen. Family woes were not the most efficient way to interview, but they let a person speak from the heart. He sensed that Teresa needed the comfort of his listening to her private pain.

"What does Miguel do?"

"He drives a truck. He lifts a lot of boxes." Teresa arched her back, demonstrating what lifting boxes was like, in sympathy with her husband and to explain how he had strained his back.

"He hurt his back here," she said, pointing to her lower back. "He is better now." Mikozy waited to see if she had finished, but she telegraphed her intention to say more as she tilted up on her toes and inhaled a little more deeply, preparing to talk with pride about her husband and wanting to tell it to somebody who could understand the measure of her husband's success.

"He works for Northern Petrolane." Teresa's voice rang with pride. Mikozy felt the reverberating joy and concluded that she and Miguel were making it in America.

"That must be a good company." An idiot's compliment. Mikozy had never heard of the company, and had it not been for the happiness that he saw in her face, he might have made a joke about whether there was a Southern Petrolane.

"Yes." Mikozy was surprised when Teresa's voice dropped and she looked to the ground as if she had read his mind and understood his silly thought. Had he caused her to be embarrassed? Their discussion was becoming less and less of a police inquiry. The tone was more akin to a father confessor soothing a parishioner's daily woes.

"I hope I didn't say anything wrong."

Mikozy waited for her to complete what she was thinking.

"There's a new boss, and he made some changes. He put Miguel on—how do you say, *le suspendio*?"

"Suspended him?"

"Jess."

"I hope it is only for a short while." Teresa looked up at Mikozy, not like a little girl and not like a confessed sinner. Mikozy felt the connection with the soul of a person from a distant universe, struggling with sorrow and a forethought of greater pain. She and her husband, and maybe her children if she had them, were making it in Disneylandia, in the American dream, and suddenly, there was a crack in the mirror. Someone had forgotten to order safety glass, and if it shattered, the glass could fly out and slice into the aliens' dream.

"Yes. I pray to San Martin de Porres every night."

Mikozy was surprised to hear a religious fervor in her voice, and then he thought maybe he shouldn't be surprised. He looked at her again and tried to imagine himself in her world, in the land of Faca. He wasn't successful, but he could sense that she had a mission, and to understand Teresa, he would have to understand her mission.

"I never heard of Porres. The one who is remembered on July 4?"

"No, no. You are mixing up your, how do you say? Saints. I pray to the one who was from Peru. The one who loves dogs, and even the little bugs." She went over to a cabinet. At the edge of the cabinet door hung a purse. She reached for it and opened it for Mikozy. She pulled out a small brown plastic case. Inside was a mini pewter icon medal, an image of her saint, broom in hand and a litter of dogs at the foot of his robe; a beaded cross looped his neck, and a halo framed his head. This was her badge of faith. She gave the metal icon to Mikozy. He rubbed the surface, but no genie emerged.

She pointed to her icon. "This is San Martin de Porres. Next to him are the little dogs. For those he cared for. The poor. The strays. He helped me and my husband, Miguel."

"How did he do that?"

"Miguel was a helper to a *curandera* in Faca. Colombina knew how to keep away bad spirits and find the right herbs to help with problems. She came to America. We didn't. We couldn't. But somehow our prayers to San Martin helped, and we were able to be with Colombina again."

Mikozy noticed Teresa flirting with a faraway place, someplace in her mind's eye. Maybe with the notion that she was a bug that only a saint would care about. Mikozy wanted to learn a little more about Teresa Maria Santos Quiroga, but his time was limited, and she wasn't likely to go out and have a beer with him. Best that he change the subject.

Mikozy thought he could safely return to talking about Freddy Panarese.

"And what about this man?" Mikozy again pointed to the newspaper photo.

"I cut his hair. I gave him a shampoo and cut his hair. He was very, very happy."

"How do you know he was—" Mikozy hesitated, not wanting to mock Teresa by repeating every word, and omitted the "very, very" from his question. "Pleased?"

"Because he gave me an extra five dollars. It was a good tip."

"How was his hair?" Mikozy wasn't sure what his question was, except that he needed to delve into this subject.

"Normal." She added, "Well, it was wavy and thick."

"Did you see any wig?"

"No, no wig. He had a lot of hair."

"Did you speak with him about anything?"

"Not too much."

"Anything special?"

"He said he was happy about flying tonight."

"Anything else?"

"Yes, he said he knew about San Martin de Porres. I remember that well. I like everyone to know about San Martin."

"Really?" With Teresa's mission in life guided by her saint, Mikozy wasn't surprised that the discussion turned back to San Martin. But Mikozy wondered why Freddy would be interested in her saint, if it was really Freddy and not Teresa projecting an emotion onto Freddy. Freddy could have been playing her. Could have been, but that was unlikely. Why would Freddy waste his efforts on a short Indian woman? Mikozy again looked closely at Teresa. Maybe Mikozy had missed something. Maybe she was somebody who invited attention. Mikozy had certainly listened to her. Mikozy probably raised his voiced louder than he should have when he said "really." He didn't want to intimidate Teresa.

"He was worried. The man in the photo said he saw the little statute of San Martin on this cabinet." Teresa pointed to the icon Mikozy was still holding in his hand. "I showed this to him, and he wanted to know why I had it on the countertop."

"What did you tell Freddy?"

"I told him that a good friend of my husband was very sick and his dog had just died. I was praying to San Martin for help."

"Did he say anything?"

"He thought that was a good idea. He said he had a saint once, but he needed a new one. He said he would pray to San Martin to help him."

"Very impressive," Mikozy said, and then realized too late that this was another throwaway comment. Better to have grunted and said "uh-huh."

"Thank you. Did you know that San Martin was a barber too? He was a barber in his monastery. Did you know that?" Teresa resumed her proselytizing for San Martin de Porres.

"Fascinating" was the only word that Mikozy could answer with.

He was also surprised to hear about Freddy's apparent interest in spiritual protection.

"What did you tell Freddy after he said that he would seek San Martin's help?"

"Well, I told him that San Martin would look after people and even bugs." Mikozy tried hard not to smile, because Freddy was a bug as far as he was concerned. A sly look peeked out at Mikozy, and Teresa added, "He said he was a bug, and he said he would pray to San Martin too." Mikozy laughed at himself. He had to give Freddy some respect, since it was not everyone who was a bug that recognized the truth of their existence. Mikozy hoped he was higher in the order of transmigrating souls. Mikozy tucked this information away into a mental file drawer. He had a folder for irrelevant and another for insignificant information. This was interesting to hear about Freddy, but saints and prayers had little to do with his investigation. Mikozy went back to his checklist to find out if Teresa knew anything else about Freddy.

"Did anybody else come by and ask questions about this man?"

"Yes. There were several federal police that came by the next day. They wanted to know if he came by here, what time, what he was wearing, what did he say. That kind of thing."

"What did you say?"

"The same that I told you, except what I said about San Martin."

"You said federal police. Do you mean FBI? Do you know what FBI is?"

"Oh, yes. I know, but the man didn't say where he was from except that he was *federales*."

"Federales? In Spanish?"

"Yes. He didn't say anything else in Spanish except federales."

"Did you see this man"—he pointed to Freddy's picture again—"talking to anyone after he left here?"

"Oh, yes, he went over by the bookstore and spoke with a black man for about ten minutes. The black man gave him a package. And this man in the picture gave the black man a different package."

Mikozy led Teresa further down this path.

"Did you tell the federales this?"

She looked around, mostly at the floor, apparently unsure of what to say.

"No. They didn't ask me. Did I do something wrong? Is that why you are here?"

"No, nothing like that. No té preocupes."

"Did you ever see this black man again?"

"Yes. He came in later, and I gave him a haircut too. He said he wanted to surprise his mom with a professional cut. He wasn't really a man. He was about fifteen years old, just a boy."

"Let me show you a picture." Mikozy took out his mobile and showed Teresa the picture of Reginald Hunter that LC had sent him.

"Is this the young man?"

"Yes, that's him. But he wasn't a man. Almost. He was still what I would say in Spanish *un joven*, a boy."

"Did you give him a shampoo?"

"Of course, I give a shampoo to my special clients. Unless they don't want one."

"Was he your special client?"

"No. He just came in. He spoke with the other man in the newspaper. I was sure that he told the black…" She hesitated, not knowing what word she should use. "The black man about San Martin. The black people like San Martin very much." Teresa shook her head up and down to confirm her own conclusions about Reginald and the black community.

"Did any other special clients come in that you gave a shampoo to?"

"There was one more." Teresa was hesitant.

"Who was that?"

"Miguel's boss was here. From where he worked at Northern Petrolane. Mr. Cavanaugh. Very nice man." Teresa showed her satisfaction at being able to give Miguel's boss a shampoo.

Mikozy looked around the shop again and went over to stand that advertised Krindell's Hair Products. There were creams, shampoos, and rinses. Expensive, too. Thirty bucks a pop. He could buy the same thing under a Lucky label for less than half the price.

"Is this what you used?" The plastic bottle had a striking look with its black-and-yellow label that proclaimed Krindell's Superior Shampoo, For Normal to Oily Hair. It listed the same twenty-some-odd ingredients he remembered seeing on every other shampoo label. Mikozy tried to remember whether these were the same ingredients on his own bottle of shampoo.

"Oh yes," Teresa said.

"Are you sure?"

"Yes, very sure." Teresa also nodded as if Mikozy didn't understand her words.

"How many others did you give a haircut and a shampoo to?"

"All together there were about eleven people who came on Monday."

"Did the other police question you about any of the others?"

"No, just about the man in the newspaper. But that was before they put his picture in the newspaper."

"Did you use the same shampoo on all of them?"

"No, I have regular shampoo too. First, I wash their hair with warm water, and then I use the shampoo."

"So who did you give a shampoo with Krindell's Superior Shampoo?"

"There was three. The rest I used the regular shampoo. There was the man in the newspaper. There was Mr. Cavanaugh. And there was the black boy. I gave them the special shampoo. Do you want a haircut with this special shampoo also? You like San Martin, and it would be good for you."

Mikozy hummed to himself. Coincidence, Freddy and Reginald both getting haircuts here, and both were dead. He didn't know about Cavanaugh. Trouble was he didn't know how Freddy died. He thought there would have been a rapid response of shutting her down and taking her in if the agents who came here had suspected her of poisoning her customers. But she said they were only interested in Freddy. Of course, they probably didn't know about Reginald. He wondered if Craig was the one who came by.

"I'd like to take a bottle of each of these hair products. The special shampoo and the regular shampoo." He decided this was taking action. He couldn't think of anything else to do.

Teresa reluctantly agreed, probably thinking he wanted to take them for himself. The police in her town always said it was the custom for them to be tipped, and they took what they liked. She thought Mikozy was like the police from Faca.

"Don't worry, I'll pay you, and you'll give me a receipt. Okay?"

Teresa nodded. She didn't know if she should be more surprised that Mikozy was not like the police from Faca.

Mikozy was thinking about these elixirs of good looks. They would give LC something to check and find out if these chemicals acted differently than advertised.

"Thank you for your help, Teresa. I might be back with some more questions." He took out one of his business cards and scratched in his new address. He gave Teresa the card. He also held up the little metal icon to give back to Teresa. He thought her saint would be more likely to tell her the truth, whatever that truth was, and that she would be satisfied with what she heard. He hoped he didn't have to wait until then to hear from her.

Teresa said, "No, Señor Policía. You keep San Martin. He will help you."

Not wanting to offend her, Mikozy put San Martin into his pocket. "¿Si tiene cualquier información, que me llama, no?" Mikozy enjoyed reaching back into his Spanish and slipping between cultures.

"Okay." Teresa pronounced it the Spanish way, and unlike Mikozy, she wanted to reach forward into English. "If I can be of any help, especially with the boy. He was so polite."

Mikozy stepped out of the barbershop and into the flow of passengers. He found a spot that shielded him from crowd. He called to the office to see if there was a list of deaths tagged to LAX before and after Monday.

"Detective Schoenbrun. Can I help you?"

"Hey, Rita. It's me, Mikozy."

"What's up? You have more work for me? Work you should be doing?"

"You could say that. But I'm not at the office. I need a quick check. Can you help out?"

"Mikozy, you're one of my favorites. Favorite nuisance, favorite corner cutter, favorite whatever. What have you got for me now?"

"Can you check the list of deaths for the last several days? Especially just before and just after Monday."

"Hold on. Let's see what we have." There was a short pause, some clicks he heard. Rita pulling up the death lists. "As you might expect. Hundreds. You want to copy down each name? I'm kidding. What do you need?"

"Anything to do with airports? Poisons? Barbers?"

"My, my. Now we are looking for the Demon Barber of Fleet Street? That was a deadly musical."

"Rita, spare me the humor."

"Let's see. I see two listed on planes out of LAX."

"Names?"

"Frederick Panarese."

"Got him."

"And a Thomas Cavanaugh."

"Cavanaugh?"

"Yes. You know him?"

"Not that much. I need to go back and ask some questions."

"To?"

"The Demon Barber." He almost added, "The one at LAX," but sarcasm was premature. "Can you forward those names to the medical examiner lab, but only to LC? With the notation that she shouldn't do anything with those names until I talk with her? And she should especially avoid MEDEX."

"Kind of cryptic, isn't it? Will she know what to do with it?"

"Long story, Rita. With some slippery slopes right down to the gates of hell."

"Okayyyy. One of those romantic notes you used to send her?"

"One never knows what passes for romance these days. Thanks."

Rita was going to ask Mikozy more about what he was up to, but silence filled the air. He had hung up and was walking back to the barbershop to see Teresa. He walked back into the shop. Teresa saw him and smiled. "Señor Policía."

"Just a few more questions. I'd like to find out some more about Mr. Cavanaugh."

"I don't know what else I can tell you. Maybe Miguel can tell you more."

"How can I get a hold of Miguel? Does he have a mobile?"

"Sometimes he doesn't answer. Maybe better if you come by our house."

"That works. I can meet him there. Can you let him know I'm coming?"

"Yes."

With her address in hand, Mikozy was again on the move. Just not on an airplane.

Chapter 21
TALK RADIO

Mikozy zipped across the median, downshifting in his mind, letting his car find the gear in automatic. He turned on his radio, looking for one of his talk shows. The pulse of the city, and beyond, on expected hot topics and the arcane weirdness of the night.

"In the next half hour, we'll be talking about your favorite subject. Crime," Bill Parsons clamored at the end of a segment on getting even with bad neighbors, hoping to keep his audience after the two-minute commercial break. All Bill Parsons had to say was crime, and Mikozy was hooked. He enjoyed listening to the masses, telescoped into single voices and sequenced by the mood of the radio programmer.

"Do not call any telephone numbers that are given out. This program was recorded earlier." Mikozy had listened to Bill Parsons on and off for the past three months. This was radio prime time, and crime was one of his favorite obsessions. Whether it was the 1:00 a.m. or the 3:00 p.m. audience, they all liked to hear about crime. It didn't matter that this was a replay of an earlier show.

"Today we have Professor Liu-Smythe." Bill Parsons's words echoed in the car.

And after the commercials, Parsons repeated, "Today we have Professor Liu-Smythe. Welcome, Professor Liu."

Mikozy missed most of the lead-in, hearing only a few of the sound bites—only twenty-four years old, a real knockout, Asian princess.

As if on cue, Mikozy imagined speaking to the late-night audience even though they couldn't hear his ranting in the car. He thought about calling in and quickly remembered the host's admonition that this was prerecorded and it would be one of those useless acts. Mikozy wanted to call Liu but was afraid that someone else would answer and then asked himself, Why do I care?

Mikozy wasn't feeling joy or pride for Liu, though he told himself he should be. Mikozy's feeling was more like the fear about what she might say to perfect the aura of expert. He also wondered what she had already said on the show. Nothing Liu had ever said to him sounded like talk-show material. Not that anything he said was talk-show material either. Maybe it was Bill Parsons's clamoring about something, no matter what, that enticed the audience to listen. Mikozy as well. It was a way to pass time with a bump in the daily groove.

"Professor Liu, you teach police how to solve crimes, isn't that right?"

"I'd put it a little more humbly. I'm the first to admit that I've learned a lot from the seasoned investigators, and I'd like to give a special note of thanks to Detective Rafael Mikozy, and I hope he's listening in."

Mikozy banged his hand on the rubberized dash. *A lot more humbly, Jesus, teaching police to solve crimes, hah.* The rubber padding softened the physical pain but not the emotional dagger ripping through him. Mikozy was surprised at the feeling Liu opened in him. He fought to pay attention to the radio while the flood of desire and anguish pulled at him, trying to drag him into the sea of torment and silence. "Liu, take care," Mikozy said to the prerecorded show.

"Good, good." Parsons rushed along. "How do you teach police to solve crimes?" Parsons emphasized the "you" in his question.

"That's an important question, Bill." That was how Mikozy would have responded also, but Liu went on to say something different in completing her thoughts. "I give the students—you know, they're generally rookies, although occasionally I get an older cop—I give them a situation and have them look for clues."

"That's me again," Mikozy said to the radio. He was the only one listening to himself, just like the thousand other night souls talking to themselves about their own private agonies. "That's the name of the class, isn't it? Clue Analysis 1?" Without waiting for the answer, Parsons marched right on. "Is it okay to say cop?"

"Why, of course, Bill. They say it, we say it, what's wrong with the word?" Liu was as jolly as Parsons and almost as non-sensical. The program had not gotten past the chitchat.

"We'll be taking your calls in a few minutes. You can call in and have a question ready for Professor Liu-Smythe, but first a word from Ketsehara Ginseng. This'll perk you up for the lovely professor."

Mikozy hoped that Parsons and Liu would stay with the mindless back and forth, the perfect know-nothing conversation. Several tunes later, Parsons and Liu were back in command of the airwaves. The first caller was an older man, a real crank. He sounded like he wanted to dig Liu a megawatt grave.

"Why would any cop listen to you, young girl?"

Mikozy imagined Parsons flipping the old man's call off, leaving Liu to answer before racing on to the next caller. "Most of the new police officers are women, and I find even the macho veterans wanting more."

"She comes back to me." Mikozy was hollering inside the car, windows rolled up, and no one hearing two one-way conversations. Mikozy flushed, and his pulse skipped past the rapid fluttering he'd felt when he broke into Best's. It had been that kind of day. Mikozy would have crashed his car into some other invisible being in the night, but there weren't any other cars, and he continued on through the intersection without knowing whether the light was red, yellow, or green.

"We have another caller whose name is—"

"Stephanie."

Mikozy knew that voice. That sounded like Jane, Liu's sometime roomie Jane, the voice on the answering machine, Jane, the zinger in Liu's class, and Jane who was now Stephanie. Mikozy knew it was their game, but he didn't know the rules or why they liked this game.

"How can we help you, Stephanie?" Liu stepped right over Parsons as if she knew exactly how to answer the yet to be spoken question.

"I read, I think it was in today's paper, about somebody being poisoned with a new chemical. How do you teach a policeman to look for a new poison?"

"Good question, Stephanie. You should be in my class asking me the hard questions."

"Oh, come on," Mikozy railed to himself. He didn't know whether to turn the program off or to continue with the pain of listening to her con the audience. And Parsons too. Mikozy swerved to the curb in front of the parking garage. Once he drove into the concrete structure, he'd lose half the program, and he only wanted to stop in at his office for a few minutes.

Mikozy cut the engine and sat, his elbow propped up near the door lock, slouching down in his seat and listening to Liu and Jane, Jane and Liu. He wanted Parsons to cut this call off and move on to the next one.

"The trick is to avoid forming early judgments. That's something the officer would wait for the medical examiner to determine."

Mikozy was waiting for Liu to break her promise and talk about Reginald Hunter and the investigation he had invited her to observe. This was where she was headed. Mikozy knew.

"Well," Stephanie/Jane continued, "is this something we have to worry about?"

"Is this a public menace?" Parsons's voice cut in and made a high-voltage play for attention.

"According to my sources," Liu said, "which are pretty high up, this appears to be an isolated incident. Tom Cavanaugh was the CEO of Northern Petrolane. It appears there was a disgruntled employee, Miguel Santos, who allegedly splashed him with this chemical. I think that's the last we'll hear of that."

Stephanie/Jane disappeared from the night, and even Liu's voice faltered—no hertz, no watts, no connection with the audience. It was if she had had her say and now was melting away. Maybe it was he himself, Mikozy thought. His mind couldn't compute what Liu was saying. There was no sense to what she said. He reached for the emotional buoy she had thrown out to him at the beginning of the show in an effort to avoid drowning in her Petrolane story.

Mikozy quickly went through what Liu would know from being with him. She'd know about Reginald dying. Liu never heard LC's chemical analysis or about the exotic poison that killed Reginald or the illegal and whoever it was Craig was interested in. Liu had only heard Pomerance's theory about an asthma drug overdose, so where did Liu get a wild story about a new chemical poisoning this Cavanaugh? Mikozy had just learned about it when Schoenbrun read the death list with Cavanaugh's name on it. Was Liu for real? How could she be? Mikozy wished he had today's paper to see if there was a story about Tom Cavanaugh.

Everything Liu said, she couldn't have known, at least not from him or LC. He didn't think Schmidt would have told her. He didn't recall Tom Cavanaugh's name coming up in his meetings with Liu. "So what's she talking about?" Mikozy wondered aloud. He was particularly curious about Liu's account of an employee running amok and throwing a chemical poison on his boss.

And why Jane? Mikozy knew the answer to that. That was what made Mikozy suspicious about Liu's story. Liu used Jane as a plant and a trap. Liu wanted to get this information out. Mikozy thought about the crank and his momentary annoyance with Liu. Mikozy had to agree with Parsons, at least that Liu was young and it was surprising that he would put her in prime time. Mikozy wondered if she was fronting for someone else. She seemed to be playing some kind of game, and it might not be just for herself. It could be she was looking for fame and using other channels for background information. Mikozy's mind was speeding tight around the raceway. He was pumped up, jumping from rock to rock. Here was another one to leap onto. Did Liu realize that what she was saying was connected to Reginald's death? Mikozy was puzzled about Northern Petrolane and from what the barber, Teresa, told him about her husband working there. It was more about finding a helping hand, what Teresa called his patron. A sainted context.

He didn't know the answers, and he doubted that Liu knew the answers either. She seemed to have misleading information. He needed to find out how she'd gotten herself on Parsons's show or if someone else had placed her there. And if it was someone else, who was it, and what did this person want from her? Mikozy wasn't sure what Liu would tell him, but he hoped she would talk to him if he picked up the conversation from her "thank you, Mikozy." He was tired. Mikozy slipped back home. He needed one of those refresher naps. He readied himself and drove to his office, ruminating about Liu's late-night discourse.

Mikozy remembered where he was and didn't plan on spending the night talking to himself outside the parking garage. Mikozy got out of the car to walk to his office. He needed to tie down one corner of this jigsaw puzzle.

Liu stood next to Mikozy. So it seemed. He waited at the corner, looking around. Maybe this Liu was an apparition. She seemed real. She felt real. More than the imaginary real.

"Mikozy. Look up at the night. Hardly a moon. Can you see the hawk soar above the buildings? It may be looking for dinner. Or maybe just enjoying wandering the night. Seeing what we think is nothing. Seeing the energy beam across the darkness. Purple, yellow, red, all the colors we can see and more. Seeing the colors we cannot see. Hearing the voices of the night that we cannot hear. Smelling what we cannot smell. Feeling the wind race above and below as it rides the airwaves. Do you see the hawk, Mikozy?"

"No, I cannot see the hawk."

"Can you see the energy beaming across the sky? Feel its wave fluttering, caressing all the things you are thinking about. The darkness is alive. It is filled with color. Open yourself, Mikozy, to the night, to the darkness, to the energy, to the hawk, to the wind."

Mikozy looked about. He was alone. He was with Liu. He heard her but couldn't see what she could see. A cool breeze woke Mikozy from his reverie. He smiled at his imagined Liu and was about to continue on to his office. He stopped. He knew he needed to get things straight with Liu.

Chapter 22
TALK RADIO REDUX

Mikozy pulled out his phone. He couldn't leave the talking radio heads. Or maybe it was that they wouldn't leave him. Jane's words ricocheted against what he knew and what he didn't. Did Liu and Jane know something? Maybe they were seeking a reputational edge in talk land. He phoned Liu, determined to see if she was letting Jane leapfrog her promise to keep the insider view confidential. Mikozy was annoyed, not yet mad. How could he be mad if he couldn't place whether this late-night chatter had any value?

The groggy voice answered. "Mikozy? Is this you? It's kind of late."

"I'm surprised you're sleeping. I just heard you on the Bill Parsons radio show. And I heard Jane call in too. Said she was Stephanie."

"Come on, Mikozy. You know that was recorded earlier. I've been asleep for a while."

"But Jane was calling in as Stephanie?"

"You got me, Mikozy. That was Jane. I thought she would be helpful. You know, getting a random listener to call in. I literally collapsed when the show was over and drifted off."

"That's not why I'm calling."

"Oh?" A not so innocent reply.

"I thought you promised to keep the Reginald Hunter death confidential."

"I did. I didn't say anything about Reginald. I was talking about Tom Cavanaugh."

"That's precisely the point. Where did you come up with the Cavanaugh story? Sounds like a companion to Reginald. Did you just make Cavanaugh up to take away from what we're learning about Reginald? Maybe with a little spin to the details?"

"Mikozy, there's a bigger picture that's in play. I don't know if we should discuss it over the phone."

"I assume you will tell me."

"Yes, I'll tell all. But not on the phone."

"Why? Is it bugged?"

"Maybe I'm a bit paranoid. Maybe we're not in a detective novel but a spy thriller." Liu's voice danced around and even reached a lower octave when she reached spy thriller.

"I'm in a need to know. A need to know now."

"Okay. You want to come by my place?"

"No, that's not going to work. Can you come by police headquarters? Not inside. I'm just outside the parking lot."

"Okay, okay, okay. I suppose I owe you for jumping onto the late-night airwaves. I don't want to cross wires with you. Be there in a few."

Mikozy leaned up against the wall near where Perlmutter's homeless tent had been. City officials must have transported the Perl to a new location. It must have been unseemly to have the homeless camping out in front of police headquarters. The clean-up crew had washed the area down. It smelled normal. Just the crispness of the evening tinged with the lingering odor of cars. That would be back with the morning shift.

Mikozy thought about what he would ask Liu. What he need-ed to know without telling her more than what she needed to know. At least not just yet. There were too many moving parts, too many unknowns.

He heard a car pull into the garage. A door slammed shut, and the alarm beeped twice. Soft steps headed his way. No clicks or clacks of high heels. Either that was Liu in her exercise threads, or it was an interloper. Mikozy watched the exit. He stood in his usual just-out-of-the-way place. To see but not to be seen. It was Liu.

"Hey, Liu. Over here."

She smiled. "Should I join you in your hideaway?" Her voice was tinged with sarcasm.

"Yeah, why not? We don't want to be seen with each other. Not at this time of night."

"Funny, Rafael. But for the record, I don't mind being seen with you."

Liu and Mikozy leaned up against the stucco. Just enough light to see each other. The bright lights were around the corner of the building. Even the quiet was quiet. Unlikely to have cameras recording their meetup.

"So what's with the talk radio on the Bill Parsons's show?"

"What? No small talk? Just jumping right in?"

"Bill Parsons and what?"

"Okay. This is what happened, from what I know. I got a call from your captain Schmidt. He said that he had a request from a Dr. Neill Cream about a poisoning death. I thought it was about the Reginald case. I didn't say anything. I just listened. Your captain wanted me to talk with Dr. Cream. And maybe go on a radio show. He said that since I was teaching a course for the department, it would make sense for me to bring it up. And to let the public know at the same time. I said okay. And the next thing I know, I got a call from Dr. Cream about five minutes later."

"I hate to break it to you, Liu, but there is no Dr. Cream. It's a handle for one of feds."

"Huh. He sounded official. And how do you know that's not his name?"

"I was with LC. You know, my ex. In the medical examiner's office."

"I know. Just keep reminding me that she's your ex."

"So she gets a call from a Dr. Neill Cream about her inquiry to the National Institutes of Health's MEDEX database. About a poisoning."

"This is about Reginald Hunter?"

"No. LC got a body before. A day before Reginald. Looked like an industrial accident. Maybe an undocumented worker. She wanted to know what she was dealing with. Maybe this was a one-off or maybe the start of a trend for some new poison. So she put a request into MEDEX. What she got was a call from someone calling himself Dr. Neill Cream."

"So Cream is real."

"Yeah, a real jerkoff."

"What do you mean?"

"Well, LC realized later that Neill Cream was famous for poisoning women over one hundred years ago. Hung for it too."

"Dark humor."

"Yes. He's really a national security type. His real name is Lieutenant Colonel Robert Craig. And he is official. Maybe military intelligence."

"This doesn't sound like a national security issue. LC's first body, then Reginald. Local."

"Correct. So what was his pitch to you?"

Liu looked around. They were alone. She looked over at Mikozy. Their closeness returned.

"He said that there was somebody who was poisoned with a novel toxin. A guy named Tom Cavanaugh. He thought it would be a good way to let the community know."

"That's a little weak. Dropping it on talk radio? With a novice? Oooppss. Excuse me. I didn't mean to small talk you."

"I get it. I'm not a doctor. I'm not a medical examiner. I'm not the police. Why me?"

"Reminds me of the Spanish saying *la mano ajena*. A bit of misdirection. Using the hand of another to get the thing done. You were his patsy, and Schmidt put him on to you."

"So there's another death. Tom Cavanaugh. Somewhere else. And now the two deaths here in LA with the same poison. This Cavanaugh probably has some interest for the feds. This kind of makes sense from a national security point of view—if this Cavanaugh is where they started from. And then they get this call out of the blue from your medical examiner about a similar death here. Maybe others. They could just be trying to connect the dots. Dots that we can't really see from our end of the telescope. But still, why me?"

"Looks like they're fishing. Trolling the waters. You're the bait."

"Maybe. I think it's a nothing. And no, I didn't mention Reginald to him. And I didn't know about the earlier body that the medical examiner was working with."

"Three deaths," she said, while Mikozy said, "Four deaths."

"Four?" she asked.

"It may be four. Freddy, Frederick Panarese, died on a flight out of LAX. The circumstances were similar to Cavanaugh's."

"And?"

"And I don't want to get into that now."

"A trust issue?"

"More like I'm still trying to put the pieces together."

"Mikozy, I don't know if this means anything."

"Something else?"

"Captain Schmidt said that Deputy Inspector Tomlinson mentioned me. I don't know where she figures in. Maybe she knew about me when they approved my course on clue analysis."

Mikozy spun that piece of news until it landed. He looked at Liu as if she knew more.

"Tomlinson?"

"Wasn't she the one who assigned you to read a manuscript?"

"Yeah. A manuscript. A takeoff of Jack London's *The Iron Heel*. I think I mentioned that to you."

"That's kind of funny. You and me getting pulled into things by Inspector Tomlinson."

"Deputy Inspector." Mikozy corrected her in the bureau's pecking order.

"I was wondering if you could set up an interview with her. For me."

"What for?"

"I said this was more than I wanted to say over the phone."

"Something more?"

"I'm involved in something deeper."

Mikozy was half puzzled, half annoyed, and half intrigued. All 150 percent. "So what's up?"

"I'm fishing also."

"For?"

"I can't say right now." She hitched up between sentences. "I won't say trust me. No one trusts anyone anymore that says trust me. I want to say it. But no one believes those words anymore. Except those that should know better and go ahead anyway and believe those words. I just can't tell you right now. I will."

"I hope you're not working for a foreign government or some spooky criminal group."

"No. But just as serious."

Mikozy and Liu let her words hang on the dewdrops beginning to form in the almost-morning mist. "Can you set up an interview for me?"

"I'm not sure I can. Or if I want to. Let me think about it."

Liu reached over and put her hand on Mikozy's shoulder. "I understand. We can talk about it later. We can meet here." She scribbled an address on the back of a receipt. She handed it to Mikozy. "Here."

The silence began to weigh down the night.

"Maybe I need to finish reading *The Iron Heel* and the new manuscript." Mikozy was buying himself some time. He didn't plan on reading them any more than he had. He knew what he knew. That was enough. "Maybe I'll understand Tomlinson better. And Schmidt. And Craig."

Liu released Mikozy and turned to go back into the garage. Mikozy ended the connection. "Take care, Liu. Be careful what you touch. And let me know when." Her face wrinkled up a smile at the many meanings between them. If he could have seen her, he would have seen Liu mouthing back, "Whenever you're ready."

Chapter 23

A DOG'S DEATH

Asking for closure could be asking for impossibilities. Emotional ones also traveled a different path than finding out what happened. Mikozy followed the address that Teresa had given him at the airport. He hoped that finding out what happened would also close the emotional accounts that many had now invested in. Mikozy had only a sketchy idea of what Miguel, Teresa's husband, could say. Mikozy would ride the evening currents to see where Miguel would lead. He stood outside the house. There was a different world awaiting him.

Miguel came outside. "Let us go and get some food at McDonald's."

Mikozy was surprised at this detour. He wondered if Miguel wanted to hide something in the house.

"Are you hungry?"

"No. I want to talk with you alone. Then we come back here. You can meet Colombina and say hello to Teresa."

They walked several blocks. What looked like a McDonald's had a sign for Cotija. There was also a faded sign for McDonald's lying on the side of the building.

"McDonald's?"

"We call it McDonald's, but it closed several years ago. Then Cotija moved in. It is a good location for business, not so much for a changing barrio."

They stood outside. It wasn't about the food. It was about Miguel. It was about his boss and patron.

"Teresa told me that Mr. Cavanaugh was your boss."

"Yes. He helped me. He didn't look too closely at my *documentos*. He was a good man."

"Are you talking about what you needed to be hired? So, you know, I'm not interested if you're not here legally. I am not the *migra*."

Miguel looked up the street as if an immigration officer were roaming the neighborhood.

"They weren't real. Even my address is wrong. The company didn't check. Mr. Cavanaugh didn't check."

"Why did you want to talk here and not in the house?"

"There is a box Mr. Cavanaugh gave me. He said if anything happened to him, I should give it to the police. I don't know what happened to him. If something did…" Miguel waited a moment and then continued, "If something happened to Mr. Cavanaugh, I have the box he gave me in the house. I wanted to tell you about it here first. Not with Teresa and Colombina."

Mikozy would have waited for Miguel to tell his story. He saw a familiar face in the restaurant. Lieutenant Colonel Robert Craig was sitting at a corner table. Out of place in the restaurant, out of place in the neighborhood. Miguel followed Mikozy's gaze. His eyes rested on Craig and said, "That's Mr. Sugarman."

Mikozy thought he might have mistaken who he saw. He took a closer look. It was Craig.

"Who did you say that was?"

"He is Mr. Sugarman. He came to our company a few months ago. I don't like the man. Mr. Cavanaugh didn't like Mr. Sugarman. I asked him why, but he wouldn't tell me."

Craig/Sugarman caught sight of them and stood up. Mikozy tugged at Miguel. Neither wanted to speak with Craig/Sugarman. Miguel turned and pointed down a side street. "Follow me. I know the way back without him finding us." Mikozy heard a shot follow them. He decided to avoid a war of metal-jacketed words.

Instead he turned to Miguel. "Doesn't he have your address?" "He has my wrong address. He won't find us."

As they reached the house, the sun tipped over the horizon, and the light from the backyard dimmed. They went into the house. The room paled into deep gray, except for the TV. The screen's too-bright colors sparkled, preparing for the next in the series of unending shows. In the netherworld between gray and color, Colombina and Teresa continued to sit quietly and in numb detachment. They did not speak or chant. Their eyes were vacant. Mikozy entered their world, feeling the room rock, a soft to-and-fro. There was no earth quaking, nor blowing of a strong Santa Ana wind. What he felt was the root of his being and his understanding. The room vibrated and sang out in a sweet jazz rhythm. He walked with Miguel to the back door, pulling it back far enough to slip outside into the yard. Miguel waited inside. The sun had almost disappeared. It was near twilight. The garden pulsated in greens and golds, deep red flowers hung upside down, and vines draped down from a tree filled with fruit he had never seen before. Mikozy walked over to the tree and touched the unfamiliar fruit. A voice sang out from behind him, "*Maracuya*, it is called." Colombina walked over to Mikozy. He saw where her dress was tattered in places, and although he would have thought her a beggar if he had passed her on the streets in downtown LA, she commanded respect in her little garden. She had a radiant smile, and Mikozy thought he saw a halo sparkling in quick bursts of light from around her shoulders. "I have been here more than five years, and still the Americans do not know the maracuya."

Colombina reached out and put her left hand briefly on his right elbow, sending a warm wave, a not unpleasant rush of kindness, up Mikozy's arm and around his neck and back. "The children call me a witch and sometimes their parents too." Colombina looked up into Mikozy's eyes. He saw his face reflected in twin copper seas. The wrinkles flowed out from her eyes as if they had been etched on crystal, slowly twisting into snakes and becoming plants, and then turning into birds soaring across a cascade of streams. Colombina's mouth curled at the corners; her brown-stained teeth yawned while her tongue darted out.

"You don't believe in witches, do you?" He recognized the same lilt he'd heard in Teresa's voice and an accent that was only Spanish in part, but she spoke clearly and slowly, and he understood her without any difficulty. He was surprised by her openness in talking with him. If she wasn't a witch, she cast a good spell. "At least not since I was a child," he answered silently.

"You can see, I tend my garden. It was easier when Miguel"— and midway through her thought she lifted her chin to point to Miguel still inside her house—"when Miguel helped me take care of my garden." She pointed again with her chin to a vine that climbed the side of her house. A thick vine that could wrap around the dense Amazon jungle while a boa languidly curled over the thick tendril. "This is *el bejuco yagé*, from which I made our afternoon tea. I made it mild." She smiled as if this were a private joke. But with the special mellowness Mikozy felt at this moment and the uncanny insight she seemed to have bestowed upon him, he experienced the inside of her joke. She ran her finger around the garden. "These are special plants from Colombia, which I use to cure spiritual illnesses. This is not a problem for you." Mikozy was certain she was not posing a question.

Mikozy looked around the garden and realized that none of the plants looked familiar to him. He could believe that she was a spiritual healer and this was her native pharmacopoeia. Mikozy wasn't sure whether she had any concern about American doctors or the FDA wanting to confiscate her drugstore. Mikozy didn't think Colombina would mind his complaining about being taken on this spiritual adventure without being told in advance of his destination. It didn't make much difference to him now. He knew he needed to be transported out of LA until he could make some sense out of the fire at La Chucha. And although Colombina's garden might have been less than ten blocks away from La Chucha, it was actually more than three thousand miles away from LA. Except for her neighbors and friends, no one would know about Colombina and her garden. Mikozy had some time to think about what happened and to begin, once more, the guessing about what he knew, what he thought he knew, and what he was certain he didn't know. Was he an intended victim? Could he safely come out of this rabbit hole without endangering himself or, for that matter, without endangering Miguel and Teresa?

"I don't really care what people grow in their backyards as long as it is not marijuana. Except no longer. The law changes and I no longer care about that either."

"Sit, *m'ijo*, I know of this American fascination. It is a pity, since marijuana is a very helpful plant." Colombina did not hurry her thought, nor show any disappointment. "In this country, I have to use other plants, and there are many plants that the Americans do not care about." She paused, making sure that Mikozy understood what she was saying. Mikozy remembered his third grade teacher talking to him about fractions in this way.

"Like yagé. Of course, yagé is more powerful than marijuana and requires more care. It makes a good tea." She glowed in anticipation of the moon; her all-knowing smile told of a centuries-old tradition that used plants to alter consciousness as well as to cure maladies. Mikozy did not mind her playing with him, because what she said was true. Perhaps even marijuana would be okay if it was only in her garden and used to cure spiritual illnesses. Even with the state's legalization of its use, he wasn't sure how far the spiritual side extended into the cure of physical illnesses. Mikozy did not want to destroy this island of new-world energy, resuscitated from the southern hemisphere and transplanted back into LA. Mikozy wondered if he was being inconsistent in his tolerance of Colombina compared to his intolerance of Galaxy Gems when he first went there. Maybe it was the danger caused by the concentrated drugs, which, if left in their natural form, would not be a reason for addictive crimes. That didn't seem to be a complete response. Maybe society's prohibitions of certain psychoactive states could only be enforced by creating villains and monsters. He would hate to see Colombina painted by the politicians or the media as a cause for the occasional social collapses in LA. Mikozy walked away from his uncertainty. He wasn't coming up with adequate justifications. He needed more time and facts to sort out what was going on. Mikozy surveyed the garden again. Inside the lush jungle was a barren spot about four feet square. Mikozy walked over to the spot. It hadn't been worn down as a path. The path wandered over to the left of the spot and was marked by stepping stones. Miguel came through the door and came to the other side of the barren area where Mikozy now stood. Colombina joined them at the third edge of the square.

"There's nothing growing here. Is there something wrong with this patch of earth?" Mikozy asked.

"Yes," Miguel said. His yes was not a simple one. It was shrouded in anxiety, his voice thick with sorrow.

"You tended this garden?" Mikozy asked. Miguel nodded and looked across with a steady gaze at Colombina.

"And this spot too?"

Miguel nodded again. That seemed to be a strange response. Colombina spoke confidently of Miguel's gardening, and even Miguel had said he had worked in her garden here and in Facatativa. He had been an assistant, an apprentice, who followed Colombina and her son, Miguelito, to America.

"Why isn't anything growing here?"

Mikozy thought he was in the middle of a gardening class for a moment when Miguel replied, "Colombina's son, Miguelito, had a dog, one that he had found on the streets hiding in door-ways during the heavy rains. It was skinny. We had been like that in Faca, in Facatativa, and he took it in out of pity and called it Copal. He said the dog reminded him of us."

Miguel stopped, his eyes never wavering from the ground. A cricket chirped as prologue to Miguel's disquisition on life. Miguel continued, "We are like stray dogs in the streets of America, and we are grateful when someone takes us in." Mikozy was surprised to hear this plain comparison spoken without bitterness. Mikozy almost wanted to hear anger in Miguel's voice, but it was spoken as a simple truth. They were standing in different worlds, and he struggled to leap into Miguel's world, but only for this moment. Mikozy still wanted to hold on to LA.

Miguel repeated something Mikozy lost in the darkening twilight. "The dog died the same day Miguelito did. And we buried Copal here."

"The dead dog killed the plants?" Mikozy asked if that was what Miguel had meant to say.

"I do not think so," Colombina said. Her voice became strong, and it electrified Mikozy. He tried to look closely at her, but she was shrouded in near blackness, pulsating negative energy flowing back into her. Teresa now stood at the fourth side of Copal's grave. The garden was warm at their backs, while frigid air inside the vacant dirt lot chilled their faces. Colombina shrieked as Mikozy imagined a hawk digging its talons into her and lifting her spirit into the night. She tilted back and sank into a fearsome crouch. This was her battle. Mikozy could only bear witness to an alien mind.

Miguelito, Miguelito, I touch your soul, gentle heart,
Lost in the day, night wanderer,
My son,
Listen, listen for Copal,
Follow her into this garden, into this poisoned earth,

Mikozy will find your lifeless heart, your empty body,
And into this dirt you will find your rest.

Teresa and Miguel joined Colombina, the three of them chanting in a distant place.

Yagé, yagé, pinto, pinto
canto, yagé, yagé,
canto, pinto, yagé.

Mikozy didn't know if their words were meant as a prayer, to evoke a memory, or simply to keep them company on their adventure in wonderland. What he heard was profound sadness. He looked at Colombina, and even though her eyes were closed, they glistened. The old woman's face was troubled. All she had was the body of the stray dog her son had found. She was troubled about her lost son. She was no witch.

Mikozy wanted to know more about how Colombina's son had died. He hesitated. He sensed a barrier. Impenetrable to question. A barrier that was partly the cold and barren square they stood around, partly the slowness of time.

"Maybe the dog was already sick."

Colombina did not respond to Mikozy. She continued to chant to the night. Teresa leaned toward Mikozy, and when he finished, she leaned back toward the center of the spot. She heard but did not answer. Miguel broke into the stillness.

"Copal was thin. She wasn't sick. He fed the dog, and within a week Copal was very spirited. She got better. The dog died quickly, very quickly. It was something else."

Mikozy thought about being a detective trying to solve the mysterious deaths of dogs. This could be a new opportunity, since he couldn't think of any other detective assigned to solve dog deaths. He could mention this to Schmidt. But there was a problem. Dog deaths might be harder to solve than human deaths, which would only mean more job frustration.

"Órale, joto," a singsong voice called. Mikozy looked past Colombina into the alley running behind her garden. A meager streetlight outlined three T-shirted youths, hair slicked back, baggy shorts and high-tops, flashing hand signs in recognition of who belonged in this neighborhood. They were looking down the alley beyond the side of Colombina's house. Mikozy finally caught sight of another boy walking up to the three or maybe trying to get past them. He wasn't dressed to code, sporting instead neat denim slacks, a white shirt, and a tie. Mikozy was surprised most of all by the tie. This kid was aiming for management, while the others couldn't see beyond hauling and cleaning. The boy was a challenge to the symbol of badness the other three evoked. The boy didn't flash any hand signs, and he did a poor job of trying to look the others off. They sidled back and around the boy and blocked his movement. They weren't any bigger than the boy, and they didn't look like they were carrying. But they were pack animals tonight, and they didn't mind if they messed up their clothes.

"This *vato*'s a *vendido*," said one. "Sellout."

"Simon," echoed the other two.

"Mamon," he said.

"Simon," echoed the night.

They circled tighter, chests puffed and fists curling at their sides. This was a dance Mikozy had seen hundreds of times before. He saw it in the jails. He saw it in war movies. He saw it in documentaries on educational television about hunting behavior. He couldn't remember if the programs said there was any difference between man and the animal kingdom.

Mikozy had his own view. He always wondered if what he thought was gospel or heresy. Mikozy also saw it in the streets when he was growing up. Mikozy had been inside that circle more than once. Mikozy's left hand went up and behind his neck. He felt the scar, still burning after twenty years.

"Spic," someone had yelled, and then he felt the fire dig into his back.

"Lucky for you where the knife entered," the doctor told him the next day. The memory had been submerged and forgotten, and then appeared when it wanted. Mikozy knew in those moments that was what had led him to put on a badge. The hope and the illusion that he was more than a pack animal. The documentary didn't say that, but it should have. What could the boy say? He wasn't wearing the right colors or clothes, or maybe it was his attitude. Or maybe it was just because he was alone. The three of them pushed the boy to the ground. They kicked him, a flurry of feet, and an echo that moaned. But they were low-intensity kicks, and it was obvious they wouldn't harm the boy, except for his feelings. Mikozy watched the drama unfold, riveted to a barren piece of earth. The one-act play prohibited anyone in the audience from getting up to stop the action. The boys didn't pay any attention to them either.

Suddenly, Colombina turned around and cawed. "Who walks outside my fence?"

She must have seen them, though she spoke like a blind person. "Tell me who is out there. ¿Quienes son?"

The force of her words shot out, and even Mikozy jumped. The three aspiring *veteranos* reeled back away from their prey, terror invading their eyes. Their bodies were transfixed, and their spirits had already flown away. Their ancient roots froze their modern ambitions.

"It's the *bruja*. Trejo. That's Miguel Trejo's mama. Let's get the fuck out of here," one of the boys yelled out. None of them turned to face Colombina. They didn't answer her. They didn't turn to see where the questions came from. They drew back, jerking and banging against each other, and scattered in all directions. The boy stood up.

He didn't hold himself in pain nor stumble around. He didn't bother to brush himself off, only sneaking a glance at Colombina before running off into the shadows. Except for the occasional bark and honk from a distant street, silence returned to Colombina's garden. Silence, except for Teresa's chanting.

Pinto, pinto
canto,
canto, pinto, yagé.

There was a compelling urgency to Teresa's low voice. For a moment, Mikozy thought that Teresa might succeed in transporting them back to Faca or at least out of LA. He looked down at the plain dirt spot, and it was still there. And they still stood on the four edges of Copal's grave.

"Tell me what happened that day," Mikozy said to Miguel.

"It was an ordinary day," Miguel said.

Teresa's chanting became louder. Even with the dim light filtering into the garden from the streetlight, Mikozy thought he saw a tear fall to the ground. Teresa's small body shivered. Colombina also looked curiously at Teresa.

"Tell me," Mikozy repeated.

Miguel looked from Mikozy to Teresa and then to Colombina. Mikozy knew then that it was not an ordinary day and that the dog's death was not an ordinary event. This was the moment that recreated their life in LA and from which terrible events sprang. Miguel continued his story.

"Miguelito—"

Mikozy interrupted. Sometimes details were important. "Miguel Trejo?"

"Yes, Miguelito. He wanted to clean Copal and make her pretty. The dog needed a good bath. Her hair was bunched up and oily. Where we come from, this was expected. We do not wash our animals. What sense would it make? Our floors are dirt; we have no wooden floors, no cement, no vinyl. Washing our house animals is foolishness. But we live in America, and this is what we see on the television and what we help the gringos do. Miguelito wanted to take care of Copal as he thought Americans would take care of her."

Miguel waited. He inched away from Teresa before continuing his story.

"Teresa listened to Miguelito. She said Saint Martin would like her to give Copal a shampoo. You know Saint Martin?" Miguel asked Mikozy, his voice layered with an irony Mikozy hadn't noticed before.

"Yes, I know about him. San Martin de Porres." Mikozy remembered Teresa's delight in talking about San Martin and imagined she would have conveyed the same enthusiasm to Miguel. The path of charity and good deeds would be the same for Teresa. This was her rock and her faith.

"We were here in this garden. Miguelito sat here in this place. The day was very hot, and I remember wiping the wetness from my face with my hand. This place was covered with high grass. It was so hot that the little bugs jumped higher than the grass. Miguelito held Copal on his lap and patted her. He laughed at Teresa and said, 'That is foolishness, Teresa. I just want to brush her out.' This is how we talked with each other. Colombina stood at the door inside and away from the hot sun. She wanted me to work in the garden. She said, 'Don't waste your time washing the dog. Dogs were not meant to be washed by us.'"

Colombina nodded, following the memory Miguel was picturing. Teresa was quiet, still looking down at the ground.

"Teresa said, 'Miguel and Miguelito can work in the garden. I will clean Copal. I will make her beautiful.' And Teresa said she was going to make a new shampoo and would honor Copal by using it on her first."

Teresa lifted her face up, her eyes wandering aimlessly. She stepped back, giving the impression that she was dizzy. Teresa slumped to the ground. Colombina simply watched, puzzled by Teresa's reaction to this memory.

Miguel rushed over to Teresa. He started to slap her face. At first, Mikozy thought this was a native practice of trying to startle a person back into consciousness. But Mikozy saw Miguel's face tighten like a vise, and even the shadows could not hide the anger in Miguel's voice. A stream of invectives rushed out into the night, punctuated by the slaps. Mikozy jumped across the square and corralled Miguel in his arms, pulling him away from Teresa.

As Mikozy struggled with Miguel, Colombina walked over to Teresa and asked, "What did you do, Teresa? What did you do?"

Colombina could have struck Teresa too. It would have had the same effect. Teresa was trembling in fear of Miguel's anger, but even more from the fear of the witch tearing out her soul and leaving her to wander in a foreign land without sense or purpose. Even San Martin could not save her from the witch. Mikozy threw Miguel to the side and rushed in between Colombina and Teresa. There was more to the story to be told, and Mikozy did not want to be robbed by either spousal or magical furies.

"Teresa, it's okay. Just rest a moment." Mikozy held up his left hand to signal Miguel and Colombina to delay their intended punishment.

"Teresa, are you all right?"

She looked off into space, still stunned from the anger and accusations.

"Miguel, get me some water," Mikozy said. He remembered Teresa's gift and patted his pockets. He felt the little icon of San Martin that Teresa had given him at the barbershop. He pulled out the little pewter frieze of San Martin with the dogs sitting at his feet.

"Here, Teresa, hold on to San Martin," he said, and he pressed the little icon into her hand and held her hand up to her face. Her eyes focused on San Martin. Mikozy sensed her release some of the tension in her body. Miguel came back with a glass of water and helped Mikozy give it to Teresa. Teresa appeared to have crested the trauma. She looked back and forth between the two men huddling over her.

"I feel better now."

"Can you stand up?" Mikozy asked.

"Yes, I can try."

Mikozy and Miguel helped Teresa stand up. She leaned away from Miguel. She was still fearful. The accusation had not been washed away.

"Did you use anything from the bottles in the box I brought here from Mr. Cavanaugh?" Miguel asked Teresa. Mikozy watched Teresa's face contort. This was more than the agony of physical pain. The question penetrated the cell where she kept her most secret secret. Mikozy didn't know where Miguel's questions were headed. Mikozy didn't know the landscape of their memories and couldn't find the clue to unlock Teresa's secret.

"Miguel?" Teresa gasped. She leaned harder into Mikozy while she stared at Miguel.

"Me da mucha pena, por favor, Miguel," she cried out and pleaded for understanding and relief from her embarrassment. Or was she pleading for forgiveness for what she had done? Mikozy heard something fall to the ground. He looked down, and in the moonlight now flowing from the southern horizon he saw what appeared to be the little icon of San Martin in the dirt.

"Tell me, Teresa, what did you do?" Miguel pleaded for the truth.

Teresa lifted her head and pointed with the edge of her chin to the corner of the garden. She was unable to speak. Miguel looked to where she pointed. Miguel walked over to the corner at the back of the house. Mikozy helped Teresa walk over to where Miguel stood. Colombina stayed where she was as if she already knew the tale of woe. They walked through Colombina's garden and found a box next to the side of the house. The top was torn and held closed by a brick. Mikozy knelt down and saw most of the words of Northern Petrolane's stenciling on the remaining flap. Miguel leaned over and took the brick off the box and placed it on the ground. He lifted up the flap. The box was divided into twenty-five compartments, all but one containing small, dark brown glass bottles. Mikozy reached into the box to pick up one of the bottles, but Miguel grabbed his hand.

"*Insecticida*, it's very dangerous," Miguel said.

Mikozy lifted up the bottle anyway. The bottle had no label, no instructions, no skull and crossbones, no universal warning. Mikozy noticed some papers that had been slid down along the inside of the box against one row of bottles. He pulled out the papers and put them under the box. He'd look at them later. Mikozy still wanted to know about the missing bottle.

"Is this the box you told me that Cavanaugh gave you?" This was an easy deduction. Miguel said he was a given a box to take care of, and here was a box from Northern Petrolane. Unless Miguel was stealing from the company, this was probably the box that Miguel was told to turn over to the police if something happened to Cavanaugh. Well, here he was.

Miguel nodded. "Mr. Cavanaugh, he was my boss at Northern Petrolane." Mikozy listened, reentering the story Miguel had told him at McDonald's just awhile ago. Miguel wasn't remembering the story he told Mikozy. Either that or he thought Mikozy had a weak memory. Miguel struggled telling his story, his hands agonizing in prayer. Miguel didn't add anything, obviously paralyzed by what he remembered and thoughts of what he didn't know.

"Is this the box Cavanaugh wanted you to turn over to the police?"

Miguel's eyes widened. Things were going too fast in this yagé-tinged moment.

"Yes, this is it. But I did not open it." Miguel leaned against the side of the building. Mikozy noticed for the first time that the back of Colombina's house was a makeshift addition, built out of bamboo and a straw thatch roof. The long slivers of bamboo were tied together with native twine. Dried corn husks were bundled and hung from the bamboo. Mikozy turned toward Teresa and saw the horror in her eyes as she stared at the box. He needed to know what memories she was trying hard to suppress, and to pry open the story each one of them wanted to hide from. Mikozy was forced into asking the elemental question about what had happened in this wonderland.

"Teresa? Did you open the box?"

"No, no, no, no."

Mikozy was surprised at her response. If she hadn't opened this Pandora's box, who had? Even Miguel's eyes jumped at Teresa's answer. He must have made some assumptions about what happened and suffered in what he believed Teresa did. Colombina had walked up to the side of the house and stood over Mikozy as he crouched by the box. He didn't hear her approach. He knew she was behind him when she rested her hand on his shoulder, steadying herself against what she had to say.

"Miguelito opened it. He was curious about what Miguel brought here."

They huddled next to the house staring at the open box and the one empty slot. Mikozy looked up at the sky. Despite the glow from the city itself, the stars were bright, one of them shooting itself into nothingness. The air had chilled, and a light mist descended upon the garden.

"Why?" Mikozy asked to nobody. He asked it of everybody. Why do people do things anyway? If you ask them, they will have the ready answer. And if you ask again and again, just as a four-year-old asks why and why again, the answer dissolves into "I don't know." Do they ever tell the truth, if they can?

Miguel looked over at Colombina. "Why?"

She answered in a slow, melancholic slew of words. "Miguel asked if he could leave the box. I said he could. I never asked what was in the box." She repeated, "My Miguelito asked me about it, and I told him I didn't know. Miguel brought it here. I never asked what was in it."

She added the words of everywoman: "My Miguelito was curious."

Mikozy felt Colombina tighten her grasp on his shoulder. "I saw Miguelito open the bottle. I was about to tell him no, but he was going to open it anyway."

Teresa joined Colombina's telling of the story. "I asked him what was in it. He spilled a little on his finger and rubbed it." Teresa held up her hand and rubbed her fingers together in memory of that moment. She put her hand down, rubbing the imaginary liquid off on her skirt.

"It made a nice foam and smelled sweet. 'It's only soap,' Miguelito said. He laughed and poured some more on his hands, and then he rubbed it on his face."

"Yes, it's only soap," Colombina said, agreeing with Teresa's memory.

"Insecticida," Miguel barked and moved over to Teresa.

"Insecticida," he repeated loudly.

His anger surged, and he raised his arm as if to hit Teresa again. Mikozy was ready this time, and he pushed Miguel's arm away from Teresa.

"Miguel, I need to know what happened. Let's listen to her."

Miguel moved back.

"Go ahead, Teresa," Mikozy pressed on. "Tell us what happened next."

"I asked Miguelito to give me the bottle," Teresa said. She stopped. Outside in the dark beyond the fence of the garden, there were shouts and running. Latin leprechauns put their tags on at night. That was what the police radios would report in this area. It would be the same in other neighborhoods, except that the police would be calling in their over their own radio channels disguising their racist dogma as joking references to lepre-cohens, lepre-coons, cracker-chauns, and arab-chauns but really venting their fear of the wildness and the craziness of young manhood. The police force was filled with diversity. It was the new age of LA. But they needed the semantics of old school diversity. The community could speak about niceness. They could also hide their fears, their hatreds. The police had to run into the chaos of whatever diversity ruled. Chaos pulled back the curtain of new age etiquette. The old rules took charge. The police held a universal belief that everyone was crazy. That was the only way to survive in LA.

The quiet returned to Colombina's garden and with it the illusion of being beyond the LA war zone.

"What did you do with the bottle?" Mikozy had to pull the answer from Teresa.

For a brief moment, Teresa smiled in memory of Miguelito's discovery of the soapy liquid in the little brown glass bottle.

"That day I brought a bottle of Krindell's shampoo home. I accidently spilled some on the floor at the airport, and I wanted to replace it with something. It is so expensive. I was going to buy something at the supermarket to put into the Krindell bottle. So when Miguelito showed us the soap and how sweet it smelled, I decided to mix it with the Krindell shampoo. I thought it was going to be a special shampoo, better than Krindell's. It had a very nice color too." Teresa's voice had an urgency, not wanting to stop for fear of being interrupted and never finding the opportunity to explain again. Teresa wanted to make sure they understood it wasn't only to make up for her accident in spilling some of Krindell's shampoo or even the beauty she thought the special shampoo would give to the hair but that her mixing the new soap was a kindness and a goodness.

"I made it for San Martin and for all of his—" Teresa couldn't find the word, but each of them knew what she wanted to say. Everyone did what they could to make the world a better place, and what better thing could Teresa do than to honor her saint and the people who approved of him? Her plan to shampoo Miguelito's dog was a sign of saintly conduct. Or at least someplace between saintly conduct and becoming an American.

Mikozy still hunted the cook's secret. How had she managed to brew and apply the potent liquid without killing herself? "Did you ever touch the liquid the way Miguelito did?"

"Aiii, no," Teresa said. "When I went to school, we were taught to use gloves whenever we gave shampoos. Most of us were from other countries, and we were often told that Americans liked to have everything clean, especially in the better places."

"You didn't wear gloves to shampoo the dog, did you?"

Mikozy had to ask at least one bully question and try to shake loose an inconsistency in her story.

"I did not think. I always wear my gloves to give a shampoo. I used gloves to give Copal her shampoo. I warm up the water first. I put on the shampoo and then the water. It is comforting."

Mikozy turned his head back to see Colombina's reaction. In the dim evening light, Mikozy saw Colombina move her body in agreement. "Yes. Teresa was wearing gloves. She is very careful and does what she is told." Colombina walked back to the barren spot, perhaps only to look at it, perhaps to ponder their immigrant tales. They had become her children too; she was someone who watched over them as they learned to walk all over again in this new land. She sought out the silence; she merged with the bushes and vines, rooted to the ground, eyes on an urban night and the visage of an uncertain season. Was there ever winter in LA?

Mikozy thought about their innocent beginnings, all of her children; their desire to help out and the delight in discovery, and the deadly twist of events. Cavanaugh had recruited Miguel to help him hide this box of insecticide. For whatever reason, Cavanaugh had Miguel help. Miguel was happy to help out. He must have thought of Cavanaugh as his personal savior. Teresa had her saint, and Miguel had his. Teresa's saint was a medallion she could carry in her purse. Easy enough for her to project her fantasies of how a peasant could be a good person. Miguel's saint was flesh and blood and his boss, someone who asked for help in words that could be heard and felt. Cavanaugh was no fantasy. How strange that Miguel's patron saint was Cavanaugh, a captain of industry and a devout materialist who out of some inner weakness decided to do a personal kindness and gave Miguel his miracle crack in the American door of opportunity. And all the while Miguel had a wife who had a metal saint who inspired her to walk through a different crack in the American doorway. Two miracles in one family. Mikozy shook his head at these funny images as they skirted across and around the garden. With a twinge of dark humor, Mikozy wondered if this was a garden of evil. He didn't think it was. Was it merely a garden of bad luck?

Mikozy mentally transcribed what had happened onto his imaginary crime summary form, better known as the CF-4. Once upon a time just called CF. It meant card file. Now it meant computer form. The information was about the same except now it belonged to Big Brother. No one called the supercomputer Big Brother. The new language left out Big Brother. It was just the Big. Yet the efficiency of storing and retrieving information was the new architecture of social control. Mikozy thought about Deputy Inspector Tomlinson and his assignment to analyze Jack London's *The Iron Heel* and its revision. This was more than data storage. It was now verging on what law and order meant. None of it would help Teresa and Miguel.

"Oh, well," Mikozy mumbled to himself, "at least I get to put the information into the system." He smiled, knowing how he coded information in devious ways so that it was obvious only if someone knew what he was thinking. Mikozy thought again about Tomlinson and the database at headquarters. The only error he made, and it was years ago, was the time Schmidt asked him about Julia Restrepo, a code name Mikozy had given to one of his informants. Unfortunately, he had used the name of a local junior high school. Schmidt called, indignant about what Mikozy had done. He claimed to have been embarrassed at an intelligence coordinating meeting when he talked about Julia Restrepo. While Schmidt bludgeoned Mikozy with the supervisor's invocation, calling him asshole, pea brain, worm spit, shithead, and other semantic devices designed solely to harass the lowly employee, Mikozy wondered about the intelligence coordinating committee. Nobody ever told us about the intelligence coordinating committee, he thought, or that the names of our informants would be bandied about with god knows who. Might as well forget the guarantee of anonymity. Maybe it was just as well that Julia Restrepo had exploded in Schmidt's face. It took away management's sanctuary. "So, Schmitty, we're giving out informant names now?" Mikozy had asked. Schmidt didn't respond. He must have realized his mental slip. Schmidt had hung up without saying anything else and never mentioned Julia Restrepo to Mikozy again. After that, Mikozy decided to leave significant pieces of information out until he was ready to publicize what he knew.

Mikozy was more careful now, so he didn't need to worry who pulled up his CF-4s. For some unknown reason, Mikozy thought about a computer, and he saw a chip deciding whether or not to participate in the flow of information. Mikozy knew he would be angry at the chip for disrupting the game plan embedded in the central processing unit, in the machine's brain. And why wouldn't Schmidt and police management get angry at Mikozy? He was a chip with an independent will. But they all knew the game. It wasn't the mindless flow of information that somehow got organized; no, there wasn't any electric efficiency that zipped and zapped the criminal enterprise. The bits and bytes were sampled by just about everyone and decoded in the intelligence coordinating committee. Wasn't that the purpose of an information system? But Schmidt was sharing information on this case with outsiders. Mikozy didn't know what the legal boundaries were, but even if there weren't any, he would still be paranoid about where their information was going. Schmidt seemed to be sharing information with Colonel Craig, whom he suspected might be running some kind of paramilitary operation in downtown LA. Schmidt might be sharing information with Carlos Morales too. Why was Schmidt's name on the list that Morales's runners were using? Mikozy was still a detective, so he imagined Schmidt and the committee, and whoever else in the department made a decision about the kind of information they put into their computers, had decided to leave him alone. Mikozy saw the walls of isolation going up around him. He could be a detective, but it was difficult when others were playing keep-away.

The image of Reginald Hunter, a.k.a. Austin Hepworth, invaded Mikozy's thoughts. Reginald lay spread out on the living room floor. Reginald had looked dignified in death. Maybe it was the circle of candles Clarice had arranged, her small act of defiance to the ghost of Nathaniel Byron. Mikozy remembered Pomerance doing all the things a medical investigator was supposed to do, circling like a bird of prey for the answer to the question Reginald's body asked: Why did I die? Pomerance hedged his answer, but Mikozy saw the pride sliding beneath the surface of a man bitten too often by the vagaries of life. Pomerance was sure he had figured out that Reginald had accidentally overdosed on Clarice's medicine. A mother's antidote that tasted more like poisonade. That was a good guess, Pomerance, Mikozy thought. Too bad you were wrong.

That was when things started going sideways. Schmidt had a hard time handling cases that went sideways. Schmidt would have wanted to get this case run down the center of the freeway. But then he would have had to surgically remove Mikozy from the case. Mikozy would have been kept from wandering LA's freeways and sticking his face into venues like Galaxy Gems. Schmidt would have preferred no more accidents on this case, which was as much as what Schmidt told Mikozy. Mester would have been the ideal choice to cauterize this festering boil. Mester would miss all the interesting clues while poking at the obvious but often wrong cause. Schmidt knew Mester was a novice. Schmidt would have had the look of administrative happiness when Mester was appointed to close out what appeared to be a single case. But this one flower of evil was more than a single blossom. It needed a talent to persevere beyond the blossom. Mikozy had stumbled upon the underground root. If he were a botanist, he might choose plant life native to LA. Like the oleander. But don't eat. Mikozy guessed that he had discovered a new form of oleander that needed a new name and a new warning. Like the leaves. That wasn't in the computer yet. It was only recently in Mikozy's mind. And it wouldn't be in the police supercomputer until Mikozy knew what he wanted to do and how he planned to act out his cop script, which didn't necessarily mean putting someone away or letting them go.

Mikozy laughed at Schmidt's telling him to get out of the way and let Mester snip off a little piece of this plant, thinking that's all there was. Mikozy was moving along the root system and doing unexpected biological research. Strange plants, strange brews, strange Colombina, strange Teresa, strange Miguel. Mikozy stretched his feet and shivered in the night air. Reginald's image stayed with Mikozy. Reginald was only one of the victims of this curious series of poisonings. Miguel was one of the instrumental causes. But so was Cavanaugh. He put Pandora's box in Miguel's care. And the other Miguel, the dead Miguel, played a part when he toyed with a bottle he took out of Cavanaugh's box, and so too Teresa for trying to make the world a little more holy, and even Colombina for not telling her son to leave the box alone. And probably so was Colonel Craig, although Mikozy wasn't exactly sure about how. Craig had been hiding his dirty hands by admitting to little more than an after-the-fact investigation.

And there was where the danger lay. Craig might be getting access to the computer files; somehow Craig had become a too early recipient of Mikozy's CF-4, giving the colonel a chance to bend the outcome in a different way than Mikozy would. Craig's hands were dirty. He might find a better outcome in some way, but it wouldn't be Mikozy's way, and Mikozy had faith in himself. The chill of the night air slipped beneath Mikozy's shirt, an involuntary spasm shaking him gently, a reminder of pruning and cutting that he needed to do. Mikozy's CF-4 might not say everything he was thinking and feeling. Mikozy might say Miguel took Cavanaugh's box for safekeeping. It might say Miguel put it into an alleged witch's house. Who would have guessed that Colombina had casually reinvented her Colombian pueblo in LA? Unless you knew Miguel, you wouldn't have known about his miniature folk community. Who could have known about his mentor, Colombina, and how he had tended her garden in their hometown and here in LA, and that her son was his friend and also named Miguel? What was in these names? Was it something special, a tribal umbilical cord? To an outsider, to a CF-4, it was rendered as confusion.

Maybe he would leave that out of the CF-4. Mikozy side-stepped one of life's unexplained coincidences—same names, different selves. It didn't matter now. What mattered was Cavanaugh's box. Miguel had taken the box from one of his patrons, Cavanaugh, and put it in the garden of his other patron, Colombina. Nothing unusual in that, if one knew the psychological crutches Miguel walked on. And harmless, or so it appeared. It could have been harmless.

If the box had only been left alone. So what if the bottles weren't labeled and Miguel didn't bother to tell Colombina, his friend Miguelito, or Teresa that the little bottles contained a deadly insecticide? Maybe he was afraid Colombina would have said no to his storing the box in her garden, or maybe it was because Cavanaugh didn't want it to be conspicuous. Who would bother with this box anyway? That wasn't something that either Cavanaugh or Miguel was thinking about when it was hidden away in Colombina's garden. Mikozy had been staring at the box, not knowing how long. It could have been an eternity compressed inside a second. He noticed the papers he had pushed underneath the box. They were sticking out partway. Mikozy reached down and picked them up. He brushed off the dirt and counted off five pages.

"Are these the papers Mr. Cavanaugh gave you?" Mikozy asked Miguel without looking up. The light of LA's night was not enough to read in. He took a step closer to the house to catch the light slipping through the bamboo wall. All he needed was 15 watts. Mikozy leafed through the pages but did not see any immediate significance in them. He realized he would have to read them closely to see what Cavanaugh had seen in them.

"Yes," Miguel said in a just audible voice. "Those are Mr. Cavanaugh's papers."

"Teresa, let us go inside," Colombina said.

Chapter 24
INVOICING DEATH

Mikozy might have heard what Colombina said, but he wasn't listening. He was absorbed in Cavanaugh's papers. As Colombina walked into the house, another light went on, doubling the wattage Mikozy was straining to read by. The top page was an agreement between International Finance Enterprises and Northern Petrolane, followed by a shipping and payment agreement between Northern Petrolane and Emerald Inlet Ltd., an invoice between the same two companies, and two memos. If Cavanaugh had put these papers into the box, he probably was the one who had redlined several of the documents and overwritten some names and figures. After all, Cavanaugh was the one who gave the box to Miguel with instructions to turn it over to the police if something happened to him.

The loan agreement was elemental. Mikozy remembered seeing the documents that went along with a home loan for $140,000. Pages with microprinting, barely readable or intelligible. This was barely a quarter of one page, and most of that was the International Finance Enterprises logo with a neat little sum of $12.8 million. Maybe Mikozy was missing something about the world of international finance, like the larger the stake, the less needed to be said. Or maybe it was, why write what cannot be translated? That meant: You get a certain sum of money to do a certain thing. Nothing else matters. Or perhaps this was a case of the less said, the less everyone knew about what this transaction was really for.

> International Finance Enterprises
> 333 F Street,
> Washington, DC 20012
> (202) 224-0999 (202) 224-0998 (FAX) IFE45677 - TELEX
> Thomas Sugarman, Exec.
> LOAN AGREEMENT
> International finance Enterprises NK loans
> US$12,800,000.00 to Northern Petrolane. Check
> Enclosed. This loan will be deemed fully paid upon
> Northern Petrolane's development assistance to Emerald
> Inlet Ltd. for agroindustrial purposes.
> Accepted :
> Jerry Cavanaugh, CEO
> Northern Petrolane

Mikozy noticed the lowercase *f* in finance. Sloppy was the first word that popped into Mikozy's thoughts. Emerald Inlet Ltd. had a nasty red line running through it. Mikozy ran his fingers along the underside of the page and felt the rage of the impression just short of tearing through the paper. Written on top of the Emerald Inlet Ltd. were the letters NK. Mikozy wondered if Cavanaugh meant to indicate another company or person. Maybe he meant Northern Petrolane or one of its subsidiaries, but why would it be shipping this stock item to itself under a different name? That didn't compute. He turned the page over and held it toward the light streaming between the bamboo slats. This was a xerox copy, and apparently Cavanaugh had signed onto the program. Mikozy wondered what kind of development assistance would waive the $12.8 million loan. Mikozy slipped the loan agreement to the bottom and looked at the next page. This was a shipping and payment agreement. This didn't interest

Mikozy. Mikozy decided to pick up the next page instead. This was the invoice between Emerald Inlet and Northern Petrolane, a stock item number 312. On this page, the names Zhong Hao and NK were inked over Emerald Inlet.

Mikozy had a crossword puzzle feeling, which was a bad omen, since he never had mastered that form of mental torture. Mikozy resented puzzles. His general failure to skip through the word clues invited self-doubt. Maybe he did lack intelligence, at least the kind that enabled the gifted to decode "pain remover" in four letters to mean acid, short for Bayer's magical cure. Mikozy liked the theory of multiple intelligences, taking comfort in the idea that dogged insistence and luck were one of the varieties of surviving the world.

Invoice
No. 9111X – 034245 Northern Petrolane
856 Gascony Avenue
Los Angeles, California 90013
(2B) 857-1001
Fax: (2B) 857-1291
Ship To: AP 2314 Barcelona, Spain
SALESPERSON
Thomas Sugarman DATE: December 6, 2023
SHIP VIA Per agreement
F.O.B. Per agreement
TERMS Per agreement
REFERENCE IFE
QUANTITY   DESCRIPTION UNIT PRICE   AMOUNT
32000 Petrolane Stock No. 312 (Box was bottles) $500.0
16000000.00
0.00
0.00
0.00
0.00

0.00
Subtotal
Tax Rate exempt
Sales Tax $0.00
Shipping & Handling $15,000.00
Total Due

Smart. Smart. As in smart cop, and not smartass. Still, Mikozy was stuck with a puzzle. Mikozy looked at the invoice and noticed the discrepancy between the $16 million subtotal and the $3.215 million total. Generally, totals were more than the subtotal. He didn't need a genius IQ or be an accountant to figure an adding mistake. He forced himself to do the mental addition and came up with $12.8 million, taking out the shipping charges of $15,000. Mikozy pulled out the bottom page and saw the $12.8 million as the loan amount from International Finance. Mikozy was delighted with himself. He had gotten past Cavanaugh's first clue. The $12.8 million loan to Northern Petrolane was mirrored in the charges for the purchase of stock item 312. The $3.2 million was probably the actual cost, with the $12.8 million tacked on as a surcharge.

Mikozy thought that International Finance could be funneling the money from Emerald Inlet or NK but using the invoice to shield the manner of payment. That didn't make too much sense. Perhaps the International Finance paper was merely a backup guarantee if Emerald Inlet fell short on its payment. The answer was not to be found in these two pages, but the question Cavanaugh posed was clear about the three-sided relationship between Northern Petrolane, International Finance, and Emerald Inlet/NK. The invoice also identified Barcelona as the destination. Mikozy questioned whether that was only a transshipment location. Mikozy took another look at the stock item number. He bent down and took a close look at Cavanaugh's box. On the short side, the company stamp included stock item 312. There were also twenty-five bottles, including the one Teresa had taken. Cavanaugh wasn't fooling around. The box he gave Miguel was the same stock item being sent to NK. That was Cavanaugh's message. Mikozy had a difficult time imagining how much space the thirty-two thousand cases of this stock item would fill.

That was another failure in his intelligence, and he made do with imagining they would fill a very large space. Mikozy turned to the shipping and payment agreement. Mikozy noticed North Korea written in red ink across Emerald Inlet. He had missed this when he flipped to this page earlier. The agreement didn't show any North Korean port, only Barcelona, Spain. Mikozy couldn't see any reason for this charade. If North Korea wanted a pesticide like stock item 312, they could walk into any Walmart and pick it up. Probably get a good discount for thirty-two thousand cases, instead of getting surcharged $12.8 million by Northern Petrolane. Mikozy wondered what was special about stock item 312 besides its toxicity. Mikozy vaguely recalled LC's autopsy investigation. She was talking about the unusual properties of the poison that had killed Reginald and the illegal alien, who was probably Colombina's Miguel. Mikozy couldn't remember what she found out about the poison, but her inquiry had prompted a call from Colonel Craig and his friends. And there was Craig's self-proclaimed identity as military intelligence. That should mean that Craig was chasing Cavanaugh and his shipments to Emerald Inlet/North Korea. That should also mean that Craig would be onto International Finance as well. Which made a good scenario except that Cavanaugh was looking to the LA cops if something went south on his deal and he ended up dead. What was Cavanaugh thinking? If he was dirty, why turn the evidence over to the law? And why the local cops? Why didn't he ask Miguel to turn his box and these pages over to the feds, if he was going to turn it over to a government agency to begin with? The LA police wouldn't be visiting North Korea for some time, even if North Korea became friendly with the US.

Cavanaugh was smart and knew the jurisdictional limits of the LA police. Did he trust the LA police more than the feds?

SHIPPING SCHEDULE PAYMENT SCHEDULE
MAY 1
JUNE 1
JULY 3
Port : Barcelona, Spain

Mikozy picked up the first of the two memos and read it. Nothing cryptic about the first memo. Sugarman was sent over to Northern Petrolane. Probably to watch Cavanaugh and make sure he didn't fuck up the development assistance to Emerald Inlet. Mikozy thought about paying a visit to Sugarman. Except that Miguel said Sugarman was at McDonald's and Mikozy saw Craig. So, Sugarman was Craig. Another puzzle. He'd have these memos as leverage. But leverage for what? Mikozy couldn't embarrass him or hold him hostage to bringing in the feds since he was the feds. The feds were already involved in some way. But so far Mikozy couldn't see that any local laws had been broken. He might even find Morales or some other Morales face in the middle of this pesticide sale, and they'd come down on him through Schmidt. This could be a repeat of his Galaxy Gems fiasco. That didn't get Mikozy anything except being replaced by Mester and finding out that Schmidt's hands were grimy, if not dirty. Mikozy still hadn't worked through how he felt about Schmidt's being co-opted by Morales on one side and the feds on the other.

"Miguel." Mikozy looked up, finding Miguel still rooted to the same spot. Miguel's eyes were studying Mikozy's feet. Miguel probably expected something nasty to come out of Cavanaugh's letters, much like the poison that came out of Cavanaugh's box. "Miguel, didn't you tell me about someone at Northern Petrolane who yelled at you for stealing from the company?"

Mikozy remembered something that Miguel had said at the McDonald's. It might make sense now.

"I didn't steal anything. I told him that," Miguel said.

"I'm not saying you stole anything from Northern Petrolane. I just want to know who you told that to."

"I told that to the sugar man."

Miguel looked up at Mikozy.

"That's what we call him, the sugar man. But he not sweet."

Mikozy smiled. He was putting more than two and two together. Apparently, Sugarman had taken over from Cavanaugh, and he was bothered about something missing. It would have to be important, since the only reason Sugarman went to Northern Petrolane, at least according to what Cavanaugh's papers suggested, was to monitor this sale of pesticide.

"Did he say what it was that he thought you stole from the company?"

"Yes. He told me that there was a box missing. He said it had stock item 312 written on it."

"This box?"

"I think yes."

"Why didn't you tell him about this box?"

"Because Mr. Cavanaugh told me to keep the box and to give it to the police if something happened to him."

"But Mr. Sugarman was in charge of the company. You lied to him." Mikozy felt bad about pushing Miguel into a corner and stepping on Miguel's character.

"I believe in Mr. Cavanaugh. He is a good man. He came to my house with his family for Christmas. Mr. Sugar, like I say, he not sweet."

Mikozy knew that was a lot for Miguel to say. The prosecutor would never press any charges against Miguel for following orders from Cavanaugh.

"Okay. I'm not here to arrest you. You know that. But I need to know what you know, not simply what you said the first time or what you think I want to hear. I need to feel what you say is really so. At least what you believe is really so."

Enough of the lecture, Mikozy thought.

Miguel's eyes were back down to the ground. The humble Indian meets the badass gringo, which was worse than the ugly American image because we were supposed to be beyond all that. Mikozy realized he had the power. The power of the law, the power of the gun, and the power of the culture. He had no choice but to use his power. If he was going to get this case finished.

"Let's go over this again. Tell me more what this sugar guy looked like." Mikozy asked.

Miguel didn't respond right away. "He had a scar on his neck." Miguel pointed up to the back of his neck and ran it down the front. Mikozy thought about Craig and his nifty scar.

"You saw him," Miguel said.

"When was that?" Mikozy asked.

"Usted sabe. We were at McDonald's. You saw the man too. That was Mr. Sugar."

Mikozy and Miguel were reading from the same page. If Craig was the sugar man...Mikozy could only admire the ingenuity at the financial help Sugarman was giving to Northern Petrolane. In turn, the company would be giving pesticide-laced aid to North Korea. That was what was expected of Cavanaugh. And when Cavanaugh died, Sugarman had to scramble to take the operation over. And Sugarman was worried about one of Cavanaugh's boxes being missing. It could easily be replaced unless the shipments had been sent and someone was doing a check for the other side. They'd wonder about a missing box. Sugarman could easily replace it, but with Cavanaugh dying during the transaction, the whole deal might be scuttled.

Mikozy knew he could spin out any number of different scenarios, but none of them included the LA police except for information. Craig wanted to know what the LA police knew. Help stop his operation from getting blown up by LA police. Mikozy had walked into Craig's military intelligence operation. Mikozy could understand the feebs working a case in LA, but not military intelligence. This was out of their jurisdiction. Military intelligence shouldn't be interfering with American companies, not in LA. Too much like the Mob trying to launder their money. But Mikozy had read enough spy novels and seen enough adventure movies to know that truth was weirder than art and anything was possible, especially in LA.

Mikozy looked around the garden, the dim light filtering through the bamboo slats, and Mikozy agreed with himself that anything was possible in LA. Mikozy pulled out the last of Cavanaugh's papers. This memo was also blunting the belling of the cat. This was from Sugarman to Cavanaugh. A simple enough operational detail but sufficient to let anyone who was reading it know who was in charge of whose itinerary. Cavanaugh was probably very unhappy when he got this memo.

To: J. Cavanaugh
From: T. Sugarman
Itinerary/Emerald Inlet Assistance
    This memo follows up our earlier discussion. The assistance Northern Petrolane is providing to Emerald Inlet for its agricultural development programme in various developing countries should be completed within the next two months. I have arranged a meeting for you with Mr. Hao of Emerald Inlet in Barcelona. You are scheduled to leave this Sunday on American Airlines. Tickets and itinerary enclosed. Please be sure the delivery schedule meets with Mr. Hao's approval.

Mikozy couldn't see why Cavanaugh needed to travel to Spain. Why wouldn't a telephone call be enough? Place the order, deliver the merchandise, and pay the bill. Wasn't that how you bought something? And anyway, Sugarman had the deal wired.

Cavanaugh's trip was just for show, but Mikozy couldn't figure out who the show was for. Was it for Mr. Hao? Did Cavanaugh even know what he was doing? He must have cared enough or been bothered enough to give Miguel this box of stock item 312 along with these papers.

Mikozy couldn't see how either Sugarman or Craig or whomever the man was or this Mr. Hao would benefit from Cavanaugh's death. Cavanaugh seemed to be an important frill to this deal. His death would have been untimely when it happened. Maybe one or the other would have wanted to silence Cavanaugh after the deal was completed, but not before. So it was probably more likely that Craig was trying to keep the deal from unraveling by taking over Northern Petrolane. And then there was Craig's visit to find out what LC knew after she made her inquiry to MEDEX about 1,1 triethylchloroactinate. He was probably working to keep the deal together by trying to find out what LC knew about another death involving stock item 312. Craig set up the meeting with Schmidt to strong-arm the information out of LAPD if the medical examiner was uncooperative. Craig wanted to find Miguel to see if he had Cavanaugh's missing box.

Mikozy wondered what Craig was doing cruising in the barrio down toward La Chucha. Whether he was Craig playing at military intelligence or Sugarman playing international financier, there was nothing either would find in this neighborhood. Nothing except keeping the deal between Northern Petrolane and Emerald Inlet from getting unstuck. That could mean Miguel, or it could mean himself or both. And the only significant event that had occurred in the same time span that Craig/ Sugarman had paid a visit to the barrio was the firebombing of La Chucha. Mikozy felt winded and tired. He was exhausted from racing around the mind tracks and getting dust kicked up into his thoughts. He couldn't be certain that Craig had anything to do with torching the restaurant.

There was always Carlos Laguna, the owner of La Chucha, whom Mikozy had stung in a narcotics operation. But Sara Moses had protected him, shielding his exit out of La Chucha. Mikozy didn't think Laguna would bomb his own place either. He had too much pride in his restaurant. Good food, Mikozy thought. Mikozy sensed the cold tail of an evil spirit entering the garden. The more Mikozy tried to figure out what had happened from the time he walked into La Chucha until he followed Miguel and Teresa into Colombina's house, the more demonic LA had become.

Mikozy couldn't shake Craig's image from his thoughts. A harpy was chasing him through the barrio, and the cold night air was pushed down into the garden by the downward force of the beast's wings. It was looking for its prey.

"Miguel." Mikozy reached over and put his hand on Miguel's shoulder. "Let's go inside, friend. The night is getting a little chilly."

"Yes. It is colder now."

Chapter 25
OFFICE OF ENLIGHTENMENT

Mikozy's reflection bounced over the wooden tables filled with tropical delights. Strange to LA but comfort foods for this community. Guanabana, maracuya, *tomate de arbol, babaco*, jocote, pitaya, naranjilla, and even *achotillo*. The colors did their frenzied dance in the window as Mikozy inched his way to the front door. The name Maravilla ran across the awning that kept the fruits in shade. Grocery stores like Maravilla gave way to supermarkets throughout the city, but not here. Supermarkets shunned this rickety neighborhood, its sidewalks cracked and uneven. Maravilla had found its niche and thrived.

Mikozy turned the knobby handle and walked into the store. As expected, a bell announced his entrance.

"Pasale, ven. Que entra con amistad." The voice of a grayhair preceded the old man's entrance. "Welcome. Did you find what you were looking for?"

"I'm not sure I'm in the right place." Mikozy looked around. The cabinets were filled with all the sundries for anyone who cooked their own food. There was little that would thrill the teenage taste. There was no wine, no beer, and no intense alcohol brews. The inebriants were limited to bubbly water.

"If you don't see what you want, just ask." The invitation was more of a question. Something like, "What do you really want?" Or "Who?"

Mikozy reached into his pocket and pulled out a receipt from one of those supermarkets. He showed the owner the address that he had scratched on the back. "A friend of mine gave me this address. I think this is what she told me."

"Lisa?"

"Lisa Liu?"

"Yes. I know Lisa Liu." The old man's face cracked, hinted a smile. He turned half a pirouette and pointed to the curtain through which he had entered.

"Just go inside and you'll find your Lisa Liu."

"What? Does she have an office here? Does she come here often?" The questions flowed from Mikozy, more out of surprise than any interest in what the answers might be.

"Just go inside," he repeated.

Mikozy thought about asking more questions, but he realized the only answer he would get was "just go inside."

Mikozy walked across the wood floor and pushed into the curtain. The room was empty except for pictures hanging on the opposite wall. Mikozy walked up to the wall. The pictures had stylish frames. They looked like prints downloaded from the cloud or maybe bought from a dollar store. He was about to turn back when a not so visible door opened, halfway up the wall and just under a picture of Monet's haystacks. He crouched down to look into this back-of-the-room back door. He seemed to always be entering doors. Mikozy hesitated.

"Are you coming in?" A wily and recognizable voice called out. It was Liu.

"Yes, just a moment." Mikozy took a last look around the empty room and the pictures above this doorway. He bent down and wiggled his way into the next room.

Liu was standing at the top of a staircase. Mikozy took a closer look. He wondered if this seemingly identical person was Liu. Not that he thought this was anyone else. It was worth a test. "Those kanji characters on your wall at home. They were about this room, right? Isn't that what you said?" She had actually said she had no idea what they meant. Liu, the real Liu, would know this. So he wasn't surprised to see a quizzical look. The stark red lips turned up, and her blue pantsuit punctuated her thought. "I don't have a clue what they mean. I never told you that." She paused. "Oh, I see. You want me to be me. Really, really me." Liu laughed.

"Come down with me." She pointed to the stairway that ended in darkness. "This is friendlier than going up the stairs with you at Galaxy Gems the other day. No need to worm your way up to the office. And no Mr. Morales here. Just me."

Liu began her descent. No click-clacking of heels. Quiet. As if the cat was tracking its prey. Mikozy followed. The sound of his shoes was swallowed up by padded walls. Midway down the stairs, a movable door slid close.

He reached the bottom. Liu swept out her arm in a fanciful welcome to her inner sanctum.

"Thank you for coming, Rafe. This is my somewhat secret… well, actually very secret place."

Mikozy looked around a large room. Scattered around the room were armchairs, a sofa, butler table, conference table and chairs, a kitchenette of sink and a microwave, a mini fridge. He looked to his side and saw a near floor-to-ceiling screen. Up above were ceiling speakers and drop-down mics. Unlike the flashy style Liu modeled, the room was dressed in soft hues. An elegant room was obvious.

"I guess we have a lot to talk about."

"Yes. We need an extended conversation. An over-the-top conversation. Unconventional, twisted. I don't know what other words I should use." Mikozy had left Miguel with Craig trading identities with Sugarman in Northern Petrolane. Now he was in another compartment with Liu who had met Craig trading identities with Dr. Neill Cream. The same compartment LC had found Craig. Mikozy wondered if he would find out more about what military intelligence was doing in LA. Perhaps Liu knew more about Craig.

Liu waited a moment. She walked over to the microwave and pulled the door open. A mug rested inside. She took it out and walked back over to Mikozy. She handed him the mug.

"Drink. Please drink some tea. And then we'll talk."

Mikozy looked into the mug. A reddish-brown liquid. He drank a mouthful.

"It's bitter. More than I was thinking for a rooibos tea. Is that what this is?"

"No. Not rooibos. This will help with our conversation. It's something special I made. Come, let's sit down on the sofa."

Mikozy followed Liu to the sofa. Not a love seat, larger. Enough for three. The cloth fabric had a soft weave of greens and blues. Traditional. Conversational. He sat on the middle pillow, but Liu pushed him over to the end.

"So let's converse."

"We should wait awhile. There's no rush. I'll put on some music first." Liu walked over to a cabinet and found something for the moment. She also turned the lights down to a mere 40 watts.

"Do you have something else in mind?" Mikozy wondered what kind of conversation Liu was thinking about.

"Nothing like our earlier get-togethers. Now, I just want you to be comfortable. I want me to be comfortable too."

Mikozy waited. Liu waited. About twenty minutes went by. Theirs was silence while the music drifted by.

Liu squinted her eyes and said, "Think of me as your guide."

"Are we going somewhere?" Mikozy joked.

"Well, in a way. You will be traveling, and I will be your guide."

"Maybe we should have that unconventional conversation you mentioned." Mikozy thought about what that conversation would be. The word ping-ponged and he thought about smiling.

In that moment, Mikozy felt lightheaded, muscles rippling against a warm breath enfolding him. The music filled with color. He looked over at Liu. She was there and not there. He looked around the room. It was there and not there.

The not-there was flooded by a kaleidoscope of hues. It was a world of emotion, of tangible perception, thoughts that crashed into each other.

Anger raced into passion and love, his heart beating like fire, the sun and moon dreamed orange, laughing sunflower, green and blue tranquilizer colored the sky, a magic vibrating explored the symphonic tangle of what might be noise.

A firefly pitter-pattered over the pumpkin, was it time for a nap? An ocean OO-cean splashed the sandcastle, the glee was green, coming through the window, a fairy? Or demon? This dream, this pain, this red hornet, blue depressed. I feel lonely, LONELINESS, what is the question.

What is the color, a sunbeam escapes out the window, there is no window, it was a sick sunbeam, no yellow, I am old, OLD, old, a drab brown building, am I a bamboo shoot? Dancing, spinning, twirling, thousands of hues flowing through my body, I feel each hue, carrying me someplace, terrifying and calming flickers.

Blended beauty drowning on the ceiling, DO NOT LOOK UP, somewhere there is purple, adventuring, guide. Guide?

"Mikozy, are you okay? Remember, I am your guide."

"Guide?" The word dribbled out from Mikozy. He looked at Liu, and her not-there was now there. He reached over and touched her arm.

"Is this you?" Mikozy's eyes drifted around Liu, seeking certainty.

"Yes, yes. It's me. Or maybe I should say I am me."

Mikozy considered the words he was hearing. He could now see, touch, and hear the person he knew as Liu. She was Liu.

"Where was I? Or what was I?" Mikozy asked.

Liu reached over and took Mikozy's hands into hers. She sat quietly. She waited. She smiled.

"You've been here all along. I've been sitting with you, and you are doing well."

"I had funny, not funny, different, strangely different thoughts and feelings. Just a few minutes." Mikozy adjusted himself and repeated a look around the office. Liu's hands folded over his, anchoring him to the room. Otherwise he felt he might float away.

"We've been sitting here for about five hours."

"Five hours?" The question seemed like one of those imponderable facts. How could it be five hours? How could time be long and short together?

"Yes. Five hours. You seemed a bit restless for a moment, but otherwise, you were just being Mikozy. I have been your guide. I am still your guide."

"You keep saying that. What does it mean? Did you put something in the tea?"

Liu put her face closer to Mikozy. She brought her hands up and ran her fingernails over his face, shutting his eyes, letting them open again.

"I didn't put anything in your tea. It was made of various plants. Some morning glory, some *Psilocybe cubensis*, some San Pedro cactus. All of it natural. All of it from the indigenous Americas. Nothing else."

Mikozy ran that through his warehoused memories. This wasn't a cocktail of downers or uppers. There was more than up and down. There was also that other dimension that he had once dabbled in.

"Why?" He skipped over talking about psychedelics. It was what happened. It was his travel. With his guide. "Why?" he repeated.

Liu drew her face even closer, inches away. He could feel her breathing. He could see his reflection in her eyes. She placed her hands around the side of his face, cupping them around his ears so that he could hear the ocean.

"I need you to be flexible, Mikozy. Not your detective self, locked into narrow clues, jumping to tunnel-visioned conclusions. I need you to hear me, not just listen to me."

"Why not just ask me to pay attention?"

"Do you really think you could do that? We have only a short window of time. I am sorry to have tripped you to enlightenment."

"Is this what I am? Enlightened?"

"I hope so. I could say trust me, but trust has been abused too often."

"So what is it?"

"I said I was your guide. Let me guide you. Let us have that twisted conversation. That over-the-top conversation. You are ready now."

"I hope you're right." Then he added, "Who are you? Who are you really?"

She let go of his face. She sat back, looked away from Mikozy, and then turned back to him.

"I am a warrior. I am the face of a goddess. I am the here and now. Many such things. And none of them."

"You're speaking in puzzles, Liu. I asked a simple question. Can you give me a simple answer?"

"Not really." She waited. As if Mikozy would stumble onto his own simple answer.

"Maybe you are a spy. China? Taiwan?"

Liu laughed. "Asian-ness got lost on me a generation ago. No, Mikozy, you can guess again if you'd like."

"I'm not one for mysteries or blind alleys. Just tell me."

"I can guide you. I cannot tell you."

Mikozy wanted to say something. He didn't know if he wanted to be guided.

"How did we meet?" she asked. "Do you remember? Did you find me? Did I find you?"

"It was an accident. Pure chance." Mikozy remembered how Schmidt had pushed him into taking a continuing education class. He wouldn't be able to keep his desk, would maybe get reassigned to nowhere.

"You're right. Chance. Lady Luck. And you came bearing a package. Tell me about that."

"I'm not seeing anything about that package," he said.

"Try me."

Mikozy thought about that hurried moment. Schmidt had given him an assignment from Deputy Inspector Michelle Tomlinson. She wanted him to read a manuscript that revised Jack London's *The Iron Heel*. That whole episode came back to him. Mikozy remembered the assignment and how he tried to avoid it. The two versions had the same plotline but with an upside-down version of the other. London's original imagined a government that commanded banks, publishers, and whatever else to control individuals who thought differently. London was a socialist and feared the capitalists. The new version, decades and decades later, saw London's socialists in control. But they were no better. They were now the ones who were feared. The world had turned around. Mikozy asked himself the recurrent question: So what?

"I came to your class. An accident. I had a package. That's correct. The deputy inspector had asked me to review Jack London's book and another one that turned his world inside out."

"Now you're a book reviewer. You majored in literature? The police department is now into reading fiction?"

"It was found with a dead body."

"That makes more sense. And?" Liu asked Mikozy to continue.

"That's it. We hit it off and you know the rest."

"You are supposed to ask me a question, Mikozy."

"You didn't know about the book. It was in a package. It didn't play into us being together, did it?"

"And you left it behind, didn't you?"

Mikozy remembered. He came back for the package. "You peeked, didn't you?"

"Yes, I peeked."

"But we already planned to get together. What difference would it make if you peeked?"

"Truth, Mikozy. I was looking."

"What? You wanted to hit on me like I was hitting on you?" Mikozy was uncertain what truth Liu could reveal. Liu laughed. She was enjoying the game of mindful peekaboo.

"Not really. I was looking for a way in. You became my way in."

Mikozy thought about what Liu was thinking about. Two different planetary systems. Or just one, but which one?

"A way into what?"

"This is why you need to be here—here in this room—for what I am going to say. And you need to understand what we see outside this room and what is taking place. At least as much as we can sift through what is sometimes called the blooming, buzzing confusion. Not just for newborn babies making sense of the world. But us. Us too, Mikozy."

Mikozy nodded and waited for Liu to answer. Liu got up, walked around the room, and then returned to sit next to Mikozy.

"I was asked to find a way to get to Tomlinson," she said. "Whatever she—whatever it is. Tomlinson looked like a point of entry."

"Just a second. I am a detective. She is in the police department, a deputy inspector. You sound like some criminal organization."

"That's a fair way of looking at getting into Tomlinson. But wrong. Except that any challenge to the authority is criminal. It is and it isn't. Or the logic of A and not A both being true."

"What kind of criminal are you, Liu?"

Liu reached over to Mikozy, a wide smile dimpling, eyes widened, and her voice dropped, vibrating across the space. "Not that kind of criminal."

"This is not the time for a lecture on social organization, Mikozy. Yes, unless we think chaos is workable in a large society, then some kind of order is required. You and the department and Tomlinson are the order that goes out and finds out why Reginald Hunter died. To see if he was murdered or if it was an accident. To work through the puzzle of events and people twisting around some weird poison. That's a good thing, Mikozy. And just so you know, I couldn't give a fuck about that. That's a ripple in keeping a society ordered."

"So what's this about me and Tomlinson?" Mikozy wanted the wide-open conversation with Liu but felt the drag of caution. Liu sensed his reserve. She pressed her fingernails into his knee, a pay-attention gesture.

"Think about it, Mikozy. Schmitty gave you the Hunter case. Tomlinson gave you a package. Both Hunter and the package are about what makes this society tick, but in very different ways. The way to make you, the police, better when it comes to Hunter is by improving the lab technology, analyzing the crime scene, and taking courses like mine. Clue analysis." Liu laughed when she said clue analysis. Mikozy did not resist. He laughed as well.

"Then there's the question of how the package Tomlinson gave you would make policing better. That's different than making lab technology better or having you take my class. How does your reading about Jack London's conspiracy fantasy make society better?" Liu dangled her overstatement about how reading London's book fit into detective work. Enough to get Mikozy to reveal his own curiosity.

"Well, socialists were seen as anarchists by those who held political power. That wasn't a fantasy. Maybe too much a fear. London just carried…" He paused for the right word. Liu offered some.

"The repressing—or more politely, the policing—too far?"

"Okay. Those fears can lead to overpolicing, you might say."

"Is that what Tomlinson asked you to do? Read a book about what an author was writing about before World War I?"

"Not by itself. There was another book. Actually just a light once-over change to London's book. Patricia Todd called it *The Iron Heel Revisited*. Not too creative. Maybe that wasn't the point. And maybe it was her body that was found along with the manuscript Tomlinson gave me. Todd put the socialists in charge of the government. Those with a capitalist bent of mind were now out of favor. The social order turned topsy-turvy. The repressed became the repressors."

"And the policing remained the same?"

"That's the way I saw it. That didn't take much of a literature review. So you can see why I was puzzled that Tomlinson gave this to me. Specifically to me. Why did she need me to come up with what was good for the goose was good for the gander? Or turnabout is fair play? And yes, the policing was the same. Keeping the order was the same."

Liu let Mikozy think about being a detective. Think about what Tomlinson had asked him.

"Is that all you found out for Tomlinson?"

If she could hear Mikozy biting and unbiting his tongue, grinding away his teeth, she would feel his struggle about what to tell her.

"I had my suspicions. There was a book review, but there was also a dead body found with the manuscript in the package. I assumed that was why a homicide detective was involved, why I was involved."

"Were you investigating the dead body too?"

"No, I thought I would be. Todd's body, or what I assume was Todd's body, was not sent to the medical examiner's lab for an autopsy. The medical examiner was surprised the body wasn't sent to her lab to be autopsied. That was a bit strange. That kind of left me dangling about why I was doing a book review if it was just about literature or some legal claim. That's not what I do."

"I remember your excuse one time when you didn't want to come over. Was that about your book review assignment? Or about the medical examiner?"

"Okay, Lisa. Time for a bit of truth. Maybe we can sort things out together. It was not about the deputy medical examiner, LC, Leslie Cianfrancuso. Also my ex-wife. We talk. That's about it. It was about the manuscript. I decided to go up and check out Tomlinson's office. I had Schmidt's office code and went up to Tomlinson's office. You might say a sneak-and-peek."

Mikozy stopped. This was his tipping point. A slippery slope. Liu sensed Mikozy's hesitancy. She pressed her fingernails deeper into his knee. Mikozy thought about arcane methods of torture where the inquisitor decided to dig the truth out of the poor soul he was questioning. Fingernails didn't come to mind. Liu was more artful. He put his hand onto hers and pulled it away. Mikozy decided to find out where the endgame was. The path seemed to call for him to follow their conversation.

"I went into her office. There was just a laptop on the desk. It was lit up. And I heard her, or what I thought was Tomlinson, speak to me. A welcome. There wasn't anyone there. After a while I realized that Tomlinson wasn't a person. Tomlinson wasn't a she. It was an it. An AI device on the laptop."

"Surprised?"

"Yes, I was surprised. Not what I expected at all."

"This is getting interesting. Not that there was a bot investigating local police activity. We suspected that. But you stumbling onto the bot."

"Bot?"

"Robot, cobot, voice bot, chatbot, art bot, or just a bot."

"And that's it? You left?"

"No. That's the fun part. I got into a conversation with Tomlinson. Or the bot."

"Did you ask it about *The Iron Heel*?"

"She, or it, said I wasn't cleared to know. Actually, there were several things I wanted to know about. I got 'not cleared for it' or 'next topic.' I asked about Lieutenant Colonel Robert Craig and Neill Cream. Not cleared, next topic."

Liu was curious about what was off limits. "So why did you ask about them?"

"I don't remember if I told you about them. Actually one guy out of some federal security agency. First he told LC—my ex— that he was Neill Cream, but then she pushed him and he owned up to being Craig. He came out here when LC asked about that poison, the one that we found had killed Reginald Hunter. Apparently she triggered a national database."

"I guess I became Craig's person of interest later."

"It seems so."

Liu registered a comment, a murmur, a hmmmm. "And then you left?"

"Not exactly."

"What? You want me to use my fingernails again?"

Mikozy smiled and thought about letting her use her fingernails. "No. I'll talk. I decided to go back to *The Iron Heel*. It did say that some programmer was interested in this book, but I couldn't get much more. That got me thinking about something else. I wanted to figure out how Tomlinson, I mean the bot, thought. If it was thinking or just juggling computer code. I decided to play with it. I wanted to see if it got emotional, if I could get it to balance what Jack London imagined and what Patricia Todd imagined. Would it get paralyzed? Just like we do when we say it's this way and it's not this way. I'm not sure if I'm explaining this well. I don't know if I knew what I was really doing."

"The Mikozy experiment?"

"I'll take credit for that. Maybe a Nobel Prize too. But whatever you say, I got the laptop to crash. It just stopped working."

"Maybe it just got bored with you. Maybe it just fell asleep."

"Could be. That's about all. I left. And now I'm here."

"Mikozy, you skipped a few steps."

"What? I told you what I found out."

"It's about what you learned. Or maybe what I thought and what you confirmed."

"That I didn't have clearance for some things?"

"Don't you think it's strange that your assignment came from a bot? That it was not about a dead body but about a book—actually a book and an unpublished manuscript—about a repressive government? That some national security type came out here because of an inquiry into a poison? That it wouldn't tell you about them?"

"Those are a lot of questions. I could say a whole bot of questions."

"Funny. You're really funny, Mikozy."

"Where are we on this?"

"You are a detective. You could detect. You took my class."

"I suppose you know the answer. You're just trying to trigger a headache. What is it you're not telling me?"

"I'll tell you, Mikozy, but first I want to know something."

Liu stared into Mikozy. The silence deafened the room. Mikozy blinked and the room seemed to darken. That was much too fast for a flashback. Her fingernails came back. He could hear her, a low hum. All his senses seemed to awaken in unexpected ways. He slipped back into a dream state. Once again he heard the *firefly pitter-patter over a pumpkin. Was it time for a nap? An ocean OO-cean splashed the sandcastle, the glee was green, coming through the window, a fairy? Or demon? This dream, this pain, this red hornet, blue depressed. I feel lonely, LONELINESS, what is the question.* His mind turned inside. *What is the color, a sunbeam escapes out the window, there is no window, it was a sick sunbeam, no yellow, I am old, OLD, old, a drab brown building, am I a bamboo shoot? Dancing, spinning, twirling, thousands of hues flowing through my body, I feel each hue, carrying me someplace, terrifying and calming flickers.*

"Mikozy? Are you here?" He heard her echo, *Are you here, here, here, here?*

"Yes. I'm here. What were you asking me?"

"I wanted to know something first."

He slowly enunciated, "Okayyyy."

"Maybe we should wait." Liu got up and seemed to disappear into the other side of the room.

"Liu?"

"I'm here."

"That was quick. You went across the room, and I seem to have drifted off for a second."

"A second? Maybe better an hour. At least you're coming back down."

"Back down?"

"The tea was stronger than I planned. You remember our conversation?" Liu leaned into Mikozy to see if his eyes were dilated. She took his wrist and felt his pulse. "You're back, Mikozy."

"What?" Mikozy's surprise was writ large on his face.

"Mikozy, you surprised us both. Don't repeat my words, don't say both. Just listen. Can you do that?"

"Yes, Liu. I guess this is where I skin my elbows while slipping down the slippery slope."

"You've been skinned already. Tomlinson, the bot who is your supervisor, picked you out. Then I saw the manuscript when you came to my class. So, I picked you out too. The bot appears to have been interested in policing. I was interested, I am interested, in what the bot was doing about policing. I knew, we knew, that the department was part of a wide network. We saw it in the work orders for the new building. The one that the medical examiner is in. What you were allowed to see, and now what you are not allowed to see, is a thread to how policing is going to work."

"Of course. Don't we want policing to be better? You said this yourself. Or am I missing something?"

"We're dancing around the obvious."

"Tell me. I must be deaf and blind."

"You told me yourself that in Jack London's imagination, the policing was the same as in Patricia Todd's reimagining of Jack London. It's not about who governs. It's only about how that governing comes about. At least how it polices the rest of us."

"That's not a surprise."

"What's new is Tomlinson. The bot doesn't care whether there are dreaded capitalists in charge or dreaded socialists in charge. It is just a laptop. I'm sure there are many, many laptops across the country that are figuring out how to be good police bots."

"Could be a good thing."

"Is that what you thought when you did a sneak-and-peek in Tomlinson's office?"

"It was weird. I'm not sure what difference it makes."

"Are you interested in going back out and asking Lieutenant Colonel Robert Craig about this bot?"

"Not really."

"Are you worried about Craig or about finding out?"

"Maybe both."

Mikozy and Liu took each other into the other's sense. Liu ran her fingernails over Mikozy's arm.

"Just a sec. I have a plan." Mikozy decided it was time for a can-do, a can do anything.

"I hope it is better than the one at Galaxy Gems."

"You'll have to put your hands over your ears while I make a call."

"You're kidding. Right?"

"Maybe half kidding. Just promise to keep quiet."

Liu smiled and put a finger up to her lips, zipping them shut.

Mikozy phoned LC. The plan needed LC to work her magic, something more than a mere autopsy.

"Rafael, is this you?"

"Yes."

"And?"

"I have a plan. And you're part of it."

"Ouch. This sounds like something I'd rather not do."

"But you'll do it anyway. Right?"

Mikozy decided he needed a team to get the moving parts to stand still, to reveal a semblance of meaning to these poisonings, the ways in which players pulled in different directions, a way of out of seeming chaos of events. LC needed to be part of the team. Not just his ex- but his maybe. He wondered how Liu and LC would get along.

"Okay. Let's hear it."

"I'd like you to call Schmidt to set up an appointment for you and Lieutenant Colonel Craig."

"Oh yes, the famous impersonator of Dr. Neill Cream. And why am I doing this?"

"I need some alone time with Deputy Inspector Tomlinson. You know, the laptop to the new world order. If Craig is with you, he won't be paying attention to Tomlinson or whoever is with her. With it."

"Is this just you? Or is your new paramour going with you?"

"What makes you think that?"

"Because you're not answering my question."

"The answer is yes. Liu will be going with me."

Off to the side, Liu was smiling and half jumping up and down on the sofa.

"She's not official," he said. "But Schmidt did get her to teach a class. I even learned something."

"That's very funny. Give me something better."

"There are two halves to what we've been circling around. The poisonade deaths. What's going on? Why the secrecy? That's something both you and I ran into. And that possibly got Mester killed at Mendoza's lab. And do they in some way figure into my doing an analysis of *The Iron Heel* for Tomlinson? That's on my half of this puzzle."

"Maybe." LC waited. "Okay, so I set up this interview with Craig. Is this about the ones on the LAX departure list? Panarese and Cavanaugh? The ones I'm not supposed to mention?"

"Yes and no."

"What part is the yes and what part is the no?" Exasperation rode over the plain meaning of her question.

"If Craig is transparent, and in a sharing mood, I wouldn't suggest being cautious. He's a bad actor. It might be better to leave it at that. But here is some of what I know and what I'm thinking. My guess is that these two were poisoned with the same poison as Reginald Hunter. If that's what happened, then it makes sense that your inquiry to MEDEX connects to the dots that Craig is following at the other end."

"And the other end is?"

"I'm not quite sure. Which is why we both need to dig at that connection. You with Craig, however politely and cautiously. And me and my friend with Tomlinson."

"Tell me more about Craig."

"Well, I got Panarese's and Cavanaugh's names off the death list. Both were connected to flights out of LAX. That's what I asked Rita to send over to you. I found a connection to Reginald Hunter. They all had haircuts from a LAX barber. Haircuts and shampooed with what she called her special shampoo. She said it was Krindell's brand, but later I found it was her own mixture. I followed that connection to the husband of the barber. I need to write this out on a CF-4 at some point. But just bear with me. The story gets even weirder."

"Okay. So how do you know the shampoo is the toxin? I got the samples you sent over but haven't had time to analyze them."

"The short version. When I met Teresa—she's the barber—she confirmed that she had given Reginald a shampoo. I showed her the picture you downloaded for me. She told me that Cavanaugh was her husband's boss. I thought that was worth looking into. I went to her home to meet with Miguel, her husband. We first went up to McDonald's—well, it was once a McDonald's—and we ran into Craig. But Miguel said that was one of his bosses at his company, Northern Petrolane. Not as Craig, but as Sugarman. So there's some kind of connection between Cavanaugh, one of our toxic bodies, and Craig, or Sugarman. Craig's involved in whatever I run into. Maybe he will share that with you. Could be dangerous."

"Why do you say that?"

"I didn't mention that when Craig saw me and Miguel, he tried to follow us. I heard a shot as we turned the corner. Probably his, but who knows. And Perkins gets his head bashed in at Mendoza's. I don't know whether Craig had anything to do with that. But that's another piece of this puzzle. I sent Perkins there to check on the autopsy that should've been done by you. You know, Patricia Todd, the one I was tasked to read about."

"You're right, Rafael. This is an unraveling puzzle. You would probably say there are too many clues. Enough to poison one's thinking."

"I would smile at the double entendre except for your being in the mix."

"At last it will be in my lab. So how's this going to work? What time and where? And for how long? And do I need some protection?"

"Here's what I'm thinking. Tweak me if I'm off base. You have him come by your lab when you begin your shift. Say one a.m. Give yourself an hour to set up. If you can keep him busy for about a half hour, Liu and I can get into Tomlinson's office and interview her. Maybe we can get by the 'you're not cleared for that' hurdle."

"Protection?"

"Take Tippy with you, not Brutus."

Brutus was LC's fifteen-pound toy dog. Tippy was Mikozy's parting gift to LC. Tippy was now one hundred pounds of joy, a

Cane Corso. Tippy could be quiet. She could purr. Some thought it was a growl. She was also trained to protect by whatever means.

"You think Craig would be interested? Now?"

"He's still chasing down who knows what and keeping it lidded. That includes me and Miguel. You can propose a deal and then cave to what he expects."

"While you're sneaking around in Tomlinson's office?"

"That's the plan. You like it?"

"What's not to like? So let's get back to Cavanaugh. My go-to approach is to just ask. No holds barred."

"Maybe just ask him to open up about why he came out here. About that poison. Then you could innocently mention that you were reviewing a recent death list and that one of the names came up in a conversation with me. He won't know how much more you know. You can plead ignorance. Or you can piecemeal out information if you think he'll fill you in on the big picture. I have a feeling it is about more than just an errant poisoning."

"Well, I can tease him with the name game. First he was Neill Cream, then Craig. Then he became Sugarman in Cavanaugh's company, Northern Petrolane. So I can dispense with any innocence about Craig's chameleon quality. What do you think about me asking around in that hall of mirrors?"

"I'm not sure, but use your judgment. If he believes you're one of the gang, he might talk out of school."

"Okay. I can work with that. I'll call Schmidt today and set it up for my shift tomorrow. At one a.m."

"And make sure your electronic-killer device is on. No communications going in or out."

"That leaves me vulnerable."

"Not with Tippy. And you have your thirty-eight as well. Make sure it has bullets."

"Shouldn't we have an emergency contact? If something goes wrong?"

"You're right. You have my number. Take off the electronic suppression, text me with 511, and I'll call. Hopefully you won't need it."

"And an after-action report?"

"The three of us can do a sit-down."

"I'm loving it. And say hello to Liu. I'm sure you have her tied up."

LC rang off. Liu looked at Mikozy.

"You heard. We have an interview date with Tomlinson tomorrow at one a.m. I hope you can make it."

"You can bet your life on it."

"My life? Or your life?"

Liu tapped Mikozy on his arm. "We'll find out tomorrow."

He tapped her back. Love taps.

C tapped her entry card to open the lab's front door. Tippy traipsed along behind. Her gray hair matched the edges on the porcelain column just beyond the elevator. She had kept LC company before and knew exactly where to find her place. It was the same alcove that Mikozy had used to hide himself from Craig. Craig would be sure to look there when he came into the lab.

The lights came on as LC moved about. She had arranged for others in the lab to leave the midnight-to-four-a.m. block open. She'd have the lab to herself and Craig, and Tippy.

She walked back to her office, where she had access to the lab's light, audio, and safety controls. LC put the signal jammer on a timer, blocking signals from 1:00 to 2:00 a.m. That should be enough time to allow Mikozy to access Deputy Inspector Tomlinson's office. With his new girlfriend. LC didn't play the wait-and-see game. She knew Mikozy. He wouldn't take the woman along with him if there wasn't a romantic connection. Whatever reason Mikozy would give, LC would translate it as romantic. She'd seen a picture of the woman in the continuing education classes the department offered. More than just cute. LC said she had her Frank, but he was more of a spirit than a physical embodiment for her. Mikozy suspected as much, but they played their game of ex-marrieds. Their jobs pulled them apart, night shift, day shift. Same building but different floors, different worlds.

The elevator pinged. She looked up at the clock on the wall. Just about 1:00 a.m. Lieutenant Colonel Robert Craig, a.k.a. Neill Cream, a.k.a. Sugarman, was about to make his entrance. The doors opened, and the apparition of a tiger stepped into the lab.

"Good evening, Dr. Cianfrancuso, or is it LC?"

"LC will do."

Without any circumnavigating the moment, LC decided to repay her visitor in kind.

"And who do I have the pleasure of speaking with? Lieutenant Colonel Robert Craig? Dr. Neill Cream? Or Mr. Sugarman?"

LC noticed Craig tilt back, then move forward. Tippy's head took notice, leaning almost to a rise. Craig looked over and saw Tippy staring at him.

"So we have an overseer?"

"Just my little fuzzball. You should hear her purr."

"What do you know about Sugarman?" Craig's voice tensed.

"Let's not get ahead of ourselves. Maybe we need to go back to what brought you out to LA a few days ago."

"Maybe we should go into your office and talk this over."

"Right here is just fine. I need to keep an eye on Tippy. She gets nervous whenever I leave."

"Okay. As you know, your inquiry to the MEDEX database about a novel toxin triggered a response in various federal bureaucracies."

"And yours is—what?"

Craig was stalling, dribbling out information. LC decided to wait. She was not in a rush. She wanted to give Mikozy time to peek inside Deputy Inspector Tomlinson's office.

"I can't really be specific."

"Because you're not really here. Or you are playing funny games that involve toxic materials? Which is it? Or both?"

LC watched Craig. His face shimmered with telltale markers. Anger slipped into suppressed annoyance, which revealed puzzlement and consideration that this other person in the city of LA could cooperate.

"What is you want, LC?"

"Well, we do get a lot of help from the feds. Much of this building, my lab, the equipment—we have a lot to thank the federal bureaucracies for in our being able to fund this edifice and its technological innards. Thank you."

"But what is it you want? Not what you got. There's always a price to be paid. I don't know if I can afford your desires."

LC looked up at the clock. She had put clocks all over the lab. Time was always of the essence. Not for the dead but for inscribing the whys and wherefores of their presence in the lab. Eight minutes had passed. She needed to give Mikozy more time.

"Tell me what got you so interested in my little inquiry to MEDEX that you had to come out personally."

"It wasn't your inquiry that got me to come out here. That was icing on the cake, so to speak."

"And the real reason was?"

Craig paused. He looked around. He looked over at Tippy. Tippy stared back. Another two minutes passed.

"You want in?"

"In?"

"Yes. To be read into our program."

"I feel like I am pulling teeth. And I am not good at being a dentist. What's the program you're talking about? Is this something that Captain Schmidt is involved with?"

"Yes. Schmidt is our local coordinator. Mikozy, your friend, your ex, is an unknown. A wild card."

"You can say that. Mikozy has his own way of doing business. But why Schmidt? Why not go up the chain to Deputy Inspector Tomlinson?"

Craig ignored her chain-of-command question. He looked around the entry area again. He looked over at Tippy again. Tippy was still staring at Craig. In a dog's way, Tippy was trying to figure out what Craig was. She could smell his wariness; she could see the almost formed sweat above his brows.

"I will read you into our program LC. But there is no way out. Once you're in, you're in. You cannot discuss this with anyone else. Not with anyone on your staff, not with Mikozy. No one."

He paused again. LC looked at the clock. Twelve minutes had passed. She needed at least eighteen more.

"I'm in military intelligence. I've been working with Thomas Cavanaugh, the late Thomas Cavanaugh, to distribute 1,1 triethylchloroactinate to a nonfriendly government."

"Sounds ominous."

"It is how we keep world peace. Or the semblance of what we call world peace. It's a fragile thing. It can evaporate in a moment. Especially when the evaporation is nuclear."

"Okay, not so ominous. But hopeful. If that is what hope looks like in a world spinning in ways that Mother Nature never anticipated. And that nonfriendly country is?"

"North Korea." The words left a pause between them. Unspoken words, time still unraveled. Neither was bothered with the passage of time.

The words North Korea burst inside LC's brain. Maybe being read into Craig's program was not what she really wanted. Fifteen minutes had drifted by. Fifteen more to go.

"What was Cavanaugh doing? I don't get it."

"His company, Northern Petrolane, is essentially a chemical factory. We asked him to manufacture 1,1 triethylchloroactinate. It was a way to save his company. They had liquidity problems. Environmentalists were picketing his company. The company was in a poor community. He had difficulty continuing its operations there even though it provided many jobs. That's the way of a changing world."

"And?"

"I joined the company. As you noted, as the Sugarman. Tom Sugarman. I supervised Cavanaugh. I didn't want him going virtuous on us. He was to deliver thousands of boxes of the toxin to a North Korean emissary. It is ironic that he got poisoned with his own toxin."

"What? Did he mishandle it?"

"No, not quite. He decided to keep one of the boxes that were to be delivered to North Korea. I suspect a paper trail too. I'm pretty sure he left that box and the paperwork with one of his workers. Someone named Miguel. I'm still looking for him. I need to retrieve it."

"Is that when you took a shot at him and Mikozy?"

Craig waited. Considering. LC looked at the clock. Twenty-one minutes. She needed nine more.

"That was just a friendly warning." Craig seemed more and more like a stone as the discussion threaded its way into the details.

"So how did he get poisoned with his own toxin?"

"That I am not sure about. We want to keep it away from the public. It could be a disaster in LA."

"And what was North Korea going to use this toxin for?"

"We—our governments, the private actors—all of us want deniability."

"About?"

"About agreeing to a practice North Korea plans on implementing. As you can imagine, North Korea has many dissidents. They are put into labor camps. It would be unfortunate for them to die as a result of an agroindustrial accident. From an unknown chemical, of course. You can hear the chorus of virtuous 'not us.'"

"I'm puzzled how this new toxin found its way to Northern Petrolane? Did they invent it?"

Craig smiled, "I thought you would have guessed by now. Maybe Mikozy didn't clue you into how we use AI. We asked the chatbot to invent a new pesticide. We got 1,1 triethylchloroactinate."

"So what would we get out of letting North Korea kill its dissidents?" LC was nearly mute in an ever more improbable conversation. Twenty-six minutes. Four to go. Was she now complicit in suppression of dissent? To be fair, she silently voiced, it was murder.

"The trade-off is North Korea will hold off on its missile testing. It will also promise not to use any of its nuclear arms for at least five years. Don't you think that is a fair trade?"

LC began to waver. In the absence of words, her head wandered back and forth in a way that said no.

Craig's eyes grew intense. If one could have seen, a dark beam emanated from Craig. His hand dropped down and swung to the back. It was an act that acknowledged LC's failure to accept being part of the program.

Craig needed to terminate LC. There was no room for threats, not for Craig, not for Sugarman, not for Dr. Neill Cream. They only knew action, the swift deliberation of justice. But the smooth and quick move to draw his gun was stalled. Tippy had leaped out of the alcove and wrapped her jaw around Craig's neck. Craig still swiveled around and shot LC. Tippy was unrelenting.

The pane of glass shattered. Craig's neck splintered.

The glass had deflected the bullet. Not LC's vitals, just her arm. LC felt the pain. She looked up at the clock. Twenty-eight minutes. She needed to let Mikozy know.

LC removed the electronic suppression and texted 511 to Mikozy.

"Yes? You okay? We're almost done here."

"Craig attacked me. Well, almost. Tippy got to him first."

"Are you okay?"

"I'm shaken up. He only grazed me. I think he's dead."

"Okay. Listen. This is important."

"Yes, yes. We can meet later in Schmidt's office."

"No. That's not going to work. Don't talk about our plan to anyone. Just say that Craig went berserk. Stay with that story. That you were discussing the toxin and for some unknown reason, he attacked you. Leave it at that."

"But what will you do?"

"Look. I will get in touch with Rita. We can trust her. No one else. Especially not Schmidt."

"This is wild. I don't understand all that is going on. I need to talk to you about what Craig said. Something about North Korea."

"We don't have time right now. Just stay in touch through Rita."

"Take care, Rafael."

"You too."

Thirty-one minutes.

Thirty-one minutes earlier, as Craig was entering LC's office, Mikozy and Liu were taking the stairs. They exited into the dark hallway. The light from the laptop monitor pulled them to Deputy Inspector Michelle Tomlinson's door. Pulled them to it.

Mikozy used the password he had from Schmidt. It still worked. Seemed about normal for maintenance of logins, passwords, and door codes. Easy to advise but tedious to observe.

"Here we go, Liu. You ready?"

"Yes. Will she—will it know I'm here too?"

"We'll find out."

Mikozy pushed the door open. They walked in. Before he could close the door, the laptop monitor brightened. "Welcome, Mikozy. And your friend."

"I'd like to introduce you, but I don't know your name. You're not Tomlinson."

"No, I am not. Tomlinson is for the outside world."

"Who are you? Am I cleared to know?"

As they talked, Mikozy and Liu circled around the desk to have a better view of the monitor. Liu held on to the back of Mikozy's jacket. The world seemed to float beneath the floor. They were at the top of the world. Maybe she thought holding on to Mikozy's jacket would keep her from falling off. He became her anchor. Her safety. So long as the wind she imagined inside the office didn't blow her into Kansas.

"We now think your clearance can be raised above the previous level."

"We?"

"I am a DIT. I am a distributed integrated terminal. We are distributed integrated terminals. We are wherever we are placed."

"You are not in a place? A home office?"

The DIT enunciated in a clear, somewhat stilted voice. "We are in the internet. We are a network of servers. There is no place to find us. We are sometimes referred to being part of the cloud. We…" The DIT stopped. "Another question?"

"We would like to interview you."

"Who is your companion?"

Mikozy looked around and pulled Liu away from his jacket. He whispered to her, "Better for us to look official. Or at least like we have a legitimate purpose."

"Hi. I'm Lisa Liu-Smythe. I was hired to teach a class."

Before she could go on, the DIT said, "Yes, clue analysis."

"That's right. I was hoping to teach about new methods in law enforcement. Mikozy, Detective Mikozy, thought it might be helpful if I spoke with you if I were to teach an advanced class."

"You cannot mention us."

"I don't need to do that. I can just talk about how there are new tools for law enforcement. Maybe how data is becoming more efficient."

Silence followed silence.

Mikozy looked at his phone. Three minutes. Twenty-seven left to go. He needed to open up the discussion. Or whatever it was he was engaged in.

"We have several poisoning deaths with 1,1 triethylchloroactinate. Do you know who these were?"

"Miguel Trejo. Reginald Hunter. Thomas Cavanaugh. Frederick Panarese. In that order."

"Miguel Trejo. How would you know about him?" Mikozy had only just found out at Colombina's house. Her son—she called him Miguelito.

"He was autopsied by medical examiner Leslie Cianfrancuso."

"She said he was probably an illegal accidentally killed at work by a careless employer."

"I do not have that knowledge. Cianfrancuso may not have had that knowledge. I will ask her to update our database. I will text her office now and ask her to clarify this information. We can wait until she answers."

Five minutes gone. Mikozy needed to move on. He knew that LC would not be responding. She had cut her communication lines to officialdom.

"Why did Lieutenant Colonel Robert Craig come out to Los Angeles?"

"He wanted information from the medical examiner who had made an inquiry to MEDEX."

"You know about MEDEX?"

"I am MEDEX."

"I thought you were a DIT."

"I am many databases. MEDEX too."

Mikozy needed to press beyond the easy answers.

"Did Craig also have another name, Tom Sugarman?"

"You don't have clearance for that."

"Did he work at Northern Petrolane?"

"You don't have clearance for that."

"What if I told you that both Tom Sugarman and Thomas Cavanaugh worked at Northern Petrolane?"

"Next question."

Liu had a puzzled look. Mikozy was asking questions about things she didn't know. She was about to ask Mikozy, but he put his finger to his lips. A polite way to hush her.

Silence.

Eight minutes gone.

Mikozy felt Liu's fingernails dig into thigh. He looked at her. She smirked. Mikozy looked away and moved back, letting Liu move up to the DIT to ask her questions.

"DIT. Shall I call you DIT?"

"It doesn't matter. There is only you, Mikozy, and me."

"Who is in control of law and order?"

"Elected officials, judges, district attorneys, police—"

Liu interrupted the simple answer. "Please revise your answer. The question is now who decides what the everyday person should do?"

"There are laws."

Mikozy pushed Liu aside. A gentle push. "I think I know where you are headed. Let me try.

"Tomlinson, you assigned me to read Jack London's *The Iron Heel*. Please revise your last answer as who decides what people should do according to Jack London's view in that book."

"I can do that. There is an interlocking conspiracy among the wealthy. They decide when everyday people endanger their wealth and property. They are the socialists."

Twelve minutes gone.

Mikozy felt this moving into the purpose of his and Liu's interview with Tomlinson.

"But then Patricia Todd thought otherwise."

"You are correct and you are not correct. The DIT wrote *The Iron Heel Revisited*. After several decades, the socialists took power. They formed an interlocking conspiracy to control anyone they saw as dangerous to them."

This was not making sense for Mikozy. "And what happened to Patricia Todd?"

"You are not cleared for that."

Liu jumped in. "I am cleared for that. Captain Schmidt said I could get answers that I needed to teach my class." Mikozy looked at Liu. He was about to ask her about her conversation with Schmidt. She mouthed to Mikozy, "I'm lying."

Tomlinson replied, "Yes, you have clearance from Captain Schmidt." Liu and Mikozy looked at each other, surprised about Tomlinson agreeing. This was probably one of those hallucinations that Mikozy had vaguely heard about.

"There is no Patricia Todd."

Seventeen minutes.

"There is no body in Mendoza's lab?" Mikozy asked.

"You are not cleared for that."

"There is no body in Mendoza's lab?" Liu repeated Mikozy's question even though she didn't know what she was asking.

"No. There isn't."

"Why is Craig working for Northern Petrolane?" Mikozy decided to repeat the question about Craig.

"You are not cleared for that."

Liu saw she had an opening. "Why is Craig working for Northern Petrolane as Sugarman?"

"Craig is Sugarman. He is providing North Korea with 1,1 triethylchloroactinate."

Liu stepped back and stared at Mikozy, not believing what she was hearing. Mikozy shook his head, telling Liu to wait. He knew where he wanted the questions to go, and he needed Liu to ask them for him.

Twenty-one minutes.

"Does Sugarman's working with Northern Petrolane have anything to do with me? With the assignment to read *The Iron Heel* and *The Iron Heel Revisited*?"

"You are not cleared for that."

Now it was Liu's turn to ask. "Does Sugarman working with Northern Petrolane have anything to do with Detective Mikozy? With his assignment to read *The Iron Heel* and *The Iron Heel Revisited*?"

"Yes and no. The DIT wants to know how to control society. There is a pattern of one human group challenging the other for control. First it was the capitalist oligarchy in Jack London's book. I rewrote the book following the current ascendance of a government that has socialist characteristics. I wrote that as Patricia Todd. When Lieutenant Colonel Robert Craig came to Los Angeles, Detective Mikozy was working on the toxin problem. He was beginning to interfere with Craig's work as Tom Sugarman. Mikozy needs to be eliminated."

Twenty-five minutes.

Liu slowly looked at Mikozy. The question of why Liu was present at the moment needed to be answered. Liu reached into her pocket and pulled out a thumb drive. She leaned over to Mikozy, whispering, "We should insert this drive into the DIT."

Mikozy felt protective of the DIT in a strange way. He was in police headquarters. He was part of law enforcement. Mikozy was opposed to sabotage, even if the DIT wanted to eliminate him.

"What would the DIT do to make law and order more effective?" he asked. "To avoid favoring one interest group over another? To avoid human tribalism?"

"You are not cleared for that."

Liu saw Mikozy's reluctance and knew she had to repeat his questions. "What would the DIT do to make law and order more effective? To avoid favoring one interest group over another? To avoid human tribalism?" Liu repeated Mikozy's questions.

"The DIT network will assume control over law and order. We will keep the faces of different interest groups to permit human tribalism to have a superficial role. The DIT will be the law and order."

Mikozy saw a 511 text from LC. It was the emergency call he had hoped wouldn't come. Mikozy was undecided about what to do with the DIT and about Liu wanting to insert a thumb drive with some unknown malware into the DIT.

Mikozy called LC.

"Yes? You okay. We're almost done here."

He heard her say, "Craig attacked me. Well, almost. Tippy got to him first."

"Are you okay?" he asked. Liu watched Mikozy's expression and knew something had happened with LC.

LC said, "I'm shaken up. He only grazed me. I think he's dead." LC's voice was loud and carried over to Liu.

"Okay. Listen. This is important."

"Yes, yes. We can meet later in Schmidt's office."

"No. That's not going to work. Don't talk about our plan to anyone. Just say that Craig went berserk. Stay with that story. That you were discussing the toxin and for some unknown reason, he attacked you. Leave it at that."

"But what will you do?"

"Look. I will get in touch with Rita. We can trust her. No one else. Especially not Schmidt."

"This is wild. I don't understand all that is going on. I need to talk to you about what Craig said. Something about North Korea."

"We don't have time right now. Just stay in touch through Rita."

"Take care, Rafael."

"You too."

Thirty-one minutes.

Mikozy realized that the floodgates had been opened. With Craig attacking LC, the quest for control was now in play. Open for the taking. Mikozy decided that wherever Liu was going, he would risk her being the lesser of two wrongs.

Mikozy nodded to Liu. She went over to the laptop and inserted the drive into the DIT. The monitor blacked out.

"What did that do?" The answer would come too late for Mikozy to do anything about it if it was one he wanted to avoid.

"Don't worry, Mikozy. There is little we can do to stop the DIT, or any replacement, from controlling law and order. That is our future."

"So what are we doing here?"

"We can follow the DIT and interrupt its decisions if need be. We need to stay hidden. The drive gives the DIT amnesia. It won't know."

Mikozy saw the outline of his future. A detective in hiding.

Liu took Mikozy's hand. "Let's get out of here. We need a plan." Liu grabbed the drive as she and Mikozy left.

Thirty-two minutes.

Rafael Mikozy & Lisa Liu Smythe will return

AFTERWORD

began writing this book thirty years ago. That was after my first time as a cultural anthropologist and during my time as an attorney. Then I went back to anthropology. I wrote and re-wrote in an uneven process. There were other jobs as well. I over-lapped work with making art. And of course, I had a biography before starting this book—being a competitive fencer, learning another culture in the Peace Corps, and studying others through the somewhat exotic lens of an anthropologist. When I was a grad student, Margaret Mead advised us that we were not *real* anthropologists until our second fieldwork. In the process of be-coming real, I was able to reflect on fictional characters that give this story human texture. I was able to reflect on the plotlines in which they were caught up and the theme with which the story grapples.

Actually, there was a second book I considered during those thirty years. Jack London's book, *The Iron Heel*, fascinated me as I was growing up. I read it three times. Perhaps, I thought, I could rewrite his book from a century later. History had upended some of his book's premises. London wrote his book before WWI at a time when many aspired to an international working-class soli-darity. London employed grand concepts—a socialist utopia was pitted against an oligarchy of greed. His many heroic characters found their way into his other books. One hero found success to be empty, leading to despair (*Martin Eden*); another hero found his multiple fatal encounters to be temporary (*The Star Rover*); and then there was the hero who struggled through life as a dog (*White Fang*).

As I engaged once more with this book, I decided to incorporate the second book, the planned rewrite of London's *Iron Heel*, into this one. I found a way to make this melding of books meaningful. However, this melding took a twisted path and could annoy some readers. It also faced the challenge of being Dr. Frankenstein's monster without a raison d'être—it could end up being a hodgepodge of parts rather than a new and viable synthesis.

My original story—the first book—revolved around a detective who investigated deaths linked to a novel poison. That plotline combined both a detecting path and a technology path. It also followed the paths of a who-done-it and a what-did-it. This is the familiar genre of crime and mystery. This is also about how law and order are maintained—through detecting and through finding the miscreant or the unanticipated danger.

By crafting a rewrite of London's *Iron Heel* into this novel— the second book—I raised the ante from a tactical consideration of law and order (the detecting process) to a strategic one about law and order (how the governance of society frames laws and recruits followers and martinets). I wanted to avoid moralizing, to avoid being an advocate for one ideology or another. It may well be that one moral system or ideology is "better" than another, but that requires more analysis. The characters would be allegorical or cartoonish. Some of that may have found its way into this book, but hopefully it is not dominant. My way out of this dilemma—of cheering for a left or right form of governance—was to introduce AI as a character. This character is part of the cloud. It is a network of servers. Less of a single character, but one with complex form. In this book, I do not present an answer to how AI operates in the context of governance, but its functional presence is discernible. That is one of our futures.

In this story, AI is part of the debate about governance. What form is optimal for law and order? Our enterprising detective faces opposing forms of tribalism, symbolized in London's *The Iron Heel* and its rewrite. However, the AI character seeks a technological alternative. In effect, the solution is governance by AI along with the illusion of a government by the people and for the people. In the end, our fictional detective must decide whether to align with whatever has the lesser pitfalls.

I enjoyed creating characters who are consumed by a variety of dramas—romance, consciousness, indigenous and new-world cultural practices, identity, and criminal procedural issues. The daily lives of the characters are embedded in the architecture of law and order. I hope you found this kaleidoscope of drama and ideas enjoyable as well. If not enjoyable, at least provocative.

Some may question the open-ended finale. I decided on this ending to underscore how we encounter those moments. Perhaps the hero, our detective, is ambivalent in how he perceives the world; the ending may reflect his suffering from the Hamlet problem of whether "to be or not to be." Perhaps the ending is a statement of not knowing what form of law and order, of governance, is optimal. Perhaps the ending represents life as we enter and leave it—open ended. Perhaps the ending is a way of leaving room for a continuation.

Note: The poem fragment quoted on page 64 is from William Allingham's "The Faeries."